The Iron Girl

ELLEN HART

ST. MARTIN'S MINOTAUR ☙ NEW YORK

THE IRON GIRL. Copyright © 2005 by Ellen Hart. All rights reserved. Printed in
the United States of America. No part of this book may be used or reproduced
in any manner whatsoever without written permission except in the case of
brief quotations embodied in critical articles or reviews. For information,
address St. Martin's Press, 175 Fifth Avenue, New York, N.Y. 10010.

www.minotaurbooks.com

Library of Congress Cataloging-in-Publication Data

Hart, Ellen.
     The iron girl / Ellen Hart.
          p. cm.
     ISBN-13: 978-0-312-31750-8
     ISBN-10: 0-312-31750-6
     1. Lawless, Jane (Fictitious character)—Fiction. 2. Women detectives—
Minnesota—Minneapolis—Fiction. 3. Mass murder investigation—Fiction.
4. Restaurateurs—Fiction. 5. Lesbians—Fiction. 6. Minneapolis (Minn.)—
Fiction. I. Title.

PS3558.A6775 I76 2005
813'.54—dc22

                                                    2005046568

First St. Martin's Minotaur Paperback Edition: June 2006

          D 10 9 8 7 6 5 4 3 2

For Lori Lake and Diane Thompson.
Introverts Unite!
We should start an organization—
except introverts don't join anything.
Oh well.
Here's to homemade apple pie and
carefully planned spontaneity—and to
many more years of great conversations and
growing friendship.

Author's Note

Some books are harder to write than others. Because of the emotional backstory in this novel, this was one of those books. In the past I've occasionally used music to set the tone for a chapter or a scene. But during the writing of this novel, I used music constantly—as a way to get up for the writing day, as a way into the emotions of the characters, and as a way to relax at the end of the day. I was introduced to three amazing artists this past year, and because of them, this has been a year of true musical rebirth in my life. You'd think I'd been hermetically sealed in a box for the past twenty years, but the truth is, before January of 2004, none of this music was even on my radar screen. Since I shamelessly plundered their artistry—relied on it daily for so many reasons—it seemed wrong not to thank these wonderful artists for the hours of enjoyment and inspiration they've brought. So, with respect and great affection, I'd like to thank Cheryl Wheeler and the Indigo Girls—Emily Saliers and Amy Ray. You guys rock!

Simoneau Family Tree

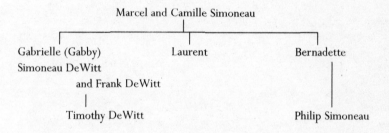

Marcel and Camille Simoneau

Gabrielle (Gabby)
Simoneau DeWitt
and Frank DeWitt

Laurent

Bernadette

Timothy DeWitt

Philip Simoneau

We live in our own souls as in an unmapped region,
a few acres of which we have cleared for our habitation;
while of the nature of those nearest us
we know but the boundaries that march with ours.

—Edith Wharton, *The Touchstone*

Christine

August 16, 1987

It was a sweltering August afternoon the day Christine approached the front door of the Simoneau mansion for the first time. Cicadas twanged their harsh summer song as heat rose off the ground in waves. Waiting under the front portico, she scanned the front yard. The rest of the Twin Cities might look as if it was about to dry up and blow away, but the grounds here looked as green and watered as a spring garden.

Christine Kane was in her mid-thirties. She'd been a real estate agent for eleven years. She'd recently changed agencies, moving from a discount broker to McBride Realty. Her new boss, Bill McBride, had lured her away from her old company by promising to help her establish herself in the tonier sections of Minneapolis and St. Paul—specifically, Kenwood and Summit Avenue. She'd always made a good living, but her love of architecture, of the old, majestic houses of the Twin Cities had prompted her to try a new direction.

The Simoneaus' home was located on a lovely bend in the Lake of the Isles Parkway. The house, which looked like a miniature medieval castle, complete with tower and faux battlements, faced the lake. Christine had done some research on the Simoneaus. Back in the sixties, they'd been one of the richest families in the Twin Cities. After the death of Marcel Simoneau in 1974, the family fortune had dwindled—but dwindled by rich people's standards, not ordinary mortals like Christine.

Marcel Simoneau was originally from New Orleans. He'd made an early fortune by producing and selling bootleg whiskey during Prohibition. By the time the United States entered the Second World War, his legitimate manufacturing business, Simoneau Fire and Machine, was well established.

In the early forties, S.F.&M. received a bunch of government contracts to produce firefighting equipment for the military. After the war, due to a variety of high-placed political connections, the government contracts kept coming. Simoneau expanded into wire and cable production, and finally, into fiber optics. Camille Simoneau, Marcel's widow, was no longer involved in the company. None of the Simoneaus' three children—two daughters and a son—had gone into the business.

As Christine waited for the door to be answered, she set her briefcase down on the granite steps. It wasn't really that heavy, but she wasn't feeling well today, so it felt as if it was stuffed with bricks. She was mildly surprised that the house wasn't better staffed. She stepped to the edge of the portico and looked up at the blazing sun, then moved back and pressed the doorbell again. The relentless heat was making her feel faint. She assumed the interior of the mansion was air-conditioned and that she'd revive once she got inside. She had good news for Bernadette, Camille's oldest daughter, and wanted to deliver it in person.

After two more rings, Philip Simoneau, Bernadette's only child, appeared at the front door. He was home for the summer from Yale. He'd graduated in the spring with a degree in economics and planned to return in the fall for his master's. Christine had gotten to know him over the past couple of weeks. He was bright and friendly, and often quite funny. He liked to mimic snooty upper-class Eastern accents, especially FDR. Given a bit of prodding, he'd even break into a pretty fair Eleanor Roosevelt. He was handling the daily details of the sale of his mother's house, although Camille Simoneau, his grandmother, insisted that she be kept in the loop.

Philip and Bernadette had lived for years in a large Tudor on Irving Avenue, just behind the mansion. If Philip had a father, he wasn't in the picture now, nor did anyone ever mention his name. Christine took the cue and kept her curiosity in check.

For personal reasons—reasons to which Christine wasn't privy—Bernadette had decided to sell her house and move in with her mother. McBride Realty, specifically Bill McBride, handled all of the Simoneaus' real estate holdings. Just last year, Bill had sold several properties Camille owned up on the North

4

Shore. After getting permission from Camille, he turned the Irving Avenue listing over to Christine.

To date, Christine had attended two official meetings with Camille, Bernadette, Philip, and Bill, but most of the time she dealt directly with Philip. Camille insisted that he had a good mind for business, much better than her daughter's, and wanted him to oversee the transaction. Every now and then, Christine got the feeling that Philip was inching the conversation toward a more personal level, but something always stopped him.

"Christine, hi," said Philip, smiling with a cigarette holder clenched in his teeth—another FDR affectation. When dressed formally, he was Mr. Preppy. Navy blazers with gold buttons, khaki slacks. When dressed more casually, as he was today, he was a slob, wearing old ripped cutoffs and faded Yale T-shirts. "How did the inspection go?" Sensing that something was wrong, he added quickly, "Are you okay? You look kind of pale."

"I'm a little dizzy."

"Ditzy?" He grinned.

"Dizzy, Philip. Dizzy." She picked up her briefcase. "It's probably the heat." He held the door open for her.

Christine lowered herself onto the first chair she found. "Don't you have a butler?"

"They're called 'house managers' now. Yeah, we had one. Merrill Kovlatch. Nice guy. He walked out last week."

"Why?"

"He and my uncle Laurent got into a fight over the security system my grandmother wants to install. In a nutshell, Laurent wanted one kind and he wanted another. Guess who won?"

"Does Laurent live here?"

"Nah. Lives in Florida. He and a buddy of his own a couple of dance clubs down there. But he spends a lot of time in Minnesota." He paused to exhale cigarette smoke. "He's a strange guy. Grandmother hasn't gotten around to hiring a new house manager yet. This is the third one she's lost in two years."

"Because of Laurent?"

"Pretty much."

Christine pressed hard against the bridge of her nose.

"Hey, you really aren't feeling well. Can I get you something? A glass of water?"

"Water would be great."

5

He excused himself and dashed back into the bowels of the house.

Just getting away from the nearly one-hundred-degree heat was helping her feel better. When Christine was younger, she thought of herself as a human lizard, lazing around on hot rocks in the full summer sun, totally in her element. But that love of the summer sun had repercussions. She was paying for it now.

Philip was back in short order. "Here," he said. "I brought you lemonade. Maybe your blood sugar is low."

Christine held the glass to her cheek, relishing the chill. She wondered idly if she might have a fever.

"We could go back to my grandfather's study. It's more comfortable there. That's where I've been working."

"I thought you had the summer off."

"Oh, yeah, well. The house manager was supposed to help manage my grandmother's financial affairs, but Merrill's background was in interior decoration. It's probably a good thing he's gone. The books are a mess."

Christine rose slowly, feeling a bit more steady now. "If you carry my briefcase, I think I'll be fine."

The interior of the Simoneau mansion was as majestic as she'd expected. The floors were a polished gray marble. A wrought-iron balustrade capped by a bronze handrail curved its way to the open second floor. The rug in the foyer was a bold Jacquard design—black and white diamonds bordered by two strips, one red and one green.

Christine followed Philip to the rear of the house, glancing at the artwork on the hallway walls. She wasn't sure, but she thought one of the paintings might be a small Degas. Entering the study, she found that the room overlooked the back garden. At the far end of the yard she could see a three-car garage with a gatehouse on top.

"So," said Philip, setting Christine's briefcase next to a wing-back chair, then moving behind a sleek ebony desk, " 'Be sincere, be brief, be seated'—as FDR used to say. How did the inspection go?"

Christine sat down and crossed her legs. Thanks to the weather, her white linen slacks and jacket already looked like limp rags. "It's just what I'd hoped for."

The Irving Avenue house had undergone a top-to-bottom private inspection. It was all part of the information Christine would provide potential buyers.

"I brought the stat sheet with me. Is your mother around?"

"No. She woke up depressed, so she went shopping. It's what she always does

when she's feeling down." He pulled the cigarette holder out of his mouth, blew smoke into the air.

"Well, then I'll tell you the good news. I expected the house would sell in the 200,000- to 300,000-dollar range, but with a little work, we could list it in the high three hundreds. Maybe even a little more."

"How much work are we talking about?"

She opened her briefcase and removed a file.

"Wait, I think my grandmother should hear this."

"Is she home?"

"Not sure. Let me go see if I can find her."

Christine sat for a while looking out the window at a couple of squirrels chasing each other around the trunk of a tree, but when he didn't come back, she got up and walked across the hall to an even larger room. This one appeared to be a gallery. Paintings were hung on all four walls from eye level all the way up to the ceiling. Her gaze locked on one hanging next to a window. Could it actually be a Picasso? Moving closer, she bent forward and searched for a signature.

"What are you doing?" demanded a voice from behind her.

She turned around. A man in a bright orange, green, and yellow Hawaiian print shirt stood in the open doorway. He was dark-haired, like Philip, but the resemblance ended there. Where Philip was tall and lean, this guy was short and fleshy, not quite fat, but approaching it. Christine had no idea who he was. "I was just looking—"

"You've got no business in here." A muscle pulsed in his cheek.

Whoever the man was, he seemed wound pretty tight. "My name's Christine Kane. I'm the real estate agent—"

"I know the cover story. I've seen you talking to Philip."

She wasn't sure what he meant.

Stepping into the room, he kicked the door shut with his foot. "I'm Laurent."

"Oh." Philip said he was strange, but strange covered a lot of territory.

"McBride's our real estate guy. I don't like being lied to."

Christine trusted her gut instincts, and her instinct told her she didn't want to be alone with this jerk. She wasn't comfortable with the closed door, but she also didn't want to make a big deal out of it. He was, after all, the son of a major client.

"How come you're so interested in the artwork?" he demanded.

"I'm not. I mean, I came in here because I was waiting for Philip to come back with your mother."

"Mother's not home. Try again." He moved over to a glass curio cabinet.

Christine wasn't sure why she felt so ill at ease, but she couldn't shake the sense that being alone with him wasn't a good idea. She took a few steps toward the door. "Well, nice meeting you. I think I'd better go see what happened to Philip."

"What do you and my nephew talk about?"

That stopped her. "We talk about your sister's house. I'm not lying. I'm the agent who's selling it. I work for McBride Realty."

"Right." He opened the glass top of the cabinet and removed a long, narrow, elaborately jeweled silver ornament. "Philip has this tendency to mess with stuff that's none of his business. I don't like people prying into my affairs, Christine. As a matter of fact, it pisses me off big time." A quick smile was followed by a quick frown.

Christine wondered if there was something truly wrong with him. "If you've got problems with your nephew, you should take it up with him."

"But I'd rather take it up with you."

That was it. "Sorry, can't help." She turned, but before she could get to the door, Laurent edged in front of her.

"Get out of my way." She wanted out of the room, and she wanted out now. "If you don't leave me alone——"

"You'll what?"

"I'll scream bloody murder. I mean it."

When she tried to force her way past him, he pulled a razor-thin dagger from the ornament and shoved her back against the wall. Her shoulder clipped the edge of one of the gilded frames, sending a painting crashing to the floor.

Pressing the dagger to her throat, Laurent grunted. "Shut up."

"What's going on in here?" said Philip, bursting into the room. "Shit." Seeing the painting on the floor, he bent to pick it up. When he turned around, his mouth dropped open.

Laurent didn't move. "Uh-oh, Christine. Guess I'm busted."

Christine was too terrified to do anything other than hold her breath and hope Laurent's hand didn't slip.

"What the hell are you doing?" demanded Philip.

"Chatting with your friend," said Laurent.

"Are you freakin' nuts? Laurent, put that thing down!"

"Not until you both promise to stay out of my business."

"What the hell are you talking about?"

8

"She knows. Don't you, Christine?" Laurent pressed the flat of the dagger against her throat. "All I'd have to do is flick the edge up and . . . bye-bye Blondie."

"Laurent, please," pleaded Philip. "I don't know what you think she's done. She's here because she's selling Mom's house. That's all."

Laurent stared at Christine for a second, then stepped back and released her. "You're in way over your heads, children. FYI—stay out of things that don't concern you." He straightened his Hawaiian shirt and left the room, slamming the door behind him.

Suddenly, Christine's legs didn't feel all that steady.

Philip helped her over to the couch. "God, I'm so sorry. He's a total freak. You have every right to press charges."

"I'm okay."

"No you're not."

She took a couple deep breaths. It had all happened so fast.

"I've never seen him act like that before. Not that I'm making excuses. I think we should call the police. Really." He started to get up.

Christine knew it was the right thing to do, but she stopped him. "Let me think about it, okay?"

"What's to think about? He attacked you. If I hadn't come in when I did—" As he stared at her, the light dawned in his eyes. "Oh, shit. I get it. It's your job." He shook his head and groaned. "You're right. My grandmother would blow a gasket if you pressed charges. And I suppose that would create big problems for you with McBride. God, what a total . . . I mean, screw this." He sat with his head in his hands, chewing on his lower lip. "Look, I won't pressure you. Whatever you decide to do is fine by me. Just know that if you need a witness to what just happened, you've got one."

"Thanks."

"And, just in case—" He stood and walked over to the cabinet. Removing a rectangular leather box, he returned to the couch, sat down and opened it. Inside were two derringers with matching carved-ivory grips.

"I want you to take one of these."

"Philip, no. I could never—"

"If you decide not to involve the police, that means you'll still have to come here occasionally until the house is sold. I don't know how long Laurent plans to stick around. He came up this time for my aunt Gabby's funeral, but that was weeks ago. I don't know why he stuck around, but I do know he's terrified of

9

guns, spiders, and thunderstorms. Always has been. These derringers belonged to my grandfather. They're both loaded. Two bullets, that's all you've got, but just the sight of it would be enough to give Laurent a coronary. Do me a favor. Put it in your pocket when you know you're coming here. It would make me feel so much better just knowing you have it."

Christine took it from his hand. She hated even the idea of a gun, let alone the reality. "I don't know——"

"Please," he said, closing his hand over hers. "For me. Just keep it with you. You'll probably never need to use it. Take the bullets out if you want, but be ready to flash it, okay? Man——" He laughed, almost giggled. "I'd love to be there to see the look on Laurent's face if you ever do."

Late March

1

Jane had just come through the front door when the phone rang. She dumped her luggage in the foyer and rushed to answer the cordless in the living room.

"Hello?" she said, sinking down on the couch, trying to catch her breath. The luggage had been heavy and she'd carried it all in at once.

"Janey? I've been calling you for hours!"

It was Cordelia, Jane's oldest friend.

"The plane was late," said Jane, dropping her head back against the couch cushion. "We were supposed to land around eight-thirty, but didn't get in until closer to ten."

"Why didn't you answer your cell?"

Jane knew she was truly home when Cordelia's golden tones began ranting about one thing or another. The cell phone, for instance, was a running battle. Jane understood the value of cell phones, but rebelled at the idea of being at everyone's beck and call all hours of the day and night. The wee hours of the morning were when Cordelia was most prone to call.

Cordelia Thorn was the artistic director of the Allen Grimby Repertory Theater in St. Paul, and a woman who loved the night. She felt that sunrise, in general, was highly overrated, and didn't understand why poets rhapsodized about morning dew and all that crap.

"I turned my cell phone off," said Jane.

"You drive me insane!"

"Besides, you can't use a cell phone on a plane, Cordelia. It's against the law."

"That's why the clever little people who make them provide you with an 'on' button."

"I forgot."

"Right. Like I believe that. It's your reclusive nature leaking out, Janey. You should really see someone about that. A therapist. An exorcist?"

"Don't I even merit a 'welcome home'? I've been gone ten days." On the other hand, she and Cordelia had hardly been out of touch. Cordelia had called daily for a "romantic update."

Jane had spent spring break with her new love, Kenzie Mullroy. Kenzie was a professor of cultural anthropology at Chadwick State College in Chadwick, Nebraska. They'd only been together a little over four months, but already Jane knew it was serious. She wasn't one to leap into bed with virtual strangers, partly because she'd been in a wonderful, committed relationship for almost ten years—until her partner's death in 1987. It was hard to measure a new relationship against that one, especially since it had attained the rosy patina of "long ago," of remembrance and not everyday routine. Many of the rough edges had been worn down by time, although not all of them. But what stood out in Jane's memory was the intensity of the love she and Christine had felt for each other. Jane's brushes with romance over the years had mostly faltered. It hadn't been her choice, it was just the way it had worked out.

Cordelia, who was serially monogamous—with oodles and oodles of serials, most of them brimming with melodrama—didn't understand Jane's reticence about dating. Jane didn't like to talk about it. Maybe she felt guilty that she'd been able to go on living when Christine's life had ended so abruptly, and at such a young age. Or maybe there were other, less obvious reasons. But none of them were anybody's business but her own.

"Just sit tight," said Cordelia. "I'm bringing someone over."

"I just walked in the door!"

"So?"

"I'm exhausted. And I have to call Evelyn Bratrude and go pick up Mouse." Mouse was Jane's dog, a chocolate-colored Lab. He'd been staying with a neighbor while she'd been gone.

"Evelyn goes to bed right after 'Law & Order.' If you call her now, you'll wake her up. Go get him in the morning."

She had a point. "But I'm filthy. What I need is a shower and a good night's sleep."

"Okay, *take* a shower and a five-minute power nap. It's still early, Janey. It's not even midnight."

Jane groaned. "All right, I'll bite. Who do you want to bring over?"

"It's a surprise."

"I don't like surprises."

"Bet you'll like this one. Like I always say, unexpected invitations are dancing lessons from God."

"To what am I being invited?"

"Nothing less than your future, dearheart." With that, she hung up.

Cordelia lived in a downtown loft. Jane lived in a house in Linden Hills. Doing a mental calculation, Jane figured she had about fifteen minutes to shower, wash and dry her hair, dig up some clean clothes, and make herself presentable. But she wasn't in the mood to rush. Instead of heading up to the bathroom, she drifted down to the basement.

After Christine's death, Jane had boxed up her belongings and stored them in a room next to the laundry. It had been too painful to sort through at the time. Over the years, she'd come down occasionally and opened a box or two, but she could never bring herself to make any final decisions about what to toss or what to save. Intellectually, she knew that Christine lived in her heart, not in her old shoes. It was just "stuff," and stuff could be discarded.

After returning from her visit with Kenzie, Jane felt that she not only needed to *try*, but to succeed this time at making peace with the past—saying good-bye to Christine in a way she'd never been able to before. Part of this new effort to move on was to deal with the detritus of her partner's life.

Jane switched on the light and stood for a moment staring at the boxes. It didn't take but five seconds for the feelings to hit. It was like darts being tossed at her skin. All the chaos of emotions she kept locked behind a shelf in her brain came tumbling out. Closing her eyes, she thought of Kenzie, of what they were building together. Jane had lost her mother when she was thirteen. Loss seemed to be one of the few permanent elements in her life. But if loss had taught her anything, it should have taught her to let go. Move on. What she held in her hand now was a tender, fragile but growing new love. This was the second chance she'd been hoping for. It was unthinkable that she'd let a memory mess it up.

When she opened her eyes, the world fell back into place. The boxes came back into focus. There were twenty-six in all. A person's life reduced to twenty-six boxes. Pathetic. Except they hardly summed up Christine.

Willing herself to move farther into the room, Jane ran her hand along the dusty tops. She opened one, but the photograph of Christine that met her eyes caused her to close it back up. How long would it take for these ruins to grow mute?

The next box contained Christine's drawings. She'd been a good artist, working both in watercolor and pastels. The top drawing was one she'd done of Jane a few weeks after they'd first met. The sight of it gave jane's heart such a twist that she immediately looked away. "Damn it all," she whispered, slamming the top shut.

She walked into the laundry room, checked the dryer and found one lone sock. Working up her courage, she returned to the storage room.

"Come on, Lawless. Show some guts." Spying a box with the words "Real Estate" written across the front, she pulled it free and carried it over to a chair. She figured that Christine's job was the least likely area of her life to turn on the water faucet behind Jane's eyes. Removing the top, she found a bunch of file folders stuffed down next to Christine's soft-sided leather briefcase, the one she took with her to appointments.

Jane moved the box to the floor so she could sit down on the chair. She lifted the briefcase out, then unclipped the leather straps and flipped the cover back. Inside, she found Christine's date book. She paged through it, seeing personal notations along with notes about business appointments. In late August, the appointments stopped. Jane took a deep breath, holding it until the wave of sadness passed. Nothing in these boxes would be free of emotion. After a few seconds, she placed the date book on the floor and rummaged around to see what else was inside. It was mainly junk. Pens. A package of chewing gum. A stick of lip gloss. A hairbrush. Steno notebook. A packet of business cards. An unopened can of Dr Pepper.

At the bottom of the briefcase she found a white paper sack. Her eyes opened wide with surprise when she saw what was inside.

It was a gun. A small derringer with a carved-ivory handle. Because it was so light, Jane wondered if it might be a toy. She examined it more closely. Not only was it real, but it was loaded. Christine hated guns. Finding one in her briefcase made no sense at all.

"What on earth," she whispered, her mind returning to the last few weeks of Christine's life. She'd been trying to get Bernadette Simoneau's house in shape so it could go on the market. The only reason Jane remembered the name of the woman Christine had been working with was because of what had happened to the Simoneau family shortly after Christine had been admitted to the hospital. The bloody horror of that night in late August was an eerie image virtually all Minnesotans carried around with them. It had been the single most infamous murder case in Minnesota history.

Jane had always thought Christine knew nothing about the dark, twisted, Simoneau family. And yet here she was carrying a gun when she visited the mansion. That told a far different story. Selling Bernadette's house had been her focus during the last weeks before she died. Christine said it was the biggest potential business connection she'd ever made. But if she felt the need to carry a gun, it was not only possible but likely that she knew more about what was going on in that family than she'd ever let on.

"More secrets," whispered Jane, feeling something clench in the center of her chest. Christine had been a master at keeping secrets.

Beyond her own feelings, finding the gun raised other issues. What had Christine known about the Simoneaus? Could that knowledge have altered what happened at the trial? Maybe Jane was jumping to conclusions, but something inside her, call it instinct or a sixth sense, told her that the gun was a message—a tantalizing, frightening, yet irresistible tug to look more closely at the last days of Christine's life.

What Jane had come home from Nebraska hoping to put behind her, now flashed inside her mind like a neon sign. She knew in her gut that this was exactly the wrong direction to take, the wrong time to get sucked back into her dead partner's past, and yet she also knew the gun represented a larger mystery she would feel compelled to unravel, wherever it might lead.

2

Jane was in the kitchen opening a beer when she heard several loud thumps on the front door. Returning to the foyer, she found Cordelia standing outside, holding a pizza box.

Jane's hand rose to her hip. "You said you were bringing over my future."

"Pizza's in your future," said Cordelia, bumping past her into the house. "As long as I'm alive and kicking."

Since returning from Switzerland, where her sister was filming a movie, Cordelia had taken to wearing a trench coat and a man's felt hat. The hat, when combined with her three-inch heels and her six-foot tall, two-hundred-pound-plus frame, made her new look highly imposing. Underneath the coat, she wore a pair of pale gray rayon slacks and a black silk blouse with a plunging neckline. Tonight, bright red lipstick and gold earrings completed the ensemble.

"You know," said Jane, following her into the living room. "You're kind of an amalgam these days."

"Of what?"

"Humphrey Bogart and Lauren Bacall."

Cordelia stared down her nose, the edges of her lips curling into a satisfied smile. "You've caught my idiom precisely."

The film her sister was shooting was a psychological spy drama. Michael Douglas, the main star of the movie, had given the hat to Cordelia during one of her visits to the set. Jane assumed that was why she never took it off—not even in the house. She pinned her long auburn curls up under it.

"I thought you were bringing someone over," said Jane.

"We drove separately. The War Machine tends to make great time on the freeway. All I have to do is move up behind a car and it zooms out of my way."

Last fall, Cordelia had traded in her old black Buick for a used Hummer. She might go broke putting gasoline in the thing, but in a strange way, it suited her.

"Did you get your shower?" asked Cordelia, eyeing Jane's frayed jeans, white Reeboks, and black turtleneck sweater, the one with the rip in the cuff.

"Can't you tell I'm all spiffed up?"

"Grand of you to make such an effort," she said dryly.

"Listen, before . . . *whoever* . . . gets here, I want to ask you something. Can you think of a reason why Christine might have owned a gun before she died?"

Cordelia did a double take. "Christine? You just came back from visiting *Kenzie*. Didn't we switch topics kind of abruptly?"

"Just answer the question."

She pulled her hand out of her pocket and adjusted the hat. "She hated guns, Janey. Everybody knew that."

"Okay, then why did I just find a gun in her briefcase? I went downstairs to look through some of the boxes you helped me pack after she died."

"Dare I ask why?"

"I'm going to get rid of it. All of it."

Cordelia stared back at her with a kind of soft worry.

"Don't look at me like that. It's about time, don't you think?"

"Time is relative. If it's what you want—"

"It is."

"Well, then, fine."

"Fine. What about the gun?"

20

"I'd say someone else, maybe one of your more unsavory renters, must have hidden it down there."

"I thought of that. Except the box I found it in had the same dust on it as all the others. I'm pretty sure it hasn't been touched."

"Then . . ." She seemed at a loss for words. A rare state of affairs.

"I found it inside her briefcase, the one she was using right before she went into the hospital."

Cordelia sat down on the couch. "Boy, you got me. Unless . . . well, maybe . . . you know. Maybe she had it because . . ." She didn't finish the sentence.

Jane knew what she was thinking. "No, Christine and I talked about that. She told me she'd never take her own life. She felt it would be wrong."

"Yeah. That sounds like her."

"So why did she have it?"

Before Cordelia could answer, the doorbell chimed. "I better get that," she said. "It's probably Judah."

"Judah?" repeated Jane.

"Judah Johanson. His mother was Jewish, father Norwegian. Kind of an intriguing Minnesota mix."

As Cordelia rushed back to the front door, Jane opened the box of pizza. The smell of anchovies nearly knocked her over.

Cordelia returned a few seconds later with a tall man in tow. His wispy blondish-white hair softened the otherwise hard angles of his face. He wasn't terribly attractive, and yet there was something appealing about him. His most prominent feature, other than his lightbulb-shaped head, was his amused expression. When he offered Jane his hand, she noticed the diamond pinky ring. The baggy brown cardigan and worn-out-looking blue cords certainly didn't suggest wealth, but the size of the ring spoke volumes.

"Nice to finally meet you," said Judah. For such a big guy, his voice was surprisingly high. "Cordelia's told me so much about you. All good, of course."

"Of course," said Jane. She nodded for him to sit down.

Cordelia sat on one end of the couch, while Judah perched on the other. Jane took the rocking chair by the fireplace.

"Judah's a doctor," said Cordelia.

"I'm an anesthesiologist," replied Judah.

"Really," said Jane. She wasn't sure why she needed an anesthesiologist in her future.

"But he's also a kick-ass businessman," added Cordelia.

"I own a company called Jump House Rentals. You've seen these big brightly colored inflatable castles that people put out in their yards for their children's birthday parties? The kids climb in, jump around and have a ball. We're busy constantly. I've made a small fortune in the last few years."

"Good for you," said Jane.

"Judah also helped a friend start a coffeehouse," said Cordelia.

"Well, it's actually more of a coffee *kiosk,*" replied Judah. "You probably know what I mean, Jane They're carts. My friend serves coffee and pastries. He's got several of them up and running now. In St. Petersburg."

"Not the one in Florida," added Cordelia. "The one in Russia."

Jane nodded, smiling through her confusion.

"Judah's latest great idea is what he's here to tell you about," said Cordelia, barely containing her enthusiasm. "I came on board last week as a silent partner."

Jane's eyebrows shot upward. *"Silent?"*

"Your point?" said Cordelia, narrowing her eyes.

"Cordelia is just trying to be supportive because she's a good friend," said Judah. "I don't expect her to shoulder any of the workload or make any of the important decisions. But she did lead me to you. She told me you've been thinking about opening another restaurant."

It was true. Jane had toyed with the idea. She'd even gone so far as to check out several buildings in St. Cloud and one in Rochester. None of the locations had interested her.

"Are you familiar with that old movie theater on 28th just off Hennepin?" asked Judah.

"The Xanadu?" said Jane. "Sure. It's a dump." It had been closed for years. If it hadn't been a rare art deco design, it would have been bulldozed long ago.

"I bought it," said Judah with a proud smile. "In January. It's just the place I've been looking for."

"This is so cool," said Cordelia, nearly erupting out of her seat. "He's planning to turn it into a bar and restaurant. But not just *any* bar and restaurant. This one will have a live orchestra. And a dance floor peopled with elegant diners."

"Um, not to put a damper on things," said Jane, "but where do you plan to get the elegant diners?" It was an honest question. Minnesota was the land of the terminally casual.

"Well, first, I should tell you that it's a theme restaurant," said Judah. "All the music will be jazz from the twenties and thirties. Everything will have an art deco flavor, including the food. The main dining room will only be open in the evenings. To get in, you'll have to be dressed formally—tuxedos and evening dress."

Jane laughed out loud. "Okay." *Dream on,* she thought.

"No, really," said Cordelia. "You'll drive up to the front doors and a valet will park your car. All part of the price of admission."

Judah nodded eagerly. "Next to the theater is a run-down building that was once used as a dentist's office. We're in the process of gutting it, and adding a covered walkway to the side of the Xanadu Club. I'm going to call it Fay's Vintage Formal Wear. All the clothing will be available for rental. It won't really be vintage clothing, but it will look like it. I'm having it made to order by a costume shop in Prague—an old friend owns it, Fay Gutemann. It will work like this: People can pull up in their jeans and T-shirts, run into Fay's, and for a nominal fee, deck themselves out in a faux vintage tuxedo or an elegant evening dress. We'll provide feather boas, costume jewelry, shoes, top hats, canes—whatever strikes their fancy. With the addition of a small computer chip in all the rentals, nobody will walk out of the club without returning the merchandise."

"And on the dance floor," continued Cordelia, "there will be dance instructors teaching people the Lindy, the fox-trot, the Argentine tango, the Charleston, the rumba—"

"We'll even have conga lines," said Judah. "I've already got a contractor in place and the interior is being redesigned by an architect, another friend of mine, this one from New York. What I don't have is a restauranteur, someone who can take over the food part—and help design the kitchen."

Jane had to admit she was intrigued. "What kind of food are we talking about?"

"Nothing too fancy or pricey. Steaks. Seafood. Chops. But I want everything to be beautifully presented—with an art deco flair. I'm thinking that we should look at some old menus, maybe update them in an innovative way. The person I'm looking for will be doing the hands-on running of the restaurant, at least for the first couple of years. I need someone who can get behind the vision, Jane. Someone who can set the tone. I hope that person is you."

"Janey, this is the opportunity of a lifetime," said Cordelia, her eyes nearly popping out of their sockets.

"I've done a ton of research," said Judah. "I'd be happy to provide you with a copy. The Uptown area is about to undergo another renaissance. New condos are scheduled to be built along the railroad tracks. It's already one of the hottest areas in town for new restaurants—or just about any other commercial endeavor. The demographics are great. Lots of young people with good incomes. But I would imagine we won't just draw from the Uptown crowd. People from all over the metro area will want to come to the Xanadu Club." He paused, studying Jane's face. "I'm not asking for money, Jane, although if you want to invest I won't turn it down. What I really need is a partner. I know we could draw up a contract that would work for both of us—something that would be mutually lucrative. What do you say? Will you at least think about it? Maybe you could come down tomorrow afternoon and look at the building. My architect friend is in town right now. He's free after four."

Jane had to admit the project sounded fascinating. "I'll need some time to study your research."

"Sure. No problem. I figure it will be at least eight months to a year before it's up and running. But I need a formal commitment in the next month or so."

Jane looked at Cordelia, then back at Judah. "I'll want to pass whatever contract we work out by my lawyer."

"Of course," said Judah.

She hesitated. "I'm not saying yes or no, but . . . if it's as good as it sounds, I'm in."

Cordelia leapt off the couch and threw her hat in the air. "Yeeeee-haaaaaa!!!! This calls for champagne."

"Oh," said Judah, raising a finger. "I don't drink, remember?" Smiling a bit sheepishly, he added, "I'm also a vegetarian."

Jane cocked her head. "A nondrinking vegetarian is about to open up a steak house and bar?"

"I think I am," said Judah. "Yes."

"Well, break out the fruit juice, then," cried Cordelia. "We've got to toast our partnership with something."

Jane glanced at Judah. He seemed so pleased, his face flushed with excitement, that she decided it wasn't the time to point out that the word "silent" and the word "Cordelia" couldn't realistically coexist in the same sentence.

3

By eight the next morning, Jane had picked up Mouse from Evelyn Bratrude's house and was on her way to her restaurant. The Lyme House was located on the south shore of Lake Harriet, directly across the water from the bandstand. It was a two-story log structure, one she'd designed herself with the help of one of Minnesota's best-known architects, Lars Peterssen. The Lyme Public House, otherwise known as the pub, was located on the first floor, with the main dining room on the second, overlooking the lake. A wide deck wrapped around the dining area, creating a space for outside dining during the summertime.

"You wanna go for a run?" asked Jane, waiting for Mouse to spring out of her Mini. He was still a young dog and needed lots of exercise. After the two weeks she'd spent in Nebraska with Kenzie—visiting all the local restaurants and making lots of great homemade meals—Jane needed exercise badly. She crouched down and scratched his back. Mouse buried his head in her stomach and kept it there longer than usual. This was the first time they'd been separated since she'd found him last winter. She hugged him close. "I missed you, too," she said, kissing the top of his head. She had a lot to do today, but Mouse came first.

For the next half hour, they alternately trotted and raced around the lake. It was a glorious day. With temperatures in the fifties, the last of the snow would be gone soon.

Jane had no specific plans to visit Kenzie again. After the school year was done at the end of May, Kenzie was scheduled to teach a month-long seminar in Vermont. In July, she would fly to Minnesota to spend the entire month with Jane. Jane couldn't wait to get her on home turf. On the the plane ride back home from Nebraska, she'd begun to make notes, things she wanted to show Kenzie, places she wanted to take her. She already missed her like crazy. Long-distance romances had their moments, but the separation part was going to be tough. Tomorrow night, when she called her, Jane would tell her about the potential new business deal. The more Jane thought about Judah Johanson and the Xanadu Club, the more excited she got.

But first things first.

"Hey there, Mr. Mouse," she said, coming to a stop below the restaurant. She bent over, resting her hands on her thighs. She was winded from the run. "We gotta get inside. Get down to work. My desk is probably piled high. What do you say? You ready for a nap on the couch?" During the design stage of the restaurant, Jane made sure her office had room for a comfortable couch, a bathroom with a shower, and a fireplace—all necessities for this home-away-from-home.

Mouse sat down in front of her and lifted his paw.

She shook it. "I'm sure we can find you a treat in the kitchen." At the mention of the word he jumped up and barked. She yanked his leash and the two of them climbed the stairs to the deck.

Jane was greeted warmly by her staff. It felt good to get home, to be back at work. She wondered how hard it would be to start up another restaurant and still have time for her first love. But she had great confidence in the group of people she had running The Lyme House. She might never be in a better position to branch out.

After finding Mouse a bowl of meat scraps, she unlocked her office and sat down behind the desk. Flipping through her Rolodex, she located the number she wanted. She needed to talk to a friend of her father's—Jake Marrone. Jake did background checks on people for a fee. Once she got him on the line, she asked him to dig up everything he could on Dr. Judah Johanson. She explained about his side business—Jump House Rentals—and that he'd just purchased the old Xanadu theater on 28th Street. She wanted anything and everything, including his shoe size. He told her it would take a few days, but that he'd get back to her.

By noon, she needed a break. As hard as she tried, she couldn't seem to get her mind off the gun she'd found last night in Christine's briefcase. While she watched Mouse lick his paw, a thought occurred to her. She grabbed the Yellow Pages and flipped through it until she found McBride Reality. Sure enough, it was still in business, still located on 50th and Bryant. She punched in the number. After talking to the receptionist, she was passed through to Bill.

"McBride."

"This is Jane Lawless. Do you remember me?"

"Well of course I do," boomed the now friendly voice. "You were—" He hesitated, searching for the name in his mental database. "Christine Kane's . . . friend."

"Right."

"Well, this is certainly a surprise. How are you, Jane?"

"I'm good, thanks. Actually, I know this request comes out of the blue, but I was hoping you'd have a few minutes to talk to me this afternoon."

The line went silent. Then: "Is this a real estate matter?"

"No. Personal."

Another pause.

"Well, of course," said Bill. "But . . . can you give me some idea what you want to talk about?"

"I'd rather come by, talk to you in person."

"Okay," he said drawing out the word. "I've got an appointment in a few minutes. I should be free by three. Would that work for you?"

"Three is great," said Jane. "See you then."

The exterior of McBride Reality hadn't changed much since Christine had worked there. The building was redbrick, one story, with broad windows flanking the front door. A large picture of Bill, happy and smiling standing next to a "Sold" sign, obscured most of one window.

The receptionist greeted Jane and told her that Bill was in his office. She pointed down the hall to the last door on the right.

Bill was sitting behind a desk, working on his laptop, when Jane gave a soft knock on the open door.

"Hey there." He stood and smiled. It was a practiced smile, not a genuine one. Jane had never really liked Bill. She thought he was a phony and a braggart. She knew enough about business to realize that he had to present a pleasant, positive face even when he didn't feel like it, but in his case, it always seemed forced. Maybe he just wasn't much of an actor. He'd put on weight since the last time she'd seen him. He must be in his sixties now. His hair was still strawberry blond, but had thinned considerably. His belly, once flat, now spilled over his belt.

She entered and shook his hand. "I appreciate you making time for me today."

"No problem." He nodded to a chair. "Like I always told Christine, anything I can ever do for you, just ask. That's the kind of guy I am." His expression softened. "I still remember her fondly, you know. Always will. I had big plans for her. I'm just so sorry her life had to end so soon."

For the first time, Jane felt she saw genuine emotion in his eyes. Maybe he wasn't such a bad guy after all. She found herself feeling grateful for the comment.

"So, what did you want to talk to me about?" He sat down, closing the cover of the laptop.

Jane plunged right in. "I was down in my basement last night going through some of Christine's belongings when I came across her old briefcase. Did you know she was carrying a gun before she died?"

He seemed truly surprised. "Hell no. I had no idea."

"She never talked to you about it?"

"Never. I don't mind telling you, if she was meeting clients with a gun on her, I would've put a stop to it good and fast."

"Do you have any idea why she might have felt she needed one?"

He seemed at a loss. "What kind of gun was it?"

"A derringer. Quite small."

"Did she have a permit?"

"Don't know." It was a good question. "Actually, I have a theory. Mind if I run it past you?"

Bill leaned back in his chair. "Go ahead."

29

"Well, right before she went into the hospital, she'd been working almost exclusively with the Simoneau family."

"Yeah, okay. I see where you're headed. But as far as I know, Christine knew nothing about the problems in that family. She had nothing to fear from any of them."

"You're sure?"

"As sure as I can be without asking her. We both know that's not possible."

"Were *you* frightened? I mean, you were there a lot, too. You were good friends with Camille Simoneau."

"Jane, this is the absolute truth. I had no idea what was going on behind the scenes in that house. Nobody did. Camille and I may have been friendly, but we were hardly friends. She certainly never confided any personal details of her life to me."

"But you testified at the trial, didn't you?"

"As a character witness, that's all."

"I didn't really follow it. I was still recovering from Christine's death." She tapped her nails on the arm of her chair, wishing now that she had. "Do you know what happened to Laurent and Bernadette Simoneau?"

"No idea. If they were smart, they probably headed for the hills. Reporters dogged them constantly."

"What about the child? Seems I remember a little boy being involved."

"Timmy? Let me think. He must have been about three when it happened. I suppose he's in college now. He's going to be one very rich kid when he turns twenty-one. One third of the estate will go to him."

"Does he live with his aunt and uncle?"

"God, no. Timmy's father hated that family. Last I heard, Timmy was living with his dad in Willmar. Frank DeWitt wanted his son to grow up normally. The Simoneaus had lots of fine qualities, but none of them were exactly normal. Especially Bernadette and Laurent."

"Have you seen either of them since the trial?"

"Well, I sold the Irving Avenue house for Bernie, but Lord, it wasn't easy. The place seemed to be tainted by what happened at the mansion. Nobody wanted to go near it." Bill leaned forward and placed his hands palms down on the desktop. "Believe me when I tell you that I have no desire to ever set foot in either of those houses again." He picked up a pencil and began to tap it nervously against the side of his coffee mug. "I suppose I can understand your curiosity about Christine and the gun, but if you'd take a little advice from an old guy who's lived a little longer than you, just let it go. There's no way to make sense of it now and that was a time nobody wants to revisit."

Jane sat in the chair and stared out the window. "I suppose you're right."

"But?"

She looked down at Christine's ruby ring. She wore it now. "I guess I'm having a hard time letting go. To be honest, it bugs me—I mean, really *bugs* the hell out of me because she must have felt she needed to keep whatever caused her to carry that gun a secret from me. It makes me wonder what else she kept secret."

Bill looked at her hard. "You loved her a lot."

"Of course I did," said Jane. Why the hell was she trying to explain all this to him? She shifted in her chair and began again. "I packed all her belongings away after she died, never really sorted through any of it. Maybe, as I go through it now, I'll find something that will shed some light on why she had the gun."

Bill folded his hands on top of the desk. "You know, every now and then I read about you in the local newspaper. You seem to have a gift for solving crimes. I assume you must help your father—him being a defense attorney."

"It's more a matter of being at the wrong place at the wrong time on a few too many occasions. I'm just lucky someone hasn't blown my head off." She was feeling uncomfortable and wanted to cut the conversation short.

Bill scrutinized her face. "Okay. Well, I wish you luck. If there's any way I can help, don't hesitate to call. I might be able to explain Christine's business affairs. Beyond that, I'm afraid you're on your own."

Nothing new in that, thought Jane. "Thanks for your time."

"No problemo." He rose from his chair. "And if you're ever in the market for a real estate agent . . ."

She grimaced, but tried to cover. "I remember." She repeated the old slogan: "Sell with pride. Call Bill McBride."

He snapped his fingers and pointed at her. "That's my girl."

What an ass. She rarely reacted when people called her a girl. She was in her early forties so it didn't exactly fit. But when Bill said it, she had the urge to deck him. Time to go, she thought. Before she got arrested for assault.

4

That night, Jane stayed at the restaurant until just after eleven. She spent the early part of the dinner rush working the dining room, meeting and greeting guests, and later, expediting orders in the kitchen. While it felt great to be back, as the evening wore on, a nagging sense of loneliness began to tug at her. For her relationship with Kenzie to work, she would have to figure out a way to deal with it. Maybe the loneliness would always be worse after they'd been together. All Jane knew was, when it came time to leave, instead of heading home, she and Mouse drove downtown to Cordelia's loft.

Riding up in the freight elevator, Jane told Mouse to be a good boy. Cordelia had three cats and Mouse was young, playful, and naive when it came to the ways of the feline. He didn't have a mean bone in his body and he didn't understand stealth, manipulation, haughty disregard, or plain old condescension.

Melville, the smallest of Cordelia's brood, was essentially polite but aloof, while Blanche, named for Blanche DuBois in a *Streetcar Named Desire,* lavished affection on everyone. Cordelia found her "disgustingly easy." Apparently, when it came to cats, such behavior was suspect. Lucifer, the one who'd once belonged to a deranged cook, presented the only real threat. Jane kept out of his way and hoped that Mouse would do the same. So far, Lucifer only lurked around the edges of the loft when Mouse was over. He was big, ornery, and autocratic, used to ruling the cat contingent, if not Cordelia herself.

"Just watch out for the striped tabby," said Jane. "Between you and me, I think he's got a screw loose."

Jane knocked on the door. A few seconds later, Cordelia appeared, dressed in jeans and a red-and-black-plaid shirt. And of course, "the hat."

"Hey, have you been raiding my closet?" asked Jane, smiling at the shirt.

"Heavens," said Cordelia, shuddering. She stood back as Jane and Mouse walked in. "You know I wear this shirt when I need to feel strong."

"And what do you need to feel strong *about?*" Jane saw the open laptop sitting on Cordelia's desk.

"None of your business." Cordelia stepped over to the drinks cart and poured them each a glass of wine. "We're in rehearsals as of this afternoon for the fall repertory season. We did our first read-through today."

"What play?"

"Ibsen's last. *When We Dead Awaken*. It went pretty well. I will say that the repertory company this year is the best I've ever assembled. I don't have to spend my time pushing people to do the work they should have done in acting school."

"What are the other plays?"

Cordelia made herself comfortable on her couch. Patting the space next to her, she motioned for Mouse to join her. But before he could jump up, Lucifer leapt up next to her and bared his teeth.

"Now now," said Cordelia. "Get a grip, dear. Mummy doesn't like it when you snarl."

Mouse backed up, not sure what to do.

"Come sit by me," said Jane. She eased down onto one of the overstuffed easy chairs, careful not to spill her wine.

Cordelia's loft was sixty feet by eighty, with twelve-foot-high ceilings. A series of small-paned factory windows comprised one entire wall. The view of downtown Minneapolis was spectacular, especially at night with the lights off, when being in the loft was a little like riding a magic carpet. Cordelia, being a typical theatrical megalomaniac, probably felt she owned the city.

The loft itself was entirely open, except for the platform bedroom and bathroom, which had been walled in for privacy, and sections divided by tri-fold Japanese screens. Cordelia tended to "borrow" props from the theater to change the look of the place. There'd been her Egyptian period. Her Roman period. Her more recent Bloomsbury period. Her French cafe period. Tonight, the loft was cluttered with Greek pillars, no doubt painted plaster. The theater had done Aristophanes' *Lysistrate* last winter.

"We're doing a new play by Adriana Sanchez. It's called *Frigid*."

"Sounds fun."

"Actually, it is. It's a comedy. And then we're doing Somerset Maugham's *The Circle*."

"You've got your hands full."

"Oh, I'm not directing them all. I don't have a death wish. I'm just doing the Ibsen. It's one of my favorites."

"What are you working on over there?" Jane nodded to the desk.

"Nothing." Her eyes rose innocently to the ceiling.

"Your nose will grow if you lie."

"Okay then, it's *something*."

Jane stared back expectantly.

"E-mail. If you must know, it's to Marian."

Marian, Cordelia's newest girlfriend, was the owner of a muffler shop near the university. She'd accompanied Cordelia on her European tour last fall.

"Is she out of town?" asked Jane.

"No. Just out of sorts."

"Uh oh."

"I'm not talking about it."

"Okay."

"We'll work it out."

"Sure you will."

"It's private. Personal."

"I get it."

"Painful."

"Right."

"You can use thumbscrews for all I care, put a contract out on my life, but this mouth remains mum. Deal with it."

"I will," said Jane. Sensing that Cordelia needed more, she added, "As hard as it will be for me, I promise not to beg."

"Good."

"Now, can we move on to what I came here for?"

Blanche oozed her way into Jane's lap.

"*Shocking* behavior," said Cordelia. "Simply shocking."

"Marian or Blanche?"

"Blanche, of course. She should be stripped of her cat credentials."

"I need to talk to you about the Simoneau murders. I know you read several books on the subject. I remember seeing them in your bookcase."

"Is that a veiled comment on my reading habits? True crime stories are mother's milk to me, Jane. Jane Rule is a goddess. And yes, you're right. I followed the trial religiously. But that was a long time ago."

"You don't remember much?"

She tapped her head. "Mind like a Venus flytrap."

"Just give me the high points."

"Is this about the gun you found in Christine's briefcase?"

Jane shrugged.

"Well," she sighed. "I suppose a short tutorial can't hurt. I mean, the crime has already been solved. You can't possibly get in trouble over this one."

"Exactly. So, what happened? I know the basics—three murders. Two family members and the cook."

"Right." Cordelia settled herself more comfortably. "Back in '87, there were"—she counted on her fingers—"seven family members living in the Simoneau mansion, plus, of course, the poor cook. Camille Simoneau, the matriarch of the family, and her two adult children: Bernadette, who was in her early forties at the time, and Laurent, in is mid-thirties. Bernadette had a son, Philip, who'd just graduated from college. Camille had a third child, Gabrielle—everyone called her Gabby. She died the month before the murders. That's why Laurent was in town. He lived somewhere in the south, but had come up for the funeral. Gabby had a young son, Timothy, and a husband, can't recall his name. John or Henry or Frank. Something generic. The husband and the boy were living at the house when Gabby died. Apparently, Camille had hired a nanny to take care of the child because her daughter was sick and the husband had to work. Actually, the nanny—a woman named Cathcart, I believe—was the one who found the bodies."

"Wasn't there a pool boy?"

"No pool and no pool boy, Jane. But there was a part-time handyman who lived on the property. He was a law student. He took care of the place—mowed the lawn, shoveled snow, and did light maintenance around the house. In return, he was allowed to live in the gatehouse free of rent. His name was Dexter Haynes."

The light of memory was beginning to flicker. "I remember now. He was the murderer."

"Sentenced to three life terms in prison."

"You think he was innocent?"

"No."

"So what happened that night?"

"Well," said Cordelia, warming to the subject, "nobody really knows for sure, but the theory goes that Camille was murdered first. Can't recall the exact time, but it was early evening—seven or eight. Fierce thunderstorm that night. There was no forced entry, so it was most likely somebody she knew. She was bludgeoned with a crowbar. Very brutally. If I recall, they found blood spatter on the ceiling. The next two murders were supposedly committed to cover up the first, at least that was the police theory. Philip, Camille's grandson—Bernadette's son—got home a little after the first murder occurred. The murderer must have been waiting for him. From the blood patterns on the floors and area rugs, the police determined that Philip fought back."

"Against a crowbar?"

"A gun. Dexter had to have known where the guns were kept because he was in the house a lot. Philip was shot twice. First in the chest, then in the head, but neither killed him. Or killed him fast enough, I suppose. He dragged himself up the entrance hall steps into the foyer, and from there it looks like there was a fight. But he was weakened by the bullets, and the murderer finished him off with a hammer. His body was found halfway up the central staircase. Again,

37

horribly bloody. So then, the story goes, Dexter went into the kitchen. The cook, a woman named Hanson, was home taking care of the little boy. The nanny had gone out that night to have dinner with a friend, leaving the child behind. Mrs. Hanson lived in a small room right off the kitchen. Maybe Dexter heard the child cry out. Who knows? Whatever it was, something alerted him to their presence. The cook was hacked to death with one of the kitchen knives."

Jane winced. "What happened to the little boy?"

"That's the really gruesome part. Apparently, he must have walked around that bloody scene all by himself. His clothing was soaked with blood."

Jane was beginning to feel nauseous. It was one of the most violent stories she'd ever heard.

"The knife came from the Simoneau kitchen. That was proved later. The gun belonged to Marcel Simoneau. The hammer and crowbar came from Dexter's toolbox, which was in the dining room. At trial, Dexter said he'd brought it in the day before because he was working on a bunch of the windows. They wouldn't open. He said he left the toolbox in the main house because he wasn't done. He figured he'd be back in the morning. But, of course, the next day the watch was found. And then, all hell broke loose."

"What watch?"

"They found Marcel Simoneau's watch in the gatehouse. For a month or so prior to the murders, jewelry and a few small sculptures had gone missing. All of it worth big bucks. Camille contacted the police, but nothing came of it. When the pocket watch was found in the gatehouse it wasn't a huge leap to assume that Dexter was the thief. The assumption was that Camille confronted him about it and fired him, told him she intended to press charges. According to the theory, he must have flipped out. He found Camille in the living room that night and, in a fit of rage, bludgeoned her to death."

"Did he have an alibi?"

"Not much of one. The gatehouse wasn't air-conditioned and it had been a hideously hot summer."

Jane nodded, the comment bringing it all back to her.

"He insisted he'd gone to a movie to cool off. But he paid cash and didn't have the ticket stub. Nobody at the theater remembered him. Dexter is African American. He was good-looking. Articulate. And he was a third-year law student at William Mitchell, close to the top of his class. He had a lot to lose."

Jane took a few seconds to mull it over. "How did he explain the watch?"

"He said it was planted."

"By whom?"

"The cops. Camille was pressuring them to find the thief. He was an easy scapegoat. Of course, everyone figured it was just a way to get himself off the hook. I mean, even I thought it was pathetically transparent."

"Were there any eyewitnesses to the murders?"

"If you don't count the little boy, then no, none. But two of the weapons belonged to Dexter. His prints were all over them."

"Bloody prints?"

"No, he wore his work gloves. They were found out in the back garden."

"But he must have been covered in blood. Did they find his clothes?"

"Nope. No clothes were ever found. No blood in his car. No blood in the gatehouse. And no fibers or hairs at the scene that couldn't be explained by the fact that he worked inside the house fairly often."

"So they prosecuted Haynes on the basis of a stolen watch? That's all?"

"It was apparently enough."

"Weren't there any other suspects? What about the rest of the family?"

"They were one bunch of weird people, Janey. Especially Camille's kids—Bernadette and Laurent. Suffice it to say, in the end, the case against Dexter must have seemed the strongest and that's what the D.A. went with. The jury convicted him after only two days of deliberation. For a capital murder case, with multiple counts of murder one, it was some kind of record."

It was a lot to think about, and at the top of it all was Christine. What had she known, or feared, that had caused her to carry a gun? Maybe it had nothing to do with the Simoneau family. And yet, every time Jane tried to separate it from what Christine had been working on those last few weeks, something in her gut told her she'd taken a wrong turn. Jane had learned over the years to trust her instincts, and that instinct almost screamed at her now that the answer she was looking for lay bound up in one bloody night in late August, 1987.

5

On the way back to her house, Jane drove south on Hennepin. She took a right on 27th and headed toward Lake of the Isles. She'd driven past the Simoneau place several times earlier in the day, but she wanted to get out this time and take a closer look.

The night was breezy and the air was filled with early springtime chill. She turned up the heat in her Mini, twisting around to look at Mouse. "Any opinions on what I should do about the gun in Christine's briefcase?" She waited for several cars to speed past, then turned right onto the parkway. "You never knew her, but you would've liked her. She's the one who brought Bean and Gulliver home, our first two dogs. Those two little guys helped get me up in the morning after she died, and believe me, right about then, that was a big deal."

She could feel Mouse's breath against the back of her neck. "Sit down, boy. We'll get out in just a minute and go for a walk. I want to show you a house, a very spooky old place." When she looked back again, he was curled up on the seat.

She pulled the Mini to the curb a few minutes later, half a block from the mansion. During the day, the paths around Lake of the Isles were filled with joggers and bikers, but at this time of night, the paths were empty.

A light burned in the tower window toward the rear of the house, but the rest of the place was dark. Jane hooked Mouse's leash to his collar and the two of them set off up the sidewalk. In the moonlight, the building rose up like a medieval castle, out of time and space. Darkness hid the worst of the decay, but even at night, anyone could see that the place was a dump.

"Christine told me this house is a replica of a place called Stronvar Hall in Scotland." She wondered why, when she couldn't remember what she had for breakfast, she could pull that arcane piece of information from her memory.

As they walked along, she saw that patches of the lawn were nothing but mud, while other sections were soggy, matted weeds. She wondered who owned it now. Back in the mid-eighties, the house had been a true Kenwood showpiece. Jane assumed the neighborhood wasn't particularly happy with the current state of affairs.

Mouse was examining a particularly enthralling spot along the wrought-iron fence when a car came barreling around the corner and pulled to a stop in the driveway next to the house. At first, Jane thought it was a police car, but looking closer, she realized it was a cab. A man got out of the backseat as the trunk popped open. Stopping by the front window, the man—short and heavy, wearing a raincoat and baseball cap—paid the driver. He muttered under his breath as he walked around to the trunk and, with some difficulty, lifted out three heavy pieces of luggage and dragged them over to the side.

The cab backed up and sped off, leaving the man standing in the dark.

He stood there a moment, glaring after the car, then flung his arms in the air and screamed, "Freakin' fascist state!"

Jane yanked Mouse away from the fence.

Turning his glare on Jane, he said, "Who the hell are you?"

"Me? I'm just out for a walk with my dog."

"Oh hell, since you're here, you might as well help me carry these inside."

Jane was a bit startled.

He picked up two of the bags, leaving the third—the heaviest—for her. Puffing up the walk to the front portico, he glanced over his shoulder to make sure she was following. He tapped the code into the security pad next to the door, then cursed when it refused to open. "Damn it all, she's locked me out again." He banged on the door with his fist.

"Your wife?" asked Jane.

"My witch of a sister," he said, banging louder.

"You aren't, by any chance . . . Laurent Simoneau."

"What if I am?"

Mouse growled.

"That dog of yours bite?"

"No," said Jane, patting Mouse's head. "He's very friendly. He'll wait for me on the steps."

A light came on inside. An instant later, the door creaked back, revealing an equally squat, heavyset woman. Except for the different genders, they could have been twins. They looked like dark-haired Hummels—chubby cheeks, thick legs, oversized feet.

"What are you doing home?" demanded the woman.

Jane assumed she was Bernadette Simoneau, although she made no attempt to introduce herself. She was wearing a flimsy cotton bathrobe tossed over a long, baggy T-shirt. Not Hummel-wear, to be sure, but then it was the middle of the night.

"This entire day has been nothing but one long nightmare," said Laurent, nodding for Jane to follow him inside.

Bernadette held the door for Jane. She didn't seem to find anything unusual in a total stranger hefting her brother's luggage into the house.

Jane struggled up the stairs behind Laurent to the entrance hall. Looking up, she saw that it was lighted by an impressive, cobweb-covered crystal chandelier. The room on her left was cavernous, but had a sparse, strangely empty feel to it, while the room to the right was equally large, but was cluttered with books, clothes, and tons of assorted junk. It looked like a garage sale in progress, except that it wasn't very well organized. It seemed odd to find such vastly different approaches to housekeeping in the same home.

"Who's the *woman?*" asked Bernadette, as if Jane wasn't in the room.

"Just a kind stranger," said Laurent, letting his suitcases drop to the floor. Collapsing into a chair, he added, "I spent most of the day in FBI custody."

Jane turned to look at him. He was sweating, his black hair matted

43

to his forehead beneath the baseball cap. He had on tiny round glasses. Glancing back at Bernadette, she saw that she was wearing equally tiny glasses, but hers were square.

"I simply did what I had to do," said Laurent, heaving a sigh. "I keep forgetting that this isn't a free country anymore." He flapped a finger under his nose, sniffed, then continued, "I fell asleep in my seat because the plane was late taking off. I woke up just as we got out to the runway. That's when I had the premonition. I just knew the plane was going to crash. So I stood up in my seat and demanded that they let me off. Made a real fuss, I did. I didn't care. That plane wasn't going to take off with *me* on it."

"Oh, lord," said Bernadette. She started to walk away.

"Stay here and listen to this. Don't think it couldn't happen to you!"

"You want my opinion," said Bernadette, in her low, whiskey voice. "The FBI should have locked you up. They would have done the world a big favor."

Laurent went on, ignoring her now and addressing his tale of woe to Jane. "They brought the plane back to the gate. This guy in a cheap suit was waiting for me—along with a couple of cops. They put me in an airless room and interrogated me for hours. Me! As if I'm some terrorist. I told them I wanted to talk to my lawyer, but they just kept asking me the same questions, over and over again. I explained, patiently, that I'd had a vision. That plane was going to crash and I wasn't about to allow Sunrise Airlines to lead me like a lamb to the slaughter. I didn't care what they did to me. At least I was alive."

"I'm going back to bed," said Bernadette, shuffling off. She was a quarter of the way up the open staircase when she stopped and turned around. "Tell that woman to leave."

"Maybe I will, and maybe I won't."

Glancing at Jane, she said, "What's your name?"

"Lawless. Jane Lawless."

"Why is that so familiar?" Her eyes searched the air for an answer.

"You any relation to that defense attorney in St. Paul?" asked Laurent.

"He's my father."

"*That's* why I know the name," said Bernadette, clomping back down the stairs. She seemed to want a closer look now that the

44

stranger had morphed into something other than a bellboy. She moved up close, peering over the top of her glasses. "Yes, yes. Mmm."

Jane just stood there feeling like a drop of pond water under a microscope.

"You've got lovely hands," she said, finally, holding up her own stubby fingers, then hiding them behind her back. "And your eyes. What color are they?"

"Sort of blue-violet," said Jane. "My brother's are the same color. It runs in the family."

"Yes, yes. I see."

"Actually," said Jane, "you knew my partner. Christine Kane."

"Kane . . . Kane," repeated Bernadette, tasting the word. "We don't know any Kanes, do we, Laurent?"

"She was the real estate agent who was helping you sell your house back in 1987," said Jane.

"Oh, sure. The *blonde,*" said Laurent, sounding bored. "You remember."

"She died," said Bernadette.

"She did," said Jane.

"She was your *business* partner?" asked Bernadette.

"She was a dyke," muttered Laurent. "I knew it the moment I laid eyes on her."

Bernadette turned to her brother, then back to Jane. Her face puckered.

Jane decided to jump in. "Can I ask you two something?"

They both blinked.

"I was going through some of Christine's things recently and I found a gun in her briefcase. It was the briefcase she was using right before she died. Since she was working exclusively on the sale of your house back then, I was wondering if either of you knew why she might think she needed to carry a gun."

The two Hummels exchanged glances.

"Describe it," said Laurent.

"Small. Carved-ivory handle. I think it might be a derringer."

"Never seen a gun like that," he said, shoving his hands into the pockets of his raincoat. "She certainly never pulled it on me."

45

"Don't be an ass," said Bernadette. "Why would she pull a gun on you?"

Laurent smiled, then frowned, all in the space of a few seconds. "We can't help you."

"I just thought—"

He stood up. "I think you should leave."

"All right," said Jane. "I, ah . . . I'm sorry you had such a bad day."

He removed a handkerchief from his pocket and coughed into it a couple of times. "I'm back in the bosom of my family," he wheezed, casting a sidelong glance at his sister. "Can life get any better?"

Christine

August 21, 1987

10:45 A.M.

Christine stood talking to a contractor in front of the Irving Avenue house when a white limo pulled up to the curb. The driver hopped out and opened the rear door, revealing two women sitting far apart in the backseat. It was another scorching August morning. Dexter Haynes, the handyman employed part-time by the Simoneaus, was in the backyard mowing the lawn. The smell of newly cut grass lingered heavy and sweet in the sticky summer air.

Waving, Christine waited as Camille and her daughter Bernadette got out. Camille was dressed, as always, in black—this morning, a tailored silk designer suit. Camille was a slight woman. The entire family was small—except for Philip, who towered over all of them at five-foot-ten.

Camille was in her late sixties, still an attractive woman, but from what Christine had been able to gather, content with her single status. The only comment of a personal nature she'd ever made was that she'd lived through one marriage, adapted to the quirks of one man, and had no desire to repeat the experience. She enjoyed her position as the matriarch of the family. She was an extremely gracious woman, projecting the quiet confidence of royalty. She had a reputation for being devout, an old-world Catholic by education and temperament, who'd brought her children up to know the difference between right and wrong. It was clear that they often disappointed both her and God, but Camille appeared to have a deeply forgiving nature. She was fond of saying that God loved the saint as well as the sinner, and so did she. She always wore a small gold cross around her neck, a gift from her husband before his death. She touched it often when she spoke, as if it reassured her—a direct link to the divine.

In contrast, Bernadette was a soft, fleshy woman, still darkly pretty, but disintegrating fast into middle age. She always deferred to her mother when they were together. Even apart, Bernadette tended to avoid eye contact and slip down inside of herself, which meant that Christine didn't have a very good read on her yet. She'd seen flashes of Bernadette's temper, intensely acidic flashes that surprised her. But in general, Camille's oldest child kept a low profile. Christine was curious what kind of mother she'd been to Philip.

"Miss Kane," called Camille, floating up the sidewalk. "I'm sorry we're late. A police officer dropped by just as we were leaving the house. Couldn't be avoided." Her Estée Lauder perfume preceded her.

Bernadette often looked uncomfortable in her clothing. Today she wore a yellow sleeveless sundress and white sandals. Unlike her mother, whose salt-and-pepper hair was cut in a neatly trimmed pageboy, Bernadette's hair was long and straight, black and shiny as a crow's. Christine thought it was beautiful.

After introducing the contractor, Christine stood back as the man explained the repairs that needed to be made to the exterior of the house. Bernadette fidgeted with her rings, looking bored and restless. Once they were finished in the front, they all walked around to the back of the house, where the contractor pointed out sections of soffits that needed to be replaced.

While Christine listened, she smiled at Dexter as he came past, pushing the power mower across the long expanse of lawn. She'd only talked to him a couple of times, but he seemed friendly enough. He was in amazing shape. The sweat on his broad, dark brown shoulders glistened in the sunlight.

The group was about to head inside when a red Ford Mustang sailed into the driveway and came to a stop in front of the garage. A gray-haired man in a light blue sport coat and dark glasses got out and motioned for Camille to join him in the drive.

"Will you excuse me a moment?" she asked, looking pained.

The contractor took the chance to excuse himself, saying there were a couple more things he wanted to check in the house.

Sitting down on a covered swing away from the bright sun, Bernadette gazed at her mother as she talked to the man driving the Mustang. "That guy's a P.I.," she said.

It was hard to hear her over the power mower, so Christine sat down next to her.

"Mom hired him a couple of weeks ago."

"You said he's a P.I.?"

"We've had a bunch of thefts from the house recently. Jewelry, mainly. A few sculptures."

"Has your mother talked to the police?"

"Oh, sure. That's why the cop came by this morning. But they haven't done much, so she decided to cover all her bases and hire someone private. So far, he hasn't come up with anything either. There were a lot of people in the house for my sister's wake. Mom assumes the thefts took place that night." She paused, looking down at her black-painted fingernails. A smile crept around the corners of her mouth. "Did you ever meet Gabby?"

Christine shook her head.

"No, you wouldn't have, I guess." Her gaze drifted to the top of the elm tree high above their heads. "I miss her a lot. She was the only person in this entire family who was on my side. Nobody gets their way around Mom. At least, nobody used to." Switching her gaze to Dexter, she continued, "I'm not getting any younger, you know." She followed him with her eyes as he bent down to remove the grass catcher. She seemed to enjoy watching him.

Christine wasn't sure what to say.

Moving closer to Christine, Bernadette said, "Can I trust you with a secret?"

"Uhm——"

"I'm completely deranged right now. Totally out of my mind. Ever been in love?"

"Yes." Christine was surprised by her choice of words, and also amused. Bernadette did indeed have a personality. It just wasn't what Christine had expected.

Tossing her mother a surly look, Bernadette went on. "I'm getting married."

"You are?"

"We'll set a date as soon as he gets out."

"Out of where?"

"Prison."

Christine turned, pulling down her sunglasses to get a better look. "He's in prison?"

"We met because I was writing this friend of his. Brad, the friend, is a poet. So's Kev. Brad lives in Montana and he turned me on to Kev's poetry. Kev's in Stillwater for grand theft auto. Brad thought that, like, we lived so close to each

51

other that we should get to know one another. I promised that I'd read some of Kev's stuff, and that's how it started. I just fell head over heels in love with him."

"When does he get out?"

"End of the week. I've got a trust fund. Mom owns this place, not me. She pretends that I've got some say about it, but I don't. Kev and I can buy a place anywhere we want. Start a new life."

"Well," said Christine, pushing her sunglasses back up on her nose, "that's . . . wonderful." *Mainly for Kev.*

"Yeah, it is." Bernadette caught her mother looking at her. "Remember, don't say a word. I like you so I'm trusting you, but we better change the subject." She pulled away and stretched her arms out in front of her. "Yeah, it was pretty sad about Gabby. She started having heart problems when she was in junior high. Just bad luck, really, because there's no other heart disease in the family. She was the youngest of us, but she died a month ago. She left behind a son, little Timmy, and a husband. Nice guy, but kind of dull, you know what I mean? They all moved into my mother's house a few years back. Gabby couldn't handle Timmy by herself anymore, and Frank, that's her husband, is a schoolteacher, so he was away during the day. Mother hired a nanny to help out. Little Timmy is a sweet kid, and now he's lost his mom. He adored her, you know. We all did."

It was like someone had pulled a cork out of a bottle. Christine had never heard Bernadette so much as put three sentences together, and now she couldn't seem to shut up. "I'm sorry," said Christine.

"She was my best friend."

"Are you close to your brother?"

"Laurent's a bastard."

Christine agreed, but was amazed to hear Bernadette state it so flatly.

"I wish he'd leave, go back to Florida. Not that those dance clubs of his make much money. I wouldn't be at all surprised to find out Laurent robs banks for a living. Mom's been incredibly generous with all of us, but Laurent always has his hand out. It's upsetting, you know what I mean? He's a leech. At least I have a career."

Christine wasn't aware that Bernadette had a job.

"I write short stories."

"Oh, I see."

"I got a real way with words."

"Have you published any of them?"

"Not yet. But I will."

Christine had been feeling a little nauseous all morning, but it seemed to be getting worse. She leaned her head against the swing's back cushion. "Philip is a great guy. You're lucky to have such a wonderful son."

Bernadette nodded. Her jaw clenched and she looked away.

Christine could tell she was done talking.

As soon as Camille was finished with the P.I., they all gathered inside the house. The contractor spent the next twenty minutes suggesting areas where fresh paint or drywall replacement would improve the look of the place. Camille seemed distracted now. She listened patiently, but made very few comment. Before she and her daughter left, she took Christine aside and told her to authorize whatever she felt needed to be done.

Christine was grateful for the carte blanche. It made her job much easier. After the bid was formalized, she slipped it into her briefcase, thanking the contractor for his time. She'd worked with him before and knew that he was expensive, but that the job would get done right and on time, a growing rarity in the construction industry. She stayed behind to make sure the house was locked up tight. It was hard to leave the cool interior for the blast furnace outside, but the only way to get to her car was to brave it. Thankfully, the nausea she'd felt earlier had eased up.

As she came down the back steps, she was suddenly stopped by a searing pain in her abdomen. She rocked forward, catching herself on the handrail, inching her way down the rest of the steps to the bottom. Out of the corner of her eye, she saw Dexter cut the engine on the lawn mower and race toward her, but before he could reach her, the pain exploded again. She felt her legs give way, saw the ground rush at her.

One Month Later

6

On a sunny late-April morning, Jane stood outside the old Xanadu theater, gazing up at a glass and metal tower, one that looked like a stylized radio wave. Years ago, it had glowed pink and turquoise in the night sky. By this time next year, it would glow again. She couldn't believe that a building she'd admired for so long was soon to become her second restaurant in the Twin Cities.

Below the tower was a marquee that formed a triangle over the round, arched entrance. Right now, the marquee was blank, but soon the words "Under Construction" would announce that something new was about to be introduced into the Uptown area. The word "XANADU" was written in distinctive, bold yellow neon deco lettering on top of the marquee triangle.

The upper part of the building was a stepped pyramid design, using blocks of brown-tinted cast concrete to create a sort of Mayan temple effect. The usual deco geometric elements—bold sun rays, strings of zigzags, stylized eagles and flowers—were all present in the facade. In addition, two massive stone-helmeted men with drawn swords had been set into the concrete as a bas relief on either side of the doorway. The entire structure reeked of energy, optimism, and the soaring spirits of Americans between the two world wars.

Since her initial meeting with Judah Johanson, everything had fallen into place so smoothly, Jane almost felt as if the cosmos was telling her it was the right move. Not that she entirely trusted the cosmos. The background check she'd initiated on Judah had proved to her that he was not only a gifted physician, but an honest entrepreneur. Of course, this was a much larger venture than either of them had ever taken on before, but that was part of what excited her.

Jane had so many ideas she didn't know where to start. Judah had already developed the basic structure—the dance band playing early jazz, the Fred Astaire/Ginger Rogers clothes, the art deco mood, etc.—but without great food the club didn't have a chance. Like any good movie or theater piece, where the writing was what made the difference between the ho hum and the unforgettable, Jane believed that food would be the heart of the Xanadu Club experience.

Drawing open one of the heavy glass doors, she was met by a cacophony of sawing and hammering sounds. The old concession area had already been torn out, but the huge screen and all the seats were still in place. It was like an intricate puzzle. Most of the deco artwork would be restored. The basic footprint would remain intact.

Hearing the phone in the pocket of her jeans give a jingle, she fished it out and glanced at the caller I.D. The call was from her neighbor, Evelyn Bratrude.

"Hello?" said Jane.

"Jane, hi. Sorry to bother you."

"Not a problem. I'm down at the Xanadu theater. I've got a meeting with my partner and Cordelia in about fifteen minutes."

"How's it coming?" asked Evelyn.

"It's going great guns." Jane covered her ear and walked back to the doorway, away from the center of the noise. "What's up?"

"You just got a UPS delivery. Since you weren't home, they brought it over here."

"What's it say on the box?"

"Bergeron Books. It's from someplace in Florida."

Jane had looked everywhere for information on the Simoneau murder trial. All the true crime stuff written back in the late eighties and early nineties was out of print. The downtown library said they had a few books on the subject, but when she drove down to check them out, she found they'd all been checked out and never returned. She'd finally located a used bookstore online that said they would hunt down whatever they could.

"I'll stop by this afternoon and pick it up. Will that work for you?"

"I'll be home all day," said Evelyn. "By the way, it's pretty heavy. If it's all books in there, I'd say you've got your work cut out for you."

Jane laughed. "I think you're right. See you in a couple of hours."

She'd been sorting through the boxes in her basement for the last few weeks and she was making good progress, but it was a slow process. She thought about Christine pretty much all the time now. It might not be healthy, but it was apparently the wall of fire she had to walk through to get to the other side.

As she flipped the phone closed, she noticed a young woman outside on 28th taking pictures of the building. It occurred to her that she might be from one of the local newspapers.

Pushing open the glass door, Jane stepped outside.

The young woman took one last shot, then lowered the camera. "Hi," she said, smiling. "I hope you don't mind. This building is incredible."

Jane's eyes widened and then froze. A shiver of recognition slid along the edges of her spine.

"This city is so full of cool architecture."

Jane's mouth opened but nothing came out. She knew she was staring. She had to be dreaming.

"Is something wrong?" asked the woman.

Jane had immersed herself so totally in Christine that her eyes must be playing tricks on her. Giving her head a stiff shake, she glanced away, trying to realign herself in time and space. When she looked back, the woman was still there.

"I'm Greta Hoffman. Do you work here?"

"Yes. No. I mean . . ." She felt like an idiot, but couldn't stop herself from gawking. "I'm sorry . . . if I seem . . ." She stared into the young woman's eyes. This time she saw the differences. The nose was a little sharper. The mouth a little fuller. But the honey-gold slightly wavy hair, the shape of the face, the light blue eyes were all dead on. "You look a lot like someone I once knew." The Christine Jane was seeing wasn't the one in her mid-thirties, the woman who had grown so terribly ill, but the Christine in her mid-twenties—the woman Jane had met and fallen in love with. It almost hurt Jane physically to keep looking at her, but she couldn't tear her eyes away.

"Gee, I'm sorry," said Greta. "I didn't think . . . I mean, I must really look like her."

"You do," whispered Jane.

"I'm sorry. Really. I'll leave."

"No." She reached out to stop her. "Don't go."

The young woman seemed torn. "Look, I just wanted to take some pictures. I like old buildings."

"Nothing wrong with that."

"This theater must be closed, huh?"

"It's being renovated, turned into a restaurant and dance club."

"By you?"

She nodded. "My name's Jane."

"Wow. Very cool." She hesitated. "I'm an art student. I just got accepted to the College of Art and Design."

"Congratulations."

"Thanks. I start in June. I want to be a professional photographer. A photojournalist, really. I'm a huge fan of Eddie Adams, Margaret Bourke-White, Carol Guzy. Oh, and I was amazed by the stuff Stan Honda did of 9/11. Did you see it? I'm talking too much, aren't I? God, I'm such a nerd sometimes. But you seemed so startled. I didn't mean to upset you. Really." She appeared truly distraught at Jane's reaction.

"It's fine," said Jane, sensing that she'd scared her a little. "It's just . . . you look so much like . . . my old friend. And I've been thinking a lot about her lately."

"Yeah," said Greta, opening the black case hanging on her shoulder and tucking the camera away. "I always look like somebody's cousin or sister. I'm part German, part Norwegian. Pretty standard for Minnesota. My mom is actually about a quarter Scottish." She stopped. "I'm talking too much again, aren't I."

"It's fine," said Jane, smiling at her, wishing she'd never stop.

"Is this person I look like—"

"She's dead," said Jane. "A long time ago."

"Wow. Sorry."

Jane glanced over Greta's shoulder and saw Cordelia's Hummer rumble up to the curb across the street.

"Look," she said, thinking fast. "Would you like to have a cup of coffee? It just occurred to me that it might be a great idea to document the renovation of the Xanadu. If you're interested, I'd be willing to pay you to take pictures."

"Well, sure," said Greta, her eyes lighting up. "I'd love to. And I wouldn't ask much."

"Will you meet me at the coffeehouse up the street. Zeno? It's on Lagoon and Hennepin." She checked her watch. "In say, an hour? Could be a little more."

"This is so cool."

Jane saw Cordelia get out of the truck. Instinctively, she acted to protect her secret. She didn't want Cordelia to know she'd run into someone who looked like Christine. She couldn't put her finger on just why, she just didn't. "This may seem strange, but . . . could you leave now? Like I said, I'll see you in an hour or so."

Greta seemed confused, then stiffened. "I get it. There's someone you don't want me to meet. Someone else who knew this other woman."

"Right behind you—on the other side of the street."

She pulled the collar of her coat up around her face and said, "Your name's Jane, right?"

She nodded.

"Meet you at the coffee shop. Take your time. I won't leave without talking to you."

7

After the meeting, Jane had to make up a story about needing to get back to the Lyme House right away so that Cordelia would leave her alone and not press her to have lunch. Jane could tell that Cordelia sensed that something was up, but she let it go, for which Jane was grateful.

On her way to Zeno, Jane realized that there was something vaguely unhealthy about not wanting Cordelia to know about Greta Hoffman, but she rationalized that she didn't want Cordelia to let fly with a bunch of comments on how sick Jane's interest in her was. Jane believed it wasn't sick, it was simple curiosity. And who the hell's business was it if she simply wanted to sit and look at a woman who brought Christine back to her in a real, visceral way? Nothing would come of it. Well, maybe a friendship, if she was lucky, and what was unhealthy about that? No, it was best to keep Cordelia's big mouth out of the equation, especially until Jane's feet were a little more firmly planted on terra firma.

Through the window, Jane could see Greta sitting at a table in the back. During the meeting at the theater, she'd pretty much convinced herself that Greta couldn't possibly look as much like Christine as she'd first thought, but seeing her sitting there studying the menu almost took her breath away. It was like seeing a ghost, not one made of spirit and fog but of flesh and blood. Even Greta's voice was a little like Christine's—gentle, somewhat low, and very midwestern.

Pulling out a chair at the table, Jane sat down. Greta smiled at her, revealing a slight flaw Jane hadn't noticed before. Christine's teeth had been perfectly straight. One of Greta's front teeth was slightly crooked. Jane felt momentarily guilty for making all the comparisons, and yet, in this instance, her brain was on autopilot, cataloging every detail, every nuance.

"Have you been waiting long?" she asked. She glanced at her watch and saw that the meeting had gone a little long.

"It's not a problem. I'm new to Minneapolis, so I just walked around. This is a really great part of town."

"Would you like a sandwich or a salad? My treat."

"I had something pretty gooey and decadent over at the Starbucks in Calhoun Square, so I'm not hungry. But coffee sounds good."

Christine had a sweet tooth, too, thought Jane. Stop it! she ordered herself, frustrated by her behavior. Just let this woman be who she is.

The waitress arrived.

"A mocha," said Greta.

Jane found herself grinning. "Just coffee for me. Black." Watching the waitress walk off, she tried to define how she was feeling. Part of it was a familiar kind of excitement—misplaced, but there it was. She also felt wary. She didn't entirely trust herself. She'd been completely focused on the past for the last few weeks and now here was a young woman who looked so much like Christine, stepping right up to her in the ever so real present. It was bizarre. What she needed now was to find out more about this Greta Hoffman. The more she knew, the easier it would be to distance her from her old love, see her as a person in her own right. At least, that was the working theory.

"So, how did the meeting go?" asked Greta, still glancing at the menu.

"We're in the initial stages of the renovation, so there's a lot to talk about." Jane briefly detailed Judah's ideas.

When the coffee finally arrived, Greta said, "Hey, I didn't expect all this whipped cream." She was clearly delighted. "I'll remember this place. What's the name again?"

"Zeno," said Jane. "You said you were new to Minneapolis. Where are you from?"

"A little town in the northwestern part of the state. Dalton. Ever hear of it?"

"What's it near?"

"Fergus Falls?"

"Oh. Sure."

Greta took a sip, then continued, "Right after I graduated from high school, I got a job as a teller at a bank in Fergus. I've been there six years. I lived at home, so I could save up my money. My intention was to go to college somewhere, but I just kept putting it off. I got involved with this guy." She looked away. "It was going nowhere. Worse than nowhere. I didn't know about the College of Art and Design until a friend told me, so I checked it out. And here I am." She spread her arms.

"You said you'll be starting in June?"

"That's the plan. I won't officially start until the fall, but I can take classes this summer toward my degree. I found a one-bedroom apartment that's not too expensive. It's on 31st and Aldrich. The Peoria. Very old-fashioned, but also very cool. I just wish . . ."

"Wish what?" asked Jane.

"Well, that it had a space I could use as a darkroom. I suppose I could convert the bathroom, but, I don't know. With all the chemicals, it would smell pretty bad. I had a darkroom at home in the basement and I really miss it." She sipped her mocha, looking around the crowded room. "So what about you? Is this your first try at a restaurant?"

Jane took a few minutes to explain about the Lyme House.

"I think I drove past that place when I was looking for an apartment," said Greta. "It's the big log building on Lake Harriet, the one with the deck overlooking the lake."

"That's it. The same architect who designed the Lyme House also did the interior of this place. He's really terrific."

Greta propped her head on the heel of her hand. "Must be incredible to own something like that restaurant."

"It is. I love it."

She looked down, playing with her napkin. "This, um, woman I look so much like. If you don't mind my asking, who was she?"

"My partner."

"At the restaurant?"

"No," said Jane. "My life partner, for want of a better term. Her name was Christine Kane. We were together almost ten years. She died in 1987."

Greta's eyes stayed on Jane. She seemed to be working it out in her mind. "You're . . ."

"Gay?"

"Yeah."

"Yes, I am."

"And you and Christine were, like, lovers?"

"That was part of it, but certainly not all. In most ways, we were like any other couple. Sex was a part of the mix but not the totality. Does that make sense to you?"

"Yeah, I guess so. There was a girl in my high school who was gay. We were pretty good friends for a while. I don't think her parents knew." She looked away, biting her lower lip. "I mean, I've thought about it some. But . . ."

"What?"

"You mean you've *never* slept with a guy?"

Jane shook her head.

"Never wanted to?"

She smiled. "Not really."

"What about Christine?"

"Well, that's different story. She had a girlfriend in high school, and a boyfriend in college. She was five years older than me. We met when I was a senior at the U of M. Christine had been working as a real estate agent for a few years."

"Was it love at first sight?"

Jane laughed. "No, but pretty close. Christine already knew she was bisexual. What that meant, for her at least, was that it was the person she fell in love with, not the gender."

Greta nodded. After a second, she said, "I still don't get it."

Jane found her candor refreshing. "You don't need to."

"I'm not saying that I think being gay is evil or anything, just that it's . . . strange."

"Okay," said Jane. "I can live with that."

"Hey, did you really mean it about paying me to take photos of the renovation of the Xanadu?"

"Absolutely."

"That . . . is . . . spectacular! When do I start?"

"I think you already have."

"I can do it with a digital camera, but black-and-white thirty-five-millimeter photos are more artistic. They're also richer, in my opinion. And I can make the prints myself—as large as you want. Well, fairly large, depending on where I finally set up my darkroom. I brought all my equipment with me. It's in storage right now."

"Could we do both?" asked Jane. "The black-and-white art shots, and also some digital?"

"Great. Perfect."

Jane pulled a business card out of her wallet and handed it across to her. "Do you have a phone yet?"

"Just a cell." She wrote the number on Jane's napkin.

"How does twenty-five an hour sound?"

"Are you kidding me?"

She shrugged. "Not enough?"

"No, that's fantastic! The next thing on my agenda was to look for a part-time job."

"Well," said Jane, finally remembering the coffee that was getting cold in front of her. "I think you just found one."

8

Who the hell *are* you?" demanded Cordelia, blocking the young woman's exit from the coffee shop. Her broad, bulky presence—jewelry jangling, Medusa curls bouncing out from under her fedora—was enough to cause the younger woman to back up a couple of steps.

"Pardon me?"

"Not until you tell me what you're up to, girlfriend. Where'd you get that face?"

The woman seemed startled. "Where did I *get* it?"

Cordelia had waited for Jane to leave Zeno before she made her move. The woman had stayed behind to finish her coffee and that gave Cordelia just what she needed: an opportunity to pounce.

Jane's nose didn't exactly grow when she lied, but for Cordelia, who'd known her since high school, it might as well have. Cordelia considered Jane a lousy liar. As soon as she mentioned she had to get back to the Lyme House, Cordelia knew she was trying to get rid of her. And that made all the little gray cells in Cordelia's brain stand at rapt attention. Now she knew why. Where Jane had found this look-alike was the next question. The one after that was: What the hell did she intend to do with her? The needle on Cordelia's Sick-o-Meter was dangerously close to red alert.

For weeks, Cordelia had been worried. Jane was working hard to clean out Christine's old boxes from her basement. She'd made progress, but sometimes it seemed as if it was in the wrong direction. Cordelia had dropped by after the theater on a couple of occasions and found Jane, brandy in hand, wandering through the house staring at an old photograph, or reading an old love letter. Jane was a strong woman, generally sound-minded, but she was often blindsided by the intensity of her own feelings. Cordelia was the only person who'd ever seen her totally immobilized by grief. It was something she never wanted to see again.

Although Cordelia wasn't all that impressed by Jane's newest love, Kenzie Mullroy, at least Kenzie wasn't a goddamn ghost. And that's what this look-alike represented in Cordelia's mind—and no doubt Jane's. Something had to be done. It was time for Cordelia M. Thorn to take action.

"Don't mess with me," said Cordelia, narrowing her eyes. "I own a Hummer."

"Huh?"

"And I've got connections."

"Let me out of here," said the woman, squeezing past her. She steamed off toward the parking lot behind the Lagoon Theater.

Cordelia caught up with her as she was about to turn the corner. Pressing a hand to her shoulder, she said, "What's the deal, girlfriend?"

"If you try to hurt me, I'll scream." She pulled away, looking around for help. She was clearly frightened.

"If you try to hurt my friend Jane," said Cordelia, "you better learn to scream *loud*."

The young woman turned back to her. "Jane? You're a friend of hers?"

"I'm her *best* friend. How did she find you . . . you . . . what's your name?"

"Greta Hoffman."

"Did she tell you that you look like—"

"Yes. But I'm not that woman."

"*I* know that. *You* know that. But does Jane know it?"

"Well, *yeah*. She's not crazy."

"That has yet to be determined."

"If you're her friend, how can you be so nasty? She's not nasty—she's really nice."

"I'm *concerned*. Jane is in a very strange place right now. She's vulnerable."

"Meaning what?"

"Meaning . . . meaning—" Her hands rose to her hips. "She just . . . like . . . stumbled across you?"

"I was shooting some photos of the Xanadu theater and she came out to ask what I was doing. Turns out she wants the renovation documented, so she asked me to do it. I'm a photographer. Well, not exactly a professional one yet, but I'm about to start school. I'm not trying to hurt your friend, you know. I like her."

"Well roody toot friggin' *toot*," said Cordelia. No matter how innocent this Greta person made it sound, something about the situation smelled. And it didn't smell like Chanel Number 5. "Where are you from?"

"Dalton, Minnesota."

"Work history?"

"Is that necessary?"

Cordelia glared.

"I worked at Miner's Savings and Loan in Fergus Falls for six years—up until last week. That's when I moved down here. I start college in June."

Cordelia pulled the strap of her purse off her shoulder and removed a pen and a small notebook. Clicking open the pen, she said, "Social security number?"

"I don't have to give you that."

Lowering her voice, she said more forcefully, *"Social security number?"*

"008-993-4939."

"Date of birth?"

"You know, if Jane has any other friends like you, maybe you could tell me now. I'll print out my references so I can hand them out as necessary."

"Cute. Answer the question."

"April 11, 1980. I currently live at 3126 Aldrich Avenue. I'm five-six, one hundred and twenty-two pounds, stripped. I have a mole on my right shoulder and a scar on the index finger of my left hand—I cut

69

myself on a beer bottle when I was nineteen. No stitches. My finger-prints are on file with the Fergus Falls P.D. because I threw a brick through a guy's car window once. Long story. I won't bore you with the details, but you can get them from my parents—Wes and Jean Hoffman, 533 Leland Road, Dalton. Never served any jail time. I wear a size eight shoe. I like foreign films. My I.Q. is above average, al-though I don't know the exact number. I hate eggs. I like guys, in case you were wondering. Anything else you want to know?"

Cordelia thought about it for a second, then figured she had enough. "So . . . let me get this straight. You're saying it's just pure serendipity that you bumped into Jane?"

"What else would it be?"

Wasn't that the question of the hour.

The fright had disappeared from Greta's face, but she still seemed nervous. And she looked so damn much like Christine she even had Cordelia spooked.

"Did Jane offer you a job?"

"Yes. And I took it. Now if that's all—"

Cordelia put her hand on Greta's shoulder again. "For now. But I'm watching you, Missy."

"Goody. I live on the first floor, south side. Buy yourself a pair of binoculars and knock yourself out."

9

Calvin Dutcher stood on a bluff, gazing down at the farmhouse he was about to buy. It was small, but it would do. The land around it was of no particular interest to him. He was a salesman, not a farmer. Farmers worked too hard for too little money. Calvin was smarter than that. He liked the fact that he only needed to work part of the time to make a reasonable living. Money had never been the most important thing to him. What Calvin valued most was his time and his privacy.

Most of his days were spent on the road, listening to the radio or playing his favorite CDs. Sometimes he'd read a book while he was driving. He'd shove both arms through the steering wheel and prop the book up against the dash. His older brother told him it was dangerous, but Calvin had never had an accident, so what the hell did his brother know.

Every now and then he'd stop in a large town so he could catch a movie. Other times, if he'd had too much to drink the night before, he'd sleep in until the headache went away. But he always made it on time to his accounts. He'd been selling farm equipment for a couple of years. Since he'd grown up on a farm, learning the product line had been a snap.

This farmhouse he was gazing down on was exactly the kind of remote location he'd been searching for. He couldn't wait to show it to Greta. Once they were married, they'd move in and live happily ever after. Well, he wasn't *that* innocent. He knew they'd have problems, but they'd work them out. Greta would need to quit her job, but that was okay with Calvin. He made enough money to support them both.

He'd been gone this time a little over three weeks, but tonight he'd sleep in his own bed. He lived in Fergus Falls, had a small apartment that he kept for the half dozen days a month he wasn't out of town. It wasn't much of an apartment, but it served his purposes. When he was home, he'd bring Greta over for lunch. After they'd had sex, he'd make her a sandwich and they'd sit on the couch and talk. He liked talking to Greta. She was pretty, and she made him feel special. She had spunk, too—sometimes too much spunk, but that was okay. With Greta by his side, he felt his life could work. Before he'd met her, he was just a lonely guy on the prowl. He'd done some things he wasn't proud of. But now he had a goal—and a dream. He and Greta would have a good life together, he'd make sure of it.

The first order of business once he got back to Fergus this afternoon, even before he unloaded his bags, was to stop at the bank and see her. He rarely called while he was gone because he didn't like phones. He was never sure who else might be listening. Calvin didn't have many friends, but those he did have told him he was paranoid. They laughed at him. Calvin just shrugged. He figured when some asshole from the FBI showed up to ask them questions about their tax returns or their gun vaults, he'd be the one laughing then.

Screw 'em all. Calvin could take care of himself. He might be the quiet type, not the kind of guy who got up in other people's faces, but that didn't mean he couldn't handle himself in a fight. He always stayed at motels that had workout rooms. He cared for his body the way he'd care for a piece of expensive equipment. Except that he smoked and sometimes drank too much. But he figured he had to have a few vices, otherwise he'd end up like his old man—a man with superior values but no idea how to have a good time.

Calvin took one last look at his new house, then scrambled down the hill. An hour later, he drove his van into the parking lot at the bank. Greta was due for a review in May, which usually meant a raise. Not that it mattered anymore. Calvin intended to let her know that the house he'd told her about was now his, or would be in a few weeks. They could finally make plans to get married. Of course, it would come as a big surprise. Maybe even a shock. He figured she didn't think he'd ever settle down. He hoped the house would prove to her that he was serious.

Once inside, he scanned the row of tellers, but didn't see her. He wanted her so bad he could almost taste her skin on his tongue. It was close to four, the time when she usually ended her day.

Stepping up to the information desk, he asked Brenda Taylor, a customer service rep, where she was.

Brenda gave him a confused look. "She quit."

"Quit?"

"Sure, didn't she tell you? She gave her notice . . . let's see . . . must have been three weeks ago. She left last week. We were all really sad to see her go, you know. We had a great party over at the VFW."

A gust of panic blew through him. He felt like a fool. Greta was his girlfriend and she hadn't told him any of this. "Did she get another job offer?"

Brenda shrugged. "Didn't say."

"What *did* she say?"

"Just that it was time to move on. She seemed excited."

Calvin felt his neck get hot. "But she's still living in Dalton with her parents, right?"

"Don't know. I've got the number if you need it."

"No thanks." He turned around slowly, ran a hand through his coarse brown hair and down over his beard. He was bleeding inside from embarrassment, but he'd be damned if he'd let anybody see it.

After skidding out of the parking lot, he headed for the highway. He kept replaying a conversation he'd had with Greta right before he left. All the way to her parents' house, the knot in his stomach tightened.

Pulling at last into the driveway behind Wes Hoffman's Dodge Stratus, Calvin sat for a moment and tried to calm himself down. The palms of his hands were sweaty so he wiped them on his jeans. He might be the kind of guy who always imagined the worst, but that didn't mean it wasn't true.

Pushing out of the front seat, he walked across the scrubby grass and hopped up the steps to the front door. He leaned on the doorbell. Through the screen, he could hear the TV in the living room.

"Calvin, hi," said Mrs. Hoffman, emerging out of the dimness. There was nothing friendly in her look. She didn't even unlock the screen.

Calvin rammed his hands into his pockets. Clenching his fists, he said, "Is Greta here?"

"No, I'm sorry, she's not."

"Where is she? I've been on the road so we haven't talked in a few weeks." He tried a smile, but she didn't return it.

"The fact is . . ." She took off her reading glasses. "She's not living with us anymore, Calvin."

His heart stopped. "Where is she?"

"Well, ah, just a minute." She left him standing at the door.

Calvin felt like an outlaw, not even being allowed in. Greta had probably told her about the fight they'd had right before he left. It wasn't their first, but this one hadn't been his fault. He assumed she'd failed to mention that part.

A few seconds later, Mrs. Hoffman returned. This time she was holding an envelope. "Greta left this for you. She said if you came by, I was to give it to you." She opened the screen and handed it to him.

He glanced at his name on the outside. It was written in red ink. "Where'd she go?"

"I imagine it's all in the letter."

He stared at her coldly. "Just tell me."

"I can't, Calvin. I'm sorry. Whatever she wants you to know is in there."

Something raw and abandoned rose up in his throat. Staring down at the envelope in his hand, he turned around and stumbled back down the steps. He couldn't seem to breathe. On the way to the van he ripped the envelope open, crumpling it in his hand as he read the words scrawled on the notebook paper:

Dear Calvin: By the time you get this I'll be gone.
We both know it's not working between us. I've
decided to move on with my life. Don't be angry.

74

*This is for the best. A clean break is what we both
need. I wish you well.*

Greta

Calvin stopped dead in his tracks. Staring straight ahead but seeing nothing at all, he whispered, "Like hell it's over, Greta. Like *hell*."

10

That night at the restaurant, Jane sat down in her desk chair and kicked off her boots, then unpinned her hair from the knot at the back of her head and ran her hands through it until it hung loose around her shoulders. It had been a busy evening up in the main dining room. There was a stack of work waiting for her, but she needed a few minutes to relax. Glancing at her phone, she saw she had a message waiting. She hit the play button, then leaned back in her leather chair and closed her eyes.

"Jane, hi. It's Kenzie."

She smiled when she heard her voice.

"So how's my business mogul? Anything new on the Xanadu Club front? I assume you're off meeting and greeting at the Lyme House. Or maybe you're ankle deep in some kitchen disaster. What you see in that business is beyond me, darlin', but hey, I'm happy with a steak and baked potato, so what do I know. Listen, I thought I'd call you now because I'm not going to be home later. I'm having a beer in town with a couple of my students."

Kenzie lived in the countryside outside Chadwick. She owned a house and a barn, and although she didn't have any livestock, she did have two horses she loved beyond reason. The old farmhouse sat on twenty-six acres, miles from the nearest neighbor. She'd told Jane right up front that if the horses liked her, she was in. If they didn't, well. It was a joke, of course, but Jane figured there was probably some truth in it. Thankfully, the horses—Rocket and Ben—had taken to her immediately. Jane had never ridden a horse before, but by the time she left, she was starting to get the hang of it. Kenzie, who always wore cowboy boots, drove Jane into town one afternoon and bought her a pair. They were kind of stiff, but Kenzie assured her that the longer she wore them the more comfortable they would become. Sort of like a good relationship, she added with a completely straight face.

"So, have you found out anything new about the gun in Christine's briefcase? I assume you're still cleaning out boxes, although you're probably almost done by now."

Jane felt a pang of guilt. She should be done. And she would be, soon. She just needed a couple more days.

"Anyway, I'll talk to you tomorrow. I'll try to e-mail those photos to you before the weekend. I miss you like crazy, darlin'. I don't like this long-distance romance stuff *at all*." She paused. "Oh, hell. I hate talking to this damn thing. I don't like whispering sweet nothings into a machine. I'd say a whole lot more if you were around. Let's make a point to both be there the next time we talk." She laughed.

Jane laughed, too, shaking her head.

"Bye, babe."

Touching the phone, Jane realized she wanted to talk to her right now. She wanted to hear what Kenzie didn't want to whisper into her voice mail. Jane had been on such an emotional high when she came home from Nebraska. She couldn't imagine that glow ever dimming. But then she'd found the gun. And now there was Greta. Jane wanted to tell Kenzie about her, about her reaction to her. Not because Greta posed any threat to their relationship, just because, well, because Kenzie should know.

"Mouse? You awake?"

Mouse's head popped up. He'd been sleeping on the couch.

"This . . . idea occurred to me while I was working the dinner shift. It's about the third floor at the house. It's empty, you know. Make a perfect darkroom. Do I call Greta or don't I?"

He yawned.

It was hard to tell from that what his position was.

Digging the napkin out of her pocket, Jane punched in the number for Greta's cell phone. She resisted even a cursory examination of her motives, she simply wanted to run the idea past Greta to see what she thought.

The phone rang a few times.

"Hello?" said Greta finally. She sounded like she was chewing.

"It's Jane Lawless. We met this morning—"

"Sure, Jane," she said, swallowing what was in her mouth. "I'm hardly going to forget the name of my new employer. I've got some great news. I found this terrific photo store not far from my apartment. It sells everything I need. Some of my chemicals were a little low. And I bought more photo paper. I also picked up this spectacular used eight mega pixel digital camera with a seven power optical zoom. Actually, I'll be paying for it for the next two years, but hey, that's why artists live in garrets, right?"

"You've lost me, but if you're happy, I'm happy."

"Oh, I'm happy. Penniless, but happy."

"I've been thinking about something. This may not appeal to you, so just say no if it doesn't, but I have a third floor at my house that I used to rent out." Jane didn't mention that it was once Christine's office. "A couple of years ago I had a bad experience with a renter so I stopped offering it. But it's available. I'm not sure what you'd need for a dark-room, but it has a good water supply. A kitchen, bathroom, whatever you might need. And if the chemicals don't smell that great, you wouldn't be living around them. There's some furniture up there, but I'm sure we could move it around, even bring up a table for you. I've got one in the basement that might work."

"How much would it cost me per month?"

"Consider it a perk of the job."

"Are you kidding me? Jane, you're amazing! When can I come look at it?"

"How about tomorrow?"

"I have meetings during the day. What about tomorrow evening? What time are you done working at your restaurant?"

"Would ten be too late?"

"It's a date."

Jane gave her the address and directions from her apartment.

"You are a godsend, you know that? I'll figure out a way to thank you properly."

"No need," said Jane. "See you tomorrow night."

Earlier in the day, Jane had picked up the box of books on the Simoneau trial from her neighbor's house. For the next few minutes, she sat and dug through the box. She was beginning to feel as if all this effort was a waste of time. The more she thought about it, the more unlikely it seemed she'd ever figure out why Christine had that gun.

The first volume she picked up, *Frenzy* by Peter Hogarth, was a rather thin true crime take on the events and the personalities involved in the case. The second volume, *Death of an American Dream* by a man named Lynwood Demarell, was an in-depth study of Dexter Haynes, the young African-American law student convicted of the crimes.

She was just about to examine the third book, *Written in Blood* by Susanne Santi, when the phone rang.

"This is Jane," she said absently.

"Oh, good. You're still here." It was Axel, one of her managers, calling from upstairs. "There's a woman in the dining room who wants to talk to you."

"What's her name?"

"Sorry, the waiter who passed the message along didn't get it."

"Okay, I'll be right up."

She put the books back in the box and closed the top. "Mouse," she said, pulling on her boots, "I won't be gone long. I think we can head home early tonight. I've got some reading to do."

He turned on his back so she could scratch his belly as she passed the couch.

"You're such a lush," she said, smiling down at him.

On her way upstairs, she glanced into the pub. It seemed crowded for a Tuesday night. A rowdy group was playing a game of darts, and several regulars sat in the raised booths playing cribbage. There was no music onstage tonight. Jane usually reserved that for weekends. She had an Irish folksinger scheduled for Friday. Someone new. He'd play for three nights, and if people liked him, she would invite him back later in the summer.

When she reached the top of the stairs, she stopped at the reception desk. Axel pointed to a couple sitting at a table by the windows.

"Oh, it's Molly Stine," said Jane. She hadn't seen Molly for almost a year. Last she'd heard, Molly had moved to Fargo. "Hi stranger," said Jane, approaching the table. "Are you back for a visit?"

Molly slipped out of her chair and gave Jane a hug. She introduced the man she was with as Neil Bollinger. Jane shook his hand. She'd never met him before, but assumed he was Molly's latest. Ever since her divorce, she'd had a series of relationships, none of them lasting more than a couple of years.

"Will you excuse me?" said Neil, rising from the table. "I need to call my daughter and this might be a good time."

"We'll be right here," said Molly with a wink. She nodded for Jane to take his chair. "We gotta talk."

"About Neil?"

"He's a hunk, isn't he?" She grinned at his retreating back. "No, about something else." She leaned into the table. "I'm back from Fargo, living in Burnsville at the moment."

"Welcome home."

"Thanks. Fargo wasn't my cup of tea. *At all.* But let's not talk about that." She made a sour face, then squirmed in her chair until she found a more comfortable position. "Look, I'll try to make this quick. I ran into Cordelia a couple weeks ago. When I asked her how you were, she mentioned that you'd met a new woman, someone you were serious about. She said she hadn't seen you this happy in years."

Jane and Christine had been good friends with Molly and her second husband, Aaron Stine. Back in the mid-eighties, they had dinner together at least once a month. Molly had divorced Aaron shortly after Christine died. In the intervening years, Jane had lost track of him but had stayed friends with Molly.

"I feel really awful about this," said Molly, taking a sip of her wine. "I've got something of yours. I should have given it to you a long time ago."

"Something of *mine?*"

"Actually, the night before Christine went into the hospital, we all got together for dinner? Remember? She got sick? We had to call the paramedics."

Jane remembered all too well.

"Well, that night, she arrived at the house before you did, and right away I could tell something was wrong. She opened the trunk of her car and took out her briefcase. But, on the way to the house, it seemed so heavy that I asked her if I could carry it for her. When we got inside, she opened it and took out this package—it was wrapped in brown paper and strapping tape. She said it was a present she'd bought for your birthday, but she didn't want you to see it. She told me just to hide it, that she'd come back for it later. But then—" Molly looked down. "Then she went into the hospital. After she died, I asked Aaron what he thought we should do with it. We were fighting almost all the time by then. He said he'd take it over to you, but you were having such a hard time dealing with Christine's death that I thought it might just make things worse. So I put it in the basement, intending to give it to you later, when you were feeling better. But then my life blew apart. Aaron left. I filed for divorce. The house was put up for sale. I completely forgot about it. I must have packed it, although I don't recall doing it. I was pretty out of it right around then. When I moved to that condo down by the river, I left a lot of my stuff in storage. But when I moved back from Fargo, I figured it was time I cleaned it all out. That's when I found it again. And again, I didn't know what to do. I felt like a total shit for forgetting about it. When I saw Cordelia and she told me how happy you were, I figured maybe it was time to give it to you. Are you angry with me, Jane? I wouldn't blame you if you were."

"No, of course not."

"'Cause I really am sorry. I thought I could drop it by the restaurant tomorrow. Would that work for you?"

"Sure," said Jane, feeling a bit dazed by the prospect of a birthday present from Christine so many years after the fact. "Or I could come by your place if that would be easier."

"I've got a meeting downtown at noon. I might as well drop it off."

"Do you have any idea what's in the package?"

"Sorry. Like I said, it's heavy. That's all I know." She reached for

Jane's hand. "I guess this really takes the cake when it comes to be-lated presents, huh? But better late than never. God, I hate it when people spout platitudes at me. But who knows. In this case, maybe it's true."

11

Bernadette carried her coffee into the tower room, setting the cup on a small round table next to the La-Z-Boy. Before sitting down, she gazed out the open window, taking deep breaths, appreciating all the wonderful springtime smells wafting toward her on the soft morning breeze. She liked the word "waft" and intended to use it in a short story later in the day. She also had recently been drawn to the word "barnacle." Using the two together would give her the structure for the tale. She loved to puzzle out how to put words together to form unexpected thoughts. Bernadette believed in mystical convergence, almost as much as she believed in the beauty and the mystery of words.

Laurent had spent most of the morning banging around in his rooms at the other end of the house. She didn't have a clue what he did to make such a racket, but it was an obvious effort to annoy her. A few years back he'd bought some cymbals, tending to crash them in the middle of the night for maximum effect. The ploy was so obvious that even he stopped after a couple of weeks. Either that or he didn't like getting up at three in the morning just to ruin her night's sleep.

Ever since Bernadette and Laurent had become roommates, Laurent's entire existence had seemed like one long attempt to annoy her and get her to move out. But he could toss cherry bombs at the walls for all she cared. She had nowhere else to go.

She stirred Splenda into the coffee with a small spoon she'd placed next to the cup. The issue they were currently arguing about was their growing insolvency. And this problem wasn't minor, like the usual snits about leaving lights on all night, dirty clothes in the stairway (a common area), dirty dishes in the kitchen (another partially common area).

Bernadette and Laurent's living arrangements were unusual, but it was the only way they could figure for the two of them to coexist under one roof. They had simply divided up the mansion. Cut it in half with just a few overlaps. If they hadn't done it, there would have been another Simoneau family murder. When Bernadette stated it just that way to Laurent, he accused her of being flip, of not truly appreciating the horror of what had gone on. She appreciated it, all right, more than he realized. But she wasn't about to let him tell her how to state things. She was, after all, the wordsmith in the family. She said precisely what she wanted to say. If he couldn't appreciate her wit and erudition, the depth and breadth of her creative spirit, to hell with him.

Over the banging, Bernadette became aware of the sound of a motor. Probably someone out mowing the grass. Not *their* grass, of course. The neighbors weren't being neighborly anymore because Bernadette and Laurent had lost their lawn service last summer, due to a plethora of bounced checks. The exterior of the house was a common area. Bernadette had a bad back, so she couldn't be expected to care for the yard. Laurent said he had allergies, though Bernadette was positive it was just an excuse to get out of doing the work that needed to be done. She'd be damned if she'd take what little money she had left and spend it doing *Laurent's* work.

The perfect solution to their current financial difficulties was to sell some of the artwork. Sure it was pretty, but they couldn't eat it. Stubborn Laurent wouldn't hear of it. He said that if Bernadette tried to sell one of the paintings, he'd go to Frank DeWitt, the executor of Timothy DeWitt's estate, and tell him that little Tim's aunt was trying to erode his net worth. With the exception of their personal trusts, everything they had, the three of them owned in common.

All these years, mean old Frank had refused to allow his son to see them. Bernadette thought it was monstrous, but what could she do? She'd written little Timmy recently, inviting him to come for a visit. For once her letter hadn't been returned, so she had some hope that Timmy himself had actually received it. But she wasn't holding her breath.

The sound of the motor grew louder and more irritating. Bernadette stood and peered out the window, trying to locate the offending noise. To her surprise, she saw a motorcycle down in the drive. A young man sat astride it, helmet in his lap, gazing up at the house. Something about him seemed familiar.

Setting the coffee cup down, she pressed her hands together expectantly. Could it be? She felt like Rapunzel. In the tower. Peering out her one lone window. Trapped by wickedness. Was this little prince Timmy come to save her? The young man on the motorcycle had the same black curly hair that little Timmy'd had as a child. If it *was* little Timmy, he'd certainly grown. He was . . . She searched for the right word. And then it came to her. Little Timmy had become a stud muffin! She'd heard the term on a soap opera last week and had been determined to use it sometime soon. Now was the perfect opportunity.

"Timmy," she called from the tower window. She waved, but over the sound of the motor, he couldn't hear her. Oh, it just *had* to be little Timmy, she whispered to herself, rushing to the doorway and down the stairs.

She met Laurent in the entrance hall.

"I'm gonna tell that stupid kid out there to take a hike," he said on his way to the door.

"No, no," called Bernadette. "I think he may be our nephew."

Laurent turned to face her. "Huh?"

"Little Timmy. Remember? Gabby's little boy?"

"I know who Timmy is. Don't talk to me like I'm a moron."

Together they poked their heads outside.

"He's awfully big," whispered Laurent.

"And handsome," said Bernadette.

"I like those black motorcycle boots."

"Me, too. I wonder where he bought them."

"You really think it's him?"

"I invited him to visit us."

They inched down the steps.

The young man on the cycle cut the motor as he saw them approach. "Aunt Bernie?" he said, lifting his shades. "Uncle Laurent?"

"Little Timmy?" they said in unison.

Bernadette started to tear.

"Ah, actually, nobody calls me that anymore. It's Tim. Just . . . *Tim*. Okay?"

"What are you doing here?" asked Laurent.

Tim shrugged. "I told Dad I wanted to check out the U of M. I'm in my second year at Ridgewater College in Willmar—pre-veterinary medicine. I'm thinking I'd like to transfer here. As I was riding around the campus, I got this idea that maybe I should come see you. I read that letter you sent a few weeks ago, Aunt Bernie. You seemed so upset about that woman who visited you. What was her name?"

"Lawless," mumbled Bernadette. She hadn't told Laurent she'd written Timmy about her.

"You said it brought back a lot of bad memories, memories about . . . you know." He lowered his shades.

Bernadette's heart fluttered and almost stopped.

"Dad thinks we've put it all behind us, but that's not how it is for me. I mean, he made me go talk to a bunch of therapists when I was a kid, but I was never sure what I was supposed to say. I know I was there that night, but I can't remember a thing about it."

"Count that as a blessing," said Laurent.

"Amen," said Bernadette, feeling the tension in her shoulders ease.

"But, still, I wanted to come see you guys, and see this house again." His gaze traveled to the top of the tower. "It's . . . huge! I thought maybe I'd remember it from when I was a kid, but I don't." Switching his attention to the front yard, he added, "You two need some serious help."

"I suppose we do," said Laurent, giving Tim his meek look.

The look was so fake it made Bernadette want to puke.

Tim rested his hands on the handlebars. "Well, I've got a few hours before I need to get back. Maybe I could work for a while. You got a rake? A clippers? A lawn mower?"

"Of course," said Laurent. "But I'm not sure the lawn mower works."

"No problem. I can fix it."

"You can?" said Bernadette.

"Sure." Tim set the kickstand, then swung his leg off the cycle. "I'm really good with motors."

"You have such strong shoulders," said Bernadette. Maybe he *had* come to rescue her after all.

"I do?" His chin dropped to his chest. "Yeah, well, Dad always stressed athletics. I'm a pretty fair baseball player. And I like rock climbing a lot. Either of you ever go rock climbing?"

Bernadette and Laurent shook their heads.

"Huh. Well, let me get started on that front lawn. We can talk when I'm done."

"If you don't have to get home tonight, you're welcome to stay here," said Laurent.

"I don't think Dad would like that much."

"We've got plenty of room," said Bernadette, smiling sweetly. "And it would be so wonderful to catch up. Surely your father could let you stay for one measly night."

"Well . . ." He took off his sunglasses, glanced back at the house. "I would like to spend some time here. I kinda doubt Dad would go for it though. But . . ."

"But what," coaxed Bernadette.

"I suppose I could tell him I was bunking with a friend. I've got a bunch of pals who live in the cities."

"Our lips would be sealed," said Bernadette, making a little twisting gesture near her mouth. "You can count on us for absolute discretion."

"Let me think about it, okay?"

"What's to think about?" said Laurent, slapping him on the back. "You're home at last, my boy. Now let's go look for those tools." Reaching up to drape his arm around Tim's shoulders, he maneuvered him toward the garage.

12

The following morning, Jane walked out of the restaurant kitchen straight into Cordelia.

"Consider me the immovable object." Her fedora was pulled low over one eye.

"Does that make me the irresistible force?" Jane assumed her friend's grim demeanor was a joke.

"It makes you a credulous idiot."

"Pardon me?" She tried to dodge past her, but Cordelia was having none of it. She grabbed Jane by the shoulders and wouldn't let go.

"What the hell tripped your trigger?"

"Why didn't you tell me about Greta?"

That brought her up cold. "How could you possibly know about her?"

"Never attempt to keep secrets from Cordelia, Janey. It's useless *and* unwise."

"Don't you have something else you need to do? Isn't Hattie coming back soon?" Hattie Thorn Lester was Cordelia's two-and-a-half-year-old niece. Hattie's mother—Cordelia's younger sister, Octavia—was still filming that movie in Switzerland, but Hattie and her nanny were due back in Minneapolis any day. As unlikely as it sounded, Hattie and Cordelia had bonded in a big way. Octavia was only too pleased to have a place to dump her kid while she was off becoming a movie star. Cordelia had adopted the Auntie Mame role, one she was playing with increasing gusto.

"Don't change the subject," ordered Cordelia. "What are you up to with that woman?"

"Not a thing," said Jane. "Why do you always assume the worst?"

"Oh, let me count the ways." She let Jane go. "I find you having coffee with a woman who just *happens* to be a dead ringer for your old partner. This comes at a time when you've determined to put the past—meaning Christine—behind you. In case you forgot, you have a new love, but here you are dillydallying with a stranger."

"I wasn't dillydallying, whatever the hell that means."

"No, you offered her a job. How transparent is that? It's just a way of keeping her around, so you can—"

"What?" said Jane, looking up sharply. "What are you suggesting?"

"You tell me."

She headed for the stairs. Cordelia loved to put Jane's romantic life under a microscope, but today she'd gone too far.

Cordelia rushed to catch up. "Are you saying her physical appearance had nothing to do with that little job offer? My God, Jane. They could have been twins separated at birth."

Jane steamed down the hall to her office. "So what if it did?"

"Did you even spend one minute checking her out to see if she's for real?"

Jane had been planning to do that this morning. She hated herself for even thinking like that, but she'd been burned before. "I just met her yesterday."

"So did I, but *I've* already done some research."

"Oh, joy." Jane sat down behind her desk. She'd left Mouse at home. Evelyn Bratrude was going to take him to the dog park after lunch. "She's an ax murderer, right?"

Cordelia draped herself across a chair, crossing her legs and glaring at Jane with her one visible eye. "No, she's for real. Worked for a bank in Fergus Falls. Lived with her parents up until a few weeks ago. But something's not right, Janey."

"I'll make a note on my calendar. This was the day Cordelia warned me that Greta Hoffman was an undercover CIA operative and had successfully infiltrated my life."

"You mock me now, but you'll see. Coincidences like this just don't happen."

"Oh, please, Cordelia. Coincidences happen all the time. They're part of life." She was about to give her a couple of examples when a knock on the door interrupted her. "Come in," she called.

It was Carol Thomas, one of her bartenders. "A woman just dropped this package off for you," she said, walking over and setting it on the desk.

"Was her name Stine?"

"Yeah, I think so. She said you'd know what it was."

Jane stared at it. She'd thought of little else since last night. But last night she'd been captivated by the idea that there was a present out there from Christine, one she'd never received. Now, seeing the package on her desk, a wave of apprehension rolled over her. "Thanks, Carol."

After the bartender left, Cordelia leaned forward and looked at it. "What is it?"

"A present."

"From Molly? Isn't she great? I ran into her a few weeks ago. Did you know she'd moved back from Fargo?"

Jane nodded.

"Why do you look like that?"

"Like what?"

"Like you're about to take your first skydiving lesson. Do you know what's in the package?"

"Honestly, Cordelia, I have no idea."

"Is it ticking?"

"Yeah, in a way I think it is."

Cordelia adjusted the dozens of tiny silver bracelets on her arms. "Well? Are you going to open it or should we call in the HazMat team?"

It couldn't have looked more innocuous. Jane pulled it closer. "It's a birthday present."

"Your birthday isn't until next fall."

"A belated gift." She looked up. "From Christine."

Cordelia's eyes widened. "Are you kidding me?"

Jane briefly explained what Molly had told her last night.

"Whoa," said Cordelia, pushing her chair back. "This is getting downright spooky. You're telling me these are *all* coincidences?"

"I'd say they were cause and effect," said Jane. "Well, except for Greta. That was a coincidence."

"Right. And water runs uphill."

Jane removed a scissors from the top drawer.

When she hesitated, Cordelia said, "Well? Open it!"

"I'm working up to it."

"Work faster."

"Don't push, Cordelia."

"Are you saying I'm insensitive?"

"No, I'm saying this is hard."

Cordelia drummed her red nails on the arm of the chair. After a few more seconds, she said, "If you don't open it soon, Janey, I may explode. And then you really will need a HazMat team."

Jane cut through the wrapper and the tape. Inside, she found newspaper wrapped around a heavy object. She pulled the paper off.

"Wow, a sculpture," said Cordelia. "It looks like a Max Le Verrier. It's certainly from that era—between the two world wars."

"Who's Max Le Verrier?" Jane moved it around looking at it from different angles. It was a teenage girl wearing a sheath and kneeling on a pallet, her body thrust back, her arms straight out in front of her holding a large round orb. The details were exceptionally fine, the form a study in youthful grace. Jane thought it was lovely.

"He was a famous French sculptor, known for his bronzes of women. I think he had a foundry in Paris, or somewhere around there. Lots of it was just decorative, like bookends, or ashtrays. Our scene shop copied some of his stuff for that production of *A Long Day's Journey into Night* we did a few years back."

This sculpture was a dull rusty brown, with the exception of the ball, which looked like a large polished round agate. The base was a deep mahogany-colored marble. As Jane studied it, it struck her that she'd seen it before. "Oh, my God," she said, a jolt of adrenaline hitting her hard.

"What?" said Cordelia, sitting bolt upright.

Jane reached down into the canvas bag she'd brought with her from home. She flipped through several of the books until she found the one she'd been reading last night. "Look at this." She opened it to the center. "These are photos from the Simoneau trial. Remember the jewelry and the small sculptures that had gone missing from the house?"

"So," said Cordelia.

Jane turned the book around so Cordelia could see it. "Look at the picture on the bottom right."

Cordelia's eyes bugged out. "It's this sculpture! Lord in heaven!" She looked up, her gaze colliding with Jane's. "What on earth was Christine doing with a piece of stolen artwork?"

Slowly, trying to absorb the shock into her system, Jane shook her head. "I don't know. But this was no birthday present. She must have given it to Molly as a way of hiding it." Jane rested her elbows on the desk and leaned her head against the heels of her hands, trying to make sense of this new turn of events.

"Do you think . . ." Cordelia began. "I mean, is it possible Christine was—"

"Christine wasn't a thief, if that's what you're suggesting."

"Then how'd she get it?"

Jane didn't have an answer.

Cordelia returned her attention to the book. "It says here that it's called the *Iron Girl*. Ha! It *was* a Le Verrier piece, one of a kind. He was apparently a friend of Marcel Simoneau's. Simoneau commissioned it as a Christmas present for his wife back in 1949. It's worth thousands."

Jane ran her fingers over the rough surface. Here was more proof, if she needed any, that Christine had been involved in the Simoneau's lives.

"What are you going to do?" asked Cordelia. "Think you should show it to the police?"

"I don't know. I suppose."

"Janey, look me in the eye and tell me you're okay."

Jane sat back. A chasm had opened in her stomach and she couldn't exactly ignore the feeling. "I'll admit the gun and now this sculpture— it's a lot to absorb."

"Throw it away," said Cordelia firmly. "Treat it like it's kryptonite. This isn't good for you, dearheart. It's forcing you to revisit something that should stay buried."

"But if I don't go back there, if I don't figure out what was really going on, then I've lost her."

"That's absured."

"No it's not. Don't you get it? All the secrecy makes me question other things, too. Why didn't she tell me about any of this? What part—if any—did she play in the Simoneau murders? Who the hell *was* she!"

"You know who she was. She loved you. She was a good person. Just leave it alone."

"I can't."

Cordelia's eyes softened. After a moment, she said, "No, if I were in your shoes, I couldn't either."

"Then help me," said Jane. "God knows, I don't want to do this alone."

Cordelia closed the book. "As of this moment, I'm on the case, Janey. I'll read some of this stuff you've got. You read the rest. You make notes, I'll make notes, and then we'll have a strategy session."

That's when Jane remembered. "You're in rehearsals right now. And Hattie's coming home. It's not fair to ask you to get involved."

"You and me, we're a team, right? With my brains and your, ah . . . let me think." Her eyes rose to the ceiling. "I've got it," she said, snapping her fingers. "With my brains and your mulelike determination, we'll get to the bottom of this in no time flat."

Christine

August 21, 1987

11:20 A.M.

Christine opened her eyes to sunlight slanting in through partially open blinds. It took a few seconds for the world to filter slowly back into focus. Dexter was standing over her, his expression worried.

Bending down next to her, he said, "Are you feeling any better?"

She tried to sit up, but the pain in her stomach stopped her. "What happened?"

"You fell. You turned so pale, and then you asked me to get you out of the heat, take you somewhere cool where you could lie down."

Christine remembered falling, but after that, it was all a blur. "Where am I?"

"The Simoneau's gatehouse. It's where I live. Are you okay? Should I call a doctor?"

She eased her eyes to the right and saw that she was on a couch in a small living room. A few feet away was a desk piled high with books.

"I carried you up here. I didn't know what else to do."

Once again she tried to sit up, but the pain sliced through her. "I have some pills—"

"Where? In your briefcase?"

She nodded. "Vicodin."

He fumbled with the clips, finally finding a small orange prescription bottle. "This is pretty heavy stuff."

"Some water?" She had to hold on until the painkiller could take effect. She'd already made a doctor's appointment for later in the afternoon. She could

hear water running in the kitchen. A second later, Dexter was back. She could tell he'd turned on a fan, although she couldn't see where it was. It was blowing hot air at her, but it was better than nothing.

"How many?" he asked.

"Three."

"You sure?"

"Please," she said. Her entire body was shivering.

He shook three out.

She swallowed them greedily, then lay back against the pillow, trying to breathe into the pain the way she'd been taught. "I'll be okay in a few minutes."

He pulled up a chair and sat down. "What's wrong?" he asked tentatively. "Or shouldn't I ask?"

"Long story." She squeezed her eyes shut. The pain had never been this bad before.

"Are you going to be okay?"

She took a deep breath, then let it out slowly. "I just need a few minutes." She twisted her head slightly to look at him. He'd taken off his T-shirt and replaced it with a towel around his shoulders. His bare skin was glazed with sweat.

"Look," he said, wiping his chest. "I've got a class at noon. I need to take a shower first, but then I'll be out of your hair. You can stay here as long as you want. Jesus, if I'd just taken three Vicodin, I'd be out cold for the rest of the day."

"It doesn't work like that for me."

"No, well, whatever. You rest here as long as you want. The door locks by itself, so when you leave, just close it. Are you positive you don't want me to call someone?"

Christine remembered she'd made a date to have lunch with Jane. But that wasn't until one. "What time is it?"

"Eleven-twenty."

"No. No one."

He watched her closely. "I don't have to leave right away. Is there anything I can do for you? Are you hungry?"

She shook her head. "You're very kind."

He smiled. "Yeah, well. Mind if I make myself some lunch? I need to put some fuel in the tank before I take off."

"Go ahead."

She closed her eyes, breathing deeply, counting silently. The sound of clinking glasses in the kitchen, the refrigerator door opening and closing, a drawer pulled back, all helped to take her mind off the ball of fire in her stomach.

Dexter returned a few minutes later with a Coke and a sandwich. He sat down behind his desk. "Feel any better?" he asked, pulling the tab off the can.

"A little." She was starting to relax, always the first sign that the medication was working.

"You're getting some color back in your face. God, you really scared me." He took a bite of the sandwich, chewing it thoughtfully.

"Do you like working here?" she asked, feeling the need to interact with him. She didn't really know him, but here she was, lying on his couch. It was an awkward situation, although he was doing his best to put her at ease.

He shrugged. "It's a job and a place to live while I get my law degree."

"How long have you been living here?"

"A little over two years. I'm from Chicago originally, but I did my undergraduate work at the U of M. I like Minnesota. I may stay here if I can find the right firm." He popped a pickle into his mouth, washing it down with a gulp of Coke.

"What kind of law?"

"Business. My dad's a cop. Believe me, I don't want anything to do with the criminal courts."

"Then maybe you should stay away from business law."

He laughed. "Very funny. I think I like you."

"I've got nothing against making money," she said, shifting her position a little. "But I just think it should be done honestly."

"You sound like Philip."

"Philip Simoneau? You know him?"

"Yeah. He's an interesting guy." He finished his sandwich. Picking up the soda can, he said, "Well, better clean myself up. You holler if you need anything."

"I think I may try to sleep a little." The Vicodin was making her drowsy. Normally it didn't affect her that way, but she'd only had an apple for breakfast.

"I'll be outta here in ten minutes. Like I said, stay as long as you want. The phone's on the desk, in case you need it. You're sure I can't do anything else for you?"

"Thanks. I'll be okay."

"I hope you feel better, Christine."

A few moments later, she heard the shower burst on. She closed her eyes, tasting salt as tears reached her mouth. She didn't even have the energy to wipe them away. She'd been feeling so good for the last month, but in the past few days she'd taken a bad turn. And now this. She'd had her ups and downs before— many many ups and downs. The pain would pass, as it always had. She still had time.

Christine awoke with a start. For a second she wasn't sure where she was, then the morning rushed back to her in vivid detail.

"Dexter?" she called out, thinking he'd done something to wake her. Swinging her legs off the couch, she was embarrassed by the thought of him carrying her up here.

"Dexter?" she called again. When he didn't respond, she figured he must have left.

The pain was pretty much gone now. Checking her watch, she saw that it was going on two. "Damn," she whispered. She couldn't believe she'd slept so long. And then it hit her. She'd missed her lunch date with Jane. And if she didn't get a move on, she'd miss her appointment with her doctor, too.

She ran a hand through her hair, then stood. She felt shaky, but that was normal. The pain meds did that to her, especially when she took them on an empty stomach.

Moving over to the desk, she sat down and picked up the phone, dialing Jane's private line at the restaurant. When she was put through to her voice mail, she tried the main number.

"Lyme House," said a male voice.

"Is Jane around?"

"Who's calling please?"

"Christine."

"Oh, sure. Hang on a sec."

Christine thought she heard a clicking sound coming from the stairway down to the outside door. But before she could determine what it was, Jane came on the line.

"Hi, sweetheart. It's a zoo here today. What's up?"

"I thought you might be worried because I missed our lunch date."

"Oh . . . God! I completely forgot. We had a meltdown in the kitchen. Hey, just a second." She put her hand over the receiver.

Christine could hear her muffled voice talking to someone in the background. A second later she was back. "I'm so sorry, sweetheart. But I guess you forgot, too, huh?"

Christine was both relieved and a little put out. When Jane was at work, she lost all track of time. "Yeah, I totally spaced on it. Forgive me?"

"Always. Listen, I'm going to try to get away early tonight."

"What's that mean? Ten? Eleven?"

"Ouch. You mad at me?"

"Of course not. But I would like to see you sometime while you're still awake."

"Hey."

Christine realized she was being unfair. "Sorry. Guess I'm in a bad mood."

"Problems at work?"

"Something like that."

"I promise I'll be home by seven."

"Okay, I'll make us dinner."

"Or I could bring something home."

"No, let me take care of it. And then maybe we can go for a walk in the rose gardens."

"Sounds better and better."

"I love you, Jane."

"Oh, babe, I love you, too."

After hanging up, Christine sat for a moment, her hands buried in her hair. She took a couple of ragged breaths, trying to focus her thoughts. She wanted so badly to be with Jane right now, to tell her everything. But she had reasons for what she was doing. She needed to remember that.

Drawing her eyes away from the phone, she looked out the window. She could see the back of the main house across the garden. She didn't have much energy, so she just sat for a moment staring at the back of the house. As she was about to get up, a man came through a door on the second-floor landing, bolted across the balcony, and plunged down the stairs. He was in such a hurry and looked so furtive, pulling his snap brim hat low over his eyes, ducking his head, that Christine couldn't tear her eyes away. The man rushed toward the gatehouse through the garden path. As he passed under the window, she was surprised to see that it was Bill McBride. He was sweating furiously. Up close, he didn't look so much furtive as flat-out scared. She tapped the glass, trying to get his attention, but he just kept moving. She couldn't imagine why he was leaving the mansion by the back door. She wondered if he and Camille had had some kind of falling out. Didn't seem likely, but anything was possible. She shrugged, figuring that if it was bad news for the real estate company, she'd find out about it soon enough.

Christine didn't think Dexter would mind if she grabbed herself something to eat before she left. There wasn't much in the refrigerator except Miracle Whip, a couple packages of sliced ham, a jar of pickles, and a nearly empty jar of peanut butter. A loaf of bread sat on the counter next to the toaster. On the other side was a bag of potato chips. Nothing much appealed to her, but she knew she needed to put something in her stomach.

Feeling drained by the heat, the pain, and by the constant battle with her emotions, she leaned against the counter and ate a couple of the chips. Everything tasted like sawdust. She had to pull herself together before tonight. And that's when she heard it. The sound of a floor creaking as someone moved across it.

"Dexter?" she called again, walking back out to the living room. She nearly dropped the bag of chips when she saw a man standing by a bookcase across from the desk.

"Who the hell are you?" he asked, looking startled.

It was the same guy she'd seen with Camille Simoneau earlier in the day—the private investigator. His question seemed so arrogant that she immediately went on the offensive.

"This is a private apartment. Unless Dexter gave you permission, you have no business in here."

He shifted his stance, surveyed the room. "You his girlfriend?"

"That's none of your business."

"You're his girlfriend," he stated flatly.

Her presence was a complication he hadn't counted on. Camille had probably ordered him to check out the gatehouse. But right or wrong, Christine didn't see Dexter as the kind of man who would steal from his employer. Because of his kindness, she also had the urge to protect him. "I know who you are."

"Meaning what?"

"Camille Simoneau hired you. You're a P.I."

He chewed the inside of his cheek, considering his options.

"I think you should leave."

"Can't do that."

"Okay, then I'll call the police. You're trespassing. Maybe they'll even consider it breaking and entering."

He held up a key.

"Doesn't matter. Like I said before, you don't have Dexter's permission."

"Don't need it."

Christine stepped in front of the desk. "I guess we'll let the police decide."
She picked up the receiver.

"If you know so much," he said quickly, "then you know why I'm here."

"You think Dexter took the artwork from the mansion."

He nodded.

Christine understood his problem, she just didn't want to be the one to give
the go-ahead for an illegal search.

"Let's talk about this for a second," said the P.I. He scratched his stomach
through his checked cotton shirt, giving himself a moment to figure a way
around her. "If you believe your boyfriend is innocent, then why can't I look
around?"

"You have to ask him if you can come in here."

"Okay, okay. Then can we agree on this much? You won't tell him I was here.
I'll call him tomorrow and see what he says."

She knew he was lying. If Dexter was the thief, the call would tip him off
and he'd get rid of the evidence. On the other hand, if he was innocent, and she
thought he was, he didn't have anything to hide. But she still couldn't knowingly let this guy ransack his place. "Okay, fine."

"Great," he said with a slick smile. "Nice meeting you, Miss . . ."

"Good-bye," said Christine, still holding the receiver.

He mumbled something about ball-busting bitches and left.

13

Calvin finally caught a break. Greta's folks wouldn't tell him where she'd gone, and neither would any of her friends. But when he knocked on Barbara Norrgard's front door, to his surprise, she let him in.

Barbara taught night classes in photography for adults at a local middle school. She was attractive enough, in her late forties, with short, permed blond hair and curly bangs. But she had a mean mouth on her, and a permanently attached cigarette. Greta had taken some classes from her and that's how they'd become friends. But not real close friends. Calvin doubted that Barbara knew much about Greta's personal life, although her conversational style was more of an interrogation, so maybe she did. Calvin was suspicious of people like her. Overly friendly people who loved the sound of their own voice.

After being invited into her workroom in the basement, Calvin explained that he and Greta had been dating, but that she'd left town. He said he missed her and wanted to get in touch with her. Asked if Barbara knew where she'd gone.

"Minneapolis," she said, leaning over and rummaging through a tall trash can. "I got a note from her just the other day. She wanted to thank me for everything I'd taught her. She was such a nice girl. Very talented. I told her not to waste her gift. She must have listened because she's been accepted at MCAD."

"What's that?" he asked, standing awkwardly next to a tall worktable. He was never sure what to do with his hands.

"Minneapolis College of Art and Design."

"Oh." That sounded like Greta. She had this idea that she was going to become a professional photojournalist one day, travel all over the world taking pictures of war zones, earthquakes, stuff like that. Calvin understood dreams, but he thought she was just talking big to impress him.

"Here," said Barbara. She straightened up, handing over the envelope. "Can you make out that address? I couldn't, that's why I threw it away." She lit up a cigarette and sucked in some smoke.

Calvin held it under one of the work lights. "Looks like 3-29 A—ch, or th. Huh. And no zip. She give you a phone number?"

"Sorry." She tapped some ash into an empty coffee cup.

"Well," he said, pocketing the envelope, "this is better than nothing. Thanks."

"Always happy to do my part for young love." She winked. "When you see her, tell her hi from me."

Several hours later, Calvin took the Lyndale exit off I-94 and drove south until he hit 24th. He had looked up the address of the College of Art and Design in the Yellow Pages. Unlike Barbara, Calvin knew Minneapolis pretty well. He didn't know the names of all the side streets, but he knew where the Art Institute was, and MCAD was right next to it. And right next to the college's main building was a parking ramp.

While he sat in his van across the street and waited to see if Greta was anywhere around, he scanned a Twin Cities map book, looking for a street name that would correspond with the partial address on the envelope. On his way down from Fergus, he'd called his afternoon appointments and canceled them. While he was at it, he had canceled all his appointments for the rest of the week. He had to find Greta and make her understand that he was serious about getting married. He'd for sure apologize first for being so rough with her. He'd never meant to do that, but she'd pushed him too far the night before he left on his last trip. Calvin hoped the weeks apart would give them some perspective, some time to cool down. Never in a million years did he expect Greta to take off on him.

It was getting on toward four when Calvin finally added a last address to his list. He had four addresses in Minneapolis and the surrounding suburbs that might work. It would take a little time, but with the information Barbara had given him, he was confident he'd be able to find her.

Sitting across the street from a parking ramp waiting for Greta to show had been a stupid idea. But the time he'd spent looking at his map book hadn't. He started the motor, glanced at the side mirror, then pulled out of his parking space. He figured he'd try the closest address first.

Just as he drove past the exit ramp, he glanced in his rearview mirror and saw a beat-up, white Chevy C-10 pickup creep out onto the street behind him. "That's her," he whispered, feeling an electric sizzle of excitement. Afraid that she might recognize his silver van, he hung a quick right onto 24th. Greta took a left at the same street.

Calvin realized that if he didn't turn around and fast he'd lose her, but the car in front of him was moving like a turtle down the center of the road, which meant he was effectively blocked. He fought the urge to bang on his horn, knowing it would only draw attention. He stayed on the guy's bumper until an alley appeared on his left. Gunning the motor, he roared into the parking lot of a grocery store, turned around and was back on 24th heading west in a matter of seconds.

There were four cars between him and Greta now, and that was just about perfect. Greta waited at the light for the traffic to move past, then turned left onto Lyndale. When it was Calvin's turn, the light had just changed to yellow and was about to go red. He couldn't let her get too far ahead, so he floored it and made a sharp left in front of a UPS truck. The truck and several cars behind it screeched to a stop. Furious drivers laid on their horns. Calvin was jumpy now, looked around for the cops, glancing in the rearview mirror, waiting for the ax to drop. By all rights, he should get nailed for that last move, but his luck held.

Heading south, he maintained his distance from Greta's truck, but didn't allow the pickup to get so far away that he couldn't see where it was going. Just as they were coming up to 31st, her right turn signal came on.

Calvin slammed his palm into the steering wheel. "Gotcha!"

He didn't turn on Aldrich when she did. He drove one block farther, hung a left, and drove slowly down Bryant, watching across an open park as she got out of the truck and disappeared inside an apartment building.

14

Bernadette stood in the shadows under the stairway and watched Timmy move slowly around the living room. He'd been wandering around touching things for hours. Furniture. Photos. The wood mantel above the fireplace. He'd spent two days with them at the house, and with each passing hour he'd grown more quiet. Bernadette was concerned. She wanted to know what he was thinking, but was too afraid to ask. He'd mentioned last night at dinner that he was planning to drive back to Willmar today, but here it was, almost five in the afternoon, and he still hadn't left. Something about the look in his eyes made her old fears tiptoe from her stomach, up her esophagus, straight into her throat. Yes, that was exactly the way to phrase it.

It was the memories, she was sure of it. Pieces were coming back to him just as she'd anticipated they might, but filtered, of course, through a three-year-old's mind and memory. At least he'd made no attempt to visit the attic. She *must* keep that in mind. And a three-year-old's perceptions had to be, basically, nil. Except, if she really believed that, why had she been trembling inside ever since he'd arrived?

She watched him sink down on the couch, bend his head over his knees, and grasp the back of his neck with both hands. He stayed like that until she moved out of the shadows and cleared her throat.

"Aunt Bernie?" he said, sitting up.

"I thought you were leaving us today."

"Yeah," he said, somewhat sadly. "That's the plan."

She walked over to the sofa and settled herself down next to him. She reached out and touched his face. "You have such a strong, virile, jaw. The Simoneau men all have receding chins but yours is . . . a gift."

"From my father, I suppose." Gently lifting her hand away, he held it for a moment and said, "I need to talk to you before I go, Aunt Bernie. I'm planning to ask my dad if there isn't some way he can help you and Laurent. Float you a loan or something."

"Oh, a loan wouldn't do us any good," said Bernadette, enjoying the warmth of his hand closed around hers. "We wouldn't be able to repay it. Financially, I'm not as bad off as Laurent. I still have a little money in the bank, but it's not much, especially when a person has to maintain a castle. I'd be in great shape if I lived in some hovel in Edina, but here, the money just drains away."

"Maybe you should sell?"

"Absolutely not. The place may be in bad shape temporarily, but it's still an important house in the Twin Cities. Important people live in important houses, Tim. We're Simoneaus. No, I've got an idea up my sleeve that I hope will save us." She pressed a finger to her lips. "I must remain mum about it for the moment."

"Okay. Whatever you think is best."

"Besides, you can't trust your uncle Laurent with money. Not with his, shall we say, *inclinations*."

"Which are?" Tim raised his dark eyebrows.

"He has gambling *issues,* dear."

"Yeah, I assumed it was something like that."

"Tiny Tim," she said, looking at him fondly.

"Just . . . Tim, okay? We already discussed that."

"No, don't you remember? I used to call you Tiny Tim all the time. And I'd recite that poem to you every night. You loved it. You'd beg me to repeat it again and again."

"I don't remember." He looked like he had bad gas pains.

"Oh, darling, it's all right. You can talk to me."

"It's this house. It's . . . hard being here. And yet I wanted to come. And the funny thing is, I don't want to leave."

"Yes, I know. It's like that movie. You see dead people. It's frightening and yet compelling at the same time."

"What?" He cocked his head. "No, no. Nothing like that."

"But there *are* ghosts here."

"Yeah, I guess you could put it that way." He didn't look up. "See, I've had these dreams. Really upsetting dreams. I've never talked to anyone about them, not even my dad. The images are all tilted and screwed up, you know? But now, here, the same pictures I see in my nightmares I'm starting to see during the day. While I'm awake."

Her heart thumped a little harder. "Maybe it really is time you went home."

"Yeah, maybe. Has Laurent told you about his plans?"

The quick change in subject threw her off balance. "What . . . *plans?*"

Tim was about to explain when the sound of the front door slamming stopped him. "That's probably him now. Maybe he should tell you."

Bernadette peered around Timmy's broad chest just as Laurent reached the top of the stairs. He was sweating, wearing his blue polo shirt and matching blue shorts. Bernadette thought of it as his "blue balloon outfit," mainly because that's what it made him look like. She wished he would float away over the tallest turret and never return. He really was an unsightly mess. Perhaps Tim should take him shopping for some new clothes, try to help him devise a new look.

"Permission to enter?" asked Laurent, standing with his red-and-black Air Jordans together at the archway into the living room.

"Oh, bite me," said Bernadette. She hated it when he made a big legalistic show out of their living arrangements. It was just the way things had to be—unless they wanted to call in the national guard. "Tim was telling me about some new plan of yours. I assume it's a way to make money." She cracked a smile. "Thinking of setting up a lemonade stand in front of the house? That's about the level of your expertise." She laughed at her own joke.

Laurent dropped into a chair across from them. "You missed your calling, Bernie."

"You think I should have been a comedienne?"

"No." He winked at Tim. "A clown."

The edges of her mouth turned down.

"Sometimes I'm such a creative genius, I even amaze myself," he said, picking up a *Minnesota Monthly* and fanning his face. "I have the perfect plan to make us a small fortune."

The clown comment rankled. But the creative genius thing really stung. Bernadette was the creative one in the family, and he knew it. "What's the idea?" she asked, ready to fling darts at it until it died an unnatural death.

"You won't like it."

"Why do you say that?"

"Because I thought of it, not you."

His attempts to cast her in a negative light infuriated her. It was all part of his scheme to win Timmy over to his side. Bernadette would be damned if she'd let that happen. If she didn't like the idea, she would simply keep her mouth shut. She could always sabotage it later. "Tell me. Give us a glimpse of your genius."

"Okay. Let's go about this logically. What assets do we have left?"

"The paintings."

"Other than the artwork," he shot back angrily. "We agreed to keep those intact for Tim. It's the least we can do."

Oh, bullshit, thought Bernadette. He didn't give a flying flip for the art, or Timmy, for that matter. There was some other reason he wanted to keep his hands on the paintings. "You're not touching what's left of my trust," she shot back.

"No, you're missing the point. Our main asset is this house."

She gave him a sidelong glance.

"Let's open it up to the public. Do guided tours."

"But we live here."

"Just the main floor."

"It's a gorgeous old place," said Tim. "One of the oldest homes in Kenwood. I think, if you checked up on the history, the architecture, you might be able to make a go of it."

"No, you're missing the point, Tim. I want to do tours of the *murder scene*. Just because the people who run the Congdon mansion concession up in Duluth pretend it isn't why people come visit that place, doesn't mean we have to."

"You're a ghoul!" cried Bernadette. "You want to make money off our family tragedy!"

"Why not? It's our only real claim to fame, Bernie. Be realistic. I'm a failed dance club owner and you're a failed writer."

"I beg to differ!"

"This house combined with our family story would be irresistibly titillating to the *Enquirer* generation. It might even make us minor celebrities. We'll charge admission. Something paltry. Twenty bucks. Twenty-five. We'll provide groups with a tour guide, lots of information about the night in question. Maybe we'll take sections from the trial records and print them up into a booklet. Sell it for a profit. We can do T-shirts. Sweatshirts. Baseball caps with 'I survived the Simoneau mansion' on it. Do lots of commercial tie-ins. That's where we'll make the real money. Or how about this? We could do a reenactment! We could make a regular cottage industry out of the Simoneau mansion murders."

Bernadette was appalled.

"Tim, tell us what you think," said Laurent proudly. He obviously thought he'd hit the ball out of the ballpark.

Bernadette turned to look at her nephew.

"Well," said Tim, looking as appalled as she felt, "I really don't know what to say. I mean, I thought it would just be a straight house tour. This . . . idea . . . well, it—"

"Sucks lemons," she said, finishing his sentence. But as she sat glaring at Laurent, his comment about them becoming minor celebrities caused her to pause. "On the other hand, Laurent has a point. We really do need the money. Maybe there's a way we could do it tastefully."

They both turned to look at Tim.

"Um, I guess there might be a way."

"Good," said Laurent. "I knew you'd all see the light."

"You'd need to fix the place up a little first," said Tim. "That would take some money, but it's all doable. You'd want to close off the upper floors. The main problem, I suppose, would be the kitchen. But since you guys eat microwaved food morning, noon, and night, making a kitchen space upstairs wouldn't be a big deal. I could probably do most of the work myself."

"You could?" said Bernadette, her eyelashes fluttering.

"Actually, ever since I was little kid, I've worked summers with my uncle Herb. Herb's my dad's older brother. He owns a construction company. I help build houses. I can do pretty much everything—except, um, I'm not great with electrical stuff, but we could find someone to do it cheap, I'm sure of it."

"You are a godsend!" said Laurent, getting up and walking over to him. He grabbed Tim's head in both hands and gave him a big kiss on his forehead.

"Break out the nausea meds," mumbled Bernadette.

Still holding Tim's head, Laurent said, "Who knew our little nephew would become our savior?"

"I, ah, wouldn't go that far—"

"When can we get started?" asked Laurent.

"Well, I suppose after finals. June, maybe. I'll have to break it to Dad that I'll be staying with you. Cross your fingers that he doesn't blow a gasket."

"We'll abide by his wishes," said Bernadette primly, although she had no intention of actually doing so.

"Like hell we will." Laurent stalked the room like a tiger now. "I've got to make some notes while this is still fresh in my mind. If you'll excuse me." He made an abrupt exit, charging up the stairs to his rooms on the second floor.

After he'd gone, a hush fell over the living room.

"You're really okay with this?" asked Tim, turning to his aunt.

"I'm concerned about *you*," said Bernadette. And she truly was. "Do you think spending the summer here will be healthy for you?"

"You mean emotionally?" He shrugged. "I've lived with what happened here all my life. It's not helping to ignore it. I guess maybe ignoring it worked when I was younger, but when I close my eyes now I see such awful things. There's so much . . ." His voice trailed off.

"What?" she coaxed.

Looking away, he hesitated. After almost a minute, he said, "Blood, Aunt Bernie. On the floor. The walls. On my hands. My clothes."

"Oh my sweet Tiny Tim," she said, stroking his hair.

"It's like I'm inside the fun house at the fair. Everything is sort of warped and distorted. Faces pop out at me."

"What faces?" she asked, trying to keep her voice calm.

He shook his head. "Don't know. I strain to see them, but . . . they're always just out of reach. Kind of in a fog. I've started to remember a few things. Small things, but I feel like, if I stayed here, more would come back to me." He stared at her a moment, then smiled. "You've been great to me ever since I arrived. Thanks."

"No thanks necessary. I really want us to be a family again."

He looked down, playing with a rip in his jeans. "You know, I do kind of recall a children's poem. Something about a bathtub and bubbles. Was that the one you used to recite to me?"

She grew excited. "Yes, that's it exactly!"

"How did it go?"

"Oh, do you really want to hear it?" She felt a bit flustered. She wasn't even sure she remembered it properly. "Let's see." She coughed into her fist a couple times, then began:

> *"I had a little brother,*
> *His name was Tiny Tim.*
> *I put him in the bathtub,*
> *To teach him how to swim.*
> *He drank up all the water,*
> *He ate up all the soap.*
> *He died last night,*
> *With a bubble in his throat."*

She glanced over at him and saw that he'd moved to the edge of the couch.

"There's more," she said, sensing his excitement.

> *In came the doctor*
> *In came the nurse*
> *In came the lady with the alligator purse.*
> *Dead said the doctor*
> *Dead said the nurse,*
> *Dead said the lady with the alligator purse.*
> *Then out went the doctor,*
> *Out went the nurse,*
> *And out went the lady with the alligator purse.*

Bernadette took a little bow, feeling incredibly satisfied that she'd been able to remember it word for word. It was a wonderful poem, capturing, in her opinion, the essential morbidity in all good fairy tales.

15

Jane opened a window in her living room, allowing the evening breeze into the house. She'd spent the last hour on the phone with Kenzie. She loved the ease with which they talked. It was as if they'd known each other for years. Except, in thinking it over, Jane was afraid that ease might be compromised if she told Kenzie about Greta. They'd been talking way too much lately about Christine and everything associated with her. Kenzie was initially curious, but Jane was beginning to detect a certain frustration with the topic. For the good of their relationship, the subject needed to be tabled.

As usual, neither of them wanted the conversation to end. Jane finally brought it to a close, saying she had to talk to her father before he went to bed. She'd tried calling him earlier, but all she got was his voice mail. The main reason she had to cut Kenzie off was because Greta would be stopping by in a few minutes and she didn't want to be on the phone with her when that happened. It would just feel too weird.

Mouse seemed to sense that someone was coming. He'd been sitting in the foyer for the last ten minutes, his eyes locked on the door. Jane wasn't sure if he was reading a vibe she was giving off, or if he really was hooked into the universe in a way she couldn't begin to fathom.

When the doorbell finally rang, he stood up and wagged his tail.

"You be on your best behavior tonight," she said, patting his head as she walked past.

Drawing the door back, she tensed as her eyes met Greta's. No matter how hard she tried, she was still virtually paralyzed by the sight of her. "Come in," she said, forcing a smile.

"Who's this?" asked Greta, bending down to let Mouse sniff her hands.

"His name is M. Mouse," said Jane, shutting the door. "Mr. Mouse, or just Mouse will do."

Greta smiled. "Cool name. I love dogs."

Mouse was in heaven, closing his eyes as she scratched down the length of his back.

"He's very friendly," said Jane.

Greta gave him one more scratch, then straightened up. "You've got a really beautiful home," she said, looking around. "I sort of expected you would. What's the style called?"

"English Tudor."

"You live here all by yourself?"

"My aunt and her husband usually stay with me for a few months each year. They're away at the moment."

"Away where?" asked Greta, glancing up the stairs.

"England. My aunt owns a cottage in Lyme Regis. My mother was English."

"Huh. That explains the accent."

"What accent? I don't have an accent."

"Yeah, you do. You've got some of the Minnesota 'o's right, but there's another influence I couldn't quite put my finger on. Now I know what it is." She glanced into the dining room. "Do both of your parents live in town?"

"My mother died many years ago. My dad lives in St. Paul."

"Got it," she said, following Jane into the kitchen.

"Would you like a cup of coffee?"

She scrunched up her nose. "What are my other choices?"

"Wine. Beer. I think I've got some Coke."

Greta nodded to the bottle on the counter. "What's that?"

"Macallan? It's single malt Scotch."

"Any good?"

"I think so."

"I'll try that." Greta surveyed the kitchen, taking in the commercial stove, the large refrigerator, the hanging copper pots and pans. "You must really like to cook."

"I do," said Jane, pouring them each a small glass. "I test new recipes here sometimes."

"I thought you just *owned* the restaurant."

"I was the main chef for the first few years."

"Wow. I can't even boil water without burning it."

Jane smiled. She'd heard that one a million times. "I've got a great executive chef now. Makes life a lot easier."

"Which leaves you free to open up another restaurant."

"Yes," she said, sipping the Scotch, "I suppose it does." She realized she was staring. "Why don't I show you the apartment?"

"Lead the way," said Greta.

Behind her on the stairs, Jane could hear Greta cough. "What do you think of the Scotch?"

"Strong."

"Would you rather have something else?"

"No, I like it." She trotted behind Jane to the second floor. "I'm determined, now that I've left my old life behind, to try new things. I am so *totally* sick of small towns. I want to learn everything, go everywhere, try everything at least once. The whole world feels like it's opening up to me. Do you know what I mean?"

Jane turned to look at her. "Yes, I do."

"It's a little scary, but I'm not letting that stop me."

They paused next to a locked door halfway down the second-floor hallway. Jane fished a set of keys out of her pocket. "This stairway leads up to the third floor."

"You keep the door locked?"

"I guess I do," said Jane. "Old habits. It was always locked when I had renters." She switched on a light and started up.

Mouse bounded up next to them, reaching the top door before they did. He wagged his tail, waiting to be let in.

"He's never been up here before," said Jane.

Greta seemed surprised. "You don't *ever* use this space?"

"Not really," said Jane. She found the right key and pressed it into the lock. Opening the door, she flipped on the overhead light.

"God, this is perfect," said Greta, stepping into the room. It was L-shaped and narrow, with oatmeal-colored Berber carpeting and pine-paneled walls. "It's really warm and cozy."

Mouse ran around sniffing the furniture, wagging his tail like a metronome set to warp speed.

"It's not large, but I think it might work for you," said Jane. "There's an outside stairway. As long as you don't mind heights, you can come and go that way. And these"—she pointed to the row of windows in the living room—"overlook Lake Harriet. It's a beautiful view during the day. We could push the desk against the wall and bring up that long metal table I told you about."

Greta seemed to be mulling it over. "I'd either have to work at night, or I'd need to cover the windows."

"Up to you," said Jane.

"Seems a shame to cover them. Would you mind if I did my main printing after dark? That way the blinds might be enough?"

Jane examined the keys in her hand. "Whatever you want is fine with me. Here, let's make sure this key is the right one." She stepped over to the door leading to the outside stairs. "Yes, it works," she said, depositing the key in Greta's hand. "You can come and go as you like."

"Wow, I mean, I don't know how to thank you. You've been so incredibly generous. If it's okay, I'll bring all my stuff over in the morning."

They spent the next few minutes hauling the metal table up from the basement. Mouse seemed energized by the activity in the house. He watched everything from a safe distance, but used every pause in the action as an opportunity for affection.

"There," said Jane, crouching down and giving Mouse a hug. They'd moved the furniture around, pushed the couch and the desk against the far wall. The table stood in the center of the room.

"I still can't believe you're letting me use this space for free." Greta thought for a moment, then turned to look at Jane. "If I asked you a question, would you answer it truthfully?"

Jane stood up. "What's the question?"

"Did you offer me the job because I looked like . . . *her*."

Jane saw no reason not to be honest. "I think so, yes. Does that bother you?"

Greta shrugged. "No, guess not."

"I'm fully aware that you're not Christine," said Jane. "But I won't lie to you. You look so much like her that sometimes it just . . . it startles me."

"Do you have a picture of her around here I could look at?"

The room was beginning to feel way too small. Jane was glad for an excuse to get out. "Sure. Come down to my study."

With Mouse leading the way, they all trooped down the stairs to the first floor.

Before Jane could dig out an old photograph album, the phone rang.

"Give me a minute," she said, sitting down behind her desk and checking the caller I.D. "Oh, it's my father."

Greta dropped down on the love seat. Mouse hopped up next to her, lifting his paw to shake hands.

"Hi, Dad," said Jane.

"I will never get used to this caller I.D. thing."

"When did your plane land?" He'd been in New Orleans for the last week visiting his second wife, Marilyn. They'd been separated for several months. Marilyn had taken a leave of absence to be with her family before the death of her father. After his death, she'd never returned to the Twin Cities. Jane's dad had been very tight-lipped about their problems. She hadn't pushed him for details. Nobody in the Lawless family reacted well to being pushed to talk about something before they were ready.

"I got in two hours ago."

"You sound tired."

"I'm beat, honey. All that extra security at the airport wears me out."

"How was Marilyn?"

"Okay."

"Just okay?"

He was silent for a couple seconds. "It's not good, honey. But I don't want to get into it now."

"Sure."

"I just ran through my messages. Whatever's on your mind, it sounded important."

Jane filled him in on what had happened while he was gone. She ended with the *Iron Girl*.

"You're positive it's the same one that was stolen from the Simoneau mansion?"

"Absolutely. I'll bring the book and the statue over tomorrow so you can look at it yourself."

"No need. I trust your judgment."

"Did you ever work on that case?"

"Not directly. I did some consulting with the lead defense council. Ken Whitman. He was a good man, but he was in way over his head, in my opinion. It was one of his first criminal trials. I will say he did his damnedest to get his client off. What was his name?"

"Dexter Haynes."

"Haynes. Right."

"Did you think he was guilty?"

He sighed. "The case was difficult. The evidence against him was minimal and all circumstantial, but the murders were so horrific I think the jury felt pressured to convict. I don't know, Janey. Yeah, he probably did it."

"Is this Ken Whitman still practicing law?"

"He died, oh, maybe ten years back."

"What about Haynes?" asked Jane. "Do you know where he is?"

"Stillwater," said her father. "Far as I know, he's still there."

"Look, I understand if this sounds off the wall, but is there any way you could pull some strings, get me in to see him?"

Silence. "Why? Are you thinking Christine had something to do with the murders?"

"No, of course not. But something's not right—even you've got to admit it. I just . . . I need to talk to him."

"Oh, honey. Will you listen to your old man for once? You're getting into some troubled waters here."

"I know."

"I'm not sure you do."

"Please, Dad? I could probably figure out a way to do it myself, but if you arranged it, it would happen a lot faster."

More sighs. "Am I correct in assuming that you're going to pursue this whether I help you or not?"

"Yes."

"Honey . . ."

"While you're thinking about it, I've got one other question. Should I tell the police about finding the *Iron Girl*?"

"Oh, I suppose you could, but I doubt it would mean much. They'd never reopen the case just because one of the stolen articles turned up."

That was pretty much what she'd assumed. "So? Will you set up the interview?"

"If I do, Jane, it will be against my better judgment."

"Is that a yes?"

"Man, I used to think your mother knew how to wrap me around her little finger. Okay." He sighed. "I'll call around tomorrow. See what I can do."

"You're a sweetheart."

"Yeah yeah yeah."

"Now, you better get to bed."

"I'm already *in* bed. That's the easy part. What I need to do is figure out a way to get to sleep."

That didn't sound good. "Are you sure you don't want to talk about it?"

"Positive. Don't worry, I'm okay, honey. It's just . . . this wasn't the most pleasant week I've ever spent."

"I love you. If you need *anything*—"

"I know where to find you. 'Night sweetheart."

"'Night."

After hanging up, Jane looked up and saw that Greta was standing next to one of the bookcases. She'd found a picture of Christine.

"Sounds like you've got a nice father," said Greta.

"I do. I'm very lucky."

"He's lucky, too."

Again, Jane tried not to stare, but it was a losing battle. Greta had on tight white jeans, a navy blue tank top under a pink oxford cloth shirt. She looked terrific.

Lifting the picture frame from its place on the shelf, Greta studied it. "I do look like her. It's bizarre. She looks more like me than my sister does." Glancing back at Jane, she said, "Where was this taken?"

"Blackberry Lake. My family has a lodge up there. It's about fifty miles north of the cities. That photo was taken a couple of years before Christine died."

"Your hair was a lot longer."

"I cut it a few years ago. Thought I needed a change. It's grown back pretty fast, but I doubt I'll ever wear it that long again."

"I know this may sound strange coming out of my mouth," said Greta, "but you and Christine made a beautiful couple."

"Thanks. I thought so, too."

"I'm taller than she was."

"A bit."

Greta set the picture back down. She moved on to the next. "Who're these people?"

"My mother and father. The photo was taken just after we returned to the United States to live. We were in England until I was nine."

"Your dad looks very distinguished. And your mother. You have the same smile. And the same chestnut-colored hair." She put it back and moved to the last framed photo. "And these two?"

"My brother, Peter, and his wife, Sigrid."

"I like guys with beards. He's really cute."

"I'll tell him you think so."

"Is he younger or older?"

"Younger."

"You two close?"

"Very."

"I've got an older brother who lives in California. I don't see him much. He's married with three kids. And then I've got a younger sister in nursing school. She's married, too—one kid. I guess I'm the odd one. I never knew what I wanted to do with my life—until I found photography a couple of years ago. Then everything just fell into place. I always figured I would go to college, but I had no real focus so I kept putting it off. My parents would be happier if I was married with a couple of kids, like my brother and sister, but that seems like . . . I don't know. Like settling for something less than I want."

123

Jane pushed her hands into the pockets of her jeans and stretched her legs out in front of her.

"You and Christine ever want kids?"

"We both had careers that took so much time, it didn't seem fair to bring a child into that chaos."

"You didn't want kids," she said knowingly. "When people do, they don't care what kind of chaos they bring the kid into." She sat back down on the couch next to Mouse. "I couldn't help but overhear what you told your dad. I think I'll have to read up on that Simoneau murder case."

Jane nodded to the stack of books on the desk. "Help yourself."

"Really? You don't mind?"

"The one on top is a pretty good overview. I've already looked through it. You can take it if you want it."

"Okay, sure. Then maybe we can talk about it. On my days off, I used to watch Court TV all the time. I'm fascinated by stuff like that. Hey, you ever think you might write a book about the Simoneaus?"

Jane found it an odd question. "I'm just trying to tie up some pieces of Christine's life, things I didn't know about until recently."

"Oh."

For some reason, Jane had the sense that Greta didn't believe her.

"You have such a comfortable home," said Greta, threading her fingers behind her neck. "My mother was never very good with the comfort thing. She likes fake designer furniture that's about as comfortable as concrete." Glancing at her watch, she said, "Hey, look at the time. I better shove off. I've got a big day tomorrow." She grinned at Jane. "Thanks to you."

Jane walked her to the front door. "I gave you the set of keys, right?"

"They're in my pocket. Will you be home tomorrow morning when I bring over my stuff?"

"Probably not."

They stood awkwardly in the front hall, neither of them quite sure how to say good-bye.

Finally, Greta leaned in and gave Jane a hug. "Was that okay? I always do that with my friends. We're friends, right?"

"I'd like that," said Jane, feeling a bit flustered.

"See you soon."

After she'd gone, Jane stood in the foyer with a stupid smile on her face. When she reached up to brush a lock of hair off her forehead, she realized she was crying.

16

Calvin had never been a patient man. Sitting in his van, waiting for Greta to come out of the house she'd disappeared into a couple of hours ago, was slow torture. His plan was to watch her for at least a day, see what she was up to. Calvin had come to the conclusion that she must have some new guy in her life and that's why she'd left Fergus Falls. All the photography crap was just a cover. The idea that she'd been playing around on him behind his back made his gut coil into a fist. The longer he sat in the dark, the clearer it became that he couldn't wait. As soon as she walked out that door, she had some explaining to do.

Checking his watch, he saw that it was after midnight. What the hell had she been doing in there all that time? He'd seen lights go on and off all over the house. He'd check tomorrow to see who owned the place. If it belonged to the new boyfriend, well, there were a lot of crazy people in this world. Fires started in garages. Rocks got tossed through windows.

A light burst on over the front door. Calvin tensed. A second later, the door opened and Greta came out. She walked swiftly to her truck. Calvin was out of his van in a flash. As she unlocked the door, he made his move.

"Greta," he said softly moving up behind her.

She whirled around, looking startled. "What are you doing here?"

"We need to talk."

"Didn't you get my note?"

"Sure I got it." He squinted at her in the darkness. "You cut your hair. Why'd you do that?"

"None of your business."

"I liked it long."

"I didn't."

He took hold of her arm, but she pulled away. "Everything I had to say to you I put in that note."

He nodded to the house just as the front light went off. "You got a new boyfriend?"

"What?" Her expression hardened. "No, of course not."

"I don't believe you."

"Calvin, I *don't* have a new boyfriend."

"Then why'd you leave?"

"Because . . . because I want to go to art college."

"Bullshit."

"It's true."

He stared at her. "It's because of our fight, right?"

"Okay. Yes. Partly."

"I'm sorry, Greta. I never meant to hurt you."

"You gave me a black eye and nearly broke my arm!"

"I said I was sorry. Jeez. What do you want from me?"

"I want you to go away and leave me alone. We're no good for each other. We never were."

"Says who?"

"We argue all the time."

"That's because you're so goddamn stubborn. You never give an inch!"

"Calvin, I don't want what you want and I never will."

"Just listen a minute, okay? You don't think I'm serious about you, but I am. I'll prove it." He hesitated, imagining the look on her face when he told her his big news. "I bought that house, the one I told you about. I know you probably think I'm all talk, but I'm not. We can get married now, babe. Happily ever after, just like you want."

"It's *not* what I want," said Greta. "You never seem to get that."

127

Now he was confused. "Look, you can't possibly think you're going to make it as a photographer. That's just some stupid idea you got into you head because of Barbara Norrgard."

"She thinks I have talent."

"She tells that to *everyone,* Greta. Just talk to some of her other students like I have." It was a lie, but he could tell he'd hit a nerve.

"That's not true."

"It is. She's just a big bag of wind. You're going to end up disappointed and alone, Greta, and it will be all her fault. Sure, they'll take your money at that school. Why the hell not? You'll fart around for a few years, and then you'll get restless. You'll look around for some guy to settle down with. But you've got a guy who loves you standing right here in front of you. Why can't you see it?"

"You don't hit someone you love, Calvin."

He threw his arms in the air. "I told you," he said, louder this time. "I'm sorry. I want to marry you, Greta. I love you. I want to make a life with you."

She turned away.

He grabbed her again, this time spinning her around, pushing her against the side of the truck.

"Get away from me," she shouted.

"Not until you really *listen* to me."

"You're the one who's not listening!" She slipped past him and got as far as the rear quarter panel before he caught up and pinned her with his body.

"Let go of me!"

"Shut up," he ordered. "Shut the fuck up!"

"Help!" cried Greta. "Somebody help me!"

17

The cat colony sprawled across Cordelia as she lay on the couch in her loft reading a book about the Simoneau murders. Melville, who was perched on her stomach, kept licking his paw. The sound annoyed her, so she'd swipe at him every few seconds to get him to stop. Blanche had oozed up under her arm, but kept flipping her tail, hitting the edge of the book and making the cover rattle. And Lucifer, seeing himself no doubt as the musical maestro, sat atop her thigh, twitching his back, forming a kind of syncopated rhythm with the other two. How was she supposed to concentrate when she had the equivalent of a feline reggae band strapped to her body?

"Why don't you all run along? Find a mouse to torture instead of me."

Lucifer stopped twitching long enough to yawn. Interestingly enough, he did it in rhythm to the paw licking and the tail flipping.

"Stop!" she bellowed.

The cats blinked, but didn't miss a beat.

"Oh, for Pete's sake," she said, opening the small drawer in her coffee table with her big toe. She reached over and grabbed her earplugs. It was either that or turn Janis Joplin on and set the volume to "shatter." Both served the same purpose.

When Cordelia had finally finished the delicate earplug insertion maneuver, the doorbell rang. It was a muffled ring, of course, but still audible. "Oh, bother," she muttered.

She'd come home early from the theater in order to get a jump on her reading. Some people had no sense of timing.

"Just a minute!" she hollered, shaking off the cats.

She grabbed her fedora, dropping it at a proper slant on top of her head, then opened the door. The light in the hall had burned out several days ago and the building management, as usual, had failed to replace it in a timely manner.

"Yes?" she said, peering into the darkness. She looked up at the ceiling, then over toward the freight elevator. There didn't seem to be anyone around.

She was about to close the door when she felt a tug on her pants. Glancing down, she found Hattie standing in the semidarkness, her lower lip cranked out about six inches.

"Oh, Hattie!" she said, scooping her up in her arms and kissing her all over. "I didn't expect you until the weekend! Where's Cecily?"

Cecily Finch was Hattie's nanny. In this instance, there was a truly freaky synergy between the person and the name. Cecily looked and acted like a large, human finch. Skinny and twitchy with short, straight brown hair and bangs.

Hattie's mouth moved, but nothing came out.

"Speak up, dear. It's important to en . . . nun . . . ce . . . ate."

The little girl thumped on Cordelia's chest with her fists.

"Honey, that hurts! It's not good to hurt Auntie Cordelia. Nor is it smart."

Hattie's lips moved again.

"Really, dear, this is very annoying."

Out of the corner of her eye, Cordelia saw the freight elevator yawn open and Cecily step out. She was accompanied by several beefy men carrying an excessive amount of expensive luggage. Gone was the Finch of old. The new improved Finch looked like she'd just stepped out of *InStyle*. She was tanned and tended and poured into a tight pair of Sergio Valente jeans. Cordelia's sister, Octavia, had evidently taught her a few things about fashion.

Before Cecily had left to care for the golden child during the location shoot in Switzerland, she'd just been a normal theater major with

130

typically grungy clothing and the usual unrealistic expectations about her future on the legitimate stage. Now, in Prada pumps, who knew what she expected out of life?

Cecily mumbled something but Cordelia didn't catch it. "Why did you let Hattie come up here all by herself?"

Cecily pointed to Cordelia's ears and mumbled again.

"Speak up!"

This time, Cecily reached her little finchy hand and plucked out one of the earplugs. "Can you hear me now?"

"Oh," said Cordelia, yanking the other one out. "Sorry. Why didn't you call me? I would have picked you up at the airport."

"Hattie wanted to surprise you," said Cecily, sailing past her into the loft and showing the men where to put the bags.

"Deeya," said Hattie, twisting a strand of Cordelia's auburn curls around her finger. "I home!" Her blue eyes sparkled.

"You *are* home!" Cordelia was touched that Hattie thought of her loft as her real home. "I missed you tons and tons and tons!"

"I yuv you," she said shyly, lowering her eyes.

Cordelia danced around the room with her, flinging her this way and that, tickling her and making her shriek with delight. When she finally set her down, the little girl headed straight for the cats. She squealed when they scampered off before she could grab even one of them. "Bad kitty babies," she cried.

"I'm exhausted," said Cecily, flopping down on the couch.

"Good flight?" asked Cordelia.

"Long one. I feel like I haven't slept in days."

"What about Hattie?"

"She's running on adrenaline. We both are."

"I've got your room all ready. Clean sheets on both beds. God, but I'm thoughtful."

"You are, thanks. I think I'll clean up a little, and then Hattie and I should hit the sack. She needs a bath, but that can wait until tomorrow."

Hattie came out of the kitchen and ran up to Cordelia holding an onion in both hands like an offering.

"Sweetie, that's an onion," said Cordelia.

Her immense blue eyes were serious and intent. "I know," she whispered.

Out of the side of her mouth, Cordelia said, "What's she want with the onion?"

"She likes to own them."

"Why?"

"No idea."

Cordelia smiled indulgently at her little niece. "Hattie, darling, why do you have that onion?"

Hattie shrugged.

"Do you want to eat it?"

"No."

"Do you like the way it looks?"

"Yes."

"Hmm," said Cordelia. "This is extremely strange behavior. I approve."

"Thought you would," said Cecily.

For the next few minutes, Cordelia, Hattie, and the onion sat in a chair and read poems. Hattie was clearly fighting sleep. She probably didn't want to shut her eyes for fear that Cordelia would dissolve in a puff of smoke and be gone when she awoke in the morning. Instead of Cordelia's loft, she'd be back in Switzerland being ignored by her mother.

"You know I'll always be here for you, don't you, Hattie?"

She nodded. "I yuv my onion."

Okay. "But you yuv me more, right?"

"Deeya and my onion," she said forcefully.

"Look, Hattie. It's a matter of rational priorities. On the scale of things, that onion is unlikely to be around very long. There's guacamole, onion soup, a nice pot roast. It will give its life in the service of a great cause, and then it will . . . pass away into the great vegetable beyond."

"*My* onion," said Hattie, hugging it to her chest.

"Time for bed," called Cecily, emerging from the bathroom.

Cordelia kissed Hattie—and the onion—good night.

Once the three of them had gone off to bed, Cordelia resumed her position on the couch. She still hoped to make progress on that book before tomorrow. At least she had the couch all to herself for a change. The cats were in hiding now that "The Hattinator" had returned. They would once again be forced to take up the cudgel of their nocturnal natures and frolic only when the wee one was safely tucked away in dreamland.

Unwrapping several lumps of bubble gum, she crammed them into her mouth. The next chapter was entitled "Unanswered Questions."

She skimmed through a long boring section, a forensic examination centering on the estimated time of death of each of the three victims.

The next part introduced theories about the attic. Cordelia had never read anything about that part of the house before. If she recalled correctly, it hadn't been brought up at the trial.

Apparently, while the attic had been used mainly for storage, a space had been cleared that was about the size of a large hot tub. Above it someone had screwed a heavy hook into one of the ceiling beams. Dried blood was found on the floor beneath it, as was urine. Nobody in the house seemed to know anything about it.

The author discussed a few of the more prominent theories, then asked the obvious question: Was the attic used for torture? The blood that was found was all type A. Since DNA wasn't being used widely back then, no other information could be gleaned from its discovery. The one salient point the author came back to again and again was that none of the members of the immediate family had type A blood. The only person in the house with type A was Alice Cathcart, Timmy De-Witt's nanny. But the nanny claimed she'd never been up to the attic. She even offered to take a polygraph test.

No test was ever given.

"Wowie wow wow wow," whispered Cordelia. She resumed her now frantic gum chewing and read on.

Another unanswered issue had to do with a neighbor. The neighbor in question, an elderly woman named Lucille Olman, had lived in the home directly next to the Simoneau's.

On the night of the murders, the woman swore she saw a man exit the building around seven, come down the outside stairway from the second floor, cross through the yard, and disappear into the alley. Since it was still early, she would normally have been able to get a good look at him, but that night, dark thunderclouds had rolled in from the west, dimming the natural light. Even though her description was sketchy, she was positive she'd seen the murderer. She said the man was white, average height and weight, with sandy-colored hair.

The author of the book pointed out that the murders had occurred closer to eight, but said the neighbor remained adamant all through the trial. She insisted it was the man's demeanor that had tipped her off. He hadn't just walked down the steps, he had rushed, looking over his shoulder back at the house, tucking his head into the collar of his raincoat. He looked guilty. She admitted that she'd seen no blood on his clothing, but she figured he'd thrown the raincoat over himself as a way to hide the blood evidence.

The police interviewed her several days after the murders and felt, for multiple reasons, that her story wasn't credible. Their reasons revolved around the woman's poor eyesight, as well as her penchant for calling the police over the slightest neighborhood problem. But the woman insisted to anyone who would listen that she had been the only one who had seen the murderer—and it *wasn't* Dexter Haynes.

The gun used to kill Philip Simoneau was another question. Cordelia already knew it was a .22—not a very powerful weapon—and that it had been recovered at the scene. Philip would have undoubtedly died of the gunshot wounds, but it might have taken some time for him to bleed out. During that time, he might have been able to get to a phone to call the police. That's the reason, according to the prosecution, that he was not only shot, but bludgeoned with a hammer as he tried to crawl up the central stairs away from his killer. The forensic psychologist who testified at the trial saw more anger in the way Philip was murdered than in either of the two women. It was a point of interest. If Dexter had committed the homicides, what had Philip done to anger him?

Cordelia turned the page and nearly choked on her bubble gum. "Lord in heaven," she gasped. "Lord Lord Lord!"

She grabbed her cell phone off the coffee table and punched in Jane's number at the restaurant. "Answer it," she pleaded, blowing her gum into an ashtray. "Come on, Janey. Be there. Or be *somewhere* I can reach you!"

18

Jane had just walked down the stairs from the second floor when she heard loud, angry voices outside. She ordered Mouse to stay, then rushed to the front door. Without switching on the light, she opened the door a crack and looked out. The light from the streetlamp was enough for her to see that Greta was in trouble. She was near the back of her truck, struggling with a man.

Stepping outside, Jane shouted, "What's going on?"

"Help me!" cried Greta. She sounded terrified.

Jane flew off the steps. By the time she reached them, the man had backed up. "Are you okay?" she asked Greta, grabbing her arm.

"He's crazy!"

"Who are you?" demanded Jane. The guy looked young, late twenties, maybe. He had a dark beard and was dressed in a gray sweatshirt and dark sweatpants.

"Her boyfriend. I just wanted to talk to her."

"Didn't look like a simple conversation to me," said Jane.

Greta was shaking. Jane stepped in front of her. "I think you better leave."

"Who the hell are you?"

"A friend."

"Go away, Calvin," Greta pleaded.

"Not until we talk this out."

Turning to Greta, Jane said, "Go back to the house. Lock the door and call 911."

Calvin lunged at her, but Jane pushed him away.

"You don't wanna get physical with me, lady. I could put you in the hospital before she even picks up the phone."

"I'm sure you could," said Jane, dodging around him. "So . . . let's talk about this for a minute."

"Fuck you!"

When Greta opened the door, Mouse charged out, snarling and barking.

Calvin rocketed backward as Mouse came straight for him.

"He some kind of attack dog?" shouted Calvin, kicking at him and missing by a mile. He backed all the way across the street with Mouse at his heels.

Jane had never seen Mouse behave like that before. She silently cheered him on. "Like I said, I think you should leave."

"Fine," said Calvin. He took one last kick at Mouse then bolted for his van.

"Mouse," called Jane. "*Come.*"

Still growling, Mouse trotted across the street, back to where she was standing. "Good boy," she said, grabbing him by his collar.

As the van drove past, it slowed. The passenger window rolled down. "Tell Greta from me this isn't over."

"Stay away from her."

He gave her the finger, then gunned the motor and sped off.

Greta was in the foyer when Jane returned to the house. "You okay?"

"Thanks to you," said Greta, still breathing hard.

Kneeling down next to Mouse, Jane cupped his head in her hands and kissed him on his muzzle. In return, he licked her face, her hands, her arms. "Thank you," she said, pressing her head to his. "You're my best boy." He was full of energy after his brush with danger. He yipped a couple of times, then bounded into the dining room, nosing a ball out from under the table.

As Jane stood, she saw that Greta had a fireplace poker in her hand. "Did you call the police?"

"I couldn't just leave you out there. I watched from the window for a few seconds, then I raced around until I found a weapon. I was just about to come back outside when he took off."

"He won't bother you again tonight." Jane took the poker from her hand.

"God, that was the bravest thing I ever saw." She looked deeply into Jane's eyes. "You saved my life."

"Is he *that* dangerous?"

"I didn't think so. Honestly, I don't know what he would have done to me if you hadn't come out." She put the back of her hand to her forehead. "He's a bully, for sure, but I never thought he'd follow me down here. I broke up with him before I left Dalton. Left him a letter. Okay, maybe that was cowardly, but after what happened the last time we were together, I thought it was best."

"Sounds like he's not too thrilled with being dumped."

"Yeah," said Greta. "An understatement."

"Why don't we sit down in the living room? You look a little shaky."

"Could I have some more of that Scotch?"

Jane crossed into the kitchen and retrieved a clean glass from the cupboard. Grabbing the bottle, she returned to the living room. Greta was sitting on the couch, staring at the cold fireplace.

"Here," said Jane, pouring her a stiff drink.

"You're not having any?"

"No."

Greta took a hefty swallow. "Maybe it will calm me down."

Jane switched on a light, then sat down in the rocking chair across from her. She needed to put some distance between them. "You said something about the time you last saw him. If it's not too personal, what happened?"

"We got into a fight." She leaned forward, holding the glass in both hands, resting her arms on her knees. "Actually, it was just a variation on the same old fight. He'd asked me to pick up one of his suits at the cleaners. I forgot. Well, maybe I didn't totally forget, but I'm not his wife. I don't like being ordered around. And I don't want to do his laundry just because I get back to his apartment before he does."

"Does he do things for you?"

"He's not around much. He's a salesman and he's on the road at least

137

three weeks out of every month. But, yes, he'd do anything I asked. That's the problem. He gives more than I do. I think he figures it entitles him."

"To what?"

"Whatever he asks."

"How long have you been together?"

"Almost three years. He's twenty-nine. I'll be twenty-six in April. It's always been more casual for me. I mean, I like the . . . well . . . I mean, the sex part. He's a good lover. And he's smart. But he just never seems to get it that I'm not interested in something more permanent. Have you ever had a relationship like that?"

Jane shrugged. "Yes, I suppose."

"Apparently, he thinks I've been holding out, refusing to do my wifely duties until I got a real marriage proposal. That's not it at all. If I gave him that impression, I'm sorry. I thought I made myself clear, but I guess he either wasn't listening or he refused to hear it." She took another sip of the Scotch. "He beat me up pretty badly the last night we were together."

Jane's breath caught in her throat.

"Yeah. Time to get out, right? So, that's what I did. But now he's here. He'll calm down, I'm pretty sure of that. But at the moment, he's totally furious with me."

"You've got to be careful, Greta. I mean it."

"Oh, believe me, I will." She finished her drink, then picked up the bottle. "Mind if I have another?"

"I don't think you should drive if you do."

"Yeah, you're probably right." She stared at the bottle. "Look, I'm pretty trashed over this. If I drove back to my apartment I'd probably end up sleeping in the closet with a blanket over my head. I know this is a lot to ask, but . . . would you mind if I crashed on your couch just for tonight?"

Jane hesitated, not because she didn't want her to stay, but because she did. "Sure."

"God, thanks. You're totally amazing, you know that?"

"Why don't I get you a pillow and——"

"No," said Greta, shaking her head. "This is fine. I'll just use the quilt on the back of the couch. And the couch pillows are perfect."

Jane checked her watch. Maybe the best thing was for both of them to hit the sack. "It's late. I should let you get to bed." She stood, but Greta took hold of her hand. "Don't go. Please. I can't possibly sleep until I calm down. Would you mind if we talked a while longer? I like talking to you, Jane. Maybe we could discuss that murder trial, the one you're so interested in."

"If that's what you want."

The phone rang. "Let me get that." It had to be Cordelia. She was the only person who ever called this late. "I'll catch it in the kitchen. Make yourself comfortable. I'll be right back."

Jane made it to the kitchen by the fourth ring. "Hi, Cordelia. What's up?"

"Are you sitting down?"

"No."

"Well, I'd advise it. When I tell you what I just learned, you're going to fall over."

"What?" Jane could feel her heart rate speed up.

"I was reading this book tonight on the Simoneau murders. I saw it in a used bookstore this afternoon, so I bought it. You remember that the murder weapon was a twenty-two."

"Yes."

"Well, it was a two-shot derringer with a carved-ivory handle. Sound familiar?"

"Are you kidding me?"

"I wish. There were two guns exactly alike—a matched set that Marcel Simoneau had had made for himself by the Brovard Company in Quebec. One of them was used to kill Philip Simoneau. The other—"

"Was in Christine's briefcase."

"Bingo. In the book, they said it was lost, or stolen."

Jane was stunned. "Are you sure it's the same one?"

"I've got the picture right in front of me."

Jane took Cordelia's advice. She sat down at the kitchen table. "What's it mean, Cordelia?"

"You tell me."

"Bring the book over to the restaurant tomorrow. I want to see it."

"Why wait? I'll bring it over to your house right now."

"No." She'd said it too quickly. She might as well have set off a fireworks display.

Cordelia was silent. She smelled a rat.

Thank God, thought Jane, she didn't know the rat's name was Greta.

"What's going on, Janey?"

"Nothing."

"Try again."

"I'm tired, okay. I'm pretty much finished digging through Christine's belongings. I'd just like to be alone with my thoughts tonight."

Cordelia didn't reply for several seconds. Finally, she said, "Yeah, if that's all it is, I guess I understand."

"Thanks."

"I'll see you anon."

"Good night, Cordelia."

"Jane?"

She closed her eyes and slumped back against the chair. "What?"

"You're alone, right?"

"You're never alone when you have a dog, Cordelia."

"Don't patronize me. You know what I'm asking. You wouldn't by any chance be entertaining 'what's her name.' "

" 'What's her name' left hours ago."

"You're playing with fire, Janey."

"There's no fire here tonight, Cordelia. Believe me."

"Yeah, well."

"Good night. Sweet dreams."

"Whatever."

When Jane returned to the living room, she found Greta lying on the couch, fast asleep. The glass of Scotch was empty, resting on the floor next to the bottle. Turning off the lamp and switching on a nightlight, Jane covered her with a quilt. As she did so, Greta's eyes opened.

Jane was paralyzed as Greta's gaze searched her face. Neither of them said a word for almost a minute. Finally, Greta's eyes slowly closed. Her breathing evened out. Only then did Jane realize how furiously her heart had been beating.

Scooping up the bottle and the glass, she sat down on the rocking chair. She poured herself a drink, knowing full well that she should go to bed, but unable to tear her eyes away from the young woman on the couch. At this moment, all she wanted from the world was to be allowed to watch Greta sleep. And that's what she did, sipping her drink, and remembering.

Christine

August 21, 1987

4:10 P.M.

Christine's visit to the doctor's office had pretty much confirmed what she already knew. After explaining all the recent test results, Dr. Soller wrote out several new prescriptions, then asked her about her pain and nausea. Christine had been seeing an acupuncturist for almost a year. The woman had been able to help her with both. Soller didn't really approve of Eastern medicine, so she didn't bring it up. He told her to come back the following week for more blood tests. Beyond that she was, as she had chosen to be, on her own.

Christine left the office around four, feeling empty and deeply weary. She had a late-afternoon meeting with a plumbing contractor at Bernadette's house, and with luck, she might still be able to make it. The main thing now was to stay busy for as long as possible. She loved her job, used it as therapy, as a way to keep her life feeling normal. When she finally quit, which she feared wasn't far off, she was terrified it would throw her into a major depression. It would mean that Jane would learn the truth, and that knowledge would make everything so much more painful and urgent.

Christine had become obsessed about keeping score of "lasts." Last day at work. Last time she would drive her car. Last time she would speak to her sister in Singapore. Last time she would see a sunset, listen to Mozart, Coltrane, Dylan. She suspected she might've already seen her last winter snowfall, sat by her last winter fire. But the worst of all would be the last time she would hold Jane in her arms. The last kiss. The last touch. It was the "lasts" that drove her

145

crazy, pushed her toward the edge. She even looked at her front steps now and wondered how many more times she'd walk up and down them. When her mind started sliding in that direction, she simply couldn't keep it together.

Scraping at her tears, she got into her car, willing herself to think of something else. "Think about the plumbing contractor!" she said out loud. And then she laughed, tears streaming down her cheeks.

On her way down Minnetonka Boulevard, she decided she didn't have the energy to make dinner. Instead, she would stop at Lunds after the meeting and buy a rotisserie chicken, some potato salad, maybe a dessert. She'd pack it all in a picnic basket and they could take it over to the rose gardens—have dinner on a blanket, or sitting by the lake on a bench. Christine couldn't help herself. She wondered how many more picnics she and Jane would ever go on together.

It was getting harder and harder to hide her illness. She had to tell Jane the truth soon, but she wasn't ready yet. Early on, Christine had held out hope that she could beat the disease, or at the very least, without operations and chemo, her last years would be less of an obstacle course. But years had turned to months. She didn't know how long she had left, but she had the sense, for the first time, that it wasn't long.

Because Jane was so busy, she wasn't around to see how often Christine had gone to bed early—or slept late. Being a real estate agent meant you could set your own hours, and that had been her saving grace for the past two years. The acupuncture and the drugs kept the nausea and pain manageable, but she knew it might not last much longer. She'd lost seven pounds in the past month, and she could tell Jane was worried. She prayed Jane would forgive her when she found out the truth—forgive her for her selfishness, her silence. It wasn't just simple selfishness either. Christine had been extraordinarily, vastly, colossally selfish. The decision to keep her illness a secret had been a conscious choice, something she'd thought long and hard about. Right or wrong, it was the path she'd taken.

If she could just manage to keep the meeting with the contractor short, she might be able to squeeze in a nap before Jane got home. Pulling her Camry up to the curb in front of Bernadette's house, she slid out of the front seat and hooked her briefcase over her shoulder. Her tendency to become easily winded had been growing worse. She tried to keep her briefcase as light as possible. The doctor had explained many of the potential ramifications of her disease, but experiencing it was far different from being presented with possibilities.

Seeing Philip crouched down near the front steps, she waved.

"Hi, Christine," he shouted, taking one last hard look at the crumbling concrete, then standing up. He was dressed all in white—white tennis shoes, white socks, white shorts, and a white polo shirt. He'd propped his tennis racket against a large clay pot. Christine had suggested that the steps be replaced, but she hadn't heard back yet on whether it was a go.

"Hey," he said, smiling as she approached. "What are you doing back here?"

"I've got a meeting with a plumber." She checked her watch. "He should be here any minute."

"You're lucky," he said, picking up his racket. "You just missed Laurent."

She shivered, thinking of the derringer in her briefcase. "Good timing."

"Let's go inside. I want to ask you something."

As they mounted the steps, Christine said, "What was your uncle doing here?"

Philip held open the door for her. "I'm not sure. He's been a real pain in the ass lately. It feels almost like he's gloating."

"About what?"

"No idea."

Christine unhooked the briefcase from her shoulder and joined Philip on a window bench overlooking the side yard.

"He asked me some weird questions. Did I believe in corporal punishment? And then he hooted, like it was some big joke. All I know is, he's got some major dirt on my mom and he's about to drop it on my grandmother."

Christine wondered if it had something to do with the new man in Bernadette's life. If so, Camille Simoneau was in for an unhappy surprise.

"He's like that," continued Philip. "He's a dirt collector. Enjoys seeing other people embarrassed. That's why I steer clear of him."

"I can think of some other reasons to steer clear of him, since we're on the subject."

His eyes softened. "Are you okay? You're sort of . . ." He seemed flustered, unsure how to finish the sentence. "I mean, forgive me for saying this, but you don't seem well. You always look so pale."

"Blonds always have pale skin."

"Yeah, but . . . well, okay."

She felt a twinge of pain in her back. "Listen, Philip, if I tell you something, will you keep it to yourself, just for now?"

"Sure."

"I'm thinking of taking some time off, maybe even quitting my job. I know it would leave you and your family without an agent for this house, but I'm sure I could find someone else, another top agent from our company."

Folding his arms over his chest, he said, "Actually, that might work out for the best. I don't mean that you haven't been doing a great job for us. You have. But, the truth is, Laurent isn't the only one who's about to drop a bomb on my grandmother. I've got a couple myself. Our house isn't going to be a pleasant place for the next couple of weeks. And frankly, I'd be thrilled to hear you no longer had to work with McBride. He's a total sleaze."

That threw her. "Are we talking about the same man?"

" 'Sell with pride, call Bill McBride.' Is there another?"

"Oh. Guess not."

"You mean he's never hit on you?"

She tilted her head. "No, of course not. Well, I mean . . ." She wasn't quite sure how to respond. She usually didn't mix her personal and professional life. "See, Philip, normally I don't bring this up, but . . . I'm gay. Bill knows I've been in a relationship with a woman for years. He's been wonderful. Really."

Philip just stared at her. After a few seconds, he said, "Okay."

"Besides, he's happily married. Has a couple of great kids. He's even a deacon at his church. I doubt he'd risk all that for a simple roll in the hay." On the other hand, she had seen him play fast and loose with certain aspects of real estate law, but since it was his company and she was a new employee, she was hardly in a position to say anything.

Philip nodded. He scratched his head for a moment, then said, "Tell me, Christine. Is it . . . hard being in the closet?"

"I'm not in the closet, Philip. Everybody important in my life knows about Jane. But I don't usually announce it to my clients. Putting my sexuality on the table isn't relevant. And also I'm careful who I share that bit of information with. I need to feel a sense of safety. I wish the world was a different place, but it isn't. Not yet, at least."

"Does that mean you feel safe with me?"

She smiled. "Yeah, I guess I do."

He placed his hand over hers. "Thank you. That means a lot."

He seemed so sad that Christine said, "I hope everything goes well for you— with your grandmother, I mean, with the bombs you're about to drop."

He nodded, then sighed. "Part of it has to do with me. My grandmother insisted I go to an Ivy League college. To do that, I had to be at the top of my class in high school and do exceptionally well on my SATs. I worked like a dog, and I made it. When I got accepted to Yale, it was like a huge dream came true for her. I love my grandmother. I've always wanted to please her. And as far as I was concerned, Yale was great. I knew my academic path would have something to do with economics. Yale has one of the best economics departments in the country. Now that I've got my undergraduate degree, I'm slated to return in the fall to start work on my master's—a split major between economics and international relations. The problem is, I don't want to go."

"You want to quit school?"

"No, no. I just don't want to go back to Yale." He stood and walked over to the fireplace. Turning his back to it, he said, "It's personal. I've checked out the U of M and I can do pretty much everything I want to here."

"But surely a degree from Yale would mean more."

"Okay, true. But see, my plan is to get my M.A. at the U, then go back to Yale for my doctorate. The bottom line is, I need to stay in town for the next few years."

It must be important, thought Christine, because he was giving up a lot. She wondered if it had something to do with a woman.

"My grandmother will fight me on this, tooth and nail. It may sound strange to you, but she may even throw me out of the house."

"You're kidding."

"I wish."

"What would you do?"

He shrugged. "Get an apartment. Apply for loans. Scholarships. Find a part-time job. I'll put a workable package together if I have to. But between you and me, I don't think it will come to that."

When he looked down at her, she had the same sense she often did when talking to him—as if there was more he wanted to say, but something held him back.

"And that's not the only thing that's going to piss her off, Christine. If you're thinking of quitting, I'd encourage you to do it soon. The shit, as they say, is about to hit the fan. And I mean big time. Best that you're not around to get hit by the flying debris."

19

I still don't understand why I can't come in," said Cordelia, fussing with a fresh yellow crocus she'd sunk in a small plastic vase attached to the dash of her Hummer.

Jane sat looking out the window at the forbidding walls of Stillwater State Prison. It was Wednesday morning. It had taken her father several days to arrange for a meeting between her and Dexter Haynes. She would have been happy to take Cordelia in with her, but it simply wasn't possible. "All this stuff has to be arranged in advance. Besides, you'd never pass the background check."

It was a joke, but that did it. Cordelia was off and running. "I beg your pardon, Janey. I have never been arrested. Never had a parking ticket—that I wasn't able to coerce a friend on the police force into fixing. Never been caught speeding, thanks to my trusty radar detector. I am a model citizen. A pillar of the community. I recycle. I brush my teeth after every meal. I whistle a happy tune. My *mind* is a lethal weapon, of course, but you don't need a permit for razor-sharp intelligence."

Jane was thinking about how to respond when Cordelia grabbed her by the lapels of her field jacket and said: "I am *hungry* for experience, Janey. Getting in there would be raw. It would be real. It would be *street.* It would be, well, smelly." She turned up her nose. "On second thought, I'll wait for you out here."

"You're positive you're okay with it? I mean, you'd probably enjoy the body search."

"Are they going to do *that* to you?"

It occurred to Jane that they might, and all joking aside, it wasn't a pleasant thought. "I hope not."

"Go, Janey. Peace be with you." She turned on her CD player, leaned her head back, and was lost in the Dixie Chicks.

Once inside, Jane proceeded to the information desk. All visitors had to register before entering. Before being allowed into the secure area, one of the guards ran a metal wand over her body, just to be sure she wasn't bringing anything illegal into the building.

Jane had been granted permission to talk to Dexter Haynes on a noncontact status. That meant he would sit on one side of a Plexiglas wall, and she would sit on the other. A guard would be in the room with them at all times.

As she sat waiting for him, she felt her chest tighten. All the doors clanging shut and locking behind her had kicked in her claustrophobia. She wondered how Dexter had dealt with the confinement all these years.

When the door in the back finally opened and he walked in, Jane saw that the man she was about to speak with bore little resemblance to the photos of the young Dexter Haynes taken during the trial. While he still looked strong and fit, the scar that ran from his left ear, down across his throat, disappearing under his collar, spoke loudly of a brutal prison history. The man now seated in the chair before her was hard and battered, but there was an unmistakable sharpness in his eyes. He picked up the phone on his side of the Plexiglas.

Jane picked up hers. "Thanks for agreeing to meet with me," she said, pulling her chair closer to the counter.

He pointed to his neck. In a low, raspy voice, he said, "My voice box got cut in a fight. I can talk, but not loudly." He gave her a hard stare, sizing her up. "How come the daughter of the famous Raymond Lawless wants to talk to me? Please, lady, don't tell me you want to reopen my case. I figured we were done with that a long time ago. Too many damn do-gooders in this world, you ask me."

"No, that's not why I'm here."

"Good."

"But it does have to do with the Simoneau murders."

He made a keep-it-coming gesture with his hand.

"Many years ago, I lived with a woman. Her name was Christine Kane."

"Christine," he said, examining the word. "You gay?"

She nodded.

He thought for a minute, his eyes searching her face. "Yeah, I remember her. Pretty. Blond. Kind of sickly."

"You knew her, then?"

He shrugged. "Not really. If I recall, she fainted once while I was cutting the grass at Bernadette's place. I helped her. Always wondered what happened to her."

"She died."

"Huh. Sorry."

"Look, I know this may seem like a strange question." Jane hesitated. "Do you have any idea why she might have taken a gun from the Simoneau mansion? It was part of a set of two that Marcel Simoneau owned."

"The derringers?"

She nodded.

"That was one of my murder weapons." He cracked a smile. "You're telling me Christine had the other one?"

"I found it in her briefcase a few weeks ago."

"Well, fuck me. When did she die?"

"The night after the murders."

"No shit. Maybe she knew who killed those folks because I sure as hell didn't." He leaned closer to the glass.

Jane remembered what her father always said. There were no guilty men in prison. But what if he was telling the truth? "One more question. Do you remember seeing a statue of a young girl? She was on her knees, her head back, and she was holding a round ball. The sculpture was made of—"

"Iron," he said. His right eye twitched. "Sure, it was one of the pieces I supposedly stole."

"Well, you didn't steal this one because Christine had it."

152

"Damn," he said with a smirk. "Imagine that. The cops got something wrong."

"Do you know anything about the statue?"

"Belonged to Philip Simoneau."

"Did you know him?"

He shook his head. "He lived with da massa in da big house. I was just hired help."

"What about the watch the police found at the gatehouse? You saying you didn't steal that either?"

He studied her a moment, chewing the question over. "It was planted, Ms. Lawless."

"Call me Jane, okay?"

He passed the back of he wrist across is mouth. "Sure, whatever. Problem was, I couldn't prove it." The strain of talking had made his voice even harder to hear. "Since you're here, maybe you want my real thoughts on the subject."

"Absolutely."

He shot the guard a quick look. "Far as I can figure, the cops had a triple homicide on their hands, so what do they do? What they always do. They look around for the nearest brother. That was me, Ms. Lawless. From the start, it was more like I had to prove I was innocent rather than the other way round. You ask your father. He knows what it was like. I never had a chance."

"If you didn't do it, who did?"

"Fuck if I know. Any one of them could've done it. That family was rotten to the core. But did the cops ever investigate any of *them*? Hell, no. They were rich and they had a name. Plus, they already had a nigger on ice, so why break a sweat?"

Jane didn't believe it was that simple, but she also knew she'd be a fool to underestimate racism in the legal system.

Dexter's eye twitched again. "Sounds to me like your girlfriend was involved up to her ass."

"If you were me, and you wanted to look into the matter further, where would you start?"

He lifted his chin, regarding her with what appeared to be a mixture of frustration and pity. "If I were you," he whispered, "I'd go do something else with my time. There's no way to figure out what really

153

happened that night. Not now. It was all over and done with a long time ago. It was me, I'd suck it up and go shoot some pool. Life's too short, right?" He pushed away from the table and stood. "Guard, we're done."

20

Cordelia held up her coffee cup, motioning to the waitress for a refill. "You look unhappy, Jane. Tell Auntie Cordelia all about it."

"I have," said Jane. She'd spent the past hour minutely going over everything Dexter Haynes had said.

Jane had taken Cordelia to The Dock restaurant in Stillwater. Cordelia refused to eat at her favorite spot—the Lowell Inn—because she might run into Marian. Apparently, they were still on the outs, and Cordelia still refused to say why.

Sitting on a deck above the St. Croix River, Jane tossed her napkin over her empty plate. "But see, when it came to the most important question, he wouldn't answer me. He just blew it off, told me there was no way to figure out what really happened that night."

"Assuming he doesn't know because he wasn't there."

"What if he's innocent, Cordelia? What if there *was* a rush to judgment and he's been rotting away in prison all these years?"

"Easy to blame the police. They're our modern scapegoat. But just because we like to demonize them, doesn't mean they're always wrong."

"But sometimes the police *do* have attacks of tunnel vision. They latch on to a theory and they push to prove it. Maybe it's an honest mistake, but it's a mistake all the same."

Cordelia shrugged.

"What if Christine *was* involved?"

Cordelia stabbed the last bite of her curried chicken salad, then waved the fork in the air, mulling it over. "We already know the family was dysfunctional. You met Bernadette and Laurent a few weeks ago, right? What was your impression?"

"They were like children, Cordelia. Neither of them seemed to have a clue about appropriate social behavior. And," she said, pulling her beer bottle in front of her, "they live in this huge old castle, and for whatever reason, they're letting it crumble around them. I mean, how much energy does it take to cut the grass? To rake the yard?"

"Apparently, more than they've got." Cordelia added some cream to her coffee and stirred. "Look, I've made a mental list of potential suspects—other than Haynes. If, and I stress that word, *if,* he didn't do it, then maybe one of them did. The big question is motive." She held up two fingers. "First, there's Bernadette and her brother, Laurent." A third finger popped up. "Then, Frank DeWitt, the father of little Timmy DeWitt."

"Gabby was Timmy's mother, right? Camille Simoneau's youngest daughter, the one who died a month or so before the murders."

"Exactly."

"I wonder if her death precipitated some sort of family strife?"

"I never thought of that, but I suppose it's possible." She raised a fourth finger. "Last on the list is Alice Cathcart, the nanny, the woman who found the bodies. That's four people who belonged in the house and could come and go as they pleased, four people with close ties to the family. You know the old saying, Where there's smoke there's fire? Well, I've got a better one. Where there's family, there's tension. Tension begets silence. Silence begets secrets. And secrets beget murder."

"Not always."

"No, but just look at the news, all the trials that are covered on cable channels. They are almost *all* about secrets."

"You don't buy the stranger theory? One of those books I read tried to make it sound like the perpetrator was a total stranger."

"Oh, pull-ease. The Satanic cult? The psychotic drifter? A burglary gone bad? I don't buy any of that."

Neither did Jane. "The more I read about that night, two things seem apparent to me. First, it was a crime of passion. Philip and Camille Simoneau weren't just killed, they were butchered."

"And second?" asked Cordelia, waving a fly away from her face.

"Something significant went wrong that night. I don't know what it was, but I believe that the person who entered the house didn't necessarily intend to commit triple homicide. He didn't bring any weapons with him: He used what was available. That suggests impulse. The objects of his wrath were clearly Camille and Philip, not the cook. I think it's fair to say she was killed because she saw who he was and could have identified him later. And the fact that a little child was left unharmed either means he didn't think the child could identify him, or he had a tiny amount of humanity left inside him."

"Not very human to let a little kid wander around in that carnage."

"True," said Jane.

"But how did Christine figure into it?" asked Cordelia.

"Assuming she didn't steal the gun or the statue, then someone must have given them to her. The statue belonged to Philip. Maybe he gave both of them to her."

"But why? And why hide them?" Jane finished the beer, her eyes straying to the bridge spanning the river. "She was working mainly with Philip. I remember her talking about him. She liked him a lot."

"And we don't know who his father was, right? Every book I've ever read on the subject has mentioned the lack of a name. That could be important."

"Bernadette obviously never wanted to discuss it."

"A secret, Janey." Cordelia winked. "One of many, no doubt."

"Maybe."

"So, we've got four suspects," pronounced Cordelia, pushing back from the table, crossing her legs and adjusting her tie. People in the restaurant seemed to take the tie and the fedora in stride. When combined with her red lipstick, her shimmering eye shadow, her large gold earrings and her gorgeous olive skin, she was a striking image. Very theatrical. Very Cordelia.

"I think we can eliminate Bernadette," said Jane. "A mother wouldn't kill her own son."

Cordelia's eyebrows zoomed upward.

"She's eccentric, Cordelia. Not homicidal."

"Remains to be seen." She added more cream to her coffee, then took a sip.

Jane gazed up at the sky, watching one fat, puffy cloud float across the river valley. If only her thoughts could be as clear as the day. "What do you make of that hook in the attic ceiling? The blood and urine on the floor. I know the book you were reading the other night suggested it was a torture scene. But how could that kind of thing go on in a house like that?"

"That's always where we make our mistake," said Cordelia. "We think brutality and violence belong to the poor. But that's a load of crap. Behind those manicured lawns beat some nasty hearts and minds. The facade means nothing."

"It's not that I disagree with you," said Jane. "It's just, who in that family would be capable of torture? And for what reason?"

"Another secret. Maybe they were all part of some weird torture cult."

"You saying they *all* participated in the murders?"

She thought about it a moment, then said, "Nah, Agatha Christie's already done that. But I think that hook in the attic needs to be explained. It didn't fit into the prosecution's case, so they ignored it. But I'll bet you anything, Janey, that when we find who put that hook in the ceiling, we'll find the real murderer."

It made as much sense to Jane as the weak case brought against Dexter Haynes.

"Why don't I come over tonight after I'm done at the theater and we can work on a game plan?" said Cordelia, studying the dessert menu. "If you haven't thrown out that bulletin board I bought you last fall, we can set it up with photos, clues to pursue. Do the whole P.I. thingie."

Jane knew she was fighting a losing battle. She couldn't keep Cordelia out of her house forever. From the moment she finally figured out that Greta was using her third floor as a darkroom, Jane would be treated to a steady stream of snide comments and lurid insinuations. Cordelia didn't trust Jane's motives, and frankly, maybe she had a point.

"I don't know," said Jane, averting her eyes so that Cordelia couldn't see how guilty they looked.

"Come on, Janey. We've got to get cracking here."

"What about Hattie?"

"The Finch has her tonight. I'll be at the theater until ten. After that, I'm free as a bird."

"I'd rather do it tomorrow. Come over to the restaurant for lunch." Normally, the mention of food would get Cordelia's attention. But today, she seemed to sense dark influences behind Jane's reluctance to get together at her home.

"Don't tell me," she said, laying the menu down on the table and nailing Jane with her eyes.

"What?"

"You haven't asked Greta to move into your third-floor apartment."

"No, of course not."

" 'Cause if you did——"

"I didn't."

She heaved a sigh. "Boy, you had me going there for a second. It's bad enough that I see her over at the Xanadu all the time taking pictures. Quite honestly, she gives me the willies." Folding her arms over her ample bosom, she added, "How often *do* you see her?"

"Not often."

"Define 'not often.' "

"Don't push so hard."

"You listen to me, dearheart. That woman appeared out of the blue for a reason."

"Oh, come *on*. That's just not possible. She is what she appears to be: a young woman who came to the Twin Cities to attend MCAD. End of story. She's honest, Cordelia, as honest as you are paranoid."

"I am *not* paranoid." A second later, she picked the dessert menu back up and held it in front of her face.

"Now what?"

Out of the corner of her mouth, she whispered, "Marian. She just walked in."

Jane's attention shifted to the door. Sure enough, there was Marian standing with two men. She was a tall, rangy brunette with intense amber eyes and a shock of thick bangs, quite striking in her own sort of down-home way. She had on a pair of white overalls and a tight black T-shirt. The guys were wearing business suits.

"Pay the bill and let's get out of here," said Cordelia. She peered furtively over the menu.

"You know, for someone who can't get her own love life in order, you're awfully quick to judge."

"Oh damn. She's spotted me."

Jane sat back and watched the scene unfold. For some reason, she had the impression that Cordelia was afraid to run into Marian. What she saw on her face now was pure fury.

Marian approached the table.

Cordelia stood. She looked like she wanted to drop-kick her into the river.

"Hi," said Marian softly.

"I have nothing to say to you."

"You can be so cruel, you know that?"

"Me? *I'm* the one who's cruel after what *you* said to *me*?" She glanced down at Jane. "I'll meet you at the Hummer." Exuding wounded nobility, she turned abruptly and walked away.

21

Billy? Is that really you?" Bernadette hadn't heard Bill McBride's voice in years, but she still remembered it. Deep. Nervous. Pussy-whipped. How could she forget a voice like that? When there was nothing but silence on the other end of the line, she began to get annoyed. "Bill, speak up. You know I don't like mealy-mouthed men." She'd called him because she needed his help.

"Yes, Bernie, I'm here."

He sounded funny, like he was talking through a tin can. "Something wrong with your phone service?"

"I've got you on speakerphone. I'm in my office, working. What do you want?"

"Is that a nice way to talk to an old friend?"

"I thought I made myself clear. I never wanted to see or hear from you again. Ever."

"Well, that was *then*. This is the new millennium, Billy. A new world."

"And don't call me Billy," he said hurriedly. "Nobody calls me that anymore."

"Except me."

"What do you want?"

"I need you to come over to the house."

"Are you nuts?"

His voice sounded strangled. It made her laugh.

"You still living at the castle then?" he asked.

"Where else would I be?"

"Thought maybe you might have left town."

"Why? I haven't done anything wrong." When he didn't respond, she said, "So, when can you come?"

"We're finished, Bernie."

Her impatience shot into the stratosphere. "I want you to appraise my house, okay? That's all. I need to know how much it's worth."

"You planning to sell?"

"None of your damn business. When can I expect you?" She could hear him sigh. It sounded like air rushing out of a balloon.

"I'll have one of my associates come out tomorrow."

"No, Bill. I want you."

"Bernie——"

"I'll expect you at three this afternoon."

"I couldn't possibly come today."

"Tomorrow, then. Three o'clock."

"I've got a meeting at three."

"Four then."

"Oh, all right. But listen to me, Bernie. I'm serious. No funny business."

"Of course not. Just the usual elderberry wine."

"Not amusing."

She hung up before he could think of another excuse.

Bernadette was on a mission today. She'd taken one of the smaller paintings—a Berthe Morisot—and wrapped it in birthday paper, just in case Laurent questioned her about it on her way out the door. All she would need to say was that she was on her way to a birthday party for one of her poet friends. Laurent called them all The Potes. It was his way of dismissing her passion and her inspirational connections. It was jealousy, pure and simple. She pitied him for his lack of soul.

In the end, the wrapping didn't matter because Laurent's car was gone when she got out to the garage. She stowed the picture behind the front seat of her VW Beetle convertible, then hopped in, backed out of the drive, and zoomed off.

She'd made an appointment at the Hammond-Dillabough Gallery in Uptown. It was considered one of the finest in town. They also did appraisals. Bernadette had come to the conclusion that she'd been far too passive about her financial state. No more Mr. Nice Bernie. Writers were such pleasant people, weren't they? Well, except for the few backstabbing, petty, relentlessly egocentric bores. But they were in the minority and Bernadette was not among their number.

Sailing down Hennepin, Bernadette waved to the crowds along the street. She was secretly excited to think that her status as aging town pariah would soon change to that of "enduring local eccentric." Once Laurent got the house tours up and running, she'd find herself in a whole new world of intrigue. But to get the house in shape, and not bankrupt what was left of her trust fund, would require money. Laurent wasn't very pragmatic when it came to finances. Leave it to Bernadette to think in hard, cold, realistic terms. They needed cash and they needed it now.

Entering the gallery, Bernadette headed straight for the receptionist. A young, blond-haired man sat behind an elegant rosewood secretary. He was as thin and elegant as the desk. "May I help you?"

She glanced at his tie. "I like the pink stripe. It looks like a cotton candy cane."

He smiled. "Nice way to put it."

"Yes. Of course it is." She handed him the gift-wrapped package.

"What's this?"

"A Berthe Morisot. I have an appointment with Mr. Hammond to have it appraised."

He checked his book. "I'm sorry. I don't have that on his schedule."

"I called yesterday. Is Hammond here or isn't he?"

"He won't be in until this afternoon."

She muttered a few profanities under her breath. "Okay, I'll leave it."

The man placed it down on the desk, then carefully unwrapped it. "Oh, my," he said, studying it with great interest.

"Visual poetry, isn't it?"

"Indeed."

"Just give me a receipt. Have him call me when he's done."

"Of course." He took down all her information. "I'll just be a minute." As he disappeared into the back, Bernadette glanced around.

Most of the art was modern. She liked some of the sculpture, but the paintings all seemed trite. Like her father, Bernadette had an eye for art. There was nothing in this gallery that was worth much. Of course, she was used to the fine art hanging on the walls at home.

Returning from the back room, the receptionist said, "Thank you, Ms. . . ." He looked down at the name. "Simoneau."

No recognition at all. Bernadette used to pray for obscurity, but that part of her life was over. She couldn't change her past, couldn't bring anyone back from the dead, but she could make some bucks on it. Maybe that was cold, but she and Laurent had to support themselves somehow, didn't they? And neither of them had any particular skills. If the world wanted Jerry Springer and P. T. Barnum, well, who was she to argue?

"*Bernadette* Simoneau," she said proudly.

Still no recognition.

"Tell Mr. Hammond that I'd like his appraisal as soon as possible."

22

After the dinner rush had subsided, Jane descended to her office, where she undressed and stepped into the shower. For the next ten minutes she stood under the spray, letting the water and the steam ease the tension in her muscles. Changing finally into a pair of comfortable old jeans, a soft Donegal turtleneck, and a frayed jeans jacket, she clipped the leash to Mouse's collar and the two of them headed outside for a walk around the lake.

The night air was delicious, like drinking a cool glass of lemonade on a sweltering summer day. Some nights she felt brain dead by the end of the evening. Tonight was one of those nights.

Mouse tugged at the leash wanting to run instead of walk. Jane reined him in.

"You're younger than I am," she said as they started off down the footpath. Lampposts lit their way in the darkness. "And you've been sleeping for the last four hours." As they neared the bandstand, halfway around the lake, she spied an empty bench.

Mouse wagged his tail eagerly.

"No popcorn tonight, babe. I'll give you a treat when we get home."

Sitting down, she leaned back against the wood slats and watched the lamps cast bright yellow ribbons of light on the inky black water. Mouse tugged at the end of the leash, straining for a closer look at the ducks floating near the dock, but he eventually got tired of that and sat down on the pavement next to her, sniffing the air and watching people walk by.

The summer concerts hadn't started yet, so the area closest to the bandstand wasn't crowded. After a long winter, several dozen of the sailboats moored to the west of the concession area had been returned to the water—their owners assuming, apparently, that the lake wouldn't freeze again until next winter. In Minnesota, assuming anything about the weather was always a mark of brazen optimism.

Jane had been thinking all day about her conversation with Dexter Haynes. Maybe she was easily bamboozled—Cordelia would certainly agree with that assessment—but she had a strong feeling that Haynes was innocent. She couldn't prove it, but if she could, it would be an amazing gift to help an innocent man regain his freedom.

Over the past few years, Jane had succeeded in solving some significant crimes in the Twin Cities. In retrospect, she realized it all came down to taking stupid chances and mixing it with a large dose of luck. Still, if she couldn't figure out the whole truth about what happened that rainy August night back in '87, at least she had to try to understand Christine's role in it.

Christine hadn't actually lied to Jane about her illness during the last year of her life, her failure wasn't an act of commission, but omission. It still stung when Jane thought about how much Christine had kept hidden. Finding the *Iron Girl* and the derringer had brought those feelings of betrayal back with a bitter force. But her anger then, as now, was tempered with tenderness and the desire to protect, even if Christine didn't want to be protected. Why did people have to be an almost insane mixture of qualities?

Jane glanced down at her cowboy boots and immediately thought of Kenzie. She'd had two e-mails from her this afternoon, but it wasn't enough. She wanted to talk to her—not on the phone, but here, in town, where she could touch her, see her reactions. Waiting until July simply wasn't going to cut it.

Jane dithered a moment more before she took out her cell phone and tapped in Kenzie's home number. She wasn't sure what Kenzie had on her evening agenda. The phone rang a couple of times. Three. Four. Jane was afraid she'd missed her when the line picked up.

"Hello?" said Kenzie's voice.

"Hey, pardner. Seen any horse rustlers around your parts lately?"

She laughed. "My *parts* are perfectly safe, thanks."

"I'll bet you've got them rustlers tied up in the barn. Good thing, too. Old galoots like that can be nasty."

"God, but the Republicans must be proud of you, Jane. A liberal knowing all that John Wayne slang."

"I do my part to be ecumenical."

"How many beers have you had?"

"None. I'm sitting on a park bench in the great outdoors with my dog by my side and an ache in my heart."

She snorted. "Brother! You've been listening to way too many country-western songs. Something going on I don't know about?"

"No. Well. Yeah, maybe something. I want to send you a plane ticket. I miss you, Kenzie. Can't you come just for a day or two?"

There was a long pause.

"Just for one measly little night?" said Jane.

"You're only interested in what happens at night?"

"And the day," she added quickly.

Kenzie laughed again. "When?"

"I'll send you an open ticket. Whenever it works out, give me a call and tell me you're coming, and then hop on the plane. I'll do the rest. I'll meet you at the airport, wine you and dine you and do everything in my power to make you glad you came. I just need to see you."

Silence. Then, "You okay?"

"I will be when you come."

"You drive a hard bargain, *pardner*."

"The plane ticket will be in the mail tomorrow morning."

"Okay, I'll be in touch. But I'm not promising anything."

"Understood."

They took the usual ten minutes to actually say the word "good-bye." After Jane had hung up, she felt better. "Come on, Mouse. Time to head home."

As soon as Jane entered the house, she remembered that she'd left the heat low because she thought the day would be warmer than it turned out to be. She kept her jeans jacket on as she went into the kitchen.

Switching on a light, she let Mouse out in the backyard, then opened the cupboard and stared at a bottle of brandy. Before she could pour herself a drink, the doorbell chimed.

It had to be Cordelia. Well, at least the house was dark and quiet, so she wouldn't be subjected to the third degree. But when she opened the door, her father stood outside.

"Dad," she said, giving him a hug. She hadn't seen him since he'd left for New Orleans. "This is a surprise."

Raymond Lawless was in his late sixties. He had the bearing of a man who'd spent his life as the center of a jury's attention. He moved with vigor and confidence. Tonight, however, he seemed subdued. "I need to talk to you, honey."

"Sure." She led him into the living room.

"I got a phone call this evening," he said, unbuttoning his suit jacket as he sat down on the couch. "From Dexter Haynes. He wanted me to pass on a message to you. Honestly, Jane, I spent most of the evening wondering whether or not to tell you about it."

She was nonplussed. "What did he say?"

"The message was just two words. Alice Cathcart. He explained that you'd asked him a question and that he didn't give you an answer. Guess he thought about it and decided he'd made a mistake."

Jane lifted her arm over the back of the couch. She could tell her dad was troubled, but didn't understand why. "Why wouldn't you pass it on to me?"

"Because," he said, removing his glasses and pinching the bridge of his nose, "I'm concerned that you might be getting involved in something you should stay out of."

"The Simoneau murders."

"That and contact with Haynes. He was convicted of a triple murder, Jane. Do you *get* it that he could be dangerous? Guys like him know how to read people. It's very likely he sees you as somebody he can use."

"How?"

"If nothing else, you could provide him with a kind of sick prison entertainment. Lots of do-gooders are used that way. Listen to me, honey. Cons know how to *con*. It's how they survive. I know I don't always have a lot of good to say about the unholy mess we call our justice system, but believe me, most of the time the right person gets put in jail. Most of the time, the system works."

Arguing with him was pointless. Her father knew a lot more about the courts and the prisons then she did.

"You're playing with fire, Jane."

"You know why I'm doing it."

"Because of Christine."

She nodded.

"I can't help you there, but I doubt Haynes can either." He paused, studying her with his warm blue eyes. "What was the question you asked him?"

She shrugged. "I just said, if I wanted to do a little digging into the Simoneau family, where would be the best place to start."

"And he suggested the nanny. Interesting."

"Why do you say that?"

"Because of all the people put on the stand, she was the least forthcoming. It was clear she knew more than she was willing to tell, but she held on to whatever it was with incredible tenacity. Joe Ramerez, the D.A., got her declared a hostile witness. His examination of her was withering."

"Were you there?"

"No, but I read the transcript. Look, Janey, there's something you should know about Haynes. It isn't information that was allowed into the trial or the court record, but it appeared in all the local papers. I'm sure the jurors knew about it. It may have been one of the main reasons he was convicted."

"Tell me," she said.

Her father slipped his glasses back on. "Haynes had a juvie record. It was sealed, of course, but the contents were leaked. Apparently, he and two of his buddies were arrested for knocking off a convenience store in central Chicago back in the late seventies. Haynes was fifteen at the time. He was put on probation because it was a first offense—or at least it was the first time he got caught. But, see, it fits with what he did at the Simoneau mansion. The thefts he committed in that house provided the motive for the murders. If he'd never tried to steal before, maybe the prosecution would have had a harder time proving their case."

"But there's a good reason juvenile records are sealed. Just because someone does something dumb when he's a teenager doesn't mean the behavior will continue. I mean, I know youth isn't some overriding excuse, but when you're fifteen, you're still figuring out who you are, still thinking yourself up. By his twenties, Haynes was in law school. Top of his class."

Her father gave her a hard look. "You're not going to drop this, are you."

"I can't."

"You know, Janey, the fact is, you've got a lot more to worry about if Haynes *wasn't* the murderer. If the real killer is still out there, and if they find out you're digging into something you shouldn't be, well. You get my point."

She brushed a strand of hair away from her eyes. "Okay. I hear you."

"I said what I came to say. I can't do anything else." He put his arms around her and hugged her close. "I love you, honey. Just . . . be careful."

"I will."

She walked him to the door.

As he was about to step outside, he turned to look at her. "We should get together for dinner one night soon. You and me, and Peter and Sigrid. A family powwow."

"Just tell me when."

"I need to tell you all about Marilyn and me. I think we may be about to call it quits."

All she could do was stare at him.

"It's for the best. Really, Janey, don't worry. This has been coming for a long time. It's just . . . when a decision is made, it seems so final."

She knew her father and Marilyn had been having problems, but she hoped they would resolve them. "Why don't you stay a few more minutes. We could talk now."

He shook his head. "I need to gather my thoughts. Besides, I promised I'd call Marilyn around ten-thirty." Glancing at his watch, he added, "If I leave now, I'll just make it home in time."

She kissed him on the cheek. "You're the best dad in the world. Don't ever forget that."

His smile was wistful. "I wish I could say I was the best husband, but that would be a lie. 'Night, honey."

After he was gone, Jane stood in the foyer and thought about how happy he'd been with Marilyn for so many years. She often wondered if Christine had lived, would they still be together? It was easy to idealize a love that had ended in tragedy, when in reality, the truth was something far more mixed. Jane still remembered many of the arguments they'd had, the times when she felt disconnected and distant. Love was never perfect, but she still believed with all her heart that it had been worth it. No matter how it ended.

Hearing Mouse bark, she crossed the dining room into the kitchen and opened the back door to let him in. She bent down and gave him a good scratch up and down his back. "I promised you a treat, didn't I."

Straightening up, she opened the refrigerator and removed a plastic carton of meat scraps she'd brought home from the restaurant the previous evening. "Not every dog gets leftover filet mignon, you know." She dumped a few bites into his dog dish along with some kibble, then set it on the floor.

While he ate, she opened the upper cupboard again and grabbed the brandy and a glass. "I'll be in the living room," she said on her way out the door.

She thought about building a fire, even went so far as to find some old newspaper and kindling. But when she saw that she'd have to go outside to get more logs, she decided the brandy was enough to warm her up. As she sat down on the couch, Mouse curled up on the floor next to her. She had a lot to think about.

Three brandies later, she was lying down, one leg tossed over the back of the couch. She was feeling no pain but still awake when Mouse began to growl.

"Probably a car outside, buddy."

But it wasn't a car.

Mouse stood and stared back toward the front hall. His growling grew deeper, more menacing.

Jane sat up and turned to look. Squinting into the dimness, she saw a dark form standing at the base of the stairs.

"Hi," said Greta, taking a few steps into the living room.

Jane hadn't heard her come down the stairs. "It's okay, boy," she said, patting him on the back. "You know Greta. She's a friend. Come on in," she said, seeing that Greta was carrying some papers.

Mouse stopped growling, but he watched her carefully as she crossed the room.

It finally occurred to Jane that there was something vaguely incongruous about Greta simply appearing in her living room this late at night.

"I've got some photos to show you," she said, sitting down on the couch.

"Have you been upstairs working all this time?"

"Yup."

"I didn't see any lights on when I came in."

"I had to put paper over the windows. You said it was okay."

Jane shrugged. All her movements felt liquid and easy. "Whatever you need."

"Look at these," said Greta, handing her several pictures.

One dim light burned behind them, but it was enough for Jane to get an idea of what the photos looked like. "These are wonderful," she said, flipping through them.

"I took them this afternoon. Won't be long before that screen gets pulled out of there, and I wanted to make sure we had some good shots of it before they tear it down. This one's the best." She pointed to the second black-and-white.

Jane flipped through them one more time, then handed them back. Realizing she was holding her breath, she pressed a hand to her eyes. "Good work. Really good work."

"Thanks."

"Well, so . . ." She wasn't sure what to say. Her eyes drifted to Greta's face. "Have you heard any more from your ex-boyfriend? I've forgotten his name."

Greta leaned into the couch, resting her head against the back cushion. "Calvin. No, he won't be bothering me anymore."

"You seem awfully sure of that."

"I am."

Jane wanted to touch Greta's hair, but knew it wasn't right.

"You seem tired," said Greta.

"I suppose I am."

"You know, I've been thinking about what you did the other night. Calvin was for sure going to hurt me. If you hadn't come out when you did . . . what I mean to say is, you're incredibly brave, and I'm totally in your debt."

Jane smiled, then shook her head. "Truthfully, when I do things like that, it's not bravery. Craziness, maybe, or simple stupidity."

"No, I saw what I saw."

It wasn't a point she felt like arguing.

"I should probably leave you alone. I hope you don't mind, but I came downstairs earlier to get some ice for my Coke. You weren't home yet. I started some ice going in the freezer upstairs, but it doesn't ever seem to get cold enough."

"Maybe I need to have it looked at," said Jane. Gazing at Greta a moment more, she said, "You wear such optimistic colors."

"I do?"

"Pink the other night. A bright fuchsia sweater tonight."

"I never thought about it that way." She hesitated, then continued, "I couldn't help but notice that sculpture sitting on the kitchen counter. It's the one you told your dad about, right? The *Iron Girl*? It's really beautiful."

"Yeah, gorgeous."

"Are you making any progress on your investigation?"

Jane finished her drink. "Not much."

"Did you ever get to talk to the guy who was convicted of the murders?"

"Yes. This morning." She tried not to stare, but her eyes wouldn't cooperate. "Does your brain ever get tired, Greta?"

"Um, not really."

"Well, wait till you get to be my age."

"You're not that old."

Jane laughed. "But you are *so* young."

"No I'm not."

"No," said Jane, setting her glass down on the carpet. She could see that she'd offended her. "You're not."

Greta stood. "I think I better get home."

"You're sure about Calvin, that he won't bother you again?"

173

"I can take care of myself."

"Sure you can." She reached up and took hold of her hand. "Tell me the truth, Greta. You didn't appear out of the blue for some nefarious reason, did you? You're not going to hurt me."

"Whatever gave you that idea?"

"It's nothing," said Jane, feeling foolish for even asking the question. She'd had too much to drink.

"It's Cordelia, isn't it. She doesn't like me. She made that clear the first day we met. But . . . I don't get it. What's she got against me?"

"Oh, nothing. It's nothing. She gets these paranoid delusions every now and then. You just happened to move into her line of sight when she was having one."

Greta sat back down on the couch, closer this time. "Believe me when I tell you this, Jane. I'd never *ever* hurt you." She gazed intently into Jane's eyes. "That's a promise."

23

A dark wind blew up the street as Calvin sat in his van, waiting for Greta to get home. Since their confrontation the other night, he'd done some legwork and come up with some important information. The Linden Hills house, where Greta had been spending so much time, belonged to the same woman who owned the Lyme House restaurant on Lake Harriet. Her name was Lawless. Her father was a big-shot defense attorney in St. Paul. This Lawless woman had to be rolling in bucks because, not only did she own the Lyme House, but she was opening a new restaurant in Uptown.

Calvin had seen Greta taking photographs inside the old movie theater. He didn't know why she was doing it, but he intended to find out.

Late last night, Calvin had snuck into the Lyme House pub. By talking to some of the regulars, he'd learned that Lawless was a dyke. Apparently, she didn't even try to hide it.

He'd put it all together a few hours later, sitting in a downtown bar, smoking a butt and drinking a beer. The image of what was really going on inside that house hit him so hard, he had to run outside and puke his guts out in the alley. Greta hadn't left him for another guy. She'd left him for a woman.

The more he thought about it, the more the confusing parts of

Greta's personality were beginning to make sense. She never wanted to take care of him—do his wash, cook, grocery shop, clean the apartment. As far as he could see, she didn't have a domestic bone in her body. On the other hand, she could look super hot, and she flirted like hell with guys every place they went. Maybe it was a cover. He'd never seen her flirt with a woman.

What had really bugged him was her absolute refusal to quit her job. She was so goddamn independent. It was all there to see, but he'd been blind to it because he loved her. She sure kept him happy in bed. And he wondered about that. That's when the thought occurred to him that maybe she wasn't a dyke. Maybe she was just weak, susceptible, too young and stupid to realize what was happening until Lawless got her hooks in her.

As Calvin sat in the darkness now, staring at Greta's apartment building, he was struck by a totally disgusting thought. What if part of Lawless's lure was to pay for Greta to go to art college? Greta had always talked about college like it was the holy fucking grail. What if she was selling herself sexually to this woman for a chance at some stupid dream? Except, if that's all it was, then maybe she was still salvageable.

Calvin decided that had to be it. If he could just get to her in time, talk some sense into her, make her remember how much she really did love him, well then, maybe she still had a chance at a normal life. He wasn't sure he had the money to pay for her college, and that would remain a problem. But he'd work it out. If she got pregnant, maybe she'd forget about it and just settle down with him. The more he thought about it, the more he realized he was her only shot at salvation.

Noticing a light come on in her first-floor apartment, Calvin assumed that Greta must have parked behind the building. He sat for a few minutes finishing his cigarette. He had to plan his next move carefully. He couldn't come at her like he had the other night. If he lost his temper again, it was all over.

Flipping the cigarette into the street, he slipped the van into gear and drove off. He'd rented himself a motel room a few miles down Lyndale, but he didn't feel like turning in just yet.

Taking a left on 31st, Calvin decided he could use a couple beers. There was a bar over by the university that he liked. Half an hour later, he was seated at the counter, working his way through his first brew, when a man sat down next to him. Calvin hated really tall guys. He thought they were genetic freaks. This dude looked like a walking sequoia and had a face like a chain saw. But he seemed friendly enough. Introduced himself as Ron Johnson. Said he was a salesman for Bergstaad Marine. Sold boats off the showroom and a large outdoor lot.

They talked for a while, swapping sales stories. Mostly, Calvin figured they were lying to each other, but that was pretty standard. He wished Johnson would leave him alone, but he just kept hanging around, running his mouth.

Calvin had just finished his third beer and Johnson had just launched into his predictions for the Twins summer season, when Calvin decided to throw in the towel. He waited for the guy to take a sip of his rum and Coke, then said, "I think I better call it a night. I've got an early-morning meeting tomorrow."

"Oh, sure. Yeah, it's getting late." He checked his watch. "I'll walk out with you." Chugging the last of his drink, he threw some cash on the bar and got up.

It was close to one-thirty. The parking lot was empty except for a couple of cars near the door, Calvin's van, and Johnson's BMW.

"Nice wheels," said Calvin, eyeing the car.

"I like it. Well," said Johnson, holding out his hand, "good talking to you."

"Yeah. Good luck selling those boats." Calvin reached out to shake Johnson's hand. Before he realized what was happening, Johnson had twisted his arm behind his back and slammed him into the side of the van.

Calvin heard a gun click next to his ear.

"I got a message for you from a mutual friend. You listening?"

Calvin nodded.

"Stay away from Greta. You don't call her, you don't follow her, you don't do squat, understand?" He pulled up on Calvin's arm.

"Jesus," groaned Calvin. Another inch and his arm would break.

"We clear?" whispered Johnson, jamming the gun hard into Calvin's neck.

"Yeah. Clear."

"Get in that piece-of-shit van of yours and go back to wherever you came from. If you don't, the next guy who gets sent won't be as nice as me."

Calvin tried to swallow back the bile rushing up his throat. "Who sent you?" he rasped.

"Not your business, asshole." Johnson flipped Calvin around, then rammed his knee into Calvin's stomach.

Calvin doubled up in pain as the butt of the gun connected with his nose. He reeled back, holding his arms up to block the next punch. Instead, Johnson sent another knee into his gut. Bleeding and dazed, Calvin slid down against the side of the van.

"Be a good boy now, Cal. Just back away. Forget you ever knew her."

Johnson stood over him for a few seconds, then got in his BMW and drove out of the parking lot, taking a right onto University and disappearing into the night.

Calvin leaned his head back and closed his eyes, lifting his hand up to touch the blood dripping from his nose. Nobody needed to tell him who'd sent the goon. Lawless didn't want anybody messing with her new girl toy. Getting beat up might scare some guys off, but it didn't work like that with Calvin. With the firepower he had in his van, nobody was going to take him by surprise again—and walk away alive.

24

Moving day had finally arrived. The Association for Retarded Citizens' truck was in the drive, and a man stood outside on Jane's front steps, banging on the door. Feeling unusually old and a little hung over, Jane wondered for a moment if the truck shouldn't haul her off to that great garage sale in the sky instead of Christine's boxes. But, thankfully, the moment passed.

Half an hour later, she stood in the basement, Mouse next to her, staring at the empty space where Christine's belongings had rested for so many years. She waited for the sadness to descend, but when nothing came, she shrugged, grateful for the reprieve, and headed upstairs. What she needed was coffee.

Jane had packed everything she wanted to keep—Christine's diary with three entries in it, some sketchbooks, her real estate awards, her briefcase, some jewelry, a couple of winter scarves—into two boxes. She'd sorted through everything twice, looking for clues that might explain the *Iron Girl* and the gun, but came up empty. Lots of Christine's "stuff" was still scattered around the house—photograph albums; records and tapes; her jewelry case; an old, dead Nikon; her last address book; a few framed family photographs; books; etc. Jane had looked through all of that, too, but, again, nothing provided an answer.

As she was adding coffee to the press pot, waiting for the water to boil, it struck her that there was something she hadn't looked at in years—an old sewing basket that had belonged to Christine's grandmother. It sat on the dresser in their bedroom when Christine was alive. It contained lots of sewing stuff—a darning egg, embroidery thread, a button box, and also a few newspaper clippings her grandmother had saved. But Christine often used it to store odd bits and pieces of her life—a stone from the Mediterranean, an envelope containing pressed gingko leaves, a couple of Jane's old love letters, a feather. Jane didn't remember what was special about the feather, which bothered her a little. In going through Christine's things, she realized there was so much of their life together she'd forgotten. There were other things in the box, too, but Jane couldn't remember just what.

"Where is that sewing basket, Mouse?" She turned around and leaned against the counter. She remembered that she'd left it on the dresser for a long time after Christine's death, but had eventually moved it into the guest bedroom. From there . . .

"I think I put it on the shelf in the closet," she said, pouring the steaming water into the pot. She waited the requisite three minutes for the coffee to steep, then pressed the plunger down and poured herself a mug. "Come on. Let's check it out."

If she recalled correctly, the basket was maybe a foot wide. It was a cylinder, with the sides made of a tight wicker, and the top and bottom thin, flat wood. The whole thing had been painted a sort of shiny peach color, with decals surrounding the small silver handle on the top.

Jane grabbed a step stool from inside the linen closet on the second floor and carried it into the guest bedroom. After fortifying herself with a couple sips of caffeine, she proceeded to check out the top shelf.

"There it is," she muttered, seeing it way at the end of the shelf. Mouse was sniffing around the closet floor. As she pulled it free, she was nearly asphyxiated by a whoosh of dust. "No comments on my general housekeeping abilities," she said, giving him a stern look.

Sitting down on the bed, she opened the cover. Sure enough, she'd remembered the contents pretty accurately. As she dug around, she found a photo of herself, one Christine had taken of her diving off the end of the dock up at Blackberry Lake. A second photo showed Jane standing on the beach, barefoot with her pant legs rolled up past her ankles, about to push the rowboat into the water. Bean and Gulliver, their two dogs, were standing with their paws on the bow, watching.

As she sat there on the bed, she felt the tug of memory. "Those were good days, Mouse. Really good days."

Digging around a little more, she found the Mediterranean rock. Christine had nearly drowned in an undertow just off the coast of Cyprus. After she managed to struggle out of the water, she discovered that she had a rock in her fist. She kept the rock because she thought it had brought her luck.

Down along the side of the sewing basket, Jane found an undeveloped roll of 35mm film.

"Boy, this is old."

Mouse sniffed it.

"I wonder what's on it." She set it down on the bed and continued her search.

"Hey, here are a couple of my track ribbons." They were from high school. Christine had always been so impressed that Jane had been such a good sprinter.

"And look at this. My high school class ring. Cheap piece of junk, actually, but I loved it." Christine had worn it for the first couple years they'd been together. On their third anniversary, they'd exchanged rings. Jane had given Christine a ruby and Christine had presented Jane with a square-cut tigers eye. Both were set in gold.

"Well, that's about it, Mouse. Maybe, on our way over to the Xanadu Club this morning, we should drop the film off at the photo store, see if anything on it survived all these years."

He barked

"My feelings exactly," she said, stroking his head a couple of times and then rising from the bed.

Cordelia entered the Xanadu Club around eleven that morning with Hattie in her arms. She'd given up wearing her fedora today because she was in a black leather mood—leather pants; leather jacket; sleek, high-healed leather boots; her curly auburn hair hanging loose. She didn't think the two looks blended well. Hattie didn't exactly blend well either. When thinking about how to accessorize a leather outfit for maximum effect, the last thing a leather freak would choose was a toddler.

The little girl squealed and pointed at all the mirrors and colorful murals as they passed through the foyer into the main part of the theater. Glancing up at the balcony, Cordelia's eagle eye spotted Jane talking to Greta. They seemed to be laughing and having a gay old time. No pun intended. Cordelia didn't "do" puns.

Silently, Cordelia seethed. Since they hadn't noticed her entrance, she took the opportunity to study them. Jane was talking now, Greta listening intently. There was something in Greta's expression that bothered Cordelia, but she couldn't quite put her finger on it. The two of them walked to the edge of the balcony and sat down. They seemed to be deep in conversation.

Suddenly, Hattie shouted, "Yook!" Her pointer finger soared upward. "Ganey! Ganey! Ganey!" She rocked back and forth in Cordelia's arms.

Jane turned and looked down. Waving, she called, "Hi, Hattie. I'll be right there."

"Don't let *us* interrupt you," Cordelia shouted back.

Jane shot her a pained look, then got up and disappeared into the rear of the balcony.

"Do you know how to sneer, Hattie?" asked Cordelia, finger-brushing Hattie's wispy blond hair. Cordelia had tried to clip it back at least four times before they'd left the loft, and each time, Hattie had pulled the clip out. Cordelia was contemplating getting her a buzz cut. For all she knew, it was the height of toddler fashion. Or maybe she should check out the children's department at Dayton's for a pair of baby handcuffs. Surely *someone* made them.

"Sneering is easy, Hatts. Here, let's try it." Cordelia turned her around so that the little girl could see her face. Curling one side of her lips, she said, "*That's* sneering. Try it."

Hattie patted Cordelia's nose.

"It's easy. Just lift your lip a tiny bit. Show a little teeth. And then, at the same time, you've got to narrow your eyes. Just a smidge. In this case, we're going for understatement, not melodrama. Understatement gives us *deniability* when Ganey says we were sneering."

Hattie squirmed around to look at a man carrying a large piece of wood. "Yook!" she said pointing at him.

Jane breezed through the door at the back of the theater. "Hi, you guys," she called.

"She's putting on her best I-don't-give-a-damn-what-you-think smile," whispered Cordelia into Hattie's ear. "It's a sure sign of guilt."

"I didn't expect to see you two this morning," said Jane, hurrying down the center aisle. She gave Hattie a kiss on her cheek. "Our renovators are planning to start removing the seats this afternoon. I've scheduled an architectural salvage company to come pick them up next week."

"Yook at ma thout!" cried Hattie.

"What'd she say?" asked Jane quietly.

"Don't you understand toddler-ese?"

"Guess not."

"An ma peants," said Hattie eagerly.

"She wants you to admire her outfit—her pants and shirt."

"Oh. They're beautiful, Hattie. Really stunning."

"Yee-ahh," she said, stroking the black velour.

"I thought kids liked pastels with bunnies and Winnie the Pooh on them."

"Not Hatts. She's a miniature Goth who's big into texture."

Hattie grabbed her shirt and stuck her thumb in her mouth.

Glancing at the theater seats, Cordelia asked, "Are we selling them or giving them away?"

"Giving. Getting someone to haul them out of here free of charge will save us a bundle of money."

Cordelia switched Hattie to her other arm as Greta walked up. Two camera bags hung around her neck.

"Hi," said Greta, eyeing Cordelia's leather clothes. "You up for a role as a biker moll?"

"None of your damn business."

"Lovely," said Jane, clearing her throat. "I understand you two have already met."

"Do you ever smile?" asked Greta, "or is that perpetual pucker your only expression?"

Cordelia glowered.

"I really *really* don't like playing referee," said Jane stepping between them. "Greta, you might as well finish your shoot for today. I know you have an appointment at MCAD this afternoon."

Greta smirked at Cordelia. "I have a meeting with the president of academic affairs."

"How utterly thrilling," said Cordelia, her voice flat.

"It is, isn't it?" She nodded to Jane, then walked away.

"That woman is taunting me," said Cordelia. "I have a Hummer you know!" she shouted after her.

"You told me that," Greta shouted back, turning around and moving backward up the aisle. "Are you trying to impress me with your car smarts? The Hummer is the biggest piece of crap to come off a production line since the AMC Pacer."

"How dare you say that? The Pacer? That's an obscene comparison!"

Cordelia was about to charge off after her when Jane jumped in front of her.

"You two sound like four-year-olds. I mean, why don't you just tell her that her mother wears combat boots. That's about the level of your discourse."

"Your mother wears combat boots!" shouted Cordelia, but it was drowned out by the noise of electric saws. "The nerve of that sexless little pencil person, making rude comments about *my* Hummer! My Hummer is a technological marvel. A car to surpass all cars."

"Quasi military vehicle," Jane corrected her.

"Whatever. Janey, don't you see? Christine was never like that. She was sweet and kind and generous and loving."

"Like you."

"Yes!"

"You and Greta do bring out the worst in each other."

Cordelia was about to elaborate when Jane cut her off.

"Dad came by last night. Apparently, Dexter called him yesterday, after we talked. Remember, I asked him where I should start if I wanted to find out more about the Simoneau family. He gave Dad the answer and asked him to pass it on."

Now Cordelia was interested. She was a tad annoyed that Jane hadn't called her right away, not that she would have been home to take the call. She'd been out drinking beer and playing pool with a couple of friends until the wee hours. That's why she'd added a touch more makeup this morning around her eyes.

"So what's that answer?" asked Cordelia. "What did Dexter say?"

"Alice Cathcart."

"Ah!" she said, her eyes lighting up. "The *nanny*! If the butler didn't do it, it's always the nanny."

Jane smiled at Hattie. Hattie smiled back with her perfect white baby teeth. "So? Do you want to go talk to her with me?"

"Are you asking Hattie or me?"

"I haven't decided."

"You know where Cathcart lives?"

"One of the books I read said she was still in Minneapolis, so I looked her name up in the White Pages. Just one Alice Cathcart. It's an Eden Prairie address."

"Ah. The burbs, where the air is fresher, the grass greener, the minds narrower."

"That's a generalization, Cordelia."

"Your point is?"

Jane shook her head.

"Think it's the same woman?"

"Only one way to find out. Except"—she nodded to Hattie—"I'm not sure we should bring—"

"The Toddler Terminator," said Cordelia with a knowing nod. "No problem. I was just about to drop her off at a playdate. Give me half an hour and I'll met you at the Lyme House. We will, of course, take my vehicle."

"Of course," said Jane. As she walked away, the sawing ceased. Cordelia heard her mutter something about guided missiles and glorified tanks, but she let the comments roll off her back like . . . like . . . morning dew off . . . off . . . moose droppings, or whatever the hell that saying was. She wasn't good at nature similes. Besides, she knew Jane loved her Hummer. She had to. Not too long ago, it had saved her life.

25

Jane sat in the passenger's seat as the Hummer lumbered across 494. It didn't exactly have that old General Motors this-is-your-living room-away-from-home ride, although it was certainly the size of a living room. "Take the Highway 169 exit."

"Roger," said Cordelia. She adjusted the rearview mirror, then said, "What do you two talk about when you're together?"

"What? Who?"

"You and Greta."

"Oh."

"You looked like you were having a pretty good time up there in the balcony."

"She was telling me about a movie she saw. It was a comedy. Then we talked about *The Hours* by Michael Cunningham. We both loved the book but neither of us went to the movie."

"What else do you talk about?"

"Can we please change the subject?"

"No. I watched you two. Granted, it wasn't for very long, but it was long enough."

"For what?"

"I wasn't sure at first, but it finally came to me. A flash from the great mother spirit, so to speak. Greta has a crush on you."

Jane burst out laughing. "Oh, right."

"You don't notice things like that. You've got this odd social disconnect when it comes to libidinous vibes. She'd have to basically strip naked and jump in your bed to get your attention."

"That's ridiculous. She's straight, Cordelia."

"Yes, but she's also curious. And she likes you. *A lot.*"

"If I have a social disconnect, you suffer from come-hither hyperbole."

"Cute, but I know what it means when I see eyes glow. And her eyes were glowing when they looked at you." She slowed down as they hit the exit ramp. "I believe you, to some degree, when you tell me you're fully aware she isn't Christine. But that still leaves us with a problem."

"And that would be?"

"Even if you've convinced yourself that you're not interested in Greta, maybe she's interested in you."

"Can we *please please* drop the subject?"

They rode in silence for a couple of miles. Jane was grateful that Cordelia's rant seemed to be over—or, more accurately, sidelined until she found another opening to focus on Greta with her laserlike grumpiness. It was a strange phenomena, but Jane's problems always brought out the tender side in Cordelia. But when it came to Jane's love life, it seemed to evoke nothing but instant, and rapidly escalating, hallucinations.

After another few miles, Cordelia said, "Janey?"

"I'm not discussing it."

"No, I've moved to a new topic."

She glanced out the side window. "Good."

"Do you think I'm boring?"

Tedious, thought Jane, but never boring. "I can't even imagine you in the same universe with that word, Cordelia."

"Really?"

She turned to look at her. "Are you kidding me? What makes you think you're boring?"

"Oh, you know. Just checking."

"Do *you* think you're boring?"

"No." She didn't sound all that convinced. "It was a silly question. Just forget I asked it."

A red light appeared on the dash.

"What's that?" asked Jane.

"Oh, nothing. It's been going on and off for weeks."

"Shouldn't you have a mechanic check it out?"

"No need. This thing runs like a top."

"Tops twirl around aimlessly until they hit the floor."

Cordelia tapped the light with her finger. It went off. "See?"

"Take a left at the next stoplight," said Jane. "That should be Dutton Road."

It was just after two when they arrived at the town house complex.

"Nice digs," said Cordelia, making a quick right and coming to a stop in front of number 17. She pushed the door open and tried to get out, but the day had grown hot and her black leather clothes had stuck to the black leather seats. "Give me a hand here, will you?"

Jane circled around the back of the Hummer and grabbed Cordelia's hands, yanking her out. "You know, Cordelia, I don't mean to speak ill of your clothes, but, to be quite honest, you squeak."

"Leather always squeaks. It's part of the aesthetic."

They approached the front door cautiously.

"Maybe we should have called first," said Jane.

The town homes were three stories tall with decks on all three levels. On the bottom level, sliding glass doors opened onto a screened porch.

"No, we did the right thing," said Cordelia. "She might not have agreed to talk to us, and then where would we be? This way, if nothing else, maybe one of us can get our foot in the door. I nominate you. Those boots you're wearing look heavier than mine."

Jane rang the doorbell.

Seconds later, a white-haired woman wearing a pink sweater set and straight gray skirt appeared. "Can I help you?" she asked. She was thin and tan, with an open, friendly face.

Jane took the lead. "Are you Alice Cathcart?"

"Yes."

"My name's Jane Lawless." She turned to Cordelia. "And this is my friend, Cordelia Thorn. I wonder if we could talk with you for a few minutes."

Alice's glasses hung by a silver cord around her neck. She put them on to get a better look at her visitors. "May I ask what this is about?"

"I was wondering if you knew a friend of mine," said Jane. "Her name was Christine Kane. Many years ago she tried to sell Bernadette Simoneau's house, the one on Irving Avenue."

Her expression lost some of its friendliness. It took a few seconds before she responded. "No, I don't believe I know her."

"Blond. Attractive. She was a real estate agent working with McBride Realty."

"What is it you want, Ms. Lawless?"

"I was hoping, I mean, I'd like to speak with you about the Simoneau murders. My friend, Christine, may have been peripherally involved and I thought perhaps you could help me."

"Involved in what way?"

Jane glanced at Cordelia for support. "Christine was admitted to the hospital the day the murders took place. She died the next day. In going through her things recently, I came across a gun, a derringer, that was part of a set belonging to Marcel Simoneau. The matching gun was used in the murders. I don't know why Christine had it. I also discovered that she had one of the sculptures that was supposedly missing from the house. The *Iron Girl*. Are you familiar with it?"

Alice peered at her through the screen. After a long moment, she said, "I thought it was a lovely piece. It belonged to Philip. His grandmother gave it to him because he loved it so much."

"That's what I understand," said Jane. "My question is, Why did Christine have these things? I know this is an imposition. I also assume you don't like talking about that time in your life. But if you could just give us a few minutes of your time, we'd be very grateful."

"I don't know what I could tell you. I mean, I don't even remember your friend." She seemed torn. "Oh, well, I suppose it couldn't hurt." She hesitated another few seconds, then unlocked the screen door.

Jane and Cordelia joined her in the living room.

"Would you like tea? I've just made a fresh pot."

"That would be wonderful," said Jane.

As she left the room, Cordelia looked around at the furnishings and whispered, "Early Pottery Barn."

"You can chime in anytime you like, you know."

"You did a great job. We're in, aren't we? And your foot isn't even bruised."

When Alice returned, she carried a tray. "Do either of you take lemon or sugar?"

"Plain is fine," said Jane.

Cordelia creaked as she sat down on one end of the slipcovered sofa.

Alice glanced at her outfit. "Your name is familiar to me, Ms. Thorn, but I can't place it."

"I'm the artistic director at the Allen Grimby Repertory Theater in St. Paul."

"Yes, of course! I saw *The White Road* last winter. I believe you directed it."

"I did."

"It was luminous. Well, imagine that. It's an honor to have you in my home."

Cordelia gave a small bow.

Jane eased down on an ottoman, noticing that Alice seemed more relaxed now, thanks to Cordelia's celebrity status.

"To be quite honest," said Alice, handing cups around, "I'd like to set the record straight about an interview I gave to a young man a few years back. Perhaps it's better to let sleeping dogs lie, but it really rankled. The fellow was writing a book on the Simoneau family and asked if I'd be willing to talk to him. It was clear from the outset where he was headed with his thinking, so I only spoke to him for a few minutes and then I cut it off. He sent me a copy of the book after it was published. Once I'd read it, I felt better about keeping the conversation so short."

"He had an alternate theory of the crime?" asked Jane.

She nodded, sitting down in a wicker armchair. "He had this crazy notion that Frank DeWitt, that's Gabby's husband, committed the murders. Talked about his motives as if they were proven facts. It was all so ludicrous, it made me angry. I dumped the book in the trash."

"What was his theory?" asked Cordelia.

"Oh, he had this idea that Frank was furious at Camille Simoneau after Gabby died because she had tied up Gabby's assets in court so he couldn't inherit right away."

"Is that true?" asked Jane.

"Yes, but Frank didn't care about the money. He wasn't that kind of man. He told me it was just part of the same old game Mrs. Simoneau had been playing for years, and he'd had his fill of it."

"Did you know Frank well?" asked Cordelia.

"I took care of his son every day until the boy was three. After the murders, Frank moved to the Normandy Inn for a few weeks. I went with him to take care of Timmy. Frank needed help because he had a teaching position and he couldn't just walk away from it. He rented me a room right next to his. It was such a terrible time. Timmy would wake up at night screaming and crying. Lord knows what that child saw."

"I understand you were the one who discovered the murders," said Jane. "That must have been pretty horrible."

"Yes," she said softly, "it was. I still remember that night vividly. I came through the front door. The first thing I saw was Philip's body lying on the central stairs. I knew immediately that he was dead, so I turned and ran back outside. I made it to a neighbor's, where I placed a call to the police."

"So you never actually saw the whole scene," said Jane.

"No."

"Weren't you worried about Timmy?" asked Cordelia.

Alice glanced at both of them, then looked down at her teacup. "Yes, I was. But I guess, the awful truth is, I was more worried that the murderer might still be inside. The best thing was to get the police there as quickly as possible."

"Do you think Tim remembers any of it?" asked Jane.

"I pray every day for him, Ms. Lawless. Frank made sure Timmy saw plenty of therapists as he grew older, but according to Timmy, it's all a blank. I think it's for the best."

"Have you stayed in touch with the DeWitts?" asked Jane.

"Yes. Cards and letters. An occasional phone call. I see Timmy a few times a year now——ever since he was old enough to drive. He called me after Frank moved them to Willmar, and he kept calling for almost a year, which amazed me. He was so little, but he missed me. We really did have a mother-son relationship, but . . . it couldn't continue."

"Did Frank remarry?"

She shook her head. "It's so sad. He sends me lots of photos of Tim. I've watched him grow up in those pictures, but of course, I wanted to be closer——a more constant and real part of his life." She nodded to the framed pictures around the room.

Jane saw that there were lots of children represented in the photos. "How long have you been a nanny?"

"Since I was twenty-six. I retired when I was in my early sixties. That was ten years ago. Goodness, how time flies. I still miss the children. I think of *all* of them as my children." She took a sip of her tea. "But Timmy, he was special. He's grown into a wonderful young man."

"You testified at the trial, right?" asked Cordelia.

She nodded.

"Did you think Dexter Haynes was guilty?"

"I have no idea. Only he and God would know that."

"At the trial," said Jane, "I understand the prosecution had you declared a hostile witness. Why was that?"

She pursed her lips. "They wanted to dig into matters that had nothing to do with the murders. Family concerns that had no business being aired in open court."

"Simoneau family matters?"

"Yes."

"Let's say, hypothetically, that Dexter Haynes is innocent," said Cordelia, squeaking as she sat forward. "If he didn't do it, who do you think did?"

"Well, certainly not my Frank." She seemed embarrassed by her vehemence. Turning the teacup around in the saucer, she continued, "Frank was the best man I've ever known. Honest. Hardworking. Gabby was a very lucky woman to have such a wonderful person in her life. I wrote him after that awful book came out, told him I thought he should sue."

"Did he?" asked Cordelia, looking entirely too breathless with anticipation.

Alice shook her head.

"Boy," said Cordelia, "if somebody was messing with my legal inheritance, I'd be hopping mad. You really think Frank *wasn't*?"

"It was a much larger issue than just the money. Frank had been trying to get Timmy out of that house ever since he was born. A month after Gabby's death, he and Camille were still at a stalemate."

"But Frank had legal custody, right?" said Jane. "Couldn't he just take him?"

"You didn't know Camille. She thought of Timmy as her own.

Frank wasn't Catholic, and Camille was adamant that Timmy be raised in her faith. She wanted to have a hand in all aspects of his upbringing. To that end, she had a dozen lawyers working all the angles. If Frank left, she knew she'd never see Timmy again, so she did everything she could to prevent it."

"Frank must have hated her," said Cordelia.

She took a sip of tea. "Hate may be too strong a word. He was upset. Understandably, so. But it would have resolved itself in time."

Jane and Cordelia exchanged glances.

"As I think about it a little more," said Alice, looking up at a picture of Timmy, "I do remember that friend of yours. Short blond hair. Pretty blue eyes."

Jane nodded.

"Seems I recall Philip telling me that she'd had a run-in with Laurent."

"A run-in?" repeated Jane.

"I don't know what happened, but believe me, that Laurent was a nasty one. He couldn't stand children. He threatened me more than once, said that if I didn't keep that brat, meaning Timmy, out of his way, he'd make us both sorry."

"Bastard," said Cordelia.

"He was indeed. Thank God he didn't live in Minnesota. Unfortunately, he visited quite frequently from his home in Florida. I tried my best to keep Timmy out of his way, but that was impossible. You know what kids are like."

"I certainly do," said Cordelia with a knowing nod.

"He frightened me."

"Do you think he was dangerous?" asked Jane.

"I think Laurent was monumentally selfish and self-centered. He was . . . how do I put it? It was as if he had no impulse control. Right or wrong, if he felt like doing something, he did it. And yes, to answer your question, I think he could be dangerous."

"Did he get along with his mother?" asked Jane.

"Oh, more or less. When it came to her children, Camille was long-suffering. She put up with his tantrums, his money problems, his gambling. She always said that if you didn't judge, but simply loved a child long enough, they would eventually turn out all right."

"Do you think she meant it?"

"Oh yes, I believe she did. She loved her children and grandchildren quite deeply. She was wonderful with Timmy. He adored her."

"I don't mean to change the subject," said Jane, "but do you have any idea what that hook in the attic ceiling was used for?"

"Hook? No. None."

"There was blood and urine found——"

"I know about all that, Ms. Lawless, but I couldn't possibly be expected to monitor what went on in the attic. My job was to take care of Timmy."

Jane found the intensity of the rebuke curious.

"Getting back to Frank," said Cordelia.

Jane gave her a sharp look. She wanted the subject to sit on the table a while longer.

Cordelia ignored her. "Is there more to the story? I mean, was Frank . . . upset . . . with Camille for other reasons?"

Alice smiled. "A woman like you, someone who deals with moral issues all the time, *would* pick up on that."

"Human interest," said Cordelia. "It fascinates me. Grist for the mill, you know."

Alice nodded and sat back in the chair. Before their eyes, she seemed to physically deflate, as if something heavy pressed down on her shoulders. "After so many years of keeping it all to myself, I guess I *would* like to tell someone the truth."

"And I'm not just anyone," said Cordelia.

"To be sure," said Alice. "To be sure. I don't think it will help you to find out why your friend had that gun or the sculpture."

"You never know," said Jane, trying to hide her eagerness.

"It's not a pretty story." She set the cup and saucer down on the table next to her. Frowning, she began, "You see, during my career as a nanny, I've been in the midst of a good deal of family disfunction, but the Simoneaus went way beyond that." She drew in a breath and held it for a moment before letting it out slowly. "It all began when Gabby— that's Camille's youngest daughter—got pregnant. It was an accident. Frank and Gabby had always been extremely careful because Gabby had a weak heart. She wanted children, of course, but her doctor said that carrying a child to term would be dangerous. Very dangerous, in fact. Perhaps even life-threatening. Frank wanted to abort, but Gabby wasn't sure. She made the mistake of talking to her mother about it. From that day forward, her mother basically locked her up in that house on the lake. Frank had to move in just to see her. Camille played on every last ounce of guilt Gabby possessed. She said it was a mother's duty to protect her unborn child. God wouldn't let a mother who loved her child die in childbirth. I think, in Camille's defense, she actually believed it.

"During the pregnancy, Frank was beside himself with worry. There were lots of heated family arguments, but Frank always lost. Gabby was completely under Camille's spell, brainwashed, as Frank put it, by her mother's moral code."

"But according to what I read," said Jane, "Gabby didn't die when the baby was born."

"No," said Alice, her voice growing husky with emotion. "She died three years later. She was never the same after the birth. She couldn't even take care of Timmy, that's why they remained at the house and Camille hired me. I helped care for Gabby, as well, during her last days. She was horrified that she would be leaving Frank alone with a young son to raise, and deeply ashamed that she'd let him down. She begged Frank not to be angry with her mother. In the end, the doctors were right. The birth did speed up her death. But she also felt great satisfaction in knowing she'd brought a wonderful young son into the world and that Timmy would have a good life. She knew Frank would see to it. She was right, of course, but she could never have imagined what would happen to her family only a month after she died."

In Jane's mind, Alice had just presented her with strongest motive she'd heard so far for the murders. Frank hadn't been merely "upset" with Camille, he must have cursed her every waking breath.

"I'm surprised that the police didn't pick up on Frank's hostility to Camille," said Cordelia.

"Oh, they did. They questioned him that first night and all the next day, but the case against Dexter must have seemed more solid, so, in the end, he was arrested."

"Are you positive Frank didn't—"

Alice held up her hand. "Absolutely. He had nothing to do with those murders."

"He didn't have much of an alibi," said Jane.

"Neither did I," said Alice. "Not really. I was with a friend part of the time, but I left her around seven to do some shopping."

"Are you saying . . . you mean, your friend perjured herself?" said Cordelia.

"It was easier than trying to find people in Dayton's who saw me. I convinced her it was necessary, and once it was on the record, she couldn't go back on it without getting both of us in trouble. Still, for all anyone knows, I could have done it."

Jane was thrown by the comment. "But you didn't."

"I'm not a murderer, Ms. Lawless." She shifted in her chair, then sat forward.

Jane could tell she was growing weary of the subject.

"If you take nothing else away from this discussion," she went on, lifting a photo of Frank and Timmy off the end table next to her and gazing down at it, "just remember this: Frank had nothing to do with those deaths. He's had a hard life, through no fault of his own. He doesn't deserve any more pain."

26

Bernadette stood at the tower window and gazed down at the street. Bill McBride had just pulled up. He drove the same blah kind of car he always had. This one was Pontiac Bonneville. Beige, like his personality. No imagination, thought Bernadette. As he got out, she realized she hadn't seen him in so many years that she wouldn't have recognized him if she'd tripped over him on the street. His paunch had doubled in size, and his reddish-blond hair was a thinning cloud around his square head. What hadn't changed was the reticence in his expression as he looked up at the house.

Billy was basically a coward, someone who talked a good game, but when it came down to the real deal, had to be coaxed along, pulled by inches, nudged ever so carefully. When she first met him, he'd insisted that he'd never cheated on his wife before. Like she believed that. He always framed things with such a godawful, moralistic squint. She assumed he saw himself as a kind of superior father/husband saint. Bill McBride could *Provide*. He liked rhymes, which said it all right there, now didn't it?

Years ago, Bernadette had been pretty sure Bill was in love with her, but she could never bring herself to love someone as phenomenally dull as Bill. She told him once that he should never leave his wife because nobody else would put up with his con artist crap. He hadn't liked that much, but it was true. At least he was in a profession compatible with his skills. Selling houses was like selling cars. Once you saw the gleam in the client's eye, you had to ram the deal home—but delicately. Bill could ram delicately with the best of them, which Bernadette knew from personal experience, but the only reason he stood upright, like the rest of the male apes, was because he was pumped so full of hot air.

Well, most of the time. He *had* surprised her on several, memorable occasions.

Hearing the doorbell ring, Bernadette padded down the stairs.

Halfway down the other side of the second-floor mezzanine, Laurent stuck his head out of the door of his study. "Whoever's down there, get rid of them."

"Why should I?"

"Because I can't stand any noise or interruptions right now. I'm working on the text for the brochure." He looked like a mole who'd just stuck his head out of a hole.

"Let me see it when you're done so I can correct your English."

"You just want to get your hands on it so you can insert a lot of nonsensical words. This has to be to the point, Bernie. Hard-hitting. Professional."

"The words are only nonsensical to you because you have such a limited vocabulary."

He slammed the door.

She flipped him the bird, then continued on down the stairs. Just for old times, she'd spritzed on Bill's favorite perfume. And she'd taken care to make sure her bed was made and that the sheets were clean.

Drawing back the door, Bernadette smiled.

Bill blinked.

"Come in, Billy."

He just stood there as if his feet were glued to the granite.

"Oh, don't be like that. I won't bite."

"Promise?"

She grinned.

"You look . . . different."

"You're not exactly Elvis these days either."

"We've both put on weight."

"You think so?" Bernadette looked down at the red velvet dress she was wearing. It had an empire waist. She'd always thought it was a good look for her. Innocent and young. Sweet and lush with promise.

When Bill finally stepped over the threshold, he looked around as if his eyes hurt.

"Something wrong?"

"I haven't been back here since . . . since—"

"Oh."

"I thought, maybe, you'd left town."

"I did for a while. I couldn't stay here after what happened. But I drifted back in '89."

"Where's Laurent these days?"

"He lives here, too. He went back to Florida as soon as the trial was over. But we both landed back here. I mean, we couldn't sell the place. Nobody wanted it."

"I imagine." His eyes bounced around the rooms like Ping-Pong balls.

"Not to worry. That was a long time ago."

"I know, but how can you stand it? I could never live in a house where my mother and my son were murdered."

"It was hard at first, but . . . time takes the edge off." She shuffled into the living room and settled herself on the lumpy sofa.

Still looking around, Bill followed her. "So," he said, his eyes darting in every direction, "how've you been?"

She patted the seat next to her.

He gave his head a stiff shake.

"I've been fine, Bill. Just fine."

"The house looks kind of, well, run-down."

"Alas, the money our parents left us has just about run out."

"Maybe you should consider selling the place." His voice deepened. He'd put on his salesman voice just for her. How nice. "No. Actually, Laurent came up with this fantastic idea. At first I wasn't all that hot about it, but the more I considered it, the more it appealed to me."

He pulled his pant legs up as he sat down across the room on a footstool. "What's the idea?"

"We're going to open the house up to visitors, provide them with a guided tour of the murder scene."

Bill's mouth dropped open. "Lord, Bernie."

"We may even print a brochure to hand out—a description of the crime, the trial, the prime suspect, that sort of thing. We'll need to hire tour guides. I have a feeling we'll have some big crowds."

"You really think that's a good idea?"

"We play the cards we're dealt, right, Billy?"

He squirmed in his seat. "You know, Bernie, I didn't really want to come today. What happened between us . . . all those years ago, um, I'm sorry."

"For what?"

"It was wrong."

"Did you ever tell your wife?"

"No!"

"Coward."

"Why would I? It only lasted a few weeks. A month at the most." He wrung his hands together.

"You wanted it to last forever."

"Okay, maybe I did. But when I found out about your boyfriend—the felon . . ."

"Were you jealous?"

"Whatever happened to him?"

"Oh, Bill, it's such a long story. I thought I loved him, but after what happened to my family, he evaporated. Left the state driving my car."

"I'm sorry. I guess."

"But I understood. After just being released from jail, the last thing he wanted was to get involved in a triple homicide. Still, it hurt. I really needed him during the trial."

"You ever see him again?"

She shook her head. "I think he thought he'd finally found himself the gravy train. I didn't realize it at first, but he was greedy. He got a Rolex and a Mercedes out of the deal, so I guess he was paid well for his stud service."

"Bernie, don't say things like that."

"Why not? It's true."

"You don't like men very much, do you."

She met his questioning gaze with a hard stare. "I don't like anyone who tries to run my life." Softening her expression, she added, "I mean, if it ain't broke, don't fix it, right?"

200

"So," he said, clearing his throat, "you want me to appraise the house."

"That's the general idea."

"You know, Bernie, you really should think about doing some repairs." He nodded to the ceiling in the corner. "If you've got water damage down here, you've probably got it other places, too. The roof looks terrible. How many years since you had it replaced?"

"How the hell should I be expected to know something like that?"

"Well, you live here, I thought—"

"Just tell me what it's worth."

"It would be worth a lot more if you spent some money on it." He glared at her. "Oh, I get you. You want to take out a loan, use the property as collateral."

"No, it's more on the order of curiosity. I really don't want to touch the house. I've got another way to finance the repairs. We'll also need money to start up our tour business."

"I see."

"You hate the idea."

"It's none of my business."

"You happy with your wife, Billy?"

"We're divorced."

"Aw, poor Bill." She actually felt sorry for him.

He stood, hitching up his pants. "Okeydoke, then. I better get busy."

Bernadette sat primly as he removed a small notebook from the inner pocket of his suit coat. "How long will it take?"

"Awhile. I'll look around and then I'll mail you the results."

"You can't tell me today?"

He shook his head. "I'll have to do some research, see what the other houses in the neighborhood are going for."

As he examined the ceiling in the corner at closer range, the phone rang.

Bernadette answered: "Hello?"

"Is this Bernadette Simoneau?"

"Speaking."

"This is Oliver Hammond. I'm one of the owners of the Hammond-Dillabough Gallery in Uptown."

"Oh, yes, Mr. Hammond. Did you get a chance to appraise that painting I brought in?"

"Well, ah, yes, I did. But I'm afraid I have some bad news."

"It was in perfect shape. No nicks or anything."

"Yes, that's true."

"Then what's the problem?"

"The painting is a forgery."

Her mouth dropped open. "A *what?*"

"It's a fairly *good* forgery, but I'm afraid it has very little value."

"That can't be."

"I'm afraid it is, Ms. Simoneau. I'm sorry to be the bearer of such bad tidings. How much did you pay for it?"

"It's part of my father's collection. Marcel Simoneau. Do you know the name?"

"Oh," he said with a clutch in his voice. "Of course. Well, I'm sure he didn't know he'd purchased a fraud."

"Well, of course he didn't. He wasn't an idiot!"

"I'd be happy to look at the entire collection, if you'd like. I could come over to the house, say, tomorrow at one?"

"Fine."

"Do you have any paperwork on the provenance of the pieces in his collection?"

"The what?"

"Their history, proof of previous ownership."

"I have no idea."

"You might want to check that out before I come tomorrow."

Where the hell would she look? "I'll have to call my lawyer."

"Yes, that's a good place to start. In any event, I'll stop by at one. I'm sure I'll have better news for you then."

"Thank you, Mr. Hammond. You're very kind."

"Until tomorrow, then?"

The line clicked.

27

On her way back to the Lyme House, Jane stopped by the photo store in the Uptown mall.

"So that old film actually had some pictures on it." She'd dropped it off before heading over to the Xanadu. Standing at the counter, she wrote out a check.

"Four of them came out blank, but the rest were fine—a little darker than normal, maybe, but you can still see them." The young man who'd developed the roll glanced at Jane's driver's license and then handed her the package. "I could probably fix the darkness for you."

"Thanks. I'll let you know."

She took the package and her car keys and headed to the parking lot. Pushing through the door to the outside, her heart sank as she began to flip through the photos. They were nothing but pictures of crumbling concrete, soffits with pealing paint, a leaky toilet, the kind of shots Christine routinely took of the houses she was representing.

"Just great," she muttered, striding across the lot to her car. When she saw that the last three shots were of two men, she stopped next to a Jeep to take a closer look. Only problem was, she'd never seen either of them before.

"Damn," she muttered, stuffing them all back into the packet, feeling cheated. She was hoping for something personal, a last photo of Christine, or better yet, the two of them together. They used to set the timer on the camera and then dash into the picture at the last second, just as it clicked. There were lots of silly, blurry photos of them with ridiculous looks on their faces. Jane hadn't paid much attention to them at the time, but she treasured them now.

Unlocking the door to her Mini, she slid in. She paid the attendant in the glass cage at the edge of the lot, then she and Mouse drove straight to the restaurant.

As Mouse spun round and round trying to find just the right spot on the rug in front of the fireplace, Jane sat down behind her desk to look at the photos one more time. This time, however, she switched on her desk lamp, slipped on her reading glasses, and studied the faces more closely.

"Hey, Mouse, I think . . ." Her voice trailed off as she grabbed one of the books on the Simoneau murders from the bookcase behind her desk. Quickly locating a photo of Philip Simoneau, she put the snapshot next to it. "I know who this guy is," she said out loud. She studied all three photos a moment more. "Damn. I don't believe it. He lied to me!" She set the photos down and picked up her phone. After tapping in the number for her father's office, she waited.

"Law offices," came a familiar voice.

"Norm, hi. It's Jane."

Norm Toscalia was her father's paralegal. He knew everybody who was anybody in the local legal scene and had helped Jane out many times in the past.

"Hey, kiddo. Your dad left about an hour ago."

"That's okay. I wanted to talk to you."

"Oh?"

He sounded busy. Phones rang in the background. "My dad set up a meeting for me a few days ago with a guy in Stillwater: Dexter Haynes."

"I did the work on that one, Jane."

She'd figured as much. "I need to see him again. Right away. To-morrow if possible."

"Well . . ." He hesitated. "That might take some doing. And if he's not up for another visit, you can forget it."

"Just see what you can do, okay? It's important."

"You got it, kiddo. I'll call when I've got something nailed down—one way or the other."

"Thanks, Norm. You're my hero."

He laughed. "Jeez, I'm glad I'm somebody's hero, because I ain't makin' no friends around *here* today."

After the dinner rush was over, Jane sat in the bar for a few minutes, drinking a lager and lime. It was just after nine. When she finally returned to her office, she saw that the light in the bathroom was on. She was positive it hadn't been on when she left. "Is someone here?" she called. Mouse was sitting on the couch, his head resting on a throw pillow. He didn't seem the least bit agitated.

"Don't shoot," came Kenzie's voice. Poking her head out the door, she added, "I'm just borrowing some soap, in case you were wondering."

"My God! When did you get here?"

"Just a sec."

Jane could hear the water running. A moment later, Kenzie walked out. She looked wonderful in her tight jeans, brown leather vest, and red silk shirt. She'd let her red-gold hair grow since the last time Jane had seen her. Not that it was long. Kenzie usually wore a zip cut. It was a good look for her because she had such great bone structure in her face. She wasn't beautiful, but she had a certain confident vitality that made people's heads turn when she walked into a room. She also had a killer smile.

"God, I'm glad to see you," said Jane, wrapping her arms around her.

"Likewise, darlin'."

"You smell like my shampoo."

"Since you were busy upstairs, I decided to take a shower. Clean up a little from the flight."

"This is such a surprise. When did you get in?"

"Around seven. Caught a cab and arrived here about eight-thirty."

"How long can you stay?"

"I have to leave in the morning. Sorry, but it's better than nothing."

"I'll say." Jane grinned, holding her tight, ecstatic to have her in her arms again. "But . . . why didn't you come upstairs? I was just up there working the dinner meal."

Kenzie brushed a hand across Jane's hair. "Isn't this more fun—and more private?"

"God, I didn't think I'd see you for weeks. Will this really screw up your schedule?"

"Hey, Lawless, you're not the only one who has trouble with this long-distance romance stuff." She nuzzled Jane's neck. "So what are we going to do about it?"

"I don't know. Are you hungry?"

Her eyes flashed. "Famished."

"I mean for food."

Kenzie held her at arm's length. "Your girlfriend, the one you've been pining for, is standing right in front of you and you want to go have a burger? Jesus, Lawless. I think somebody better check your pulse, see if you're still breathing."

"I didn't say anything about a burger."

"Good." Kenzie moved in close again.

"It's just—"

"What!"

"I don't know. I was thinking what we'd do when you came. I mean, I thought, maybe . . . maybe we should have a cup of coffee first. Catch up."

"Are you nuts?"

"I hate it when people think gay relationships are just about sex."

"What *people*? I thought we were alone in here."

"Straight people. I mean, doesn't it bug you that society thinks all gays and lesbians ever think about is sex. It's not."

"Of course not."

"Our relationship is about much more than sex."

"Hell, yes."

"I care about you deeply."

"You think too much, Lawless."

"*That* from a professor?"

"Shut up."

"But you know what I mean."

"Oh, Jesus. Lawless, look. If some straight guy hadn't seen his girl in over a month, do you think they'd have a conversation about world peace before they jumped in the sack?"

Jane thought about it. "They might."

"You're hopeless."

"Not entirely." She ran her hands up and down Kenzie's back, then kissed her hard and long, the way she'd been longing to do.

"Whoa, pardner," said Kenzie, backing up and taking a gulp of air. "What happened to world peace?"

"Screw world peace," said Jane, kissing her more tenderly this time as she reached behind her and locked the door.

After a late dinner in the pub, Jane and Kenzie returned to the house. It was close to midnight when Kenzie finally carried her overnight bag into the kitchen. She set it down next to the table as Jane switched on the light over the stove.

"God, it feels good to be back here," said Kenzie, pulling Jane close. "*With* you, this time."

"Hey, that's right. The last time you were here I made us dinner, and then—"

"I left before I did something dumb."

"Like tell me the truth."

Kenzie's smile was rueful. "That's in the past. We're together now and that's all that counts."

They stood in the kitchen, wrapped in each other's arms.

"Don't leave," whispered Jane, easing back so that she could look into Kenzie's eyes. "Don't ever leave."

"I wish I could."

"You don't have tenure at Chadwick yet, right?"

Kenzie let her hand trail along Jane's jawline. "I do now, darlin'. It's official."

Jane's heart sank. "It feels like the universe is conspiring to keep us apart."

"That or Northwest Airlines. If I had to choose, I'd say the airline has the most clout."

Jane laughed. "How did I get so lucky?"

"Clean living, maybe?" She hugged her close. "I'd say it was about time we both got tapped by the luck-god."

"You mean there's a luck-god out there?"

"Sure thing. Big hairy dude. Goofy grin."

Jane closed her eyes, still smiling. "Cowboy boots?"

"Oh, sure. All the really great gods wear cowboy boots."

As she opened her eyes, the form of a woman came slowly into focus. She was standing in the dining room doorway, wearing Jane's white terry-cloth bathrobe. Jane stiffened. "Greta?"

"Huh?" said Kenzie turning around.

"Hi," said Greta, looking startled.

"Who the hell are you?" demanded Kenzie.

Greta looked at Jane. "I, ah . . . see, I was upstairs developing photos and I spilled some chemicals on my clothes. On the floor, too, but I cleaned all that up. I smelled pretty bad, so I didn't think you'd mind if I took a shower. I thought, maybe, like, I could borrow a pair of your sweatpants and a T-shirt?"

"Who *is* this woman?" demanded Kenzie. "Jesus, Lawless! She looks just like . . . I mean, Jesus!"

It was at that moment that Jane regretted not telling Kenzie about Greta. But never, in a million years, did she ever expect Greta to walk in on them.

"She's, well, actually, a friend," stammered Jane. "No relation to Christine."

Kenzie gawked. "Just separated at birth, huh? What the hell is she doing in your house, in your bathrobe, in the middle of the night?"

"I just told you," said Greta, sounding annoyed.

"Oh, sure," said Kenzie. "Everything's just crystal clear now. Thanks."

Jane pressed a hand to her forehead. "I'm letting Greta use the third floor as a darkroom. I've hired her to document the renovation of the Xanadu Club."

"Well, imagine that," said Kenzie.

"We haven't known each other long. She's from Dalton, down here to attend college. She was just standing out in front of the theater one morning, taking pictures—she wants to become a professional photographer—and, well, I hired her."

"On the spot."

"Kind of."

"How dumb do you think I am, Lawless?"

Jane had seen Kenzie's quick temper before, but it had never been directed at her. "Kenzie, listen to me. You're jumping to conclusions—and they're wrong."

"Uh huh."

"I better leave," said Greta.

"I think that's a good idea," said Jane.

As Greta backed out of the room, Kenzie picked up her overnight bag.

"You actually think I'm sleeping with her?" said Jane.

"Oh, no. I'm sure you always let virtual strangers roam around your house in the middle of the night dressed in nothing but your bathrobe."

She had a point. "I know it looks bad."

"Another bull's-eye."

"But Greta and I are just friends."

"Right. Friendly is good. I've been friendly lots of times in my life." She turned and veered into the dining room.

"I'm not sleeping with her!"

"Okay." She stopped and turned around. "Let's say I believe that."

"You have to because it's the truth."

Kenzie's hand rose to her hip. "How on earth did you find a woman who's the spitting image of Christine?"

"Like I said, she was taking pictures of the theater. We started up a conversation. And yes, I was initially drawn to her because of the way she looks. But she's not Christine. Give me some credit, okay. I'm not interested in her, Kenzie. I'm only interested in *you*."

Kenzie searched her face. The silence in the room pressed down heavily on both of them. Finally, after almost a minute, Kenzie said, "Call me a sucker, but I actually think I believe you."

"Oh, *please,* don't be angry." She reached out a tentative hand.

"I was going to sleep on the couch."

"We've got one night. Don't let this ruin it."

Kenzie narrowed her eyes. "Maybe we should have that conversation about world peace right about now."

"As long as we get to kiss and make up when it's all solved."

"Hell, I can't wait *that* long, Lawless." She grabbed Jane's hand and pulled her toward the stairs.

28

Sunlight streamed in through the partially open shades in Jane's bedroom. Turning on her side, she opened her eyes to find that Kenzie was gone. Mouse's bed in the corner of the room was also empty.

Jane swung her feet out of bed and sat up, running her hands through her hair. "Kenzie?" she called. When she got no response, she called again. The house seemed unusually silent.

"Mouse! Front and center," called Jane. He always came, unless he was outside—or eating. Food, in the scheme of things, rated at the top of his rapt attention list. She whistled a couple of times, but when he still didn't bound up the stairs and into her arms, she got up, pulled on a pair of black sweatpants, grabbed a clean, red-hooded sweatshirt from the top drawer of her dresser, and slipped into her running shoes. She stopped by the bathroom to splash some water on her face, give her teeth a quick brush, and run a comb through her hair.

On her way out the back door, she noticed that the baseball bat from the porch was gone. So was the softball. That gave her an idea of where to look.

Sprinting over to the park, Jane found Kenzie hitting balls to Mouse on the baseball diamond. Mouse barked when he saw her, locked his teeth around the ball, and raced across the grass.

"Hey, boy," said Jane, crouching down to give him a kiss and a hug. He dropped the ball at her feet, his eyes sparkling from the exercise and the excitement.

"Morning," said Kenzie. She stood a few yards away, leaning on the bat.

Jane tossed her the ball. "Morning. I didn't hear you get up."

Kenzie flipped it into the air and cracked it hard, sending it far into the outfield. Mouse skittered into action.

"How'd you sleep?" asked Jane.

"About as well as you."

They both stood and watched Mouse dive for the ball, then rocket back across the grass.

"What time does your plane leave?"

"Noon. Because of all the extra security stuff, I better get to the airport by ten."

"I'll drive you."

Kenzie made Mouse sit before she hit the next ball.

"Did you make yourself some breakfast?" asked Jane.

"I wasn't hungry. I'll grab some coffee at the airport."

Jane kicked a stone. "We okay?"

Kenzie looked up at the sky. "Yeah. Think so."

"But you're not sure."

She shrugged. "It's just . . ." She shook her head. "I don't know, Lawless. I guess, maybe I don't know you well enough yet. I thought I did."

"Meaning what?"

"Well, I thought we both wanted the same thing."

"And that is?"

"An honest, committed relationship."

"That *is* what I want."

She bent down and scooped up the ball. Standing back, she slammed another one into the outfield.

"Do you honestly think I'm sleeping with Greta?"

"No," she said, keeping her eyes on Mouse. "No, I don't think you've slept with her. Yet."

Jane's hands rose to her hips. She was starting to get angry, and that was the last thing they needed. Between Kenzie and Cordelia, she might as well do the deed because they thought she already had—or was about to.

"What is it, Kenzie? You think I possess some super sexy lesbian charisma that makes straight women melt in my arms? Because that's an absolute and total crap fantasy and you know it."

"Goodness, Jane. Such language."

"Greta isn't interested in me. And I, sure as hell, have no interest in her."

"*Okay.*"

But Jane could tell she wasn't convinced. "What am I missing? Talk to me. I'm at a loss here, truly."

"Let me ask you a question, Lawless." She pointed the bat at her. "Has Greta ever just appeared before, late at night?"

"Once. She wanted to show me some photos she'd just developed."

"Okay, and how did you feel about that?"

Jane considered it. "I was surprised. But I didn't mind. I wouldn't want her to make a habit of it."

"But you like to look at her because she's the spittin' image of Christine."

"Well, okay. Sure. But she didn't stay long."

"She doesn't have a key to your place?"

"Just the third floor. She enters from the outside."

"But there's an inside door."

"Yes."

Kenzie shoved her hands in her back pocket. "She ever spend the night?"

Jane focused her eyes on a weeping willow in the distance. "Yes. Again, once. Her ex-boyfriend tried to beat her up right outside my front door. I stopped him. She was afraid to go back to her apartment, so I let her sleep on the couch."

"Whose idea was it to spend the night?"

"Hers. *Nothing* happened. For Pete's sake, Kenzie, she's straight!"

"There's straight and then there's straight. You know what I mean, Lawless. Lots of people think they're straight until they realize there's an attraction to someone of the same sex."

"But it's not like that. And even if Greta was interested, I'm not."

Looking her square in the eyes, she said, "Okay, darlin'. I'd believe that except for one thing. If you really don't want her walking in on you late at night, why the hell don't you lock the inside door?"

Jane's mouth opened, but nothing came out.

Handing over the bat, Kenzie said, "I'll take a cab to the airport. Call me when you've got an answer."

Several hours later, Jane was sitting behind her desk at the restaurant when Cordelia blew in. She was dressed in a camouflage fatigues.

"Nice outfit."

"It's *gear*," said Cordelia curtly, pulling up a chair. "So, how's tricks?"

Jane's head rested against her hand. "Kenzie flew in last night."

"Really?" Cordelia's eyes opened a little wider. "Where is she now?"

"Flying home."

"You two have a fight?"

"She could only stay one night."

"Oh. Too bad. I assume you had a good time, then."

"Just fabooo."

"I also assume that you're not going to give me any details."

"Nope. No details. No snapshots. No film at eleven. Why the camouflage outfit . . . I mean, gear?"

"I had to stop at a sporting goods store this morning. Thought this would get me in the mood."

"Following that theme, if you went to a meat market, would you dress up as a pork chop?"

"You're in a weird mood."

"Guess I am." She glanced down at the calendar on her desk. "Have you ever looked at yourself in the mirror, Cordelia, and wondered who the hell you were?"

"Heavens, no."

"No, I suppose not."

"Vampires have no reflection at all when they look in a mirror."

"And I need to know that . . . why?"

"Just personal edification. A fascinating fact."

"Ah." Jane couldn't imagine what Cordelia would be looking for at a sporting goods store. "Were you searching for a new tent for your next trip to the Boundary Waters?"

"Yeah, right. I wouldn't go up there unless I was inside a tank with four or five flamethrowers and two AK-47s strapped to each hip. There are *moose* up there, Janey. Moose! Do you have any idea how big a moose is?"

Jane lifted one hand off the desk, suggesting a size.

"Oh, no. They're positively prehistoric. Think Tyrannosaurus rex and you're in the right ballpark." She shuddered.

"Then tell me, Cordelia. What business *do* you have in a sporting goods store?"

Cordelia stared at her a moment. "Boy, you know, you really look depressed, Janey. Something wrong?"

"Why would you think that?"

"Because you usually don't speak to me with your head in your hand."

She straightened up. "Is that better?"

"You tell me."

The phone rang.

Jane glanced at her watch. It wasn't quite noon, so it could be Kenzie. Closing her eyes, she picked up the receiver and said, "Hello?"

"Jane? Norm. I've got some good news. If you can get out to the prison by one, Haynes will see you."

Her eyes popped back open. "Great." She realized she hadn't told Cordelia about the roll of pictures. But there wasn't time now. "I'll be there. And thanks, Norm."

"*What?*" said Cordelia, nearly bursting out of her camouflage gear as Jane hung up the phone. "That call changed your mood so fast, it's gotta be something important. What's going on?"

"I have another meeting with Dexter Haynes."

"Today? Why?"

"Unless you can ride with me, I'll have to tell you later." She switched off her desk lamp and stood, scooping up her car keys.

"No can do," said Cordelia. "I've got rehearsals all day. As a matter of fact, I should leave now or I'll be late."

Jane glanced at the camouflage suit. "Aren't you going to change before you head over to the theater?"

"Why should I?"

She smiled. "I guess they already know you're eccentric."

"Well, *duh*. Besides, I have to stay late, and I wouldn't be able to change on the way to my evening appointment."

"And where, pray tell, is that?"

She wiggled her eyebrows. "You're not the only one who keeps secrets, dearheart."

The traffic on the way to Stillwater was lighter than she'd expected. Arriving a few minutes early, she sat in her car and flipped through the photos, removing the three she wanted to take in with her.

At precisely one o'clock, she was ushered into the visitor's area. She looked around, seeing only the one guard. As she sat down, the door in the back opened and Dexter came through. He nodded to her as he took a seat opposite her and picked up the phone.

"Did you see Alice Cathcart?" he asked right up front in his low, raspy voice.

"Yes. I talked to her yesterday."

"And?"

"I got an earful about Camille, her daughter Gabby, and Gabby's husband, Frank DeWitt. I didn't know the police initially centered their investigation on him."

"But I was an easier target."

"Listen, Dexter, I'm not saying there wasn't racism involved in your arrest and conviction, but that doesn't mean the police manufactured evidence. You did have that watch."

"It was planted!"

"Was it?"

"Yes!"

Jane glanced at the guard. He was reading a magazine. She fished the photos out of her back pocket and held the first one up so Haynes could see it.

"What's that?"

"Look at it."

As he leaned closer, his face froze.

It was a picture of Dexter and Philip, their arms around each other's shoulders. The watch was clearly visible on the desk behind them.

She held up the second photo, a silly shot of Philip sitting in Dexter's lap. They were both laughing, both holding a drink. And finally, she held up the last shot—a picture of Dexter's hand over Philip's. They were wearing matching gold rings. "Why did you lie to me?" asked Jane. "Or more to the point, why did you lie to the police?"

He stared at the last picture for a long time, then bowed his head. When he looked up, his eyes had gone liquid.

"Philip gave you that watch, didn't he."

He inhaled sharply.

"Were you two lovers?"

"Yes."

"But if you'd told the police—"

"I had no proof! Philip kept some love letters of mine, but I had no idea where they were. Nobody found them, so apparently he had them well hidden. If I'd told the cops Philip had given me the watch because I was his lover, because it was our fucking two-year anniversary and he wanted to give me something important, something that had great personal meaning to him to mark the day, I would not only be in prison today, but my entire family would've deserted me. Believe me when I tell you that it's better to be a murderer in the black community than to be gay."

The words hit her hard.

"Sure, I could've said we were friends, but nobody would've believed that either. Saying that someone had planted the evidence at least gave me a chance at reasonable doubt."

As a law student, he'd probably considered all the angles. And he was no doubt right, on all counts.

"But you knew these pictures existed," said Jane. "*They* would have been proof."

"Sure, but how was I supposed to get my hands on them? When I found out Christine had died, where was I supposed to look? You didn't know me from Adam. Hell, I couldn't even remember your name. If I'd told the cops to go look for the pictures and they didn't find them, then I had nothing to base a defense on."

She saw his point. "Did Philip ever talk to his grandmother about the two of you?"

"Yes. The day before he was murdered."

"And?"

"Believe it or not, the old lady was okay with it. I'm not saying she approved, but she had this amazing ability to stick by the people she loved. She confided to Philip that she'd been pretty certain her husband had been gay, but back in those days, men were more inclined to get married, have kids, hide it from the world, even from their wives, stay in the closet their whole lives. Apparently, she loved him anyway. She asked Philip to think about talking to their priest, but she didn't kick him out of the house, strike his name from her will, throw a big fit and damn him to hell. She actually hugged us both, told us that God loved the sinner as much as the saint. I had no reason to kill that woman, Jane. None! And I certainly had no reason to kill Philip. For chrissake, I loved him. I wanted to spend the rest of my life with him." He dropped the phone and covered his face with his hands. Bending low, his head almost touched the counter.

Jane gave him a minute, then tapped the glass. When he'd finally picked the phone back up, she said, "I believe you."

Tears flowed freely down his cheeks. "God," he whispered. "Nobody's ever said that to me before and really meant it." He took a handkerchief out of his pocket and wiped his nose.

"We've got to get you out of here."

"Won't happen."

"But I've got the proof you were looking for."

"Too little too late. The D.A. would look at those photos and say it was a different watch. He'd laugh you right out of his office."

Jane looked at him hard, saw the scar that ran down his neck. She might never truly understand the anger and despair he'd lived with all these years, but the injustice of seeing him behind this wall, knowing that his life had been stolen from him, left her feeling pummeled, outraged. The idea that she had to walk away and abandon him to rot in prison for the rest of his life for a crime he didn't commit appalled her. "I can't just leave it like this."

"You're a good woman, Jane. You care about people, genuinely care. That's a rare quality in this world. But the only way to get me out of this hole is to find the real murderer, and so many years after the fact, it's just not possible."

She pulled her chair a little closer. "But you must have sent me to Alice Cathcart for some reason. Tell me what it was."

Stuffing the handkerchief back in his pocket, he said, "Well, truth is,

217

I overheard a conversation she had with Frank DeWitt. Alice was in love with him."

"How could you possibly know that?"

"Oh, man, it was so obvious. Philip and I used to talk about it all the time. I mean, she just lit up around him. She must have been a good twenty years older than him, but it didn't matter. While Gabby was alive she kept it to herself, but once she was dead, Alice moved in. She was always fluttering around him, doing special things for him. When DeWitt learned that Mrs. Simoneau was tying up his inheritance in court, he blew a gasket, said he'd take Timmy and she'd never see him again. So the old lady counters, says she's got her lawyers working on a lawsuit. Apparently, she was about to ask the courts for custody, saying that Frank was an unfit father. She saw the way Alice acted around him and concluded Frank and Alice were having an affair, that it had been going on even while her daughter was dying."

"But that's not true."

"No, but Mrs. Simoneau had convinced herself it was. This all happened right before she was murdered. The reason I know about it is because I heard Alice and DeWitt talking in the garden, right under my living room window."

"You think——"

"That DeWitt killed her? Yeah, I've always thought he did. Either it was him or Alice. She loathed Camille Simoneau. They both did."

"What did they say to each other in the garden?"

He leaned back in his chair. "Alice told him she'd help him get the kid out of the house. She had some money in the bank and she offered it to him. She told him she loved him, that she'd do anything for him. She wasn't bad-looking, but she was older, and DeWitt wasn't interested. Except, I could tell he was frantic. You know that saying, 'wringing your hands'? Well, that's what he kept doing. He wasn't the most decisive guy I've ever run into. But even a milquetoast can be dangerous if his back's against a wall."

"Alice never mentioned any of that to me."

"Why would she? Look, if you've got the time and the interest, check out DeWitt. Maybe you'll get lucky and kick over a rock nobody else has noticed. But don't hold your breath. I stopped hoping for miracles a long time ago."

Christine

August 27, 1987

3:22 P.M.

Christine closed her eyes, took a deep breath, and rang the Simoneau's front-door bell. This was so much harder than she'd expected. She'd come to tell Philip, his mother, and Camille that she was leaving McBride Realty at the end of the week.

The decision had pretty much been made for her by the sudden decline in her health. She'd had periods before, lasting months, where she'd experienced very few symptoms. As much as she wanted to keep working, she knew the time had come to quit. There were other matters she needed to concentrate on now. She still believed she had a shot at beating the odds. Doctors didn't have a direct line to God. Maybe she had years left to live.

The last couple of days had been good ones. The pain and the nausea hadn't seemed as bad. But she wasn't sure how long it would last. Her professional life had always been very important to her. If she couldn't meet the standards she'd set for herself, it was time to get out.

Pushing the bell again, Christine waited. Under other circumstances, she might have enjoyed the cool morning breeze, the cloudless, late-summer sky, but not today. As she turned to look at the lake, she felt the press of life all around her. Birds sang. Cars and cyclists sailed past. Joggers hit the running path. A lone goose pecked at the grass along the shore. Watching such a glorious summertime tableau, she knew she'd made the right decision. Quit while there's still time, she told herself. You've made the right decision.

She'd talked to Bill this morning, tendered her resignation. He'd listened patiently, said he'd been concerned about her health, but he didn't press her for details. She apologized for letting him down. He told her not to give it another thought, that she should concentrate on getting well—and that there would always be a position waiting for her at McBride Realty. She was touched by his kindness, and thanked him for being such a great boss.

Before she left the office, she mentioned that she'd seen him coming out of the Simoneau mansion last week and wondered if there was some problem. She told him she was planning to stop by the mansion today to tell Camille, Bernadette, and Philip in person that she was leaving the company. Bill seemed momentarily at a loss. He stuck his finger in the collar of his shirt and pulled the fabric away from his neck. He finally said that he'd had an argument with Laurent over a business matter. That was all the explanation Christine needed. She'd seen firsthand what a scary human being Laurent was. One of the perks of leaving her job was that she'd never have to see him again.

When the Simoneau's front door still went unanswered after the third ring, Christine hoisted up her briefcase and walked around the side of the house to the back garden. She glanced across the flagstone patio, but nobody was around. She stood for a moment, looking at the garden—the riotous colors of the snapdragons and zinnias, and the more delicate beauty of the cosmos and daisies. She'd just turned to go when she heard Philip call her name.

"Christine," he shouted, trotting down the gatehouse steps. "Come here a sec. I want to tell you something."

Whatever the news was, it wasn't bad. He was positively glowing.

"You look happy."

"I am," he said, waiting for her to cross the yard. "Come in."

Dexter was waiting for them in the living room. He was wearing a striped blue-and-red rugby shirt and pale blue jeans, and he was sitting on the couch tying the laces on his white Nikes. He grinned at her. "You look like you're feeling better than the last time I saw you."

"I am, thanks." She was a little bewildered, not sure what Philip wanted to tell her.

"Christine," he began slowly, "I'd like you to meet the reason I'm not going back to Yale." He nodded at Dexter.

Christine searched their faces. "I don't . . ."

"As of today, we are an official couple."

They both held up their left hands, showing off her their new, matching gold rings.

"I had no idea . . ."

"No one does. It's our anniversary, Christine. We've been together two years. Never in my whole life did I think I'd be this happy."

Christine found herself smiling, too. "Congratulations."

"Want a glass of champagne?" asked Dexter.

"Sure. Why not?"

There was an open bottle of Dom Perignon on the desk next to a gold watch.

"I borrowed the bottle from my grandmother's wine cellar," said Philip, pouring her drink into an old jelly jar. "Thought the occasion called for something special."

"How did you manage to keep this from your family for so long?"

"Pure military stealth," said Dexter, laughing as he held up a plastic cup so that Philip could refill it.

"And some good, old-fashioned luck," added Philip. He held his coffee mug high. "A toast."

Dexter stood.

"To true love?" said Christine.

"To true love," both men replied.

They clicked their glasses together.

After taking a sip, Philip continued, "I haven't told my grandmother yet." His smile dimmed. "I'm not looking forward to it, but I think I'll feel much better once it's done."

"What about your mother?" asked Christine. "Bernadette seems pretty open, pretty, well, for lack of a better term, liberal."

"She doesn't care what I do. I could tell her I was a space alien from the planet of Zenon and she'd say 'That's nice, dear.' "

"That's an understatement," grunted Dexter. He made the Vulcan peace sign.

"We've never been close. More like roommates. My grandmother has always been the mother figure in my life."

"We'll be fine," said Dexter, slipping his arm across Philip's shoulders. "I'll make big bucks as a high-test corporate lawyer and Philip will devise new international economic theories to confound the experts. We'll be rich beyond our wildest dreams. And famous."

"Well put," said Philip. "I like the sound of that."

"And hell," added Dexter. "Even if we aren't, we'll be happy. That's more than I can say for my parents."

"Hey, Christine," said Philip. "I just had a thought. Do you have your camera with you?"

"Sure. In my briefcase."

Philip pushed Dexter down on the couch, then plopped down on top of him. Raising their glasses high with silly grins on their faces, they posed for the first shot.

Christine took another one of their hands, showing off the new rings, and finished with a more traditional picture of the two of them, standing together, their arms around each other's shoulders. "I'll make sure you each get copies."

"Keep them until we're past the grandmother hurdle," said Dexter. Glancing at his watch, he said, "Oh shit, I'm late." He grabbed his briefcase from behind his desk. As he passed Christine, he put his hand on her arm. "Thanks for being a friend."

"My pleasure. Truly. Maybe we can all get together for dinner sometime soon. I'd like you both to meet Jane."

"If she's as spectacular as you," said Dexter, "it's a date. God, after so many years of being in the closet, I feel like . . . like I've won the lottery." He shot Philip a smile that lit up the room. "Later, comrades," he said as he sailed out the door.

Philip watched his retreating back, then set his glass down. "Come on back to the house with me. There's something I want to give you."

On the way through the garden, Christine explained that she'd come by to tell everyone that she was leaving McBride Realty. "I was hoping to talk to all of you in person."

"I think everyone's out," said Philip.

Christine glanced up and saw a shadow fall across an open window on the third floor. She'd never been up there, but from the way the house was constructed, she assumed it was an attic. The shadow reappeared, lingering for a few seconds, then moved away again. She decided it must be a curtain fluttering in the breeze.

"I'm sorry you won't be our real estate agent any longer, but I'm super glad to hear you left that company."

"I know. You think Bill is a leech."

"I don't think, I know. And worse."

"Any details you'd care to share?"

"Sorry. I'll tell you all about it one day soon. Are you moving to another agency?"

"No. Just taking some time off. I haven't had a real vacation in years." She didn't like lying to him, but the truth would take too long and would probably bring him down. She didn't want to put a damper on his happiness.

Once inside the house, Philip headed for his grandfather's study. Opening the stained-glass doors of a wood cabinet, one that sat next to a tall mullioned window, Philip removed a small sculpture. "I want you to take this and keep it for me."

"I don't understand."

"I'll explain later." He handed it to her.

"Wow, it's heavy."

"It's made of iron. My grandmother gave it to me on my tenth birthday because she knew how much I loved it. My grandfather commissioned it from a friend of his, an artist who lived in Paris. It was patterned after a photo of my grandmother taken when she was about fifteen. To be honest, I'm kind of afraid that if she tosses me out, she won't let me take it. I need you to keep it for me in a safe place. It's also . . . well, it's my backup. I'm sorry to be so cryptic. I promise, I'll explain it all to you later, okay? Just make sure it's safe—and don't tell anyone you have it."

She didn't really understand what he meant, but she was happy to do him the favor.

"Here," said Philip. "Let me wrap it up."

She sat down in one of the leather chairs while he dashed around, finding an old newspaper and some tape. He made quick work of it. While he was working, she pulled one of her business cards out of her briefcase and wrote a few phone numbers on the back. "Here's how you can get in touch with me."

"Great. Thanks." He slipped it in his back pocket. "Now, let's put this package in your briefcase. That way, if someone comes home while you're leaving, you won't have to explain what it is."

As they were walking out to Christine's car, Philip said, "I really appreciate this. I trust you, Christine. It's sad, but I can't say that about many people in my life right now."

"When do you plan to talk to your grandmother?"

"Soon."

"Let me know what happens, okay?" She opened the trunk. "I still need to talk to her about quitting, you know. And your mother."

"I'll talk to them, okay. I know you don't like coming over here because of Laurent."

"That's not the way I usually do business."

"Don't worry about it." He opened the car door for her, closing it after she'd climbed in. "Laurent finally told me the dirt he has on my mother. Believe me, you're quitting at the right time—for multiple reasons. Let's just say Bill McBride is about to become persona non grata around here in a big way."

Christine was dying to know what he'd found out. "You can't even give me a little hint?"

"Not yet, but I'll be in touch."

She waved as she drove off. Glancing in the rearview mirror, she watched his figure get smaller and smaller until it disappeared into the deep afternoon shade. She couldn't have known it then, but it would be the last time she'd ever see him.

29

"Why, Rhett Butler, as ah live and breathe," said Bernadette in her most breathy southern accent.

"Cut the crap, Bernie." Bill ducked his head and looked around. "Are you going to let me in or not?"

"Why, Rhett, of course ah'll let you in. Into ma' house. Into ma' heart. Into ma' bed." She fluttered her eyes.

"Will you *please* stop that?" He looked over his shoulder again, clearly anxious that someone might see him.

Bernadette's body filled the doorway. He couldn't come in unless she stepped back, and she wasn't ready to do that just yet. He needed to loosen up, get his grove on. Stop being such a tight-ass.

"Look, I don't like coming here. But I made you a promise. I need to look at the upstairs bedrooms and the kitchen again. Unless you don't want me to do that market analysis. If that's the case, say the word and I'm gone."

"Of course I want that analysis, you big prick." She used her normal voice this time. "All I can say is, you used to be a lot more fun."

"Well, I changed, okay?"

"Remains to be seen," she said under her breath. She backed up, turned and glided up the stairs into the central foyer.

Bill followed, though at a slower pace.

"I believe you know where the kitchen is," she said coolly.

His head snapped up. "What's that supposed to mean?"

"Jeeze, but you're touchy."

"I don't like this. I never wanted to be *any* part of your life again."

"Well too bad. Welcome to Groundhog Day."

"Huh?"

"Didn't you ever see that movie."

His eyebrows knit together. "The one with Bill Murray—"

"Where the same day keeps repeating itself over and over again."

"Yeah?"

"That's my life, Billy Boy."

"You're nuts. You always were."

"But you used to like it."

He glanced at the water damage on the ceiling. "I can't believe you've let this magnificent house fall apart. It looks like you haven't done a thing to it since . . ."

"Well, we had a service come clean up the blood."

"Jesus, Bernie. *Jesus.*" Wiping the sweat off his forehead, he walked off.

"Coward," Bernie shouted to his retreating back.

The doorbell rang. "*I* wanted to change things around here," she muttered on her way back down the steps, "but Laurent would never do his share. Hell if I'm going to pay for everything while he's off gambling his money away. There's a little thing called *fairness* in this world." She threw back the door.

A thin, bearded man with a broad forehead and solemn eyes stood outside. He was dressed in tweeds and carried an umbrella.

Bernadette glanced up at the sky. Clear as a bell. "You're a pessimist."

"Excuse me?" He cleared his throat. "I'm Oliver Hammond."

"Oh, of course. Mr. Hammond." She pressed her hands together in front of her. It was one of her favorite poses. "So good of you to come by today."

"You were expecting me, right?"

"Absolutely."

Bill shouted from the other room, "The kitchen sink is clogged!"

She shouted back, "There's a plunger in the pantry!" Smiling at Mr. Hammond, she slipped her arm through his and led him into the living room. "There's artwork all over the house, but why don't we start in here."

"Of course." He removed his glasses from the pocket of his tweed jacket.

"You smell nice," she said, moving closer.

He seemed a bit rattled by the comment. "Why, thank you." Holding his glasses up to his eyes, he said, "Very impressive. Very impressive indeed. Your father assembled a wonderful collection."

"Worth lots of money."

"Undoubtedly. He liked American art I see."

"Well, yes. That's what's in this room. But he also invested in the Europeans."

"Is that a Grant Wood?" said Hammond, his elegant nose flaring with excitement. Snaking his way through the furniture, he rushed up to it. "Oh, my," he said, looking at it more closely. "Oh, my, oh my, oh my."

"Beautiful, yes?"

He moved to the next picture

"I believe that's a Seth Eastman."

"Oh, dear."

"Don't like Eastman?" She felt the same way. All those horrid clouds. "The next one is a John Lewis Krimmel. I like that one. Looks like a setting from a Jane Austen novel. I used to sit in front of it when I was a child and wonder what it would be like to live in there. I've always had a vivid imagination. Actually, Mr. Hammond, you may not know this, but I'm a published author."

"Really." He walked across the room to examine the paintings on the far wall.

"Perhaps you'd enjoy a private reading."

He turned to her with a deep frown on his face. "I'm afraid I have some bad news."

"*Bad,* you said?"

"None of these are originals."

"What?"

"They're all reproductions, and not very good ones at that."

"You mean—"

"They're worthless, Ms. Simoneau. I'm very sorry to have to tell you this, but I can't lie to you."

"But . . . my father was an astute businessman. How could they be fakes?"

Hammond walked over to her. "Let me look at the rest. Just so we've covered all the bases."

"Yes, absolutely." She led him to her father's study.

Half an hour later, they had returned to the living room.

"So, let me get this straight," said Bernadette, her hands balling into fists. "You're telling me that every painting in this entire house is a forgery?"

"Yes, I'm afraid so. As I mentioned to you on the phone, if you could get me the information on their provenance, I might be able to shed some light on how it happened."

"Oh, I have it," cried Bernadette. "My lawyer couriered it over to me yesterday. Everything is right here." She picked up a thick package from the piano bench and handed it to him.

Hammond tucked it under his arm. "I'll go through it right away."

Bernadette felt dazed, like a thick fog had descended and she couldn't see two feet in front of her.

"No need to show me the way out. I'll be in touch."

After he was gone, Bernadette moved to the center of the living room and stood there, absorbing the shock.

"What's wrong with you?" asked Bill a few minutes later, entering as he wrote in his notepad.

"My father," mumbled Bernadette.

"What about him?"

Flinging her arms in the air, she screamed, "He was a freakin' dodo! That's freakin' *what*."

30

Cordelia was all set. She had her new binoculars, the ones she'd purchased this morning from the sporting goods store, and she was
dressed in camouflage gear. As she left the Allen Grimby on her way to
the parking garage, she hummed the song "Dead Skunk" by Loudon
Wainwright III. It had been floating around in her mind all day. Perhaps
it was a portent of the evening to come. Or maybe it was just because
she'd played it for Hattie last night. Hattie had listened for a minute, then
plugged her nose and circled the potted palm like a little dervish. That
kid had a real taste for the absurd—and good music. She was a true
Thorn.

Arriving at Greta's apartment shortly after ten, Cordelia performed
the delicate surgery of squeezing her mighty Hummer between a silver
van and a puny Crown Vic. Glancing around, she eased out of the front
seat, noticing with some annoyance that the Hummer's hood had been
attacked by a bird. "Damn little disrespectful pissants," she muttered,
getting the spray cleaner and a roll of paper towels out of the backseat.
She pulled the straps of her headlamp over her auburn curls, and set
about cleaning the hood. So what if she was fussy about her stuff? The
Hummer was like her kid. It was up to her to see that it was cared
for—protected from the sordid underbelly, so to speak, of a dangerous and dirty world.

Once the hood was cleaned to her exacting specifications, she returned the cleaner and the paper towels to the backseat, but kept the headlamp strapped on, just in case. She switched off the light, however. Covert action was the name of the game tonight. She would only use the light if absolutely necessary.

Surveying the dark garden area between the two matching apartment buildings, Cordelia saw a grouping of bushes that would be a perfect place to hunker down and hide. Greta had basically invited her to bring over a pair of binoculars and watch through the windows, so in Cordelia's mind, she was just doing what she was told. If she saw Jane inside, she wasn't sure what would happen. What she'd like to do was repel down the face of the building, crash through the window, and punt Greta into the next century. There was something about the woman that just rubbed Cordelia the wrong way.

"Why don't I count the ways?" whispered Cordelia, finding a spot behind the bushes and crouching down. "Might as well have an Elizabeth Barrett Browning moment while I wait."

Not only did Greta have a mean mouth on her, but she wasn't who she pretended to be. She didn't just wander into Jane's life off the street, as it were. She'd targeted Jane for a reason. It was up to Cordelia to find out what that reason was. Hence, tonight's mission.

Removing the binoculars from the leather case, Cordelia held them up to her eyes and focused on the first-floor-front apartment. A dim light burned in the rear—probably a bedroom. She panned across the windows, delighted to find that all the blinds were open. Greta didn't appear to be home. Well, thought Cordelia, making herself a little more comfortable by snapping off a particularly pokey branch, she had all the time in the world. She had a canteen full of black cherry soda strapped to her belt, and two Nut Goodies in her right pocket. She was set for at least an hour. After that, hunger would set in, but Cordelia was in this for the long haul. No pain, no gain.

Glancing to her right, she was startled to see a man crouched in a different clump of bushes about ten feet away. He had binoculars, too. He was young. Dark-haired and bearded. And he was staring at her. She nodded to him pleasantly. "Been bird-watching long?"

"Shit, lady."

"Yeah," she said, agreeably. "It's harder at night."

Erupting out of his hiding place, the man stomped past her, cursing under his breath.

"Have a nice evening," she called after him.

Opening up one of the Nut Goodies, Cordelia watched him disappear around the side of the van. A moment later, the engine caught. Her eyes opened wide with horror as he slammed into the front of the Hummer, then pulled out onto the street.

"Stop!" she screamed, bolting after him. "Stop! Police! Stop!"

She didn't take time to examine the damage. Lunging into the front seat, she gunned the motor and sped off, honking her horn and screaming at the top of her lungs. Roaring up behind him at the stoplight on 31st and Lyndale, she rolled the window down and shouted, "Anarchist! Nihilist! Assassin! Look what you did to my car!"

He gave her the finger as he turned the corner and peeled away.

Bouncing up and down in her seat, Cordelia shrieked, "You'll pay for this you . . . you . . . you *evildoer!*" She couldn't think of a word bad enough to describe him. She was mildly abashed that she'd resorted to one of George Bush's simpleminded imprecations, but there it was. She zoomed after him, jerking in and out of traffic.

The van took a hard left onto 46th. Cordelia was behind a couple slow-moving cars. When she finally turned, she saw the van blow through the red light on Grand, never even making a pretense of stopping.

"You just ran a light!" she shouted. "You're a menace! A plague!" She glanced in both directions as she came to the intersection, but seeing no other cars, she shot through the light and roared after him. Checking the rearview mirror, she saw that a red SUV had stopped at the light and was honking at her. "How utterly Minnesotan," she thought, seething silently. "This is a car chase, you moron! Didn't you ever see a guy movie? Dirty Harry! Arnold!! You don't obey the *laws* in a chase scene!"

Cordelia kept on the van's tail until it made a right onto Nicollet. As their respective vehicles surged through the road construction on their way toward 50th, Cordelia laid on the horn. She had no intention of letting this asshole off the hook. She'd follow him all over town—to the ends of the earth—until he stopped and gave her his insurance information and apologized.

233

The van ran a red light at 50th, turning east toward the parkway. But as it cruised down the hill, it suddenly took a right onto a quiet side street.

"Ah ha!" cried Cordelia, slapping the steering wheel.

The van came to a stop about halfway down the block. Cordelia pulled up behind it and cut the motor. She shot out of the front seat, ready for "the grand confrontation."

The bearded guy climbed down out of the van and glared at her. "What the hell do you think you're doing, lady?"

"You rammed my car!"

"Jesus, I hardly touched it! It's just my luck to run into some idiot crank like you."

"Look at this damage! It will cost me thousands to get it repaired!" She walked over to the front of the Hummer and pointed.

"I don't see any damage."

"It's right there." She switched on her headlamp.

"Where?"

"There!" she said, pointing to a small scratch.

"You chased me all over creation because of *that*?"

"I want your license number and your insurance information. Either that or I'm callin' the cops." She whipped out her cell phone.

"Oh, hell." He threw open the back of his van.

Cordelia patted the hood and caressed the bumper. "It's okay, baby. Cordelia's gonna make sure you're fixed up right as rain." When she looked up, she was staring at the wrong end of a hunting rifle.

"Get back in that piece of shit and leave," said the man. "And don't give me any more trouble or, trust me, I'll make you very sorry."

"How come everybody insults my Hummer?"

"Leave!" He flipped off the safety.

"You should just listen to yourself. You sound like a thug."

"Lady, you are one weird fuck. Now take off and don't look back." He sighted the rifle.

"I don't know how you can live with yourself after what you did. I guess that's your problem." With one last steely-eyed glare, she got back into the front seat, started the motor, and drove away.

31

After work that night, Jane returned to her house and sat on the back porch with a beer. She had a lot to think about. Kenzie. Dexter Haynes. Alice Cathcart. What to say to Greta about last night. And now something new had been dropped into the mix. A private investigator, A. J. Nolan, had stopped by the Lyme House while Jane was out. He'd left his card, telling her manager to pass on the message that he'd be in touch. That was it. No other explanation for the visit. She had called his cell twice but hadn't reached him and it bugged her. She was so deep in thought about so many things that when footsteps came down the outside stairs from the third floor, she might not have noticed if Mouse hadn't stood up and barked.

"It's okay, boy," she said, seeing Greta approach the screen door.

"Evening," said Greta, coming to a full stop outside on the steps. "Can I talk to you a sec?"

"Yes, I think we need to," said Jane.

Greta came inside and patted Mouse, then perched on the edge of the wicker couch. "I want to apologize for walking in on you last night."

"You're timing was impeccable." She tipped the beer bottle back and took several swallows.

"I never thought . . . I mean, I didn't know—" She abandoned the sentence and started again. "Who was that woman?"

"Her name is Kenzie Mullroy."

"Is she your . . . girlfirend? I'm not trying to pry. But I, well—"

"Yes, Greta. She's my girlfriend."

"Are you two, like, in love?"

"Approaching it."

"How long have you known her?"

"Since last fall."

She looked up at the moon. "I didn't realize you had someone in your life. Hope I didn't create any problems for you."

"If you did, it wasn't your fault. It was mine."

"How do you figure that?"

"I could have locked the door on the second-floor landing, but I never did."

"But . . . there was no need."

"Well, actually, I think there was. It's locked now. If you want to see me, call first on your cell, or just come downstairs and ring the bell. I'm not saying I don't want to talk to you, or that I don't enjoy looking at the photos you're taking of the Xanadu—I think you're doing a great job—but I guess I need a little warning."

"Oh." She bit her lower lip and looked down. "I get it. Really, I'm super sorry."

"Don't worry about it."

"Did Kenzie think, like, that we were . . ."

"It crossed her mind. I can't blame her. If the situation had been reversed, I sure would have jumped to some conclusions."

Greta nodded. "It's because I look like *her,* isn't it. Like Christine."

"Actually, I think anybody who showed up wearing my bathrobe in the middle of the night would have created a stir."

"Yeah, I suppose." She hesitated, then said, "Jane?"

"Hmm?"

"You look kind of down. Is it because of last night?"

She took another sip of the beer. "It's a lot of things. I went to see Dexter Haynes today."

"The guy in prison."

She nodded. "He's innocent, Greta. I found proof."

236

"How can you be so sure?"

Jane explained about Dexter's relationship with Philip Simoneau—that Christine had taken photos of them together and that, in one of the pictures, the watch Dexter supposedly lifted from the main house was sitting in plain sight on the desk. "Philip gave him the watch. It was an anniversary gift. So you see," she said, tipping her beer up to get the last drop, "he had no motive. If anything, he had a huge reason not to have committed those murders. I'm sure the real murderer is still walking the streets, a free man."

"Did Dexter give you any leads on who might have done it?"

"A couple. I've already followed up on one of them." Since Greta seemed so interested, Jane gave her the details.

"Boy," said Greta when Jane was done. "When you get your teeth into something, you don't let go."

Jane smiled, although her mood didn't change. "I'm horrified by the idea that Dexter is condemned to spend his life paying for a crime he didn't commit."

"Do you like him?"

"Yes, I guess I do." She held up her empty beer bottle. "All this talking's made me thirsty. Think I'll get another. Would you like one?"

"Sure," said Greta.

Jane entered the kitchen and opened the refrigerator door. "I've got some Leinie's or Sam Adams Red."

"You know," said Greta, pushing a hand into the pocket of her white cords, "I'd rather have a shot of that Scotch we had the other night."

"Ah, okay." Jane got down a glass and the bottle, handing them to her. Greta poured herself at least an inch, downing it in a few neat gulps.

"Hey, slow down," said Jane.

Greta poured herself another one. "It hasn't been a great day for me either."

Jane watched her toss back half of the second drink. "Problems at school?"

"No. Problems with me. I don't like myself very much right now."

"How come?"

She shook her head. "A long story. Something I'm not very proud of." Finishing the drink, she said, "You know, when I saw you last night in the kitchen with that woman, it sort of—"

"Surprised you?"

"Yeah, that but . . . other stuff, too." She set the glass down. "I guess . . . I guess I hate it that the only reason you wanted to get to know me was because I look like Christine."

"Should I have lied to you?"

"No. But, I mean, I'd like to think you like me because of me, who *I* am."

"I do," said Jane.

"No you don't. Not really."

Jane wasn't sure what to say.

"I like you a lot, Jane."

"The feeling's mutual. We're friends."

"No, you don't get it. You just don't *get* it. God, I don't know if I get it myself."

"Get what?"

She filled up the glass again.

"Don't drink that," said Jane, putting her hand over the top. "Please? You're obviously bothered by something. If it has to do with me— something I said, something I did—just tell me. I'm not mad at you because of last night."

"Maybe you should be."

"Why?"

"Because . . . because— Oh hell, I'm such a butt-head. I have no *sense.*"

"About what?"

"*You!* I like you, Jane. What I mean to say is, I think I'm attracted to you."

Jane turned to face her. "You are?"

"I think so."

"Look, Greta . . ."

"Just, one time . . . just this one time, would you . . . could I—"
She leaned over and kissed Jane softly.

Jane pulled away.

"Oh, God."

"What?"

"That was, like, so great."

Jane started to laugh, but stopped herself. "Greta, listen to me."

"Okay, here it comes. I'm too young. Too ugly. Too straight."

"You're hardly ugly."

"So if I look so much like Christine, you have to be attracted to me."

Jane rested her hip against the counter. "Nobody seems to understand this, but the fact is . . ." She struggled for a way to put it gently. "It's *because* you look like Christine that I could never be romantically interested in you. It just feels so incredibly wrong. You're *not* Christine."

"Right!"

"Being around you does bring her back to me sometimes, but if we ever got really close, the way you're suggesting, it would be . . . like I'd have to face her loss over and over and over again every time we made love. Honestly, Greta. It would kill me."

Greta just stared at her.

"I'm not that strong."

"I'd never want to hurt you. No matter what happens, please remember that."

"I believe you," said Jane. "If you think you're gay—"

"I don't know what the hell I am. All I know is, when I saw you with Kenzie last night, I was jealous. I wanted to be the one in your arms. Crazy, right? I tried to rationalize my way around it all day, but I couldn't. That's why today was such a nightmare. I mean . . . I know I still like guys. But I got to thinking about what you said the day we first met, about Christine. That she fell in love with the person, not the gender. Maybe I'm a little like that."

"Give yourself some time," said Jane. "You'll figure it out."

"Yeah. All I know is, Kenzie's a lucky woman."

This time Jane couldn't help but laugh. "I don't think she's entirely convinced of that."

"Then convince her," said Greta.

"I'd use you as a reference, but I don't think she would be amused."

They walked back out to the porch.

"Will you be at the Xanadu Club when they demolish the old screen?" asked Greta.

"When's it scheduled for?" asked Jane.

"Day after tomorrow. In the morning. I'll be there bright and early with my cameras. I wouldn't want my boss to think I'm falling down on the job."

"I'll stop by," said Jane, smiling at her.

Greta opened the screen door so Mouse could go out. "You know, I feel sort of ridiculous now. I apologize. For the kiss. For everything."

"Hey, it's not every day a beautiful young woman makes a pass at me."

"We *will* stay friends, won't we?"

Jane put her hand on Greta's shoulder. "Through thick and thin, kiddo. Through rain and sleet and snow."

"I think that's the post office."

"Oh."

Greta grinned. "See you soon."

The next morning, Jane drove through the pouring rain to the address on A. J. Nolan's business card. She figured it would be an office, but it turned out to be a home in the Powderhorn neighborhood. The house was a white clapboard two-story, with an open front porch and a wood stove vent that popped out the north wall, ran up the side of the building, and attached to the roof.

Jane parked her Mini in front of the house and got out. As she dashed up the cracked concrete sidewalk, she saw a man sitting on the porch reading the morning paper, seemingly oblivious to the weather.

Before she reached the steps, he stood and took off his reading glasses. "Can I help you?"

He was a stocky black guy with gray hair and an equally gray mustache, one that reminded Jane of a fuzzy caterpillar. A cigarette dangled from the side of his mouth.

"I'm Jane Lawless," she said, ducking under the porch roof and shaking the rain out of her hair. "You left your business card at my restaurant."

He eyed her briefly, then invited her into the house. "I got your phone messages, but I couldn't call you back last night. I was on a job."

She glanced around the living room. The furniture was old but comfortable-looking. Homey. The house smelled of bacon and fresh coffee. She assumed there was a Mrs. Nolan somewhere in the picture. "You're a P.I."

"Guilty," he said, beckoning her to follow him downstairs. "My office is in the basement," he explained, leaving a trail of Old Spice behind him as he descended the stairs. "I've worked out of the house ever since May, that's my wife, died a few years back."

Jane sat down on a banged-up leather chair in front of an equally banged-up oak desk. The room was just off the laundry, and smelled heavily of fabric softener. Filing cabinets lined one wall. A framed P.I. license hung on the opposite wall, as well as several other framed certificates. Squinting at the closest one, Jane said, "You used to be a police officer?"

"Thirty years with the MPD," he said, sitting down heavily on a squeaky rolling chair. "I retired when I was fifty-two. That was four years ago. You do the math." He pulled the cigarette out of his mouth and tapped it over an ashtray. "I'm a good friend of Norm Toscalia's. You can blame him for giving me your name. He told me you'd visited our mutual friend, Dexter Haynes, a few days ago."

"You know Haynes?"

"I was one of the homicide cops who worked the Simoneau case." Taking a pull off the cigarette, he sat back. "Haynes doesn't usually entertain strangers. But then, I suppose your last name made him curious." Studying her a moment longer, he continued, "And then, what do I hear? Haynes calls up your dad and gives him a message for you. Now that flat-out floored me. When I heard he agreed to meet with you a second time, I got to wondering what you two'd been talking about. Thought I might as well go straight to the horse's mouth. Haynes won't talk to me anymore. I don't blame him."

"You're telling me you're one of the men who helped put him away?"

"Yeah, I guess that's a fair statement. But check this out." He rose and drew back a sliding door, revealing a floor-to-ceiling bulletin board.

Jane stood to get a closer look. "You kept this? All these years?" Stuck to the board with thumbtacks were crime scene photos, a diagram of the Simoneau mansion, photos of everyone connected to the murders, evidence lists, timelines, interviews, forensic reports, autopsy results, handwritten case notes. "My God, you've got everything here."

"Everything but the perp's real name," he said, breathing smoke out his nostrils.

"You mean——"

"Haynes? Nah, never liked him for it. I did everything I could to keep him out of jail, but the primary on the case had other ideas. Haynes was black and he had the watch in his possession. Add the two together and what do you get?"

"A conviction."

"Bingo."

"You think it was racially motivated?"

"Hell, yes. Thing is, I never gave up hope I could prove his innocence. When I left the department, I made copies of the case file and I took it all with me. Not kosher, I guess, but it's water over the bridge now. Lot of good it did me." He grunted. "Haynes's lawyer was honest but inept. If the murders had happened today, you can bet the media would've descended like flies. Haynes would for sure have snagged himself a high-profile defense team. I always thought it was a shame your father didn't take the case. If he had, at least Haynes would've had a fighting chance."

"My dad does a lot of pro bono work."

He held up his hand. "Yeah, yeah, I know. I'm not blaming him, any more than I blame myself. Your father's a decent enough guy, he just happens to work for the dark side."

"You don't like defense attorneys?"

"They're the 'necessary evil' part of my job."

They both sat back down.

"Norm told me about your girlfriend, the one who died. Said she somehow got her hands on the *Iron Girl* before she died." He raised an eyebrow. "You don't know how, right?"

"No. No idea."

"I also hear she had the derringer that matched the gun that killed Philip Simoneau. Now that's a curious one. She was some kind of insurance salesman, right?"

"Real estate."

"Sure, I remember now. She was helping Bernadette sell her house." He stubbed out the cigarette. "So tell me, Ms. Lawless, what have you and old Dex been talking about?"

Jane saw no reason to hold anything back. She laid it all out for him: what she'd learned, who she'd talked to, what she thought it meant. "Is that photograph with the watch in it enough evidence to reopen the case?" she asked finally.

He lit up another cigarette, blew the match out, and tossed it in the ashtray. "Gay, huh. Never figured him for that. Fucking crazy world, I swear." He sucked in some smoke, then blew it out the side of his mouth. "To answer your question, I don't know. I'll show it to some cop friends of mine, see what they think, but my feeling is that it's nowhere near enough."

Jane was flattened by the response.

"On the other hand, it might be enough to influence some big-shot defense lawyer to take up the case. You know anybody like that?"

She smiled. "I'll see what I can do. I'm driving to Willmar this afternoon to talk to Frank DeWitt."

"Really," he said, sounding surprised. A. J. Nolan had a kind voice but merciless eyes. An odd combination. "He know you're coming?"

"No. Thought I'd just drop in on him."

"Good plan."

"I assume you've talked to him."

"At some length."

"Ever think he did it?"

He flicked some ash into the ashtray. "Yeah. And I still do. Look, since you're so interested in the case, I'm going to tell you something that never came out at the trial. Police hold stuff back. Helps them weed out the lunatics." Taking another drag, he set the cigarette down, then leaned into the desk, making a bridge of his fingers. "The little boy, Tim? You'll read in all the accounts how he was left to wander around the house. That was partially true. He did have blood all over him. But whoever the killer was took the kid upstairs before he left and locked him in the bathroom. That, in my opinion, was the act of some-one who cared about that child—or about children in general. Granted, it wasn't much, but it was something. And don't kid yourself. It's significant."

"You think DeWitt was trying to shield his son."

"Sure do. And I haven't changed my opinion. He didn't have an alibi. And he had, as you already know, the strongest motive of any we found. Course, you don't need to prove motive to convict a man of murder."

"You don't?"

"No. It helps, but it's not essential. Look," he said, pulling the ashtray in front of him, "keep me posted on what happens this afternoon. Maybe we can help each other."

That sounded great. "Deal."

He stood up and extended his hand.

Jane leaned across the desk to shake it.

"Well, imagine that. At long last we've got a Lawless working on the right side of the law."

Christine

August 27, 1987

6:30 P.M.

Christine arrived early to her dinner engagement that night. Molly and Aaron Stine had been close friends for many years. She and Jane usually had dinner with them at least once a month, sometimes more. The last time they were together, Christine had noticed a certain coolness in the way Molly and Aaron acted around each other. She hoped they weren't having marital problems—or, if they were, that it was something minor.

Jane was supposed to drive over from the restaurant around seven. It was just six-thirty, but Christine figured Molly wouldn't mind if she showed up early. She'd stopped to buy a bottle of pinot noir on the way over. As she opened the trunk to retrieve it, Molly poked her head out the front door and called, "Need any help?"

That's when Christine got an idea. "No, I'm fine."

Molly walked out to the curb anyway.

Christine grabbed her briefcase and the wine.

"Here," said Molly, lifting the briefcase off Christine's shoulder. "Let me carry that. It looks heavy and you seem beat."

Christine lied. "Yeah, there's always too much to do." She smiled.

Tonight, after she and Jane returned home, she planned to come clean about quitting. But she didn't want anybody else to know, for now. The revelation would likely lead to the conversation Christine had been dreading—telling

Jane the truth about her health. She didn't feel up to it. But then, she never would.

"Aaron's made some of his famous hummus as an appetizer."

Even the thought of food made Christine nauseous. "Great."

As they entered the front door, Molly said, "I'll just leave your briefcase in the foyer. That way you won't forget it when you go."

"Molly," said Christine, turning to look at her. "Will you do me a big favor?"

"Sure. Anything."

She pulled the package out of the briefcase. "Will you keep this for me? I, ah . . . I bought a present for Jane's birthday today. I don't want to bring it home with me because she might find it and ruin the surprise. I'll come by and get it later, okay?"

"Sure. No problem. I'll put it somewhere safe."

"Thanks."

Aaron charged out of the kitchen. "Where the hell did you put the hot pads this time?" He seemed angry, his face flushed.

"Oh, bag it, dickhead," said Molly.

"Don't start with me, lady."

"You act like you think I've discovered a new kind of torture. Hide the hot pads from Aaron."

"It did occur to me." Glancing at Christine, he said, "You look hot. I've got fresh lemonade, or I can fix you a drink."

"Something fizzy sounds good," said Christine. "Pop, or sparkling water."

Aaron shot Molly a withering look as he disappeared back into the kitchen.

"Something wrong?" asked Christine.

"Miserable bastard," muttered Molly, sticking the package in the front closet and closing the door.

"You two okay?"

"No. Let's just try to get through the evening without an all-out war erupting, okay?"

Squinting out the window, Molly said, "Jane's here. God, she's got that chef's coat on. I hope she brought something else to wear. That thing is so heavy. Maybe we should turn on the air." She opened the door before Jane could ring the bell. "Hi, hon," she said, giving Jane a one-handed hug.

"I brought some Irish Soda Bread," said Jane, handing a white sack to Molly. "Didn't know what you had planned for supper, but—"

248

"It's perfect," said Molly. "If it doesn't fit with Mr. Picky's precious menu, he can pout and the three of us can enjoy it."

Jane shot Christine a questioning look.

"Aaron," shouted Molly. "Bread."

Aaron stuck his balding head out the kitchen door. "Oh, hi, Jane. I'll be out in a minute with the appetizers. Want something to drink?"

"What are my options?"

"Lemonade. Beer. Wine. Bourbon."

"I'll take the bourbon," said Jane.

"Good choice." He withdrew his head.

"How are you?" asked Jane, giving Christine a quick kiss.

Christine was so glad to see her, she almost started to cry. Turning away, she saw for the first time how deeply affected she'd been by learning about Philip and Dexter. They were just starting their life together. Seeing their joy brought a bitter edge to the dwindling amount of time she and Jane had left.

As she turned back to Jane, she suddenly felt dizzy.

"You okay?"

Her legs turned to Jell-O. "I . . ." She felt Jane's strong arms grip her around the waist. A moment later, the world went dark.

When Christine awoke, she was on the couch in the Aaron's study. Two men in dark brown shirts and pants were leaning over her. Glancing at her left arm, she saw a blood pressure cuff.

What—"

"You fainted," said one of the men. He was thin, balding. "I'm Mark."

"Hi."

The man taking her pressure had blond hair and a pale complexion. She assumed they were paramedics.

"You're blood pressure's low," said Mark. "Tell me what you've eaten today."

She had to think. "A bowl of cornflakes. Some coffee."

"When?"

"For breakfast."

"What else?"

She felt the cuff deflate. "A can of diet Dr Pepper."

"That it?"

"I think so."

He nodded to his partner, who immediately got up and left. "You need to eat, Ms. Kane. I want you to drink some orange juice. That should make you feel a little better. But you need a real meal with protein. Vegetables. Real food. Understand?"

"Yeah."

"Do you have a headache?"

"No."

"Do you hurt anywhere?"

She shook her head.

The blond guy returned with a large glass of OJ.

"Drink this down," said Mark.

Christine felt like a four-year-old being scolded by her dad.

"Do you have any medical conditions we should know about? Diabetes? High blood pressure? Heart problems?"

Jane had moved up behind him. The worried look on her face cut Christine to her core. "No," she said, seeing the expression on Jane's face darken.

"Well," said Mark, "we could take you to the emergency room, have a doctor check you out. Your call."

"I'll be fine," said Christine, sipping the last of the juice.

"For sure, you should call your regular doc, let him know what happened. He may want to do further tests."

"Right."

The blond man crouched back down and inflated the blood pressure cuff again. The pressure on her upper arm hurt.

Everyone waited for the reading.

"Still low," he said, releasing the cuff.

"Don't stand up for a while," said Mark. He sniffed the air. "Smells pretty good in here, like somebody's cookin' some good food. I suggest you eat some of it." He stood up and turned to Jane.

Christine listened as he gave Jane instructions, but after a few seconds she rolled her head to the side because she couldn't bear to look at Jane's face. She glanced up at the African masks dotting the dark brown study walls.

Molly came in and they talked for a while. Mark said that heat could make people light-headed if they got dehydrated. After Molly mentioned Christine's bout with skin cancer, he crouched back down.

"How you doin'?"

"I feel better," she said, wishing they'd all leave.

"I hear you had skin cancer."

"Long time ago," said Christine.

"Do you know what kind it was?"

"Melanoma."

"Invasive?"

She hesitated. "No."

"You're lucky. Where?"

"On my right forearm."

He looked it over. "I'm not trying to worry you, but you really need to have this fainting spell checked out. Most likely it's nothing more than low blood pressure caused by lack of food. We see a fair amount of situations like yours. But you don't want to take chances, you know?"

The cuff tightened around her arm again.

Everyone was in the room now, waiting to hear the report.

"It's coming up," said the blond guy after a few seconds.

"Your color is a little better," said Mark, staring at her hard.

The cuff was removed.

"Thanks for your help," said Christine.

Mark smiled. "You eat some dinner now, hear?"

The two men picked up their heavy equipment cases and left the room. Molly and Aaron followed.

Glancing at the door, Christine saw that Jane had closed it. Her back was to Christine, so she couldn't see her expression.

"I'm sorry for all the fuss I caused, Jane. Really, it's so stupid." She tried to sit up, but didn't quite make it. "I mean, how could I be so dumb? I guess I just got busy and forgot to eat."

Jane turned.

Christine held her breath.

"No more," whispered Jane.

"What?"

"I've played along with this game of yours, but no more. I don't get it, Christine. I've tried to respect your space, but I can't do it anymore."

"Game? You think I'm playing games?"

"You think I don't know what's going on? You think I can live with a woman, sleep with her, love her beyond all reason and not know she's——" Her voice broke.

"How long——"

Closing her eyes, Jane said, "About six months."

"How did you find out?"

"Oh God." She lifted a trembling hand to her forehead.

Christine watched helplessly. Her heart, which had been so badly battered, was finally breaking. She reached out and gripped Jane's arm. She wanted to comfort her, but words were useless.

Christine struggled to sit up as Jane joined her on the couch, their bodies tumbling together.

"There's still time," whispered Christine.

Jane scraped the tears from her face. "How much?"

"Months? Years, maybe, if I'm lucky. How did you find out?"

Jane swallowed a couple of times. "You'd had some tests. I usually went with you to hear the results, but this one time you said I didn't need to. I guess . . . I got worried. You never seemed to have any energy anymore. So I called your doctor. Told him I was sorry I couldn't come in with you, asked him what the tests showed. Why didn't you let them do the chemo again? It worked last time. Why didn't you at least give us that chance?"

A curious buzzing noise surrounded Christine. For a few seconds, she couldn't focus on anything else.

"Answer me!" demanded Jane. Anger had replaced the anguish in her eyes.

"Sweetheart, I want to explain, but . . . I'm scared."

Jane pulled away.

"Listen to me for a second. Let's drive up to Blackberry Lake, to the cabin. Right now. Let's get in the car, go home, pack up the dogs and some clothes, and leave. I need to be alone with you. We've got to talk this through. I promise, I'll explain everything. Just give me a chance. Don't judge what I've done until you understand why."

God, she thought, staring at Jane, realizing for the first time what a wreck she'd made of both of their lives. Jane's face looked worn and bruised. "I just have to make you understand," she whispered.

I just have to.

32

Calvin was sick of living in a trashy motel, sick of the crackpots who inhabited big cities—like the human battleship in the Hummer who'd chased him last night. Worrying about Greta all the time ate at his insides like battery acid. It was no good. He was totally wasted by too much booze and too little sleep. He wanted out.

As he cruised the alley in back of Greta's apartment building, he switched off his windshield wipers. The morning rain appeared to be over. Next to a Dumpster, he saw a truck crammed with furniture. The back double doors of the apartment building were propped open with bricks. He figured it must be moving day for someone inside, but for Calvin, it was a minor miracle. If he kept loitering around the front entry, edging into the building along with the legitimate residents, he'd eventually get busted. Twice, the nosey old lady across the hall from Greta had caught him listening outside Greta's door. If she caught him again, he was sure she'd call the cops.

Calvin had beaten the odds last night, and he planned to do it again today. He'd won almost three grand playing blackjack at Mystic Lake. Casinos were like whorehouses—they could eat a man's soul, which was why he usually stayed away. But he felt rattled after getting chased by the Amazon in camouflage fatigues. He sat in his motel room for a couple of hours, feeling like he was going nuts. When he got like that, the only thing that helped was getting in his van and driving. He'd headed down to Prior Lake, to the casino, where he could lose himself in the noise and the bright lights. The money in his pocket this morning was proof that his luck had changed.

Calvin parked his van on 32nd and sprinted back down the alley. A teenage dude with bad acne and a DKNY T-shirt came down the inside steps as Calvin entered the building.

"Crappy weather for a move," said the teenager.

"Yeah," said Calvin, bolting past him. He didn't have time to exchange small talk. He headed down the quiet inner hall, his wet Reeboks squeaking on the polished granite floors. Even before he reached number 104, he could hear Greta's voice. Standing just outside her door, Calvin bent his head and listened:

"I don't know any more than I've already told you," she said, sounding frustrated.

"You're not trying hard enough," came a male voice. "Ask more questions. Dig deeper."

"She's not dumb, you know. She's going to get suspicious. And then what?"

The wood floors squeaked as someone walked around inside.

"Did she tell you *anything* else about her visit with Dexter Haynes?"

"No," said Greta. "I've told you everything. Honestly, I don't think she's planning to write a book. I asked her about it and she said she wasn't."

"She's lying."

"Maybe." Silence. "I've gotten to know her a little, you know. She's not a stranger anymore. We're friends."

"That's great. That's what I wanted."

"She's, like, really honest. She got interested in the Simoneau case because her dead partner was connected and she's not sure how."

Calvin wondered who the hell the guy was.

"Who does she think did the murders?" demanded the man.

"She doesn't know. How many ways can I tell you that? And besides, it doesn't really matter, does it? You told me *you'd* solved the case."

"I have. But I need to find out if she has information I've missed. Do you think she's holding back on you?"

"How on earth could I possibly know that?" Silence. Then, "No, I don't."

"Is she . . . I mean, is she still fascinated that you look like her dead lover?"

"I hate that. I like her, okay? I feel like I'm lying to her every time we talk."

"But does she like *you*?"

"What are you saying?"

"Is she attracted to you?"

"Christ. No."

He gave a low chuckle. "I don't believe you. Listen to me, Greta. If she wants to get, well, friendly, do you think . . ."

"What? You want me to sleep with her?"

"I need for her to trust you. Otherwise, this is a waste of time. I've been very *very* good to you, Greta. Don't forget that. I got you into MCAD. And I've promised to pay your tuition. I need some help here!"

Calvin's jaw nearly hit the floor.

"God," said Greta. "This is such a mess. I never expected to like her so much. I feel like a traitor every time I see her."

"Just hang in there for a little while longer," said the man. "You owe me that much."

He said the last words so sweetly, Calvin knew Greta would fall for it.

"Oh, all right," she said after a few seconds. "But I won't sleep with her. Clear?"

"Maybe I crossed a line. If I did, I'm sorry. But who knows? You might surprise yourself. She's certainly attractive."

"I'm not discussing it. *Who* I sleep with—who I'm attracted to—is none of your damn business."

"Sure, sure. Greta, you've been great, but you've got to understand my side of it. If she *is* working on a book—and I believe, based on what others have told me, that she is—you're the only one who can get me inside. My own book is almost done. I've been working on it day and night. But if she publishes first, she'll steal my thunder. I want the money, Greta. I've earned it."

"But you don't even have a publisher."

"Oh, but I do. Well, almost. We're negotiating with, ah, Random House. High six figures. But if they get wind of another book about to enter the pipeline, the deal will be compromised. I know my theory of the crime is the right one. I just need time to get it down on paper."

"How can you be so positive?"

"If I told you, you might carry the information back to Lawless."

"I wouldn't do that."

"Well . . ." He paused. "I suppose I can trust you. I mean, what could it hurt? It was Alice Cathcart. The nanny."

"Really? Wow."

"Yeah, wow is right."

"And you've got proof?"

"You bet. All I need."

More silence. "But . . . if you can prove it, why didn't you take the proof to the police? Get that poor innocent guy out of prison?"

"It's complicated. I've already said too much. And, hey, look at the time. I've gotta shove off, Greta. I'll be in touch."

Realizing that the door was about to open, Calvin shot up the steps to the second floor. When he heard the front door click shut, he rushed to the window on the stairs and looked down. All he could see was the back of a man in a khaki-colored raincoat and a dark blue baseball cap. "Damn," he whispered, wishing he'd caught a glimpse of the man's face.

Hurrying back down the stairs, he knocked on Greta's door. To his surprise, it flew back.

"Look, Mr.—" Greta's face froze. "Calvin?"

He pushed her inside and shut the door behind them. "What kind of sick game are you playing?"

"How . . . how did you get in here?"

"You're letting some man pimp you to that Lawless woman?"

"No! Of course not."

"He just asked you to sleep with her, Greta. In my book, that's what a pimp does. If he's a pimp, what the hell's that make *you*?"

"Shut up. You've got it all wrong."

"He's *paying* you—footing your college bills. Jesus, woman. Maybe I'm a totally fucked-up S.O.B., but that sure as hell seems like a pimp-prostitute relationship to me."

"I told him no!"

"Yeah. Uh huh." He stomped around the room. There wasn't much furniture. Just a couple of chairs that looked like they came from Goodwill. "What's happened to you, Greta? Selling yourself so you can attend college? *College!* What the hell does that mean in the scheme of things?"

"You don't understand. You never did."

"You think you're going to become some photojournalistic genius. Well, you're *not*, Greta. You're selling your soul for a bunch of romanticized bullshit."

"Get out of here." She pointed at the door. "Get out or I'll scream my bloody head off. I'll call the police on you, Calvin. I *will*. You have no right to harass me, to follow me around, to make judgments about how I live my life." She picked up a heavy pot, ready to throw it at him, but Calvin knocked it out of her hand, sending it crashing to the floor.

"Get out!" she screamed.

He lunged at her, pressing his hand over her mouth. When she stopped struggling, he pulled a Smith & Wesson out of the back of his belt and pressed it to her stomach. "Calm down!" he demanded.

She looked at the gun. "You won't use that. If you do, you'll bring everyone in this apartment building down on your head."

"Maybe it's worth it," he said. "You ever think of that?" He yanked the hammer back. "Just keep running your mouth and we'll see what I do."

"What do you *want?*" She inched backward toward the windows.

"*You*," said Calvin. "Maybe you can't see what you've become, but I can. I'm gonna save you from yourself, even if you don't want to be saved." She was really scared now. He could tell by the way her mouth twitched. "God, how could you do it, Greta? How could you cut off your beautiful long hair just so you could look like some dyke's dead girlfriend? It's sick. Beyond sick!"

"You don't know anything, Calvin."

"No?" He grabbed her arm and forced her toward the door.

"I'm not going anywhere!"

"Oh yes you are." He shoved the gun hard into her ribs. "Keep your mouth zipped and act normal. I'm putting the gun in my pocket, but I can still use it. If you try to run, if you try to alert anybody about what's happening, I'll shoot you. I will, Greta, I swear. You know why?"

She shook her head.

"Because I love you. More than anything in this world. And I don't give a damn what your reasons are for doing what you're doing. I'd rather see you dead than end up some lesbian's twisted whore."

Calvin made Greta drive the van to his motel. He sat in the backseat and held the gun on her the entire time. She looked over at it a few times, tried to get him to talk, but Calvin told her to shut up. He needed to think. He hadn't intended to grab her from her apartment, but now that it was done, he could see that it was the right thing to do.

Once inside the motel room he ordered her to lie down on the bed.

"Why?" she said, looking startled. "Calvin, no!"

"Face down." He shoved her toward it.

"You said you loved me. This isn't how you treat someone you love."

"Lie down!" When she still refused to cooperate, he picked her up and dropped her face-first on the bed. She struggled to get away, but she was too scared of the gun to push him too far.

"Calvin, just think a second. You don't want to do this."

Stripping off a piece of duct tape from a roll on the dresser, he straddled her, pulled her arms behind her back and wrapped the tape around her wrists. "Now, turn over."

"That's too tight. It will cut off my circulation."

"No it won't. I know what I'm doing." He didn't have a choice, he had to make it tight. He dragged her up against the pillows.

"Calvin, talk to me!"

He sat down on the bed next to her, touching her face. "It's going to be okay now, babe. It's like . . . like you've been brainwashed. But I'm going to deprogram you. You've heard of that, right? Just remember I'm the good guy. You may not like what I do at first, you may even fight me, but we'll find the old Greta. The real Greta. She's still in there." His hand grazed her breasts.

"Calvin, please!"

"You used to love me."

She stared at him, her lower lip quivering.

"You used to like it when I touched you."

"Not like this," she pleaded.

His hand moved lower, unzipped her jeans. He wanted her so bad he felt as if he'd blow apart if he didn't take her—right here, right now. It had been too long. She had to want it, too.

She tried to squirm away, but he held her down, covering her body with his. Burying his hands in her hair, he said, "If you fight me, it'll only make it worse. I want this to be good for both of us. This is part of the deprogramming." He tried to kiss her, but she kept thrashing her face from side to side.

"Okay, be like that." He ripped open her blouse.

"God," she cried.

"You want it rough, that's what you'll get."

When he was finally done, he rolled over on the bed next to her, his heart hammering inside his chest. He'd never come that hard before, never felt so turned on in his entire life. "God, but I love you, Greta." He looked over at her. She was crying so softly he could barely hear her. Her eyes were squeezed shut.

"I hate you," she whispered, her body shuddering.

Calvin fixed his eyes on the ceiling. It was hard for him to see her like this. It wasn't what he wanted. But in time, she'd see the wisdom in what he was doing.

"This is tough love, Greta. You'll thank me one day." He lay there for a few minutes, fighting the urge to sleep. Finally, sliding one hand behind his head, he said, "Tomorrow, I drive up to Fergus. I close on the farmhouse in the morning. I'll need to leave at first light. But I'll be back by mid-afternoon. And then we can officially start the rest of our lives together. Oh, Greta, you're gonna love this place. It's got a humongous kitchen, three bedrooms, a bathroom that needs a little work, but hell, I can take care of that in a couple of weekends." Turning on his side, he stroked her arm. "And there's this big garden patch out back. Already plowed and ready for seed. I figure we can plant all kinds of stuff. Corn. Peas. Tomatoes. I suppose you'll want flowers. The place sits on forty-three acres, so it's real private. Just what I want—what you want, too. Right, hon?"

Her head was turned away. He couldn't hear her response.

"I said, *right, hon?*"

"Right."

"We'll head up there tomorrow night. God, it will be so great." He smiled. A moment later, he pushed off the bed. "You hungry?"

She looked up at him with swollen eyes.

"Sure you are. I think I'll go get us a pizza and some beer. I'll even have them put mushrooms on it. I hate that prehistoric crap, but I know you love them, and I want you to be happy." He kissed her on the forehead.

Before he left, he wrapped her ankles with the duct tape. She didn't resist. "That's good, babe. I think we're already making some progress."

Flipping open his billfold, he saw all the money from last night. "You know, instead of beer, maybe I'll pick us up some champagne. What do you say? We've got lots to celebrate."

She stared straight ahead and didn't respond.

"*Right,* Greta?" he said again.

"Sure," she said, turning her face to the wall.

33

That afternoon, as Jane and Cordelia drove out Highway 12 on their way to Willmar, Jane brought up the subject of A. J. Nolan.

"Hey, I used to know a guy by that name," said Cordelia. "He a cop?"

"He used to be. He's a P.I. now. How could you possibly know the man?"

"Remember when I lived in that duplex in Powderhorn? I was active in the Powderhorn Community Council. So was Nolan's wife, May. She was a real firecracker. Beautiful, too. Big mouth. Smart. A winning combination in my book. Did you get a chance to meet her?"

"He said she died."

"God, I'm sorry. That's a big loss. I always figured she'd be governor one day. I guess I lost track of her when I moved to Linden Lofts. I knew May better than Nolan, but I liked them both."

"What's the A.J. stand for?"

She shrugged. "No idea. He prefers people to call him 'Nolan,' so that's what I did."

Jane took the next few minutes to fill Cordelia in on the information Nolan had given her. Cordelia seemed interested but distracted. It didn't take long for Jane to find out why.

Half an hour out of the Twin Cities, Cordelia began to sputter non-stop about the man who'd accosted the front bumper of her Hummer yesterday evening. "And then!" she said, flinging her right arm out and nearly smacking Jane in the face, "he pulls a rifle on me!"

Jane ducked away from the hand. Driving with Cordelia, when she was in a "state," could be dangerous. "You shouldn't have chased him."

"If I *hadn't* chased him, I wouldn't have learned where he lived. And if I didn't know that, my lawyer couldn't sue him for emotional distress. It was a *ghastly* evening, Janey, one I hope never to repeat."

Jane glanced at Mouse in the backseat. He was sitting up, looking out the window, sniffing the sweet springtime air as it rushed past. Sometimes Jane wished she were more like him, always eager for each new day to begin, so trusting, sure that the day would be an adventure full of fascinating surprises. Even if all he did was walk around the lake and sleep by the fireplace in her office, he was content. He saw the world flat on, without all the torturous nuances. Maybe, in the end, he knew more about living than she did.

Cordelia snapped her fingers. "You're not paying attention."

"I am," said Jane. "Have you ever heard about road rage?"

"Are you talking about me or the little guy in the silver van."

Jane turned to look at her. "He was a little guy in a silver van?"

"Didn't I just say that?"

"Describe him."

"Oh, I don't know. Maybe late twenties, early thirties. It was dark, you know. I'm not a camera."

"What color hair?"

"I'd say dark brown or black. He had a beard."

"Stocky?"

"Very. Pumped, I'd call it. A real muscle queen."

"You never told me where this accident happened."

"No, I never did."

"Cordelia!"

"Don't shout, Janey. I could drive into a tree."

"I'll say this slowly. *Again*. Where . . . did . . . you . . . have . . . the . . . accident?"

"On a street."

"I'm not playing twenty questions. Tell me where it was!"

"In front of Greta's apartment," mumbled Cordelia. "So there. Fling me into outer darkness. Condemn me to eternal damnation."

"What were you doing there?"

"Oh, just enjoying the evening."

"In your camouflage fatigues?"

"The two aren't mutually exclusive, you know." With great dignity, she reached up and adjusted the rearview mirror.

"You were spying on her, right?"

"Well, if *I* was, so was *he*," she said indignantly. "We were both in the bushes with binoculars."

Jane turned her head slowly. "You were *what?*"

"I can't say what he was doing there, but *I* was looking out for your best interests."

"In the bushes?"

"Right."

"You're . . ."

"Amazing? Daring? Plucky? Fearless?"

"The sentence I had in mind contained the words 'screwy' and 'busybody.'"

Cordelia looked down her nose at Jane, then returned her gaze to the road.

It had to be Calvin, thought Jane. Greta had been so certain that he was gone for good, out of her life, but here was proof that he was still around.

"I know who he is," said Jane. "In case you're interested, it was Greta's ex-boyfriend. From what I know about him, you're lucky he didn't use that rifle on you."

Cordelia's eyes moved sideways. "Really?"

"Yes, really."

"Because I followed him back to his motel. I almost went up and knocked on the door."

"Where's he staying?"

"At the Woodlake Motel on Lyndale. A real dump, if you ask me." She nodded at the sign on the side of the road. "Which exit do I take?"

Jane consulted her map. "The next one. DeWitt lives in Willmar but teaches in Grass River. Take 67A. I'll direct you to the high school."

"How do you know he'll be there?"

"I called, asked some general questions. He teaches algebra and geometry. He's done at three." Jane checked her watch. "We've got about fifteen minutes."

"Piece of cake," said Cordelia, patting the Hummer's dashboard.

After getting lost—twice—they pulled into a lot across from the school, half an hour late. The building looked old but well cared for. On the west side of the four-story brownstone was a football field surrounded by bleachers. A newer, one-story addition jutted off the east side of the school. Students were milling around on the sidewalk. A few walked toward the parking lot to get in their cars. It looked like the exodus from the building was pretty much over.

"I hope he's still there," said Cordelia, climbing out of the front seat.

Jane told Mouse to stay and be a good boy. She gave him a large Milkbone and then hopped out herself. "Cross your fingers that he'll talk to us."

"What we need are fake credentials. If we could flash a badge, we could get in anywhere."

"Yes. And maybe when they catch us, they'd let stay in the same jail cell."

"You are so negative sometimes. Now, I have no idea what your strategy is, but I'm sick of getting nowhere. Far as I'm concerned, De-Witt's our boy. I'm not taking any prisoners, Janey, I'm loaded for bear."

"And you can mix metaphors with the best of them."

"Right."

Cordelia marched across the street and entered the building first, with Jane following close behind.

"We can't exactly demand that he talk to us," said Jane.

"Just watch me."

"Cordelia, stop a minute."

"What?" She whirled around.

"Dial the melodrama down just a little, okay?"

"You're too cautious."

"Except when I'm not."

"Precisely."

Jane would rather have driven to see Frank DeWitt on her own.

Cordelia always complicated these "interrogations," although Jane had to admit that she occasionally stumbled onto something important. And no matter what she wore, she made a visual splash. Today's choice of clothes was more like a belly flop. She wore a bright, paisley-patterned scarf dress drenched in long red fringe, extra-large gold hoop earrings, and three-inch red leather pumps, shoes that caused her to tower over mere mortals. Jane had no idea how she managed to walk on stilts in her tiptoes. As far as she was concerned, stiletto heals should be an Olympic event. It might be kind to think that Cordelia didn't realize how intimidating her size and general appearance could be, but the truth was, she did. She cultivated it.

"The woman I talked to on the phone said he was in room 109," said Jane.

"Right there," said Cordelia, pointing at an open door.

The classroom was empty except for a young man sitting at the front desk, writing in a notebook.

"He's too young to be DeWitt," whispered Jane.

"Unless he's had a ton of cosmetic surgery," said Cordelia.

Jane rolled her eyes.

"Well, you never *know*. This may be the wilderness, but vanity lives everywhere."

Jane started through the doorway just as Cordelia did. They became momentarily stuck.

"Will you get out of my way," grunted Cordelia.

Hearing the commotion, the young man looked over at them.

Jane backed up. "After you," she said, waving her hand to the door.

"Thank you," said Cordelia using her mellifluous Queen Elizabeth voice. Head held high, she entered the classroom.

The young man stood. "Can I help you?"

Cordelia yanked her dress back into place. "Yes, dear boy, you can."

Jane smiled at him. "We're looking for Frank DeWitt. Is he still around?"

"Yeah. He's just down the hall helping a girl with her locker. Guess it wouldn't open." He spoke to Jane, but kept stealing glances at Cordelia. "I'm Tim Dewitt, his son."

Jane tried to hide her surprise. "Nice to meet you. I'm Jane Lawless. And this is—"

"C. M. Thorn," said Cordelia, looking around the room.

Jane had never heard Cordelia introduce herself that way before. Glancing down at the desk, she saw that Tim had been doodling the same shape, over and over again—two thick spirals connected by a straight line.

$$\Upsilon\!\!\Upsilon$$

"Are you an artist?" she asked.

"Hardly." He sat back down. "It's just a form I see floating around in my mind. Ever since I was a kid." Pressing the palm of his hand against his eye, he added, "I never used to be able to draw it. But in the last few weeks, it's become totally clear to me. Odd, huh?"

Cordelia moved over to the desk. "Looks like a glyph."

"A what?" said Jane.

"A symbol. Probably astrological. I'd say it represents Aires. The Ram. I could be wrong, but I doubt it." Her attention was drawn to an algebraic equation on the chalkboard. "Heavens," she gasped.

"It's algebra," said Jane.

"It's not *human*."

Jane had so many questions she wanted to ask Tim, but it seemed beyond strange to just start grilling him out of the blue about his memories of the Simoneau murders.

Frank sailed into the room a few seconds later. "Well, that's done," he said, wiping a smudge of black off his hand with a handkerchief.

He was a frail-looking man with a high voice. Not exactly the kind of guy you'd peg for a murderer.

"Anybody ever tell you you look like Peter Yarrow," asked Cordelia, touching a fingertip to her eyebrow.

"Who?" asked Frank.

"The thin guy with the mustache and the fluffy hair who sings with the folk group Peter Paul and Mary."

"Oh," said Frank, smiling pleasantly. "I know who you mean. No, nobody's ever said that before."

Jane figured he was in his mid-fifties. He was dressed in tan chinos and a yellow oxford cloth shirt. Instead of a regular tie, he wore a bow tie—the clip-on variety.

"Is there something I can do for you?" he asked, looking at Cordelia.

"I've gotta run," said Tim, closing his notebook.

"Oh, okay," said Frank. "But let's eat out tonight. You feel like Mexican? Italian?"

"How about the Green Mill."

"Great."

"Um, Dad, I've got some stuff to do before I head up to Minneapolis on Saturday. Could I meet you at the restaurant?"

Frank's eyes lost their softness. "I thought you decided to help your uncle with that house over in Spicer."

"I talked to him. He said he won't need me for at least two more weekends. Come on, Dad. I want to go see Auntie Bernie and Uncle Laurent again. I'm a big guy. They can't hurt me. I know you don't understand, but I like them. They're nice to me. They're like little children, kind of simple."

"We'll talk about it later," said Frank, cutting him off. "I'll make reservations for six."

"Fine. Nice meeting you Ms. Lawless. C.M." He grinned at Cordelia as he passed her on his way out.

Frank turned to watch him go. When he finally switched his attention back to Jane and Cordelia, he looked at them hard. "Which one of you is Jane Lawless."

"That would be me," said Jane, surprised that he knew her full name.

"Why is that so familiar to me?" He thought for a moment, sitting down on the edge of his desk. "Oh, sure. Bernadette wrote me about you. Said you'd been to the mansion. She mentioned that your partner had helped her sell her house back in the late eighties."

"That's right," said Jane.

He slid his hands into his pockets. "And something else. What was it?" He looked down. "Oh, yeah. You found one of Marcel Simoneau's derringers in your partner's purse."

"It was briefcase," said Cordelia. "You've got a good memory."

"Actually, I do," he said. "Sometimes it's a curse."

"I was hoping you might have a few minutes to talk to us," said Jane.

He checked his watch. "I need to start our Math Club in ten minutes. But I'm all yours until then."

Cordelia perched on one of the student desks, but Jane continued to stand.

"If you've come to talk to me about the Simoneau murders, I'm afraid I don't have much new to add."

"Let us be the judge of that," said Cordelia, moving into interrogation mode.

Jane cringed. "I've been trying to understand why my partner had that gun. It's what got me involved in, well, in doing this research into the murder case. Christine wasn't a thief. And she hated firearms. As I've been working to figure out why she had it, something else dropped into my lap." She explained briefly about the *Iron Girl*.

Frank listened attentively but made no comment.

"The more I dig around, the more convinced I've become that the justice system put the wrong man behind bars."

"Do you have proof of his innocence?"

"We have," said Cordelia, giving him a steely-eyed stare.

"The problem is," said Jane, "I'm not sure it's enough to make the police reopen the case."

Frank pushed his glasses back up to the bridge of his nose. "I never believed Haynes did it. But I won't lie to you. I was relieved when the police stopped questioning me and centered all their attention on him. In case you didn't know, Haynes and I were the two prime suspects." He studied Jane for a few seconds. "Have you talked to Alice Cathcart?"

"A few days ago."

"So I assume she told you about Camille Simoneau and all the trouble she was causing me back then."

"They weren't minor issues," said Cordelia.

"No, you're right. I can't I wasn't happy to have Camille disappear from my life, though I would hardly wish murder on my worst enemy. The police needed a strong motive because they had so little physical evidence. In the end, they must have decided that watch, the one they found in Dexter's desk, was at least something they could point to, something tangible they could hold up in front of a jury. And, of course, Haynes was black. I'm sorry to say, I don't think that worked in his favor."

"If Dexter didn't do it, and you say you didn't," said Cordelia, her eyes compressed into tiny, laserlike slits, "then who did?"

"I wish I knew. At the time, I suppose I wondered most about Laurent. He always needed money, and mommy was always there to give it to him. Except, it was never very much—never enough, I'm sure."

"Did Laurent ever threaten her?"

"He wasn't stupid. As I understand it, he had a business in Florida. That was his main source of income, but he came back to stay at the mansion fairly frequently. I thought he was a horrible man. He might be nice to Tim now, but when my son was little, he was mean as the dickens. Thought Tim was a nuisance, always making too much noise. If Tim left a toy on the floor, Laurent would stomp it to pieces. He had a nasty temper and very little self-control."

"What about Bernadette?"

He shrugged. "Bernie's just plain eccentric. I didn't know her all that well because she was quite private. But she was always very vocal about her creative sensibilities. She's a writer, you know."

"We've heard that, yes," said Cordelia, sounding more and more like Joe Friday.

"I never understood why she wanted to sell her house," said Jane. "I would think that a woman in her forties wouldn't much like moving back in with her mother."

"Oh, that house, the one on Irving Avenue, never really belonged to Bernie. Camille owned it. And one day she just up and decided to sell. Told Bernadette to pack her bags and move into the mansion. Bernie was pretty passive. She did what she was told."

"But she must have resented being tossed out of her house," said Jane.

"I never heard her say anything about it. But then, like I said, she was quiet. Bookish."

"You didn't have much of an alibi for the night of the murders," said Cordelia, pulling a toothpick out of her purse and sticking it in her mouth.

"No, you're right. Alice was gone that night. I wanted to take Tim over to Loring Park, maybe buy him an ice cream on the way back. A real guy's night out. But when I got home from work, I found that he had a mild fever. I felt it was best that he stay in. The cook was taking care of him, so I left. I hated spending time in that mausoleum. I walked over to the park and had dinner somewhere along the way. Can't recall now, but I had the receipt. Gave it to the police. I spent an hour or so at the Walker looking at the artwork. Oh, and I bought Tim a book in the gift shop. I had the receipt for that, too. But, of course, the murders occurred around eight. The last receipt was for seven-thirty. I could easily have returned to the house by then. It wasn't far. But I didn't," he added, looking straight at Cordelia. "I really wish I could help you more, but that's all I know." He glanced up at the clock on the wall. "Better get going. I don't want to be late for our Math Club."

Jane thanked him for his time, all the while feeling deeply thwarted. Of all the potential suspects, Frank DeWitt seemed the most normal. She simply couldn't picture him as a killer.

"Oh, by the way," added Cordelia, "don't make any plans to leave town until our investigation is complete. We might need to talk to you again."

Frank frowned and grinned all at the same time. "Of course not. And I promise not to make any fast moves."

"Good," said Cordelia. "Jane? Come. Our business here is done."

Christine

August 27, 1987

10:12 P.M.

The night was starlit and soft as Christine and Jane sat on the dock in front of the lodge. They hadn't talked much on the way up. Christine needed time to think, and Jane needed time to cool off. As long as she stayed angry, Jane could hold herself together. Christine understood that. She also understood that Jane wouldn't be able to hold on to it much longer.

Gazing silently up at the night sky, Jane said, "You cold?"

"A little."

She ran back to the car and returned with a blanket. Draping it over their shoulders, they huddled together.

"I can smell fall in the air," said Christine. It was the sharp, dry sent of autumn that she loved so much. "Maybe we can go somewhere special for Christmas. Paris. Or northern Italy. We've got the money."

"I'd like that," said Jane. "Just the two of us."

"I've never been to Morocco. I hear it's beautiful."

"I'm sure my aunt would welcome us if we wanted to stay at her cottage. We've never been to England. Well, at the same time."

"I'd like that," said Christine. "Anywhere we go will be great, as long as we're together."

Jane looked out at the water.

"We can shop at Harrods," said Christine.

"Oh, I know lots better places to shop than that."

"You'll have to show me your England, Jane."

"I'm not sure it's there anymore. We'd have to travel up to Scotland, for sure. I love it there. It's like no other place on earth."

"Long walks on the heath."

Jane smiled.

"You could bring me armloads of heather."

"We could try to find the real *Wuthering Heights*."

"And live there for a thousand years," said Christine.

"A thousand years," repeated Jane, looking wistfully up at the moon. "Robbie Burns is one of my favorite poets. I could recite his poetry to you."

"You've memorized it?"

"Some of it."

"Why didn't I ever know that?"

Jane shrugged.

"What's your favorite?"

"Oh," she said, "there are so many."

"Pick one."

Jane felt for Christine's hand under the blanket. "You have to imagine I have a Scottish accent."

"Okay."

She cleared her throat. "Yon banks and hills of bonnie Doon, / How can you bloom so fresh and fair? / And little birds, how can you chaunt / With me so weary . . . full o' care?"

"Go on," said Christine, sensing that Jane wanted to stop.

"You'll break my heart, you warbling birds / That wanton thru the flow'ry thorns / You remind me of departed joys / Departed . . . never to return. / Oft did I rove by bonnie Doon / To see the rose and woodbine twine / And every bird sang of its love / As fondly once I sang of mine."

Jane's voice cracked.

"That's beautiful. Is there more?"

"A little."

"Finish it," said Christine, her eyes moving away.

Holding tight to Christine's hand, Jane continued, "With lightsome heart I pulled a rose / Full sweet from off its thorny tree / But my first lover stole that rose / And, ah! has left its thorns with me."

After a few seconds, Christine said, "Why'd you pick that one?"

"No reason."

"Is that how you feel?"

"No. I don't know." There was no anger or resentment in her voice.

Bowing her head, Christine watched the waves foaming around the dock posts. "I had a reason for not telling you right away."

"You said that. But you didn't say what it was."

"It was selfishness, Jane. Pure and simple. I admit it. I knew you'd try to pressure me to have the chemo, do the radiation, and I couldn't stand the idea that whatever time I had left would be spent sick as a dog, watching the light go out of your eyes, every day, a little more. More than anything, it was that. Your eyes. I knew I wasn't strong enough to watch you watching me. I thought there was time. There is time, Jane. I planned to tell you tonight, after we got home from Molly and Aaron's. I quit my job today."

"You did?"

"Can you understand that keeping my life as normal as possible was my lifeline. Doctors aren't God. I've been doing Eastern medicine, seeing an acupuncturist. Maybe I'll live to be an old lady and you'll get sick of me."

"Not funny."

"I know. I'm sorry." She felt a sudden crushing fatigue. "I don't know how much time I have left. Nobody does."

"But . . . you've lost so much weight in the last couple of months. That can't be good."

"I won't lie to you. Not anymore. The cancer's spread. I talked to my doctor last week."

"How long?" said Jane, her jaws tightening.

"He doesn't know."

"What did he say? Exactly."

"A month. Six at the most."

She turned and kissed Christie fiercely.

They held on to each other for a long time, crying at first, then listening to the rise and fall of each other's breathing as it evened out. It was the chill night air that finally drove them inside.

As the first hazy morning light appeared over the lake, Christine and Jane finally fell asleep. They were exhausted from feeling helpless, from holding each other and crying, from staring into a blizzard of darkness with no light to guide them. They'd stumbled into a place deeper than dreams, where logic meant nothing, and life seemed suspended over a great liquid silence.

275

When Christine finally woke, it was close to noon. Sunlight filled the small room. It was so strong and bright, she could almost taste it. But then that fuzzy, seasick feeling settled back over her. Easing out of bed, she found her slippers and robe and shuffled into the kitchen. The coffee was on, but Jane and the dogs had gone out. A note was propped against the salt and pepper shakers on the kitchen table.

"Couldn't sleep. Took the dogs for a walk. Back soon. Jane."

Christine was glad for the reprieve. A fragile stillness seemed to have settled over her. She wasn't sure how long it would last. Pouring herself a mug of coffee, she was just about to sit down on the couch when the phone rang. It startled her. Since yesterday, her life had turned upside down. Phones didn't seem like they should be part of her world anymore.

Picking up the receiver, she said, "Hello?"

"Christine? Is that you?"

"Philip?"

"Hey, I've got some great news."

She remembered now that she'd given him a couple of numbers where he could reach her. "What's going on?"

"Dexter and I told my grandmother last night about our relationship. And Christine, she was okay with it! I mean, she wasn't happy. She thinks it's wrong, but she didn't toss us out. She even hugged us."

"You were both there?"

"Yeah. We felt like we should tell her together."

Christine was incredibly happy for them. "Congratulations."

"That's one hurdle done. One to go."

"Good luck with . . . well, with whatever it is." In the background, she could hear shouting. "Where are you?"

"At my grandmother's house."

"Who's yelling?"

"Uncle Frank. He's really pissed at my grandmother. It started at breakfast, and now he's back for round two. I don't know all the details, but I guess my grandmother is trying to leverage the situation so that she has some say in how Timmy gets raised."

Whatever it was, it sounded ugly. "Maybe you better duck and cover."

"Yeah, good idea. I'll be in touch. The Iron Girl's safe, right?"

"Safe and sound. Just tell me when you want it back."

"I will. Thanks, Christine. Talk to you soon."

Half an hour later, Christine had just come out of the bedroom when Jane entered the lodge with the dogs. Holding on to the back of a chair, Christine said, "We have to go home."

Jane held her eyes. "Are you okay?"

"No."

Anxiety flooded her face. "I'll pack."

"No, let's just get in the car and go. I need to get to a hospital."

She didn't understand what was happening inside her body, but she knew it was bad. She watched a gust of panic blow through Jane's eyes and wanted desperately to ease it, but she couldn't, any more than she could erase the trapdoor feeling that had opened up inside her stomach.

34

That night, after the dinner meal was over, Jane eased onto a stool in the pub. Barnaby, the evening bartender, was deep in conversation with a guy at the end of the bar. Jane could easily have pulled herself a brew, but she was content to just sit and do nothing until he was free. Except, as she reached for a basket of popcorn, the conversation between Barnaby and the customer suddenly grew louder.

"I'm *sorry*, sir, but I can't serve you another drink."

Jane leaned back and tried to catch a better look at the guy he was talking to. To her amazement, she saw that it was Bill McBride. Even in the amber glow of the pub lights—lights that softened the world, created a sense of warmth and firelight—his face appeared beet red and bloated.

"Don't tell me what I can and can't do, *boy*. I want another Cutty and water. Make it a double."

Barnaby could handle even the meanest drunk. He was the unofficial pub bouncer. But in this instance, Jane felt she should intervene.

"Bill, hi," she called as she walked toward to him. "What seems to be the problem?"

"Well, looky here." He tilted backward, nearly falling off the stool. "I figured I might run into you if I sat here long enough."

"If you wanted to talk to me, you could always ask at the reception desk."

"Yeah, well. Thought I'd have a drink first."

Barnaby held up four fingers.

Four drinks to screw up his courage. Interesting.

"Yeah," he continued, wiping a hand across his mouth. "Thought maybe we should have a little chat." His words were somewhat slurred, but a man his size could easily have four drinks without sliding under the table.

She nodded to Barnaby that she'd take care of him. "Let's get out of here. Go somewhere more private."

"Right. Good idea. Lead the way, McDuff. I shall shamble along behind you."

Because of the early-morning rain—and more showers in the late afternoon—the deck was closed to diners. The sun had come out just before dark, so Jane took him upstairs. On the way through the dining room she grabbed a towel from one of the wait stations and asked a waiter to bring two coffees outside.

It was a thoroughly, disgustingly soggy evening, with temperatures in the low eighties—an early taste of summer, the only season of the year Jane hated. She was glad she had on a thin red cotton blouse. Her powder blue jeans were also pretty thin. Worn might be a better word. The breeze off the lake felt like being pummeled with a wet sock.

Seeing Bill about to sit on a chair with a puddle in it, Jane rushed to stop him. "Let me clean that off first," she said. He was wearing dark suit pants and a white dress shirt with the collar open and the tie pulled away from his neck. She tipped the chair sideways and wiped it down. While she was at it, she mopped the table and another chair for herself. "There," she said, making herself comfortable. Bill did the same.

His eyes strayed briefly to the water. "You've got a perfect setting for a restaurant, you know that? In my younger days, I worked as a line cook. That was in Spokane, before I moved my wife and kids to Minneapolis. No money in being a line cook. A friend up here was in real estate. Said if I got my license, I could work for him. And I made a success of it, too. Course, I lost my wife somewhere along the way. Mainly because I'm a bastard. Did you know I was a bastard, Jane?"

The waiter came outside with the coffee. He placed linen napkins on the table, the cups next to them.

"Yeah," said Bill, looking at the coffee with resignation. "Suppose I could use some of that."

"Thanks, Scott," said Jane.

As the waiter returned inside, Bill looked up at the canopy of stars above their heads. "I'm an old man now. What a fucking mess I've made of my life."

Jane wondered if this conversation would be nothing but a drunken walk down memory lane.

"So," said Bill, touching the coffee cup with the tips of his fingers, "have you learned why Christine had Marcel Simoneau's derringer?"

"Not yet."

"You still digging into the Simoneau murders then?"

She nodded.

He picked up the coffee and took a taste. Making a sour face, he set the cup back down. "Plan on talking to Laurent and Bernadette?"

"I'm sure I will," said Jane. "I drove to Grass River this afternoon to see Frank DeWitt."

"That right? He have anything new to add?"

"Not much."

He stared at the coffee, losing himself for a few seconds. With a start, his head snapped up. "Yeah, right, well. Got any opinions about Dexter Haynes? Think he did it?"

"No. I think he's innocent. In fact, I'm sure of it."

She had the sense that he was making small talk, but that he *was* headed somewhere.

With a sigh, he yanked a folded take-out menu out of his shirt pocket and fanned his face. "Bernie called me a couple of days ago. Asked me to stop by and do a market analysis on the mansion."

"She planning to sell?"

"Far from it." He paused, shifting in his chair. "I didn't want to go, and yet . . . I did. I was curious to see her again after all these years. But that house, ugh. It gives me the willies." Spreading out his fingers and studying them, he added, "Bernie and I go way back. I thought . . . I mean, I might as well tell you this because, if you talk to her, she'll probably blurt it out, and then you'll think, well, I mean, just cut her off, okay? Tell her you already know."

"Know what?" said Jane, wondering if he'd ever get to the point.

"That we were lovers. Back then. Long time ago, I know, but when I went over there, she acted like she wanted to get together again. It made me sick to my stomach. To think I put my marriage in danger for that *hag*."

"Not attracted anymore?" It was a rude comment, but she didn't figure he'd notice.

"Hell, I'm not that hard up. You know, Jane, Christine never knew about my relationship with Bernie. Neither did Camille. God, she would have fired my ass in a millisecond if she'd found out."

"But she never did?"

He shook his head. "Nope, but I think Laurent knew. He found out about the other men, too. Bernie had a, shall we say, *lively* social life. Laurent enjoyed dangling a sword over her head, threatening to tell mommy dearest *all*."

Jane examined the comment. Was it a motive? It might be a motive for secrecy, but losing Camille Simoneau as a client was hardly a reason for murder. Jane wasn't even sure why he was telling her about it.

Bill pushed the coffee cup away. He picked up the napkin and used it to wipe the sweat off his face. "God, it's humid." He rolled up his shirtsleeves, resting his forearms on the table. "I'm not ready for summer yet."

Jane's eyes fell to a heavy tattoo on his arm, just above his wrist. It wasn't large—maybe two inches in diameter.

"What?" he said, apparently noting some change in her expression.

"Interesting tattoo."

He rubbed his arm. "Yeah. Got it in college. Seemed like the manly thing to do at the time."

"What's it mean?"

"It's my birth sign: Aries. The Ram."

Jane's eyes rose to his. "No kidding." It was the exact same symbol Tim DeWitt had been doodling—the one he'd seen floating around inside his head since he was a child. There had to be a reason that symbol had burned itself into his memory. Nobody would be bedeviled by such a nonsensical shape for his entire life unless it was significant in some major way.

"Why are you looking at me like that?" asked Bill.

"The tattoo."

281

"Yeah? What about it?"

"Tim DeWitt remembers one just like it from when he was a child."

A tremor passed across his face. "Well, sure, he probably noticed it when I came over to talk to Camille. He was around all the time."

"The image of that tattoo has *haunted* him his entire life, Bill. There's got to be a reason, don't you think? And it's not because he casually noticed it one day when he was three years old."

"Doesn't mean anything. Not a damn thing."

If that was true, then why was Bill sweating bullets.

Sitting up straight, he said, "Are you suggesting . . . you think I had something to do with those murders?"

A voice inside her told her to get the hell away from him. Fast. "I think it's time I got back inside. I've still got lots of work to do tonight."

As she rose to go, he grabbed her hand. "I didn't kill those people, Jane. You've got to believe me."

"I do," she said, pulling her hand free.

"Okay! Okay!" he said, half standing, half swaying. "I *was* there that night! Are you happy now? But it's not what you think."

"I don't think anything."

"Yes you do." He thunked back down on the chair. Swiping at his forehead with the napkin, he said, "I was with Bernie. We were in her bedroom having sex. Tim walked in on us. That's *all*. We thought we were alone. He must have seen the tattoo then."

It was all too convenient. She didn't believe a word of it. "Sure, okay."

"I haven't convinced you."

"Sure you have."

"Oh, God," he said, dropping his head in his hands. His chest heaved, as if he was having trouble breathing. "This is a nightmare. I should never have gone back to that house. It's all so humiliating." Looking up at her with pleading eyes, he said, "You think I'm lying."

"It's not important what I think."

"Yes it is! I've got to convince you. If I tell you the whole truth, will you promise not to tell the police?"

"If you didn't commit the murders, Bill, you've got nothing to be afraid of."

He scraped a hand across his eyes. "Oh God, you're so naive. If this got out, what I did, if it made the papers, I'd be finished in this town. I might as well close down my business and move to Siberia." Keeping his head lowered, he continued, "God, I'm so so *so* ashamed of myself."

She sat down. This sounded like something she wanted to hear.

He flicked his eyes to her, then away. "Have you ever been . . . addicted to anything, Jane?"

She shrugged. It was none of his business.

"Well, I have. I was addicted to Bernie, to what we did together, what she *did* to me. Do you get it now?"

"I'm sorry—"

"*Bondage,*" he said, gritting his teeth. "S and M. Do you get it *now?*"

She nodded.

"Bernie is a dominatrix. She was in great demand back then. For all I know, she still is. She could have made a spectacular living, but she did it for free. For some reason, she singled me out. I'd never messed with it before—or since. I mean, at first, the sex was tame, but she gradually drew me in deeper and deeper. It was like being hypnotized, fed a drug that was so addictive, you couldn't live without it. I couldn't stop myself. I thought when she moved to the mansion, it was all over. But I was wrong. It heated up even more. The idea that she was doing it in her mother's house, right under her mother's nose, excited her. She took over the attic, installed a hook in the ceiling. Nobody ever went up there—it was dusty and dirty, full of boxes, old furniture, trunks, and lots of spiders. I've always been terrified of spiders. Bernie used them as part of the . . . the game."

"How does Tim fit into this?"

He sniffed, swiped at his nose with the napkin. "The night of the murders, I was at the house. We thought everyone was gone. The cook was supposed to be looking after Timmy, but he must have walked off when she wasn't looking. Right then, I was hanging from the hook, naked, my arms chained behind me in what's called a 'love swing,' a black bag over my head. Bernie was . . ." He stopped, his expression hardening. "You don't need to know what she was doing. Timmy must have come in because I heard him crying, heard Bernie say something like 'Timmy, you can't be up here.' I can only imagine what he thought, how long he'd been standing there in the doorway. I just hung there until she got back. By then, she'd put on a bathrobe to cover the leather.

She told me I had to leave. I got dressed in a matter of milliseconds and flew down the back steps from the second floor. I always parked several blocks away from the house." He put a hand up to shield his eyes. "So I was there that night, Jane. I admit it. But I didn't kill anyone. I swear."

"What time was that?"

"I was back to the office by seven-thirty. I can prove it. The barber next door was just leaving. I asked him later, just in case, if he remembered the time. He did—right to the minute."

Jane recalled the account she'd read of a neighbor of the Simoneau's who'd seen a man come down the back steps on the night of the murders. She'd put the time between seven and seven-thirty. Here was proof that she'd actually seen someone. But it wasn't the murderer, it was Bill.

"Tim must have noticed the tattoo that night, Jane. I think he was scared as hell."

Jane could easily understand why Bill wanted to keep this a secret, and why it might have branded itself into the memory of a three-year-old in some garbled way.

"Please don't tell the police. If this got out, it would ruin my life."

If that was true now, it was true back then. Sex with a client's daughter might not rise to the level of serious motive, but this sure did. "You said Laurent knew about Bernie's social life. Did he know about the bondage?"

"No, I'm sure he didn't."

"Why?"

"Because Bernie would have told me. She didn't have a death wish."

Jane wasn't sure she was getting the full story, but the confession had cost him. He was drenched in sweat.

"Now do you believe me?" he asked. "I had nothing to do with those murders!"

"I believe you," she said, feeling she had no other choice but to lie. Whether she believed him or not was beside the point. This was information she needed to discuss with Nolan.

"And you won't tell the cops?"

"That never even crossed my mind."

"Thanks, Jane. You're a good soul. Just like Christine." He stood up and moved unsteadily over to the railing. Staring at the dark water for a few seconds, he said, "I refuse to go back to that house. Bernie can get herself another real estate agent. I'm done with her for good this time. She's poison. A black widow spider. No more Bernie Simoneau in my life ever again."

35

Jane paced back and forth in the Xanadu theater's lobby. "Where could she be? She promised to be here to shoot this."

Cordelia and Judah had their backs to her. They were watching the workmen, not wanting to miss even a moment of the demolition of the huge movie screen.

"It won't be as much fun as watching a skyscraper implode," said Cordelia, using her new binoculars to view the carnage up close.

"No," agreed Judah. "But there's something intriguing about destruction, isn't there? Building takes so much time, but endings, they can happen in a second."

The seats in the theater were gone. Once the screen was down, the real work of turning the Xanadu into a dinner and dance club would begin. This was a critical juncture. Jane couldn't believe Greta would forget, or blow off the shoot to go do something else.

"She would have called if she couldn't come," she muttered to herself.

Cordelia turned around. "Janey? The crew captain just signaled five minutes. We can't exactly make them wait for her to get here. Not at the price we're paying. Maybe I should run up to Snyders and buy one of those throwaway cameras. At least we'd have something captured on film."

"Let me call her one more time," said Jane. She took the cell phone out of the pocket of her leather jacket and pressed in the number. She'd left several messages in the last half hour. She waited through five rings until the voice mail picked up. Again. "Dammit." She'd also left a couple messages for Nolan, but he hadn't called back either. Apparently, everybody in the Twin Cities was either out or unavailable.

Judah turned to look at her. "I think Cordelia's right. Somebody better go buy one of those cameras. Maybe Greta will still get here in time, but if she doesn't, I'd hate to lose this."

Jane knew he was right.

On her way out the door, Cordelia stopped and placed a hand on Jane's shoulder. "Look, dearheart, I can see you're worried. But you shouldn't be. She's okay. She probably just misplaced her phone, got caught in traffic. There's a million reasons why she could've been delayed."

Jane was grateful that Cordelia didn't use this as another opportunity to trash Greta. "You're probably right. Thanks."

"For what?"

"For the kindness. For being a good friend."

Cordelia winked. "I'll save my venom for a more propitious moment—when you don't look so wired." She squeezed Jane's arm and took off out the door.

Greta never did show. Jane spent the lunch hour in her office talking by phone to a man named Inar Rosvall, a farmer who ran an organic berry farm in Anoka. He was a new supplier and she wanted to get the delivery schedule nailed down. She assumed she'd spend the rest of the day working at the restaurant. But as she said good-bye to Rosvall, a sense of dread hit her so hard, she switched off her desk light and left.

Ten minutes later, she pulled up in front of the Peoria. She buzzed Greta's apartment several times, but got no response. Greta's truck was parked outside, so she had to be around somewhere.

Jane pressed the buzzer, this time holding it down. She didn't care who it annoyed. An elderly woman poked her head out of the security door.

"Are you looking for the woman in 104?"

"Yes," said Jane, removing her sunglasses. "We had an appointment this morning, but she never showed."

"You a friend of hers?"

"That's right. I see that her truck's here." She turned to look at it.

The old woman opened the door a little wider. Jane could see now that she was wearing a pastel cotton housedress. Behind her thick glasses, her eyes looked sharp as an eagle's. "She left yesterday afternoon. I haven't seen her since."

"Was she alone?"

"No, she was with a young man."

A jolt of fear shook her hard. "Can you describe him?"

"Not terribly tall. Dark hair and beard. Unpleasant mouth. I didn't like the look of him at all. I've seen him a couple of times listening outside her door. He's got no business doing that." She paused to examine Jane a little more closely. "Your friend didn't seem too keen to go with him."

"Did you hear anything . . . where he might have taken her?"

"They had a fight in her apartment before they left, but I didn't catch what it was about."

"Thanks," said Jane. "You've been a big help." She raced back to her car. Calvin had taken Greta against her will, she was sure of it. Right about now Jane could have kissed Cordelia for that little spy mission she'd orchestrated the other night. Because of it, Jane had a place to start her search: Calvin's motel.

As she sped down Lyndale, the world around her felt electrified. She berated herself for waiting so long. She should have gone to Greta's apartment immediately, left the demolition photos to Judah and Cordelia. If Calvin had taken her yesterday, he had a twenty-four-hour head start. They could be anywhere by now.

A few minutes later, the Mini skidded to a stop outside the Woodlake Motel. Jane opened the door and jumped out. Her heart rate picked up even more when she saw Calvin's van parked outside unit 4. She didn't have a plan, she just knew she had to get inside. She was about to knock on the door when she saw that it was open a crack. Kicking it back, she saw Greta on the bed, her arms and legs bound with duct tape. Calvin was bent over her, his finger on her neck.

"Get away from her!" she shouted, bursting into the room.

Calvin whirled around.

That's when she saw it. The blood. The bed underneath Greta was soaked with it. A gun sat on the nightstand. Acting on instinct, she lunged for it.

Calvin just stood there looking stunned. He didn't even try to fight her for it.

"What did you do to her?" she screamed.

His eyes were filled with terrified confusion. "I . . . I . . ."

"You fucking psycho!" Adrenaline shook her hard. She held the gun in both hands, trying to keep it steady, fighting the urge to pull the trigger.

"She's dead," he whispered. "God, she's dead!"

"You killed her!"

"No way. No way!"

Jane's mind hit disconnect, then shifted into reverse. She was looking at Greta but seeing Christine. It was happening all over again. Christine was dead and she couldn't do a thing to change it. "Get down on your knees," she ordered in a voice she barely recognized as her own.

"What?"

"Do it!"

Dazed, he sank down next to a chair. "I didn't shoot her. I swear. I could never hurt her. I love her!"

"If you love her, why did you tie her up?"

"I . . . I couldn't let her leave. For her own good!"

Jane was finished talking to liars. She'd spent her entire life trying to be a good person, trying to lead a respectable life. For what? What sort of world was it when a young woman could die for no reason other than that she existed, that she liked the sun. Tears filled her eyes but refused to fall.

Calvin raised his arms. "Please, I just got back. I found her like that."

"Shut up! Shut the fuck up!"

"It's true. You gotta believe me."

She pulled back the hammer. Her finger curled around the trigger. This was how it would end, she thought silently. For him, and for me.

"No!" screamed Calvin, screwing his eyes shut. "God, I didn't do it!"

From the bed came a soft moan.

Jane's eyes shifted. With one hand still holding the gun, she moved over to the bed and touched Greta's neck, feeling for a pulse. "Jesus, she's alive!" Grabbing the phone, she punched in 911.

When the line picked up, Jane said, "My name's Lawless. I'm at the Woodlake Motel on Lyndale, just off 58th in south Minneapolis. A woman's been shot. Room 4. Get someone here fast. She's bleeding badly. And send the police. The guy who did it is still here."

When she looked over at Calvin, she saw that he'd wet his pants.

36

Jane sat in the surgery waiting room staring at a fish tank, hoping to get word soon on Greta's condition. She'd been allowed to ride in the ambulance on the way to the hospital, which meant the medical staff apparently looked upon her as an official person worthy of being kept in the loop. The EMTs had done everything they could to keep Greta alive, but her face was so pale Jane feared she'd lost too much blood to survive.

The two police officers who'd arrived at the motel a few minutes after her call stayed behind to cordon off the crime scene and question Calvin.

Jane felt incredibly juiced up, hyper. If she could just go for a run, she might be able to dissipate some of the energy eating away at her insides. But instead she watched the fish swim around the tank. They looked like they were searching desperately for something they'd lost. She identified with the feeling.

A few minutes later, Cordelia burst into the waiting area. She surveyed the room until she found the quiet corner where Jane was waiting. In an instant, she was by her side.

"Details," she said, her voice a mixture of concern, sympathy, and plain old curiosity.

Jane explained what had happened. When she got to the part about how pale Greta looked in the ambulance, she broke down.

Cordelia slipped her arm around Jane's shoulders. "She's young. Strong."

"But she lost so much blood."

Cordelia rubbed her back. "Keep holding good thoughts. I will, too."

"I almost killed him, Cordelia."

"Calvin?"

She nodded.

"You mean you *wanted* to."

"No. I mean I was about to pull the trigger when Greta started to moan. I thought she was dead. Calvin said she was. So I made him get down on his knees. I would have shot him, Cordelia. Another five seconds and he was dead."

Cordelia was silent for a moment. "Jane, that's just ridiculous."

She shook her head. "It made total sense to me. I mean, it all got stirred together in my mind. Greta. Christine. He deserved to die for what he did to them."

"You mean to Greta."

"Yes," said Jane, closing her eyes. "To Greta. God."

Cordelia continued to rub her back. "Janey, listen to me. I think you need to step back from this. All of it. You're not—" She hesitated. "Your mind's not tracking very well right now. Your feelings for Christine are too close to the surface."

Jane couldn't stop shivering. When she looked up, Nolan was pulling up a chair in front of her. "How did you know I was here?"

"I called him," said Cordelia.

"You okay?" he said, looking hard at Jane.

"Yeah."

"I drove over to the Woodlake Motel. Happens that I know the detective assigned to the case. Name's Vanloh. He's a good man. They've taken Calvin Dutcher into custody. He's being held on a kidnapping charge."

"If Greta doesn't make it, it will be murder," said Jane.

"Well, that remains to be seen. The gun Dutcher had in his possession was a thirty-eight Smith and Wesson. Ms. Hoffman was shot with a nine mil. They searched his van and the motel room, but couldn't find the weapon. And there's something else that points away from him. The bathroom screen was cut. Vanloh figures that's how the shooter got in. If Dutcher had wanted to off Ms. Hoffman, why break into the room? Course, they'll check his hands for gunshot residue, but even if they find it, it won't mean much. He had a gun. They're hoping to talk to Ms. Hoffman when she wakes up."

If she wakes up, thought Jane.

Nolan sat back in his chair and crossed his arms over his barrel chest. "I'd like to hear everything you know about Hoffman and Dutcher. Vanloh will want to hear it, too, but you can start with me. First off, do you think this is related to the Simoneau matter?"

Jane and Cordelia answered at the same time. Jane said no. Cordelia said yes.

"Okay, we got a difference of opinion here. Jane, you start."

She shifted her gaze to the fish tank. In a quiet voice, she told him what she knew. Cordelia couldn't wait to chime in with her two cents, which she did, as soon as Jane was finished.

"So Greta is a mystery woman," said Nolan.

"Not in my book," said Jane. "She's just someone who happens to look a lot like a woman I once loved." Out of the corner of her eye, Jane saw a doctor in green scrubs walk toward them. It was the same man she'd talked to on the way in.

"Ms. Lawless?"

Her heart jumped into her throat. "How's she doing?"

"Holding her own. We've listed her in critical condition. She lost a lot of blood."

They all rose from their chairs.

"Is she conscious?" asked Nolan.

The doctor glanced at him. "No. Not yet."

"How much damage was done?"

"She's lucky. The first bullet entered her chest and collapsed a lung, but passed through her body. The second shot did more damage. It nicked her liver. We've gone in and repaired what we could. She's resting now. Being transfused. My prognosis for her is guarded, but given her overall physical condition, if she makes it through the next twenty-four hours, I'd say she has a good chance for a full recovery."

"What are her chances of making it through the next twenty-four hours?" asked Jane.

He adjusted his glasses. "I can't answer that." Looking at Nolan, he said, "I assume the police will contact her family."

"She's from a little town near Fergus Falls," said Cordelia.

"I'll talk to the guy heading the case," said Nolan. "He'll take care of it."

"When can I see her?" asked Jane.

"I would expect sometime tomorrow. For the rest of today and tonight, I've directed the ICU to make sure she has no visitors, except for family, of course."

"Of course," said Jane, pretty sure the sarcasm didn't penetrate his scrubs.

The doctor nodded to everyone, then walked back down the hall.

Jane stuck her hands into the pockets of her leather jacket. If she couldn't see Greta, she had no desire to stay at the hospital.

"If Dutcher didn't shoot your friend," said Nolan, glancing at his watch, "who do you think did? Did she have any enemies?"

Jane shrugged. "Not that I know of."

"Just out of curiosity, did she seem overly interested in the Simoneau murders?"

"Not *overly* interested," said Jane. "But we did talk about it."

"Did she prod you to talk about it? Or did the subject just come up in conversation because it was on your mind."

To be honest, most of the time Greta did bring it up. "She asked questions."

"And you didn't find that odd?"

"No, I guess not." And then she remembered something. "I left you a couple of messages but you never called back."

"Here," he said, removing a card from his wallet and writing a number on the back. "That's my cell. I answer it day and night. What you had before is my office number." He handed the card over. "Did you call about something specific?"

She told him about the tattoo on Bill McBride's arm, explained everything she'd learned about his relationship with Bernadette—the bondage, his fear that Camille would find out, the fact that Tim had caught Bill and Bernadette in the act and seen the tattoo.

"McBride, huh?" said Nolan, chewing it over. "So that's what the hook in the ceiling was all about. Boy, you really hit the jackpot, Jane.

Good work. Bernadette Simoneau a dominatrix." He hooted. "You know, just when you think nothing can surprise you."

"What do you think it means?" asked Cordelia.

"Don't know. Gotta ruminate on it awhile."

Jane had a splitting headache. The fact that she'd almost killed a man didn't add much to her general sense of well-being. Nolan was under the impression that he was talking to a normal, rational human being. That wasn't the case. Maybe, all along the way, she'd been lying to herself about Greta, been willingly blind. But the effort it would take to give that theory serious consideration was enough to make her head crack apart.

"I'm not feeling very well," she said, rubbing her forehead.

"You've been through it today," said Nolan. "Look, I'll keep a close eye on Vanloh, let you know if I hear anything important. And let me do some checking into this McBride character. He's a wild card, far as I can see. We never investigated him, but he deserves a hard look."

"Thanks," said Jane.

"I'll be in touch."

After he was gone, Jane sat down and slumped against the back of the chair. Looking up at Cordelia, she said, "I need you to drive me back to the motel. I left my car there."

"Sure. Then what?"

"Then," said Jane, "I go home, put on the teakettle and fix myself a nice cup of tea and strychnine."

37

Where *were* you all day?" demanded Bernadette. She was sitting in the living room—her side of the house—eating from a plastic bowl of microwaved spaghetti.

Laurent grunted, lit a cigarette, and leaned against the archway. "Taking care of business."

"Specifically?"

"We needed to find a good graphic artist and a printer to do our brochures, right? I interviewed a couple today. Think I've got it all pretty much arranged. And I've already written the copy, so we can move on it fast."

"Except we don't have any money," said Bernadette, wiping some red sauce off her chin with a paper napkin. "Thanks to our brilliant businessman father who bought a bunch of fake paintings."

"Forget it, Bernie. We'll borrow against the house. Have you had any word from McBride?"

She tilted her head back and slurped a noodle into her mouth. "Not yet. I still don't like the idea of touching the house. It's the only asset we have left."

"Yeah, well, if we can't finance this new project, we'll have to borrow against it just to survive. You planning on tightening your belt, Bernie? I'm sure as hell not."

They'd cut their expenses to the bone, with the exception of the frills. The frills were what made them feel alive. Laurent still gambled, still bought sex when he was in the mood, and still visited his therapist. The ultimate triumvirate, thought Bernadette. By comparison, her frills these days—massages, spa treatments, books—were pure vanilla. She'd always figured she could sell a painting or two when the larder got completely empty, but now that door was closed. Laurent had come up with his idea in the nick of time.

Over the past few days, Bernadette had begun to realize that the feeling of revulsion she'd initially experienced about the murder house idea was more proper than real. She was as hot to trot as her brother was about turning the house into a museum of horrors for the masses to gobble. She couldn't change the past, so why get all sentimental over it? Nobody had ever waxed sentimental over *her*.

"Have you heard from Tim?" asked Laurent.

"He'll be here first thing in the morning."

"Good." He blew smoke rings into the air. "Has he told Frank about his plans to help us with the house?"

"I don't think so."

"Wussy boy."

"Bag it, okay? Timmy is the only family we have left."

"Right. Family. A lot of good our family has ever done us. Have you been working on an idea for the lawn sign?"

She stuffed another bite of spaghetti into her mouth. "I've made a few sketches."

"Let's see them."

"Not now. I'm eating dinner."

In exasperation, he flung his arms in the air. "When your princess-ness has a few moments to spare, let me know. I'll be in my room."

"Have fun," she said, cutting a meatball in half with her plastic fork.

A few minutes later Bernadette's cell phone trilled the opening strains of "The Stars and Stripes Forever." She'd bought the phone because of that specific ringer style. Wiping the grease off her hands with the dirty napkin, she popped the phone on. "Hello?"

"Oliver Hammond here."

"Mr. Hammond, it's good of you to call back."

"I have some good news and some bad news."

"Yes?" she said expectantly.

"The paintings I looked at the other day are unquestionably fake. But after studying the information you gave me on the provenance of each piece, I can assure you that the artwork your father purchased was authentic."

"You mean——"

"Somehow, Ms. Simoneau, someone substituted those deplorable reproductions for the real thing. In other words, you've been robbed. I think this is a matter for the police."

Bernadette's heart rate dialed up to hypersonic. She stumbled to her feet.

"Do you have any idea who might have done it?" asked Hammond.

"Gotta go. You've been a big help. Big help." She clicked the phone off, dropped it into the pocket of her sweater, then, in a voice that could be heard on the other side of the moon, she screamed *"LAURENT!! GET! DOWN! HERE!"*

This ball game was about to go nuclear.

The truss still worked perfectly. So did the crank and the winch. Laurent dangled from the hook in the attic ceiling, his face looking like a boil that was about to burst. All in all, it had been a rewarding hour of effort.

"You're insane!" shrieked Laurent.

"If I am, buddy boy, you better say your prayers."

Pain was next on the evening's agenda. Always the best part. She'd cut off his shirt and pants, just for old time's sake. But she'd left his skivvies on him. This was supposed to be painful for him, not for her. Thank God he wasn't a fighter—or, frankly, all that smart. Once she'd enticed him up to the attic and got the drop on him, the taser had knocked him out. After that, it was a piece of cake.

"What are you planning?"

"To get the truth, the whole truth, and nothing but the truth, so help you God."

"I've told you a dozen times, I don't *know* what happened to those paintings!" His eyes grew suddenly huge. "What's that? What are you doing?"

"Lighting a candle. It's dark in here."

The window faced west, and the sun was fading. The only light in the room came from a sixty-watt bulb ten feet to the right of the hook. She was surprised it still worked, although she'd never used it much. In years past, when she was at the height of her game, candles were the preferred method of illumination—thick white tapers, the kind you saw in churches.

"Okay, sure. Candles are good." He wheezed a couple of times. "Bernie? It wasn't me. You've got to believe that."

"Do I? Let's give it the torture test. See if you're singing the same tune in about, oh, ten seconds." She walked around behind him, where his hands were cuffed, and waved the flame under his thumb.

His base voice instantly turned lyric soprano. *"STaaaaaaaaa-OP!"*

"The truth, Laurent."

"Shit, *Bernieeeee!*"

She held the candle to his middle finger this time, giving it another couple of seconds.

"Fucking sadist!"

"You always were good at stating the obvious."

"Okay!" he screamed. "I'll tell you. Just take it away!"

She moved in front of him and waved the flame near his plaid boxer shorts.

"I did it. Okay? I took them." Sweat poured off his body.

"You're no fun at all. I haven't even drawn blood yet."

"Jesus, Bernie!"

"How?"

"What?"

"How did you do it?"

"Just let me down and I'll tell you everything. I promise. I'm a man of my word, Bernie, you know that."

She snorted so loud she nearly ruptured her sinuses.

"Let me down, okay? I'm your brother, for God's sake!"

"How . . . did . . . you . . . do . . . it? Simple question. All I want is a simple answer."

"Oh, all right." He wheezed a couple more times, then sniffed. "I had this buddy. He worked for a gallery in Tampa Bay, restored paintings and shit. I'd take a picture of the painting, then he'd produce one, and I'd make the switch."

"What did you do with the real paintings?"

"I couldn't sell them legally, so I sort of . . . I had to . . . there's this black market. . . . I didn't ever get paid the money they were really worth. But it was enough."

"You pig!" She held the candle to his toe.

"Bernie!!!!!"

"You not only stole from me, you stole from Timmy! He's all we've got left of this miserable family. How could you do that, Laurent? How *could* you?"

"Come on, sis. Screw Timmy. When he's twenty-one, he'll be rich. Do the calculations. I figure he'll be worth over eight million dollars. I'm supposed to weep for a guy like that?"

"What about *me*?"

"I'm sorry, Bernie. I'm a creep. But I'll make it up to you, I promise. Just let me down."

"When did you start this little foray into grand theft?"

"A couple months before Mother died. I was in a bind, Bernie. Had some big debts hanging over my head."

"Did she know?"

"Mother? Hell, no. I thought for a while that Philip was on to me. I didn't believe that Kane woman was a real estate agent."

"Who did you think she was?"

"An art expert. I found her examining the paintings in the west gallery."

"She *was* a real estate agent, you douche bag!"

"Yeah, I eventually came to the same conclusion. And Philip, he didn't have a clue. He was busy with other stuff—secret stuff he wouldn't tell me about."

"Yeah, he liked secrets. A chip off the old block."

"Anyway, after Mom died, I just kept on with it."

"Right under my nose. All this time."

"I got rid of the artwork on my side of the house first. But then . . ." His voice trailed off.

"You *violated* our arrangement? You entered my side of the house without my permission!"

The cell phone in her pocket trilled "The Stars and Stripes Forever" again. Bernie yanked it free and checked the caller I.D. It was Hammond. Flipping it open she said, "Make it quick. I'm busy."

"Ms. Simoneau?"

"What?"

"*Help!*" screamed Laurent. "I'm being tortured by a crazy woman! Help me! Help! Help!"

She held the candle near his foot and shot him a cautionary look.

"Are you all right?" asked Mr. Hammond.

"Fine. I gotta—"

"Wait. There's something I forgot to mention to you before."

"Oh goody. More bad news?"

"No, this is good news. After you contact the police, I assume you know that you should also contact your insurance company. You do have insurance, don't you?"

Bernadette had to think. She was pretty sure they were still paying that bill. "Yeah."

"Then you'll be able to recover your loss."

"What?" It took a second for his words to sink in. "Fucking brilliant, Oliver!" She began to dance around the room.

"Excuse me?"

"I could kiss you!"

"That's, ah, very thoughtful of you. Of course, you do understand that you'll never be able to enjoy the beauty of those paintings again, but at least you'll receive a fair monetary settlement. I know it's not the same thing—"

"Beauty is so very important to me, Oliver."

He cleared his throat. "Well, that's all I called to say."

Before she could thank him, he'd hung up.

Her eyes rose to Laurent. "The paintings were stolen, right? We just found out, *right*? Our insurance will cover it!"

"Oh, *Looooordy,*" he shrieked. "*Salvation!*"

"*Zoooowie,*" cried Bernie, punching the air. "My jackass, jerk-off, dork of a brother ain't so dumb after all."

"Let me down!"

She cocked an eye. "I don't know. Maybe I'll let you hang up there awhile longer. Let you think about your sins."

"Bernie!"

"Stop shouting. You're giving me a headache."

"No, turn around. Look!"

Bernadette twisted her head. Out of the corner of her eye, she saw an indistinct figure standing in the doorway. Turning full around, she whispered, "Timmy! Is that you?"

Tim held his hands to the sides of his face, his eyes locked on Laurent.

Even in the dimness, she could see the look of horror in his eyes. "Honey, how long have you been standing there?"

He didn't move.

She started toward him. "You weren't supposed to arrive until tomorrow." When she reached out to touch him, he flinched.

"No," he gasped. "Get away!"

"It's okay, honey. Laurent and I were just playing. He's got a bad back, you know? Hanging up there helps it feel better."

"*Bad* bad back," called Laurent. "Ooooh, it feels so much better now. Love this truss."

Tim's eyes dropped to her face. "It's real. People said it was all my imagination, but I've dreamed this so many times. How did I know?"

She reached for his hand. He allowed her to lead him down the stairs to a bench in the open second-floor mezzanine. Still holding his hand, she said, "I lied to you, Timmy, but I did it for your own good. You did see us once, long ago. You were just a little boy. You shouldn't have come upstairs, but your nanny was gone and the cook was looking after you. When I brought you back downstairs, I balled her out good and proper. It was all her fault. She should have been more careful to keep an eye on you."

"I did see it," he breathed. "I did."

"Yes, hon. And you shouldn't have."

"I heard screams. They were muffled, but the man was in pain." He shook his head, trying to rid it of cobwebs. "It was you and Laurent?"

"Yup. Just us. Nothing scary at all. It's his back, like I said. This works better than traction."

"You guys are *so* weird."

"Can't disagree with you there."

"It's not . . . you know. It's not . . . sexual?"

"Heavens, no." She turned up her nose.

He pressed a palm to his eyes. "I see this shape."

"What shape, hon?"

He took a pen out of his pocket, grabbed a magazine and drew the symbol on the back page, next to a liquor ad. "What's it mean?"

Bernadette's eyes opened a little wider. "Hmm, interesting. Boy, you got me."

"Have you ever seen it before?"

"Nope. Never," she lied.

"I remember that, too. I dream about it."

"Well, it's probably nothing. What you need is a good cup of cocoa. You always liked that."

"I'm not a kid anymore, Aunt Bernie."

"No, of course you're not. Well, let's see. How about a G and T? I'll just run upstairs and get Laurent out of the truss, and then we'll order pizza to go with our G and Ts. Sit out on the back patio. Have a real California kind of evening. That sound okay to you?"

He seemed dazed. "I guess so."

"Great. Just sit here and your uncle and I will be right with you."

On the way back up the steps, she swore under her breath. No matter how hard you tried, the past was always there just waiting to bite you in the ass.

38

When Jane got home from the hospital, she felt like crawling into bed and hiding. Except, the person she was hiding from was herself, so where she spent the evening seemed moot.

Her tried-and-true method for stopping the voices in her head was booze. She stood for a while at the cupboard in the kitchen and stared at the bottle of brandy. She even took it down and cracked the top. But at the last minute, with Mouse pawing her leg, she decided to go for a run. Mouse needed the exercise. So did she. But no matter what she did, how hard she tried to stave it off, she'd crossed a line this afternoon and the realization of what she'd almost done nearly knocked her flat. It wasn't merely that she'd wanted to kill Calvin, it was that she had *craved* it the way a drowning man craved air.

After changing into her running shoes, Jane opened the back door. Mouse bounded out and tore around the yard a few times before she could get him to stop long enough to hook up his leash.

Forty-five minutes later, she was home, standing in the shower, wishing the water could wash away the feeling of dread in her stomach. She should be at the hospital with Greta. She wanted to be there when she woke up. *If* she woke up.

"No," she roared, letting all her anger and frustration finally come out. Covering her eyes, she crumpled against the tile and slid to the floor. She stayed like that, crying her pain into the steam and the spray, until she saw Mouse's nose press against the glass. "I'm okay," she called, pulling herself together as best she could. "I'll be right out."

As she dried off, Mouse sat extra close. Slipping on her robe, she walked down the hallway to her room. She sat down on the bed. Mouse hopped up next to her. His cold nose nuzzled her hand.

She hugged him close, pressing her face against his neck. He didn't know what was wrong, but he understood, on some level, that she was hurting, and he wanted to help. "You're the best," she whispered. He was normally too full of energy to sit still and let her just hug him, but tonight he didn't try to move away. She was grateful.

After drying her hair, she put on clean clothes—black jeans and a dark blue Oxford cloth shirt. She took her cowboy boots out of the closet and looked at them for a moment, then put them on. She felt better for the run and the shower, but only marginally.

She knew she needed to eat something. The bottle of brandy was still sitting on the kitchen counter when she fed Mouse his kibble, but after eyeing it for a few minutes, she finally put it away, grabbing a Coke and an apple from the frig instead.

It was going on eight. Outside, the sun had set. She walked around the house for a while eating the apple and turning on lights. She couldn't remember a time when she'd felt so utterly defeated. She'd been so sure that she had, at the very least, discovered a reason why the case against Dexter Haynes should be dropped. She thought about phoning Kenzie, but she wasn't sure what she'd say, so she switched on the stereo and flipped through her CDs until she found something that appealed to her—an old Tom Waits album.

Around nine, she called the hospital for an update. All they would tell her was that Greta's condition remained critical.

Dropping down on the couch with her second Coke, she stared at the empty fireplace. "Mouse," she said, watching him hop up next to her and rest his head in her lap, "I need to tell you something. I doubt I'll ever tell this to another living soul."

His right eye twitched.

Stroking his fur, she said, "I almost killed a man today. You can't know how deeply that appalls me. But there's something that appalls me even more." She sucked in some air, feeling the breath go ragged in her throat. "Mouse, I liked the feeling of that gun in my hand. The power. It was like this amazing high. Do you have any idea how terrified I am by that?"

His eyes drifted shut.

"Who *am* I?"

The phone rang.

Her first reaction was to let it go. She wasn't sure where the cordless was and didn't feel like searching for it. But when she remembered Greta, she flew off the couch and rushed back to the kitchen. Grabbing the receiver, she said, "Hello?"

"Is this Ms. Lawless?"

She didn't recognize the voice. "Yes?"

"This is Alice Cathcart. We spoke the other day."

"Oh, sure. Hi."

For a moment, Alice didn't say anything. Then, "I understand you went to see Frank yesterday."

"That's right. Did he call you?"

"No, Timmy did. I just . . . I thought I should see . . . I mean, how did it go? What did he tell you?" She sounded unsure. Even a little nervous.

"Not much I didn't already know."

"Ah. Well. That's to be expected. I'm sorry you feel the need to go to all this trouble. Frank is such a fine man. I'm sure you could tell. So caring. So kind." She waited for a response, but when she didn't get one, she said, "Have you learned anything new since we last talked?"

Jane found the tenor of the conversation odd. "Actually, I have. I understand you were in love with Frank DeWitt."

"Who told you that?"

"Is it true?"

"How could you even suggest such a thing?"

"You were overheard offering to help him get Timmy out of the house, away from Camille Simoneau."

"These are all lies!"

"I was also told that Camille was about to petition the court for custody of Timmy based on Frank's infidelity. She was prepared to claim that he was having an affair with you, that you two had been lovers before his wife died. Even if it's not true, Ms. Cathcart, your hatred of

306

Camille Simoneau must have been white hot. That goes for Frank, too. And if that's not a motive for murder, I don't know what is."

The line went dead.

"Truth hurts," said Jane, wondering what Alice would do now.

Returning to the living room, Mouse charged past her into the front hall and started to bark just as the bell rang.

"I don't need a doorbell now that I've got you," she said, smiling down at him. She squinted through the peephole and saw Cordelia standing outside holding Hattie in her arms.

As soon as the door was opened, Cordelia plowed inside. "Thought you could use some company."

"Hi, Ganey," said Hattie shyly, rubbing one eye with a fist.

"Hi, sweetheart," said Jane, giving her tummy a tickle.

Hattie squealed with delight when she saw Mouse. "Ooh, Augie!"

Cordelia set her down.

Hattie and Mouse disappeared into the living room.

Fixing Jane with a hard stare, Cordelia sighed and said, "Jane, Jane, Jane."

"Yes?"

"How are you?"

"I've been better."

"Have you heard any more about Greta?"

"Her condition hasn't changed."

"Ah. But it's probably too early for the good news. Tomorrow *is* another day."

"Thus spoke Scarlet O'Hara. Isn't it kind of late for Hattie to be up?"

"Nah, she's a night owl. Just like her dear auntie. Got any strawberry pop?"

Jane's stomach flipped over. "In the frig."

"Back in a flash."

Turning the music down, Jane folded herself into the rocking chair by the fireplace. She picked up her Coke and took a sip. Hattie and Mouse were running around the room, circling the couch. She couldn't tell who was doing the chasing and who was doing the fleeing.

"I've been mulling the situation over," said Cordelia, flopping down on the couch a few seconds later.

"And?"

"I just can't see Alice Cathcart or Frank DeWitt allowing little Tim to wander around, even for a few seconds, in a blood-soaked house. I know Nolan said the murderer eventually locked him in a bathroom upstairs, but it's still too horrible to contemplate. Nobody who cared about that kid would have allowed it." She gazed lovingly at Hattie. "It had to be someone else."

"Like?"

"I'm putting my money on Laurent. Or Bernadette. Or"—she got an intense look in her eyes—"maybe both of them did it!"

"Both of them?"

"Sure. Everybody tells us they're weird. I think we should go talk to them next. Like, how about tonight. No time like the present."

"You want to take Hattie over there?"

"Oh, I forgot. No. No way."

Hattie pulled the *Iron Girl* off the end table and lugged it over to Jane, placing it in her lap.

"Oh, that's not a toy, Hatts," said Cordelia. Out of the side of her mouth, she added, "She's got great taste. Always goes for the diamonds, never the zircons."

Hattie looked at Cordelia, then back at Jane. She pulled the sculpture off Jane's lap and, holding it in her arms like a baby doll, thunked to the floor.

"Hatts, let's find something else for you to play with," said Cordelia.

"It's okay," said Jane. "It's made of iron. She can't exactly hurt it."

"She needa byankie," said Hattie with great sadness in her voice. "She cold."

Cordelia raced back to the kitchen and returned with a hand towel. "Here's her blankie," she said, handing it to Hattie. "Now she'll be nice and warm."

"Yah," said Hattie. "She seepy."

"Then you better put her to bed."

Hattie gave a big nod.

Cordelia took a slug of her pop, then sat back down and draped her arms over the back of the couch. "Maybe we should visit the Disneyland mansion at the crack of dawn. I'll pick you up around eleven."

Jane smiled and shook her head. "If anybody's going to toss us out

308

on our ear, it's Bernadette and Laurent. I doubt they'd even let us in the door."

"Heard anything more from Nolan?"

"Nope."

Cordelia sipped her pop and grew silent.

"What are you thinking about?" asked Jane after a couple of minutes of watching Hattie play with the sculpture.

"Oh," she said, sighing, "myself."

"What about yourself?"

She sighed again. "Tell me the truth, Janey. Do you think I'm boring?"

"You asked me that before."

"I know, but maybe you were just trying to make me feel better. I can handle the truth, you know. I'm tough."

"Cordelia, look at me. Look me in the eye. You are the least boring person I know."

"Really?"

"Yes!"

" 'Cause, see . . . the fact is . . . Marian called me that. It's why we broke up. I was so hurt, I couldn't talk about it, not even to you. It cut me to the quick, Janey. She said, now that I have Hattie in my life, I couldn't be spontaneous anymore."

"That's ridiculous."

"No, actually it's not. I do have more responsibility, not that running a theater isn't a *lot*."

"Then she's pathetic."

"Yes, I think you've hit on it. I also think she was a little jealous. I admit, my life has changed, and the kind of woman I choose next will be different. For one thing, she'll need a much bigger heart. I made a mistake with Marian." Raising an eyebrow she added, "See, I admit it when I make mistakes."

"And I don't?"

"Well, it's a skill you could work on, in my opinion." Glancing down at Hattie, she exclaimed, "Oh, dear! Honey, no!"

Hattie had pealed the green felt off the bottom of the sculpture.

"Oh, Janey, I'm sorry. I'll glue it back on."

Jane bent down to pick up the shreds. "It's okay."

"Hey, what's that?" asked Cordelia. She scooped the sculpture off the floor. Stuffed into the partially hollow base was a piece of paper. Pulling it out, she flattened it against her thigh. Attached to the paper by an X of tape that had pretty much disintegrated was a key.

"What's the note say?" asked Jane, moving over to the couch to get a closer look.

"It's kind of faded." She examined the key for a few seconds, then held the note closer to her eyes. "It says, 'East wall of garage. 10 bricks from top. 16 bricks from side.' It's a treasure map! We're rich!"

It was a typical Cordelia conclusion. Grab for the sensational and fling the more obvious deduction into the dirt.

"But what garage?" she asked, her enthusiasm fading.

"The Simoneau's? This sculpture belonged to Philip, right?"

"Right," said Cordelia.

"So it could either be the garage in back of the Irving house—the one Christine was trying to sell—or the one in back of the mansion. He had access to both."

"What if it's neither?"

"Then we're screwed. I wonder what he hid."

"Diamonds! Jewels!"

"Let's be realistic," said Jane. "If it *is* one of those two garages, the chances of this key still fitting the lock are pretty slim."

"Then we'll break the door down."

"Which one?"

Hattie covered the sculpture on Cordelia's lap with the towel. "She cold." She eyed her auntie with great disdain.

"Hmm. Guess we better check them both," said Cordelia.

"An seepy," added Hattie, giving Jane a withering look.

"You're on." Jane stood up.

"Now?" said Cordelia.

"Oh, I forgot. You've got Hattie. Look, I can do it myself. I'll call you when I'm done."

"Like hell you will! You need me along for the breaking and entering parts. You always need me for that."

"I do?"

"Absolutely. We'll drop Hattie off at Sita's house."

"Who's Sita?"

"My backup babysitter."

"Sita!" cried Hattie.

Cordelia grabbed the little girl up in her arms. "You, my little sweetheart, are a genius, you know that? You may have cracked the entire case."

Hattie placed her palm on Cordelia's cheek, then flopped against her shoulder and hugged her around the neck.

"Isn't she a peach?" said Cordelia, closing her eyes and enjoying the moment.

"A real peach," agreed Jane, smiling at the two of them.

Cordelia backed her Hummer into a parking spot half a block from the Simoneau mansion. A chill night mist floated off Lake of the Isles and crept along the grassy boulevards.

"Perfect night for a break-in."

"Cordelia!"

"Don't get excited. I know this is serious."

Lights burned on the second floor of the mansion.

"Wonder what's going on inside tonight," said Cordelia as they made their way across a neighbor's lawn to the back alley.

"Kinky sex?"

"You say tomato. I say——"

"As I recall," said Jane, ducking behind a low hanging pine, "the garage sits under the gatehouse in the back. Right there." She pointed.

Cordelia bent down. "What if they rent the gatehouse out?"

"Then we'll have to be very quiet."

Cutting through the neighbor's backyard, Jane led the way to a gazebo, where they stopped to reconnoiter. The gatehouse looked about as well-maintained as the main house. The brickwork was in bad need of repair, and the shutters on the windows were either askew or had fallen off. There were no lights on. It looked deserted.

"It's brick," whispered Cordelia. "That's a good sign we've got the right place."

An alley light cast a slice of yellow light across the driveway.

Cordelia huddled close to Jane in the misty darkness. "Jeez, could this night be any more creepy? And by the way, in another ten seconds, my hair will look like spaghetti squash. Humidity and naturally curly hair don't mix."

311

"Good thing you don't have any beauty pageants scheduled for later."

"Who says I don't?"

"Well, then, I guess you'll have to rely on the intelligence portion of the event."

"Ha *ha*."

"There," whispered Jane. "A side door." It appeared to be wood, rounded at the top, with a window divided into four panes—all of them cracked. Problem was, it faced the Simoneau's house with no possibility of cover.

Jane was glad she'd put on dark clothes. Cordelia, on the other hand, was wearing a white silk blouse and tan linen slacks. A nice look, but not exactly suitable for casing garages at night.

"Let me try the key," said Jane. "If it works and I get in, run like hell and hope nobody sees you."

"Roger."

Leaving Cordelia crouched in the shadows, Jane ran flat out to the fence between the two properties, hopped it, and raced to the door. Glancing over her shoulder at the mansion, she fumbled with the key and pressed it into the lock. It went in easily about halfway, but then something stopped it. She pushed it in as far as it would go, then yanked it out, repeating the motion until the key finally went all the way in. She turned it one way and then the other, pulling it out slightly, then forcing it back in, playing with the mechanism until she heard a click. She turned the knob.

"I'm in," she whispered.

Lifting a flashlight from her back pocket, she switched it on. There were two cars parked inside—a VW Beetle convertible and an old Chrysler New Yorker. The standard garage stuff hung on the walls—hoses, rakes, rusted tools, ice chippers. She panned the light across the interior a moment more, then clicked it back off, waiting for Cordelia.

Finally, after what seemed like hours, Cordelia stumbled through the door.

"What took you so long?"

"I don't leap tall buildings, or fences, in a single bound like you do." She rubbed her back.

Jane pointed the flashlight beam at the back wall. "That's east."

"And it's brick."

"What are we waiting for?"

They cut around the cars and started the count— Jane from the top down, Cordelia from the side out.

"This is it!" whispered Cordelia, removing a loose brick.

Jane took out a pocketknife and began to loosen the bricks around it. All of them came out easily. "I'm not sure why this garage is still standing," she said, reaching down inside the wall.

"Feel anything?" asked Cordelia.

"Not yet. Maybe somebody already got to it."

"No way! Banish all negative thinking this instant!"

"Hey." Jane touched something metal. "I think I got it."

"Of course you do." After a pause, she said, "Got what?"

Jane forced out a few more bricks. "This." It was a heavy-duty steel strongbox. "Come on. Let's get out of here."

Once they were safely back inside the Hummer, Jane flipped open the metal clasps. Inside she found a bundle of letters held together by a rubber band, and a large manilla envelope folded in half. Cordelia ripped through the letters while Jane opened the envelope.

"These are love letters," crowed Cordelia. "From Dexter to Philip. My my *my*. I really shouldn't read this, but . . ." She was glued to the page.

Jane pulled some documents and several letters out of the manilla envelope. She read through them quickly. It only took a few seconds to gather what they were about.

"Cordelia?"

"Ooh," she squealed.

"You'll never guess what I found."

"Can't be as good as this."

"Bill McBride sold some property on the north shore of Lake Superior for Camille Simoneau back in '85 and '86."

"Yeah?"

"This is proof that he was working with another real estate agent up there to swindle Camille out of almost a million dollars. The two men sold the properties to a dummy company for way under the market value. Then they turned around and resold them for a huge profit."

Cordelia looked up. "They did? Who's the other guy?"

"His name was Larry Papus. Look at the dates on this? The last letter, the one that confirmed the fraud, was written three days before the murders. That means, before his death, Philip had discovered something that would not only have put McBride Realty out of business, but it would have put Bill McBride in prison."

They were silent for a moment, absorbing the revelation.

Examining the box to make sure she hadn't missed anything, she realized that it had a false bottom.

"What are you doing?" asked Cordelia.

"There's something else in here." She removed the metal divider revealing six bundles of hundred-dollar bills.

"I told you, Janey! Riches!"

Jane counted one of the bundles. "Five thousand dollars. Six bundles means there's thirty thousand dollars here. Why would such a rich young man need to squirrel away cash?"

"Mad money?" offered Cordelia. "You know, for when he saw that little bauble in the jewelry store he just *had* to have."

"We better get this information over to Nolan right away."

"Do you think it means McBride did it?"

"If we're looking for a motive, this is the mother of all motives."

"What about Frank and Alice?"

"I don't know, Cordelia. I really don't. The *Iron Girl* gave us a huge push forward, but something's still missing. We better get out of here while we still can."

"I'm down with that."

39

Looks pretty dark in there," said Cordelia, pulling the Hummer up in front of Nolan's house. "Bet he's not home."

"I'll try his cell," said Jane. She was glad she'd put his card in her pocket before she left.

The line rang a couple of times. Three. Four.

Then, "Nolan."

"Hi, it's Jane Lawless."

"Hey, kid. How ya doin'? You looked pretty gray when I left the hospital."

"Better. Thanks."

"What's goin' on?"

"There've been some developments." She filled him in on what they'd just found, leaving out the part about the money.

"Man, I need you on *my* team," said Nolan, laughing. "Ever thought of going into private investigation?"

"I like what I do," said Jane.

"Yeah, okay. We'll talk about it another time. Where are you now?"

"Sitting in front of your house."

"Great. Here's what you do. Shove all the information through the mail slot. I should be home by midnight. I'll take a look at it and call you tomorrow. It might be late in the day, but don't worry. I'll get back to you."

"Do you think McBride's our guy?"

"I don't know, but I'm gettin' a definite feeling about him, and it ain't good."

"Do you trust your feelings?"

"Hell, instinct is everything, girl. Don't let anybody ever tell you differently."

When she hung up, Cordelia said, "You didn't tell him about the money."

"No, I didn't."

"Why?"

"Because I'm going to give it to my father. He can use it to pay for some of his expenses when he forces the court to reopen Dexter's case."

"I didn't realize he'd agreed to do that."

"He hasn't," said Jane.

The following evening, Jane watched through the window of Greta's hospital room while her parents kissed her good-bye. They'd driven down from Dalton right after getting word about her injury. Jane had spoken with Greta's mom briefly when she first arrived, learned that Greta was doing much better. She would be transferred out of ICU to a room on the fifth floor in the morning. As soon as she was able to travel, the Hoffmans wanted her back home with them. Mrs. Hoffman said she was terrified of big cities. She couldn't imagine why anyone would want to live in Minneapolis. Jane considered pointing out that rural areas weren't exactly free of crime, but she let it slide.

After the Hoffman's were gone, Jane entered the room. Greta's eyes were closed. A nurse sat at a computer monitor to the right of the doorway. She nodded to Jane, then got up and left the room.

Jane approached the bed slowly. Greta looked years older, the skin around her eyes darkened and drawn. She had bruises on her arms. A cut on her lip. All compliments of Calvin, no doubt. Jane told herself to breathe, in and out, in and out, hoping the steady rhythm of her heart would dissipate the snarl of angry bees thrashing around inside her chest.

When Greta opened her eyes, Jane was standing with her hands on the bed rail, looking down at her.

"Hi," said Greta, her eyes brightening. Her voice sounded almost normal.

"How are you feeling?"

"Better."

"The doctors say you're doing great."

She glanced at the I.V. tubes. "I guess I lost a lot of blood."

"Yes, you did."

"You were there, weren't you? At the motel."

Jane nodded.

"You saved my life."

I almost let you die, thought Jane. She was hardly anybody's savior. "Have the police been in to talk to you?"

"Yeah." She shifted slightly. "A few hours ago. I told them everything I know."

"Which is?"

"I didn't see who shot me, Jane. All I remember is hearing a noise in the bathroom. Sounded like breaking glass. I was tied up on the bed, so I couldn't move. And then, this hand holding a gun pushed out of the doorway. I screamed. The center of my chest got real hot. I didn't even hear the gun go off. I think I was shot twice. All I remember is trying to twist to the side to get out of the way. I knew it was pointless. And then, I must have passed out."

"God," whispered Jane, her hands gripping the rail. "I would give anything to have prevented that."

"It's not your fault," said Greta. "It's Calvin's. He's the one who kidnapped me."

"Did he . . . hurt you?"

She swallowed hard a couple of times, fixed her eyes on the foot of the bed. "He raped me."

Jane's mouth went suddenly dry.

"I thought if he got it out of his system, he'd stop. But he . . . didn't. He went and bought some pizza, but when he got back—" She turned her face away. "He left in the morning to drive up to Fergus. He'd bought a house up near Benton and was closing on it. Whoever broke into the bathroom did it while he was gone."

"And you have no idea who it was?"

She shook her head.

"Why did Calvin take you?"

She turned her head and looked out the window. "He thought I was sleeping with you."

"That's it? That's all?"

"Well, not entirely. He thought someone was paying me to seduce you."

"Excuse me?"

She looked back at Jane. "I'm so ashamed of myself! Promise you won't hate me when I tell you the truth."

"Hate you?"

"I was hired to, well, to find out about the book you're writing."

"What book? I'm not writing a book."

"The one about the Simoneau murders."

"Greta, you *know* why I'm interested in that. It's because of Christine, because of all the stuff she kept from me before she died. It's been driving me crazy."

"But Bill said——"

"Bill?" Jane fought to keep her eyes level. "Bill McBride?"

"Yeah. He said you were working on this book. He was, too, and he already had a deal with Random House. Big money, I guess. His was almost done. He was afraid you were going to scoop him with yours, so he hired me to find out what you knew. I realize it was a sleazy thing to get involved in, but he promised to pull some strings at MCAD, get me in full-time this fall. And he promised he'd pay for my classes if I helped him. I mean, I didn't know you then. And I didn't think what he was asking me to do was all that bad."

"How did he find you?"

"I worked at a bank in Fergus, remember? He came in a few times a year because he sold homes up there, or he had a business partner who did. I don't know all the details, I just know I've known him for years. He always seemed like such a nice guy—said I looked a lot like a woman he once worked with. And then, one day, he comes to me with this deal. I hated my life in Fergus, Jane. I wanted to get away from Calvin. I just plain wanted *out,* and this was the break I'd been looking for."

Jane was speechless. She felt like a fool. Cordelia had been right all along. Greta didn't just happen into her life.

"See, Bill figured, because I looked so much like Christine, if you got a good look at me, my face would reel you in, make you want to get to know me. After you asked me to shoot pictures for you, he was thrilled, but he kept pressing me to get more information on what you were learning about the Simoneaus. I felt like a complete and utter fake, and that bothered the hell out of me because I never expected to like you so much. God, I'm so sorry!" She strained to sit up.

Jane touched her shoulder. "It's okay, Greta."

"Do you forgive me?"

"Of course I do. Bill used you. That's what he's good at. It was all a lie. I'm not writing a book, and I'll bet you he's not writing one either. He's involved in the Simoneau murders. I think he may even be the one who did it."

Her eyes looked suddenly terrified. "But . . . he told me Alice Cathcart was the real murderer. The nanny. That was the conclusion he said he'd come to in his book. He even said he had proof."

Jane recognized it for the blatant lie that it was. "I'm guessing here, Greta, but I think Bill was the one who shot you. He was probably having you followed, I don't think he trusts anyone. He hired you to keep an eye on me, but it wasn't for the reason he told you. He knew I was poking into the Simoneau murders, something he thought had been safely put to bed years ago. He was scared, afraid I might trip over something that would incriminate him."

Fear made Greta's voice sound brittle. "Have you?"

"I think so. I'll explain it to you later. Right now, I've got to go talk to a friend." Jane didn't want to worry her, but if Bill had tried to kill her once, he might try again. She had to make sure a police guard was posted on her door.

"Be careful," said Greta, squeezing Jane's hand.

"I will."

As she turned to go, Greta said, "That kiss the other night. That wasn't Bill's idea."

"I didn't think it was."

"I'm not taking it back either. But I understand what you said about Christine. And . . . I don't know. Not all guys are like Calvin."

Jane smiled. "Just be who you are, Greta. That's all I want for you. Nothing less will ever make you happy."

40

The guard's been posted on her room," said Nolan, opening Jane's car door. "McBride can't touch her now."

"Thanks." Jane felt instantly lighter. A large black van was parked directly across 57th Street, four blocks from Bill's house. She would never have pegged the van as a mobil command post.

It was all set. According to what Nolan had told her, McBride didn't own a gun. That didn't mean he didn't *have* one, it just meant he'd never filed a permit. Nolan had arranged everything. The police needed a way into the house. They couldn't get a warrant without a compelling reason and they didn't have enough on McBride yet to go to a judge. The information Jane had dug up last night might be useful in the case against Dexter, but it would take time to process. For now, the cops hoped to nail McBride for the shooting at the motel. The problem was, McBride looked like he might be about to run. The police had been watching him all day. Around noon, he'd carried some luggage out to his car, but then he'd gone back inside the house and hadn't come out again.

The big news was that CSU had found a fingerprint on a piece of brown glass behind the toilet in the motel room. It looked like someone had dropped a pint of whiskey on the bathroom floor and tried to clean it up, but had missed one piece. The print they'd found didn't belong to either Greta or Calvin. The police figured that the shooter had been drinking before he'd cut through the screen. He'd worn gloves while he was in the motel, but hadn't been wearing them when he'd been drinking from the pint. The bad news was, McBride had never been arrested, so his prints weren't on file. They'd sent a guy in plainclothes to nose around his garbage, but the bin was empty.

The theory was, if Jane could get inside his house and I.D. a gun—any gun, but preferably a nine millimeter—it would get the cops inside fast. If nothing else, she could get his fingerprints.

"Jane Lawless," said Nolan, nodding to a man who'd just come out of the van, "meet Sergeant Russ Vanloh."

Jane shook the detective's hand. He was a little shorter than Nolan, with graying brown hair, a nervous manner, and a fired-up look in his eyes.

"We're grateful for your help," said Vanloh. "Thanks to you and Nolan, we're about to put a whole different face on the Simoneau homicides. And this time, we're gonna get it right."

Agreeing to wear a wire was one of the more conspicuously suicidal decisions Jane had ever made, but both she and Nolan agreed that Bill would most likely demand to talk to his lawyer the minute a cop walked in the door. This way, the police might at least get something on tape. The trick would be to get out of the house before the situation turned ugly.

The palms of Jane's hands were covered with sweat and she felt a pressing need for a shot of brandy. Neither were good signs.

After Vanloh disappeared inside the van, Nolan said, "You still okay with this? Last chance to back out."

"I want to nail that bastard as bad as you do. I want Dexter out of prison, and I want to know why Christine had that gun and that statue."

"Okay. Had to check." Glancing up the street, he continued, "Did you bring the derringer?"

"Right here." She patted the pocket of her field jacket.

"It's not loaded, right?"

"Right."

"See if you can get him to hold it. Watch where he places his fingers. When he gives it back to you, put your own fingers somewhere else.

322

Anyway, you can start the conversation with that. Where it goes from there is up to him—and you."

Vanloh poked his head out of the van. "We're ready to set up the wire and the vest. Come in through the back here." He held the door open.

Nolan glanced at Jane. "Showtime."

While the wire was being attached, Vanloh gave Jane her final instructions.

"It'll be just you and him in there, so rule one is to protect yourself at all costs. You understand? We'll be listening, and we'll be ready with backup, but we can't get between you and a bullet."

"Don't worry. I'm not a martyr." Slipping her field jacket back on, she asked, "What about the information I gave Nolan? Is it enough to get Haynes out of prison?"

"We're working on it," said Vanloh.

Outside, Nolan clapped her on the back. "When this is over, we gotta have a long talk about your future employment."

Jane smiled at him and they shook hands.

A short time later, she rolled her Mini up to the curb in front of McBride's house. The light was on in the garage. As she passed the SUV in the drive, she saw that a couple of suitcases were stowed in the back.

"Hi," she called, seeing that Bill was standing behind a work bench toward the back of the garage. "Got a minute?"

He seemed to be deep in thought. She wasn't sure he'd even heard her.

"Bill?" she tried again.

He was looking down at an abacus, his hand frozen in midair above one of the beads. Next to him was an open bottle of Cutty Sark, about three quarters empty.

When he looked up and finally realized she'd come inside, he said, as if continuing a conversation, "My kids gave me this, you know. Long time ago. I always thought it was useless. Kept it out in the garage for years." His eyes dropped down. "Turns out, it helps."

"Helps how?" she asked, moving a few steps farther into the garage.

"Oh, you know. Taking stock. Weighing my sins against my accomplishments. I've had many *many* accomplishments, you know. But then, there's always those few major sins to screw up your average."

He'd given her an opening. "We all have our sins," she said, moving still closer. "And our secrets." She could smell the alcohol on his breath, see the lack of focus in his eyes.

"Yeah, well, there are sins and there are sins." He grabbed the bottle, took a swig. Sitting down on a stool behind the counter, he taped the abacus with his thumb. "I was a lousy husband." He pointed to a bead he'd slid to the left. "You already know that. But I was always active in charity work. I served on the board of directors of Fellowship Housing for Disadvantaged Youth for nine years. I helped pay for my younger brother to go to college." He pointed at two beads on the right. "I was a loving son—always. I loved my parents, helped them out whenever I could." He pushed another bead to the right.

"You were a good businessman."

"Yup, there's that," he said, hesitating. He looked at the abacus hard, took another swig from the bottle. "But not always ethical, right?"

She shrugged. "You tell me."

"That's what got me in the end."

Was he actually going to spill it all without a struggle?

He scowled. In a voice just above a whisper, he said, "A guy's got a right to protect himself, doesn't he?"

"I suppose."

He eyes looked scrambled. "Shit," he muttered. "What the hell are you doing here anyway?"

"I wanted to show you the gun."

"What gun?"

"Here." She handed him the derringer. "That's the one I found in Christine's briefcase. Thought you might like to see it."

With heavy, clumsy movements, he checked to see if it was loaded. "Piece of shit. No power."

"You know, Bill, I've been thinking."

"Dangerous stuff, thinking."

"I agree. I've been wondering about something you said the other night, about your tattoo."

"Yeah? What about it?"

"You said that Tim saw it when you were hanging from that hook in the ceiling. That hook's pretty high up."

"So?"

"And the attic, I'll bet it's badly lit."

"Yeah? So what?"

"And you said your arms were chained behind you."

"You got the picture right."

"Well, I was just thinking, it would be pretty difficult, maybe even impossible, for a little three-year-old to get a good look at that tattoo under those conditions."

He lifted the bottle off the counter, but set it back down without taking a drink. "Think you're pretty smart, don't you."

"All I know is, whoever killed those three people, didn't mean to do it. Everybody agrees with that. It's like . . . you got in that house and found out that Camille knew about the real estate deal and you lost it. It was a reflex. Just like you said: self-preservation trumps everything. And then, it was just like dominos. Once one fell, the others had to."

His eyes had turned cold and hard.

"Why'd you come to my restaurant the other night, Bill? You didn't have to tell me any of that stuff."

"I sure as hell had to tell you something," he grunted. "You were getting too close. I figured sooner or later you'd get around to talking to Bernie and, if I know her, she'd let it slip about our relationship just to spite me. The fact that I was keeping it all a secret would make me look suspicious. I had to head her off, had to make you think I was confiding everything to you so you'd stop looking at me as a serious suspect. If I told you I was there that night, if I bared my soul, then if you came across someone who saw me leave the house, you'd think it was the first time I left that night—after the bondage scene up in the attic."

"You went back to your office after that."

He nodded. "But when I got there, I found a message from Camille on my machine. She sounded angry, wanted me to come over. So I drove back." His voice was soaked in anger now. "It was Philip, *he* was the one behind it all. If it hadn't been for him, none of this would have happened. But does anybody ever think to blame him? Hell, no! They just want to blame me! He was the twisted fuck who set everything in motion! Put *him* in prison!"

"But . . . he's dead," said Jane.

Bill looked up at her.

She figured the police had enough on tape now to burn McBride at the stake. Time to leave. She started to back up.

"Where you going?" he asked, his voice once again conversational.

"I should probably get back to the restaurant."

"Don't you want this?" He held up the derringer.

"Oh, right."

His free hand moved under the counter and brought up a different gun.

"That's . . . a nine millimeter, right?" She hoped the cops were listening.

"It's a *real* gun," he said, tossing the derringer at her chest.

It dropped to the floor. She didn't pick it up.

"Yup, made a lot of mistakes in my life. Can't stop now though. The die is cast, and all that crap."

While he took another pull off the bottle, she stepped backward another couple of feet. She didn't like the direction the conversation was headed.

Setting the bottle back down, he studied the gun in his hand.

Jane could outrun him, but she couldn't outrun a bullet. She stood very still. "Hey, I thought of another good deed you did."

"Yeah, what?"

"The way you handled little Tim that night. You showed concern for him."

Bingo. "Right."

"Maybe that calls for another bead." Instead of moving one to the right, he hesitated, then swept the abacus off the counter. He was crying now. "You're afraid of me. God. How did this happen?"

"Should I be afraid of you, Bill?"

He racked the slide. "Yeah. Think so."

"You going to shoot me?"

"I don't know. Haven't decided yet." He stared at her for several long moments. "I can't exactly let you leave. Not with what you know."

"What I know and what I can prove are two different things."

"Yeah. Maybe." He raised the gun, looked at it. Looked back at her. Suddenly, he reared back and screamed, "Get the hell out of here!"

She turned and bolted for the door. As she hit the end of the drive, she saw Nolan running up the street.

"Get down," he yelled.

She dove for the grass as a shot exploded behind her.

Two police cruisers screeched to a stop across from her Mini. Men started shouting. Jane twisted around and looked back at the garage. Bill was on lying on the cement floor in front of the counter, the top half of his head blown off.

"You okay?" said Nolan, finally reaching her.

She turned her face away from the horror.

"It's over," he said, pulling her into his arms. "It's all over."

Christine

August 28, 1987

2:14 A.M.

By the time Christine arrived at the hospital, she was in such pain all she wanted was for the doctors to stop it. It felt like forever before the nurse came in and injected something into her I.V. Christine kept her eyes closed. She couldn't concentrate on anything but the pain. But as she felt it slowly ease, as her body grew lighter, she opened her eyes and looked around.

Jane was standing next to her, her face rigid with worry.

"I'm sorry," whispered Christine.

"Don't be," soothed Jane, bending closer. "This is exactly where you need to be. The doctors are doing lots of tests. You're scheduled for a CT scan next."

"I love you," she whispered, closing her eyes. She felt Jane's face close to hers.

"We'll get through this," whispered Jane. "We've still got time."

"Still got time," she repeated. Still time.

When she awoke hours later, it was dark outside. She was in a hospital room with the lights turned low. Using the arm not attached to the I.V., she touched the oxygen tube in her nose. Jane was sitting in a chair next to the bed, holding her hand, her head resting on top of the blanket, her beautiful dark hair spread out around her like a halo. Christine watched her for a few minutes. Her eyes were closed.

The TV was on across the room, but the sound was turned down. When Christine looked over at it, she thought she saw a picture of Camille Simoneau flutter across the screen, but it was gone so fast she assumed her mind was playing tricks on her.

"Can I have some water?" she asked, feeling intensely thirsty.

Jane jerked awake. "Hi, sweetheart," she said, smiling at her. She ran a hand through her hair, then said, "Sure." She lifted the water glass over and held the straw while Christine drank. "How're you feeling?"

She finished, then said, "Kind of goofy."

"The pain?"

"It's better. What do the doctors say?"

"They're not sure what's going on. We should get the test results by morning." She held the glass up. "More?"

Christine shook her head.

"You hungry?"

"No."

Jane brushed Christine's hair away from her forehead. "You've got a temperature."

"Maybe that's it."

"What?"

"I thought I saw Camille Simoneau on the TV. Must be seeing things, huh?"

Jane switched off the TV. "Must be."

"Did I see her picture?"

"Come on, let's talk about something else."

"Tell me."

Jane picked up Christine's hand again, lifting it to her lips. "There was . . . a problem at the Simoneau house earlier tonight."

"What kind of problem?"

"I don't know exactly. It was the lead story on the ten o'clock news. Camille's dead. She was murdered."

"What?" Pain clawed Christine's insides.

"I know she was a client of yours, and I'm sorry. But it's not worth getting upset over. Not now. We've got enough to concentrate on right here."

"What about Philip? Was he there?" She gritted her teeth and tried to sit up.

Jane pressed the nurse's button. "You're in pain."

"No, I can take it. I don't want to sleep. I want to know what happened?"

"I told you, I don't know."

"God," said Christine. She couldn't believe it. "I have to talk to Philip. You have to call him for me."

"That's Camille's grandson, right?"

"He's my friend. I just need to know he's okay."

Jane stroked her face. "It's late, sweetheart. We can try in the morning. He's got enough on his plate right now, don't you think?"

"I just . . . I just can't believe it. Why? Who would do that?"

The nurse came in holding a tray. "How are you feeling?" she asked, checking the I.V. drip. "How's the pain?"

"I'm okay." She wanted to talk to Jane.

Checking the chart at the foot of the bed, the nurse said, "I think it's time for more pain meds."

Christine didn't have the strength to fight. And maybe they were right. Keeping the pain managed was better than letting it get out of hand.

After the nurse had administered the shot and checked her vitals, she left the room.

"I'll get through this," said Christine, looking into Jane's eyes.

"I know you will," said Jane, kissing her lightly on the lips.

As the room lost its solidity, Christine continued to stare into Jane's eyes. The deeper she looked, the clearer it became that they contained worlds within worlds, all connected. Suddenly, it didn't matter if they had more time or less time because time itself was an illusion. She couldn't explain it, but as she closed her eyes, she felt profoundly comforted.

During the night and into the next day, Christine felt jostled, heard voices, opened her eyes and closed them again. The TV was on. The TV was off. Everything was stirred together, squeezed into a long, skinny stream of light and dark. She was swimming. Under the water. Approaching the surface only to float down again. More voices, deeper this time. Anxious bells. Christmas bells? And light again.

Jane's face. Eager. "Can you hear me?"

"Yes," said Christine. "I'm here." She opened her eyes. Smiled. And then she disappeared back into the fog. A fire burned. Was it inside her? She talked to her parents. She was so glad to see them she cried.

She sank deeper this time. Harder to breathe. She opened her eyes. Looked at the TV. Closed her eyes. A while later she opened them again. "Dexter?" she whispered. She saw the police holding the watch. The beautiful gold watch. But Dexter was in handcuffs. "No, that's not right."

"I'm here, sweetheart," said Jane. "What did you say?"

"Not right."

"What's not right?"

"Tell them."

"What, sweetheart? I'm listening." Jane had tears in her eyes.

Christine looked at her. "Stop the pain meds. Please."

"Are you sure?"

"Please," she said again. She drifted down. Deep down. But the light above her was brighter now. With one superhuman lunge, she broke through the surface. Jane's face appeared over her.

"Hi," she said weakly.

"Oh, Christine," said Jane, holding her hand to her lips, kissing it fiercely, tenderly.

"I'm dying, aren't I."

"No."

"Come closer."

Jane leaned in toward her.

"I get it now. Don't worry. I see it clearly. We'll never be separated. I'll always be with you. Isn't that great?"

"Great," said Jane, choking on the word.

Tears fell onto Christine's face. It felt like a blessing. A benediction. "Don't be sad. Promise me."

She nodded. "I love you."

"Love you, too," she whispered. "So grateful. For love. Every minute." She held on to Jane's eyes as long as she could. And when she finally closed her own, she felt an incredible moment of lightness, of unburdening.

Of soaring.

41

Two days later, on an overcast Monday morning, Dexter Haynes was released from Stillwater State Prison. A knot of people waited for him as he walked slowly out the door, peering up at the sky as if the light hurt his eyes. Reaching the group, he stopped for a moment and looked down at a young boy who tugged at his arm. A little girl stood to the side and gazed up at him, her eyes wide, her mouth open, like she was seeing something not quite real. One by one, the adults hugged him or shook his hand. An old woman sat patiently in a wheelchair. Dexter came to her last. Kneeling down, he took her hands in his and kissed them, held them to his face. She touched the scar on his neck. They spoke for a few minutes, both crying, both with looks of ecstasy on their faces.

Jane waited about twenty yards away, leaning against a guardrail. What she saw made everything she'd gone through worthwhile. It was the light at the end of the tunnel. You got a lot of tunnels in your life, but very few lights, and even fewer as bright as this one.

Dexter stood, whispered something into the old woman's ear, then walked over to Jane. "Thanks for coming," he said in his deep, raspy voice.

"I wouldn't have missed it for the world."

He looked around at the building, then back at her. "I owe you my life. I won't forget it."

"What are you going to do now? Where will you live?"

"Well," he said, smiling faintly, "I imagine I'll drive back to Chicago with my brother and his family. The plan is for me to stay with him until I can find a job."

"Do they know . . . *all* the details of your release?"

His nod was slow, his eyes soft and amazed. "Can you believe it? And they came anyway."

At that moment, Jane was as close to losing it as she'd ever come. She bit down hard, fighting back tears.

"Maybe it's a different world than the one I left."

"Different," she said. "Better, maybe, but there's still a long way to go."

"Yeah, I know."

When he smiled, she could see for the first time the same young man in Christine's photos. "Oh, I forgot." She slipped an envelope out of her back pocket. "I thought you might want these."

He took the envelope, opened the flap and looked inside. "My letters to Philip," he said, choking on Philip's name. He pressed a hand to his mouth. "What a waste. What a sickening waste."

"And something else," she said. She pulled a bulky paper sack out of her jacket pocket.

"What's that?"

"Thirty thousand dollars in one-hundred-dollar bills."

"I don't understand."

"It was in the strongbox we found in the Simoneau's garage. By all rights, you should have inherited Philip's part of the Simoneau estate after his death. This isn't much, but it should help."

"I'm stunned." He looked inside the sack, then folded up the top. "And grateful."

They both stood in the prison yard, listening to the hum of traffic out on the highway.

"Did you ever figure out how Christine got that derringer? Or the sculpture?" He bent down and stuffed the letters and the money sack into his case.

Jane shook her head. "I'll always wonder, I suppose, but I've learned that the past can't ever be tied up neatly with a ribbon and a bow on top."

"Yeah. If only Philip had told me about McBride, about him swindling the family, none of this would have happened."

"I wondered about that. Why didn't he tell you?"

"Oh, who the hell knows. That whole family—they were all pretty tight-lipped when it came to family business. I'm sure he *would* have told me about it—after he talked to his grandmother. We were supposed to have a late dinner the night he died. But . . . it never happened. God," he said, sighing deeply. "Makes you wonder."

"About what?"

"Oh, I don't know. Life, I guess. What happens to you. Sometimes it all seems so random."

Jane nodded. She'd had the same thoughts.

"Well," he said, glancing over his shoulder at everyone waiting for him, "I guess we got to move on."

"Guess so. That's all we can do."

He put one arm around her, stiffly, timidly. It wasn't quite a hug, but it was enough.

"Will you stay in touch?" she asked.

"If you want."

"I want that very much."

Picking up his case, he looked at her, then away, then back at her again. "Thanks," he said.

One simple word, but the whole world was in it.

As twilight settled over the Nebraska countryside, Jane drove her rental car up the dirt road to Kenzie's farmhouse. She parked in front of the barn and got out, breathing in the soft, sweet evening air. The lilacs were beginning to bloom here, several weeks ahead of Minnesota. Out in the field next to the barn, a brown-and-white pinto came galloping toward the fence. Jane wasn't used to a thousand-pound animal friend, but Ben was the horse she'd ridden when she'd come down to stay with Kenzie, and it looked like he remembered her.

She approached the fence. "Hey, there," she said. She was glad she'd remembered to stop in town and buy a sack of carrots. Ben adored them—and by association, anyone who just happened to have one in her pocket. Hopping up on the fence next to him, she took the carrot out of her jacket and broke it into three pieces. "Hungry?"

He nosed her leg.

While he chewed, she surveyed the property. Lights were on in the house, but because there was also a light burning in the barn, Jane figured that's where Kenzie was. Jane had had lots of time to think about what she would say to Kenzie, but she was still brooding about it.

"Ever feel like a complete idiot?" she asked Ben.

He nosed her arm, asking for another piece of carrot.

"You got any suggestions on how to approach this?" She stroked the side of his neck. What she knew about horses could fit in a thimble. But Ben seemed a lot like Mouse—willing to listen but not given to advice.

She sat on the fence and watched the light fade. On the plane ride down, for some reason, she'd been thinking about Christine's last hours. It was a place and a time she normally didn't go because, mostly, it was all such a painful jumble. She couldn't remember specifics, but she did remember that her last words were about love—how grateful she was for the love in her life. To Jane, it seemed that perhaps Christine was pointing the way. In the end, love was what gave life meaning.

"Well, wish me luck," she said, giving Ben the last piece of carrot, then hopping off the fence.

Entering the barn, she found Kenzie standing next to Rocket, brushing him down. She was wearing jeans and leather chaps, and a red flannel shirt. Rocket was Kenzie's favorite. He was a chestnut gelding, half Arabian, with a white patch on his nose and four white-stockinged feet. Ben was more mellow, more Jane's speed. Rocket was a lot like his name.

"Wondered when you'd get here," said Kenzie, tossing Jane an amused smile over her shoulder.

"You were expecting me?"

"Well, *yeah*."

"Been out riding?"

"Yup."

"We gonna do the cowboy thang? I talk in sentences, you give one word responses."

"Maybe."

Jane started to laugh, but stopped herself. This wasn't funny. "I owe you an apology."

"And?" She turned around, hands rising to her hips.

"And . . . you were right. When it came to Greta, I *was* playing with fire. But the thing is, I never would have slept with her."

"I know."

"You do?"

Kenzie walked over and rested her forearms on Jane's shoulders. "Yeah, I *do*. What upset me was that you didn't seem to know it—at least not last week."

"You forgive me then?"

"Hell, yes."

Jane leaned in to kiss her.

"Hey, just one minute there."

"What?"

"You gotta promise me something."

"Sure. Anything."

She cupped her hands around the back of Jane's neck. "Don't break my heart, Lawless. 'Cause, I think . . . I think you're the one."

"Which one?"

"The one all the love songs talk about."

"Oh," said Jane, drawing her close. "*That* one."